Praise for *Before Green Gables*

"Budge Wilson offers a wonderful new look at one of Canada's most cherished literary heroines."—*National Post*

"We see Anne in full verbal flight on the subject of a perfect tree, thinking in emphatic italics, thrilling to lines of poetry, and completing stories begun by the narrator in her own extravagant language."—*Winnipeg Free Press*

"A captivating story in its own right."—*The Globe and Mail*

"Wilson makes Anne Shirley speak like Montgomery's Anne Shirley and even provides a credible scenario to show how a backwoods girl with little education managed to acquire the vast, precocious vocabulary that so endeared Anne to many readers ... Wilson's book shows us that ... Anne deserves to be called a survivor ... the quintessential Canadian."—*The Vancouver Sun*

"[Wilson] shares Montgomery's ability to paint a brilliant word picture of Atlantic coastal Canada. The blossom, the autumn leaf drop, and the months of dirty, compacted snow are all vividly present and become a shaping factor in the lives of her characters."—*The Guardian* (U.K.)

"Wilson beautifully recreates Anne's voice and her spirit ... [*Before Green Gables* is] an unforgettable voyage that Wilson has expertly made possible."—*Chronicle Herald* (Halifax)

"A must for Anne fans."—*New Edinburgh News* (Ottawa)

"Profound ideas, persuasively fleshed out. L.M. Montgomery would surely have approved."—*Washington Post Book World*

"[A] lively rendering of Anne's life before Green Gables."—*The London Free Press*

"I wasn't sure how I felt about a prequel that was written one hundred years after *Anne of Green Gables*. By chapter two, Wilson had entirely won me over and swept me up, and it felt right to have a prequel." —Carolyn Weaver, host of Book Television's *Fine Print*

"It's a great read for all ages." —*The Canadian Champion* (Milton, Ontario)

"[Budge Wilson] never fails to deliver a book filled with remarkable characters, spot-on text, and a compelling story. For anyone who has loved Anne through the past hundred years, you will be delighted to read Budge Wilson's newest novel." —*Brandon Sun*

"I had the uncanny feeling that Budge Wilson must have done some channelling ... An impressive addition to the Anne canon." —*Quill & Quire*

"Wilson is truly one of Canada's finest children's authors." —*The Muskokan* (Bracebridge, Ontario)

"If you've ever wondered about Anne's background, this will give you a satisfying answer, and Lucy Maud herself would probably approve." —*North Shore News* (North Vancouver)

"*Before Green Gables* is a crisp and credible unfolding of how Anne's loving yet quick-tempered spirit may have developed ... It has been a long road for Anne, but one Wilson has traced with a good degree of spark and invention." —*The Daily Press* (Timmins, Ontario)

"Mix up some raspberry cordial and treasure this essential addition to any bookshelf." —*Daily Gleaner* (Fredericton)

"Penguin was wise entrusting this prequel to Budge Wilson. A 'kindred spirit,' Wilson brings her customary warmth, insight

into friendship, and her own love of words to the story."
—*Canadian Children's Book News*

"A quick read that will keep the reader invested in its compelling characters from start to finish."—*Publishers Weekly*

"Wilson cleverly and adroitly portrays the essence of Montgomery's famous ... orphan and gives a spectacular glimpse of her young years. Highly recommended."—*Library Journal*

"Vividly rendered ... in a style true to the original ... A must-read for fans of the Canadian classic."—Canadian Consulate General, New York

"Perfect 'I've got a cold and it's miserable outside' entertainment."—*UK Book Group*

"Like Montgomery, Wilson peppers fairy tale essences which nicely blend with realism in the story."—*Dalhousie News*

"An invaluable addition to Anne's story."—*Canadian Bookseller Magazine*

"In rendering a younger Anne than her creator gave us, Budge Wilson does not so much imitate Montgomery's writing style as pay homage to its flowery description, often generously overflowing with a gloriously excessive vocabulary."—*Barnes & Noble Review*

"A vivid picture ... of life in rural Nova Scotia..."—*Buffalo News*

"Wilson has cleverly moved the language up to date while staying within the original idiom."—*Lexis News*

PUFFIN CANADA

BEFORE GREEN GABLES

BUDGE WILSON has published more than thirty books, with twenty foreign editions appearing around the world, and her stories appear in over ninety anthologies. She has won more than twenty-five literary awards, and her previous book, *Friendships*, was a finalist for the Governor General's Literary Award. In 2004, she was made a member of the Order of Canada. She lives in Halifax.

Before Green Gables, the prequel to *Anne of Green Gables*, is fully authorized by the heirs of L.M. Montgomery.

ALSO BY BUDGE WILSON
- selected titles -

$\mathscr{B}$EFORE GREEN GABLES

BUDGE WILSON

PUFFIN
CANADA

PUFFIN CANADA

Published by the Penguin Group

Penguin Group (Canada), 90 Eglinton Avenue East, Suite 700,
Toronto, Ontario, Canada M4P 2Y3 (a division of Pearson Canada Inc.)

Penguin Group (USA) Inc., 375 Hudson Street, New York, New York 10014, U.S.A.
Penguin Books Ltd, 80 Strand, London WC2R 0RL, England
Penguin Ireland, 25 St Stephen's Green, Dublin 2, Ireland (a division of Penguin Books Ltd)
Penguin Group (Australia), 250 Camberwell Road, Camberwell, Victoria 3124, Australia
(a division of Pearson Australia Group Pty Ltd)
Penguin Books India Pvt Ltd, 11 Community Centre, Panchsheel Park,
New Delhi – 110 017, India
Penguin Group (NZ), 67 Apollo Drive, Rosedale, North Shore 0632, New Zealand
(a division of Pearson New Zealand Ltd)
Penguin Books (South Africa) (Pty) Ltd, 24 Sturdee Avenue, Rosebank,
Johannesburg 2196, South Africa

Penguin Books Ltd, Registered Offices: 80 Strand, London WC2R 0RL, England

First published in a Penguin Canada hardcover by Penguin Group (Canada),
a division of Pearson Canada Inc., 2008
Published in this edition, 2009

1 2 3 4 5 6 7 8 9 10 (WEB)

The prequel to *Anne of Green Gables* is authorized by the heirs of L.M. Montgomery.
Before Green Gables © 2008 by Budge Wilson, David Macdonald, trustee, and Ruth Macdonald.

L.M. Montgomery is a trademark of Heirs of L.M. Montgomery Inc.
Anne of Green Gables, Before Green Gables and other indicia of *Anne* are trademarks of the
Anne of Green Gables Licensing Authority Inc.

Interior illustrations copyright © Shelagh Armstrong

Manufactured in Canada.

Library and Archives Canada Cataloguing in Publication data available
upon request to the publisher.

ISBN: 978-0-14-305536-5

Visit the Penguin Group (Canada) website at **www.penguin.ca**

Special and corporate bulk purchase rates available; please see
www.penguin.ca/corporatesales or call 1-800-810-3104, ext. 477 or 474

This book is for
Alan and Glynis and Andrea

CONTENTS

Contents

Contents

Contents

$\mathscr{W}$alter Leaves for Work

Bertha Shirley stood at the door of their little yellow house, and waved goodbye to Walter as he turned on to the road that would eventually take him to the Bolingbroke High School. His arms were too full of books to wave back, but his smile told her everything she needed to know. She continued to watch him as he journeyed down the long road that led to the Hepworth house. Geoffrey Hepworth taught science at the school, and would be waiting for Walter, with the horse and buggy ready for the trip across the green marshlands and into the centre of town.

Walter had hoped to do the long journey by foot, but today was the first day of the fall term, and he had too much to carry. Usually he counted on that early morning walk to clear the cobwebs out of his head before starting his first geometry class. After the walk, and after that class, Walter always felt ready for anything. There was something so orderly, so logical, so *predictable* about geometry — in fact, about all branches of mathematics. Everything seemed to *fit*. He loved the subject he taught with the same intensity that Bertha felt for the material she'd been teaching in the same school — until last June.

Bertha stayed in the doorway long after Walter had disappeared behind the tangle of rose bushes and wild apple trees at the west corner of the Hepworth property. She wished she was with him. She was longing to step into a classroom today, and start opening the students' eyes and ears — not to

mention their brains — to the miracle of good poetry. To Wordsworth, to Keats, to the new poet Matthew Arnold. And *Shakespeare*. Supposing their new teacher didn't *care* about Shakespeare! Bertha couldn't really see why you weren't supposed to be a teacher just because you were married.

She'd asked a few people that question: "Why can't you do both?" The answer was always the same: "Because you should be home, looking after your husband." Why couldn't they look after *each other*? The house was tiny, and their meals were simple. You didn't need to dust every single surface *every day*. She'd done all the cooking on her father's farm after her mother died, and she was so good at it that she could make a whole meal — dessert and all — in twenty-five minutes. And laundry? In the summer, Walter had always helped her to wring out the sheets and to fill the big water heater on the stove. He could still do that if she changed her washday to Saturday. Bertha sighed, and turned to reenter the house.

$\mathcal{J}$essie's Revelation

"Mrs. Shirley! Mrs. Shirley!" Where was the voice coming from? Bertha looked over her shoulder and could see a figure racing down the road in the direction of the yellow house, hair escaping from its pins, apron flying. Bertha turned around again and waved. It was Jessie Gleeson. Bertha's hair always stayed put, no matter how she arranged it, regardless of what she was doing. So much of her small self was tidy — outwardly serene and orderly — that she exuded a kind of warm peacefulness. She often had some pretty untidy thoughts, but she kept most of those tucked away inside.

Jessie Gleeson was a different matter entirely. When she was running along the road, her hair would inevitably escape from its pins and combs — or whatever had been installed to keep it in place. It was typical that she had forgotten to take off her apron — and that it was flying all over the place as she raced along. And the fact that she was yelling — *yelling* — as she ran down the street would surprise no one who knew her.

When Bertha and Walter had moved into their little house in June, Jessie had made quite a few friendly calls. But she'd stopped coming. Every once in a while, when Bertha's mind had nothing better to do than to dream up worries, she wondered if she'd done anything to offend Jessie. She liked Jessie, and hoped this wasn't the case. Why the succession of eager visits and then ... nothing? Bertha smiled, and motioned Jessie to come in, when the panting woman came abreast of the house.

But Jessie just stood at the end of the lane and shook her head. She was still breathing too heavily to manage a full sentence. "Can't," she puffed. "Bread in oven. Come to my house. Children back in school. Nice and quiet. Tea's steeping."

Bertha laughed. Well, this wasn't as thrilling as teaching *Hamlet*, but it was a lot better than dusting perfectly clean shelves. She closed the door, ran down the steps and joined Jessie.

By now, Jessie had some of her voice back. "I saw Mr. Shirley striding by on his long legs — on his way to school," she said. "Figured you might be lonesome all alone in that tiny house."

"Thank you," said Bertha. "Yes. It'll be nice to have a little visit."

When they'd settled down on the two kitchen rockers, there was a brief awkward silence.

Then Jessie spoke. "Guess you wondered why I stopped coming to call."

"Well, I did wonder if ..." Bertha didn't know how to end the sentence.

"Well, stop wondering," said Jessie. "I didn't know how to explain, but suddenly I got to thinking I had to tell you anyway. When I saw Mr. Shirley drive off with Geoffrey, I knew you were alone. You're never alone ..." Her voice trailed off.

"And?"

"And I felt the courage rise in my chest. 'I'll tell her,' I thought."

"Tell me what?"

"That after a while I couldn't stand coming to your place."

"Why?" exclaimed Bertha. "*Why?*"

"I couldn't stand all that loving going on all the time. It wasn't like you were hugging or *touching* or anything. It's the way he follows your every move, even when you're just doing some simple little thing like stirring your tea. And you, too. Watching him, watching him, like he had wings."

He does have wings, thought Bertha. *She's absolutely right. And Shakespeare himself couldn't have described it any better. Jessie never got beyond the fifth class, but she's a poet.*

But Jessie was still talking.

"Maybe I wouldn't have minded that so much if Gerald had *ever*, in the twelve years of our marriage — even just *once* — looked at me like that."

"Never?" said Bertha.

"Well ..." Jessie paused for a moment. "Maybe from time to time, when ... well, *you know*. But that's different. This seems to happen to the two of you every single day, even when you're sitting on opposite sides of a room."

Bertha listened, wondering what she was going to reply to this woman.

"And he's often cross and cranky with me. Gerald, I mean. When I burn the toast or if one of the children is crying. When anything sort of gets in his way. Even when it's not my fault."

She stopped talking, and Bertha found herself able to say, "I'm sorry, Jessie."

"Well, it's not your fault, Mrs. Shirley. Or maybe even Gerald's. I know he worries about money. Six mouths are a lot to feed. He gets a lot of headaches. And working in a factory must be pretty awful. Anyway, I'm used to it. The sky won't fall. But all of a sudden, I felt like my heart couldn't survive all those adoring looks that were passing back and forth between you and your husband. So I came to a decision."

"Which was?"

"To go see you when you're alone. Or to ask you to come over to see me. I'd like to be your friend, but I think maybe this is the only way I can manage it, Mrs. Shirley."

"Which is fine with me," said Bertha, "but only if you call me Bertha. When you call me Mrs. Shirley, you put up a fence between us."

Bertha left soon after this, with a new jar of gooseberry jam in her pocket and a fresh loaf of bread under her arm. As she walked back to her house she thought about how she'd miss seeing Walter at noontime. They'd always had their lunch together last year, when she'd still been at the school. She thought about how funny-looking he was, with his broad nose, his blueberry eyes, his dark red hair — coarse and straight — the freckles on the back of his long fingers, his wide and friendly mouth. So funny-looking, and yet to her so beautiful. And yes, equipped with wings.

Bertha walked through the house to the back door, and opened it wide. She looked at the flat marshlands that led to the river, still green in the warm September air. She loved that river, with its slithery mudbanks at low tide, and its lazy, slow-moving water when the tide was high. She watched groups of dark birds flying low over the grasses, and listened to their harsh but compelling voices. *They're getting ready for their journey south. It'll be warm, maybe hot, with pelicans and palm trees and long beaches. But I don't want to follow them. I want to stay exactly where I am, looking at my beloved muddy river ambling along, and waiting for the return of Walter at four o'clock. I want things to stay exactly the same, forever.*

THREE

*W*alter Returns

At three o'clock, Walter stuffed his books and pens and chalk and pencils into his desk, and prepared to leave the school. Unlike Bertha's orderly self, Walter was untidy and absent-minded, and by tomorrow he would have forgotten exactly where he had put all those things. His whole person followed the same pattern. Even inside the school or at home, his hair looked as though he was standing on a cliff in a windstorm. An hour after he had put on one of his freshly ironed shirts, he would look as if he'd slept in his clothes; and his shirttail had a way of creeping out of his trousers when he reached into the top shelf of the cupboard to get some chalk, or when he was writing something on the upper part of the blackboard. His personality was as untidy and unpredictable as his appearance. He had a roar of a laugh, which could burst forth at the most surprising times — as, for instance, when he wrote down QED, after demonstrating the miraculous perfection of a theorem in geometry. This would be a laugh of pure joy, and had been known to make mathematicians out of some very unlikely students. His enthusiasms were contagious, and many of his students grew to love his often-unpopular subject.

Geoffrey Hepworth, his horse, and his buggy had gone ahead, while Walter had been patiently explaining a tricky equation in algebra to one of the students. By the time he was ready to leave, Walter was sorry that Geoffrey hadn't waited for him. The thirst for exercise — so strong in the early morning — had completely deserted him by the time the classroom clock told him it was three forty-five. So close to four! And he hadn't seen Bertha since half past seven. An eternity! With a marvellous lack of logic (in view of how much he revered it), he squeezed his long legs around one of the students' seats and laid his arms on the top of the desk. And thought about how much he wanted to be home in the little yellow house — RIGHT NOW. He wanted to just snap his fingers and *be there*.

Walter stared at the blank blackboard and thought about Bertha's face, with its exquisite nose (his, after all, was so huge), its perfect little chin, her enormous eyes — sometimes green, sometimes grey — and her sweet mouth with its ready smile. Walter shut his eyes and thought about her skin. Not a mark, not one single freckle — a flawless alabaster, or maybe ivory. He sighed with the wonder of it all. That these astonishing physical marvels were joined to such a warm and generous spirit, to such *intelligence*, made the whole human combination a minor miracle. But that such a person could have agreed to marry *him* — *there* was the *major* miracle. He was so weak from that particular astonishment that he had difficulty untangling himself from the undersized desk and chair, and could scarcely navigate the two miles that lay between him and the yellow house.

But eventually Walter arrived. He was almost an hour later than he had planned, and Bertha had been worried — dreaming up a school fire (centred on his side of the building), a roadway accident involving a runaway horse, a premature heart attack. But she spoke of none of this, as he enveloped her at the doorway with a long and tender hug. In the coming weeks, the neighbours who witnessed Walter's departures and arrivals were to say that when he left in the morning it was as though he was going to war, and that his arrivals in the late afternoon were like a triumphant return from a major battlefield.

On this particular day, Walter sat down in the kitchen and told Bertha about his first day back at school, as she moved around the room preparing their meal. Although he was talking about his own adventures, his eyes never left Bertha, as she cut up the cabbage, poked the boiling corned beef with a long fork, peeled potatoes, and then set the table. After checking her watch, she suddenly, in a quick and graceful movement, took the cabbage and potatoes and dropped them, one by one, into the pot of corned beef, with a kind of artistic flourish. To Walter, it was all like a performance by some acclaimed dancer, choreographed especially for him and presented in a private showing. For her part, Bertha listened to every word he spoke, even while she was busy preparing and timing the meal and moving to and fro. Later, at the table, she would comment on his account of his day, asking him questions about details of his teaching, while skillfully hiding the fact that she secretly hated mathematics, almost failed algebra in the eleventh class, and had a particularly strong distaste for geometry. *Small wonder*, she thought, as she passed the butter to Walter, *that Jessie doesn't enjoy being with Walter and me in this house. There must be altogether too much visible harmony.*

FOUR

Tea with Jessie

Several weeks passed, and it was now mid-October. Bertha had coped with her new isolation and loneliness — and her ongoing homesickness for her English classes at the high school — by going on walks in the nearby woods and marvelling at the spectacular fall colours. She loved the brilliant reds of the maples best — maybe because they were intense and exaggerated, a bit like Walter's personality. She'd never known anyone as energetic and unpredictable as he was, so full of laughter and surprises.

In spite of his strange looks, girls were attracted to Walter, and Bertha was amazed that he had chosen her over so many admiring others. As if it were yesterday, she could remember that day at Normal School, when he'd had a whole crowd of young people bent double with laughter. Suddenly he stopped talking and walked over to where she was standing on the fringes of the group, bent over, and whispered in her ear, "Let's go downtown and have a cup of tea." He took her hand, and they walked out of the room, with her feeling like Cinderella being chosen by the Prince. She'd never lost that feeling, never got used to it. She'd always thought she was colourless and dull, with her pale yellow hair and her chalk-white skin, and here she was actually *married* to this man who seemed to think she was the most beautiful woman in the world — and the most *interesting*. When she'd tell him about her walks in the woods among the wild, unbridled colours of the autumn trees, he'd listen with as much enthusiasm as if she were quoting a scene from *Romeo and Juliet*.

But today it was Monday. The weekend was over, and Walter had gone off to school again, leaving her with the dishpan and the scrub board and the recipe book and the broom and the duster. It wasn't enough. She missed him, but she also longed for the lively give-and-take of her English classes, the spirited discussions about the meaning of Hamlet's actions and inaction, the plight of Cordelia, the fall of Lady Macbeth. Bertha hated Mondays. She knew she was an unskilled and reluctant housekeeper; but she also knew that she had been a good teacher. As soon as she got into a classroom and started introducing students to the literature she loved, all her shyness dropped away from her, and she became a whole other person. And Bertha liked that person.

Walter had told her that seven separate students had told him that English classes had never been the same, had never been as exciting, since she left. It was clear that they missed her as much as she missed them. Bertha could feel some sort of cosmic injustice gnawing away at her spirit. Besides, she didn't feel well, and had been feeling like this for several weeks. Maybe she was dying of some awful wasting disease. Consumption, perhaps. She hadn't told Walter about this, because she knew he was busy, and often tired. She didn't want to worry him, to add to his load. But to tell the truth, she wished she had more of a load herself.

Jessie had always been the one to call on Bertha — to arrive at the Shirley door with an expectant and half-ashamed look on her face. Now, suddenly, it was Bertha who needed Jessie. She put a light coat on over her dress and walked quickly out the door — quickly, in case she might change her mind. Her old shyness was on her, like an extra skin, and she found it hard to walk down the road, up the Gleeson lane and steps, and then to knock on that closed door. When Jessie opened the door, Bertha said haltingly, "I thought ... you might have some tea ... on the back of your stove."

Jessie's obvious delight at hearing those words made the veil of shyness slide right off Bertha's spirit. Jessie welcomed her as though she were the Queen herself.

"Come in! Oh, come in!" Jessie cried. "I'm *so* happy to see you! And I just took some pumpkin tarts out of the oven, so we can have a really delicious party. Oh my, oh my! Such a lovely thing to happen on such a boring morning. I've been missing Jenny so much since she started school. I was deep down in the dumps, and so wishing that a miracle would happen in my kitchen. And you're it!"

Jessie had never before been approached by one of what she called "the upper ladies." She knew that Bertha was an "upper lady," even though she was younger than Jessie, and probably poorer. She had a way of speaking that was just a little bit different from her own. Not a whole lot different, but still ... And Bertha was a *schoolteacher*. Jessie had been able to muster the courage to call on Bertha, but every time she did it she found it difficult. And now — here was Bertha on her own doorstep, all of her own accord.

Bertha sized up this situation very quickly, and did all the right things. She asked Jessie questions about her childhood, her parents, her siblings, Gerald's courtship, her own children. Jessie was delighted to supply all the answers. And Bertha found herself replying to Jessie's questions with the same ease.

When Jessie turned to remove more tarts from the oven, Bertha surprised herself with some new thoughts. *This must be what it's like to have a sister.* A sister must be someone who would tell you her secrets, knowing that you'd never tell them to anyone else. And you could tell her things, too, that you'd never dream of confiding to your parents or your brothers — or your husband. Bertha came from a long line of "only children," and now that her parents were both dead, she was all alone. She didn't even have any cousins. Suddenly she found herself saying, "I'm all alone."

"Bertha! What on earth do you mean?"

"I don't have any family. No parents. No sisters or brothers, no aunts and uncles. Not even a forty-second cousin."

Jessie was so amazed that she almost spilled her tea. "Oh, my heavenly days!" she cried. "My mother had six brothers and sisters, and my father had eleven. Then they upped and had eight of their own children. I have seventeen aunts and uncles, and more first cousins than I've even tried to count. Can you imagine what it's like around here at Christmastime? Being as most of us live in Bolingbroke or close by, there are a lot of turkeys sizzling away in about ten ovens. Then the cooks cover them up — right in their pans — and we all run out and get our wagons, all wrapped up warm against the frosty air. Like a bunch of racehorses, we gallop off to my mother's house, rushing to get there before the turkeys get cold. She's got the biggest house with the biggest tables. You can't believe what it's like. All those grown-ups in their best clothes, with the women looking so pretty, making sure when we sit down that at least an inch of our petticoats are showing. And the more lace, the better. The men keep checking the time on their pocket watches so that people can admire the big clunky chains on them. It's the only time, except sometimes in church, that men haul those watches out of their chiffoneers. And all the children showing off their new toys, and little boys pulling the girls' pigtails, and a few babies crying. I've never eaten a Christmas turkey in my life without the sound of a crying baby in the background. Oh, Mrs. Shirley, dear — excuse me, Bertha — you can't believe what a wonderful day it is."

Bertha tried to push down a little tide of envy that she could feel trying to drown her. "Yes," she said, "I can imagine all of it. Noise and colour and laughter, and everyone happy — except the babies!" And then Bertha laughed so that Jessie wouldn't realize how sad she was feeling. When she was a young girl, she was the one who had had to cook the Christmas bird — and it had to be a chicken, because she and her father would never have been able to eat a whole turkey — even a tiny one. They'd get dressed up in their best clothes and sit for a while in the "best parlour" because it didn't seem right to be sitting in the kitchen on Christmas Day. The parlour was so empty and quiet and *unfamiliar* that they often couldn't think of anything to say to each other. After all, the only person who was ever invited to sit in there was the Presbyterian minister. They were both quiet people, and this was fine, most of the time. But — somehow — not on Christmas Day.

It had been Bertha's mother who had known how to laugh and sing songs and make even ordinary days seem like a party. But that had been so very long ago. She had died of consumption when Bertha was nine years old. She could remember it well, even now — the time of illness, with her mother (no longer singing, no longer laughing) lying so quietly on the pillow (embroidered with forget-me-nots and tiny leaves) under the warm quilt (pink, blue, and white, made by her mother's grandmother).

Bertha recalled all that so clearly — the white face, the listless eyes, the limp hands on top of the quilt. And her own nine-year-old self standing beside the bed, pleading, "Mother! Mother!" and getting no reply. And then the pale hand moving ever so slowly toward her. Remembering this made Bertha's eyes fill with tears. At the same moment, she caught sight of herself in a mirror that was hanging on the opposite wall. A pale, troubled face looked back at her.

Pale!

Without knowing that she was going to say it, Bertha suddenly spoke. "Maybe that's what's wrong with me," she said. Then, remembering that her mother had died on that very night she'd been thinking about, she suddenly started to cry.

Jessie left her chair and rushed across the room to hold Bertha close.

"There, there!" she crooned, in the exact voice she used to comfort her six-year-old daughter. "I'm sure there's nothing wrong with you. Every day, I see you walking over the rough ground of the marshes, looking so young and strong. I'm sure you're *fine*."

"I'm not!" said Bertha. "Sometimes I feel so terrible. Not always. But often. You know ... *sick*. Feeling as though I might throw up. But I never do. It just feels that way. My mother died of consumption. More and more, I feel sure that that's what I have."

Jessie drew away from Bertha suddenly, and stood up. "How long," she began, and then stumbled over her words, "since your last ... you know?"

"My last what?"

"Oh, *you know*. When was the last time you ..."

Jessie was finding this difficult. She did feel comfortable now with Bertha, even though she was "an upper lady." Particularly seeing her cry in her very own kitchen, with a pumpkin tart in her hand. However, some things were hard to talk about with *anyone*. But she had to try.

"Have you missed any months?"

"Months?" Bertha looked puzzled. And then, "Oh! *That!*

Well, yes, but I've never been regular. I often miss a month or two. The doctor says it's because I'm so thin."

Jessie smiled. "Well, *I* don't say it's because you're so thin. All kinds of people are even skinny, but *they* have babies, too, like everybody else."

"Babies!" Bertha's large eyes opened even wider. "What are you saying, Jessie? I don't believe you. It doesn't fit. It doesn't just happen in the morning, and I've never lost a single meal. This can sweep over me at any hour of the day, and then I feel as if I'm dying. And I fall asleep all the time. Those things must mean I'm sick. I'm thinking about my mother. She slept so much. And bursting into tears, the way I just did. That's not the sort of thing I do. But my mother did — when she was *dying*." She looked as if she might start crying again.

But Jessie had no sympathy for her now. She was actually *laughing*. "Well, you're not going to die," she said. "Sleeping a lot, getting weepy, feeling like your stomach is on a merry-go-round. It all *does* fit. Bertha, my dear, you go to see your doctor tomorrow so that he can tell you that you're going to have a baby." Then she laughed again, and said, "I've got some yarn left over from Jenny, when I was getting ready for her birth. I'm going to start knitting a little jacket this very afternoon."

It had been cloudy and damp for several days, but as Bertha walked down the road to her house, there was an odd glow in the sky, as though the sun was trying hard to pierce the clouds. *Or maybe the glow's inside* me, she thought. To her, the day seemed full of light, the sky brighter, the marsh grasses greener. And the little row of black-eyed Susans beside the front steps bedazzled her with the brilliance of their colour. She entered the house, forgetting to close the door behind her, and walked right upstairs to a room that had a big mirror on the wall. She stood in front of the mirror and looked into the eyes of her reflection. Well, was it death or was it birth — an ending or a beginning? She looked hard at herself — with honesty and intelligence. No, she didn't look like that mother of hers on her deathbed. She had to admit that. She'd always been pale, so this was nothing new. And there was certainly no sign of listlessness in those large grey-green eyes. Her blond hair, although neatly arranged, was thick, with lively little curls escaping onto her forehead. And in the late morning sunshine that was streaming in the south window, it had a definite lustre. Maybe staying alone in an empty house makes you think sad thoughts and create gloomy predictions.

Bertha now inspected the rest of her mirror self. The little pearl buttons that fastened the two sides of her bodice weren't in a perfectly straight line; they looked strained. Suddenly she recalled that she'd had difficulty fastening them this morning. She could remember muttering, "Clumsy fingers!" to herself. Well, they apparently weren't clumsy. They just had a harder job to do. She hadn't worn that dress for several months. But there had been an October chill in the air this morning, so she'd chosen warmer clothes. Bertha turned her body sideways to the mirror. "Oh my!" she exclaimed, and then, "*Yes!*"

She faced herself in the mirror again. "There's a baby in there," she whispered. "A brand-new person. Inside *me*. *Walter's child!*"

Then Bertha went downstairs to the kitchen. Her insides were doing wild somersaults, but she felt definitely hungry. After she had lunch, maybe she'd have a little nap.

"There's a miracle in progress," she murmured to herself, as she opened the kitchen cupboard.

FIVE

*W*aiting for March

The next three months were the happiest that Bertha could ever remember. The nausea that she'd been feeling dwindled to almost nothing, and then disappeared altogether. She found that she had more energy than she'd ever possessed, and she and Walter went on long walks on the weekend, sometimes even as far as the head of Chelsea Bay, where they could see the long mud flats stretching out to the wider sea. Bertha discovered that she was hungry for an odd selection of foods — peanuts, strawberry preserve, mustard pickles, russet apples. She could sit down at eleven o'clock in the morning and eat three of those apples — one right after the other. She developed two little areas of soft pink on her pale cheeks. She looked and felt wonderful.

But Bertha's most exciting moment came when she first felt the baby move. It happened in the middle of the night, and she woke Walter out of a sound sleep — even though it was exam week — in order to tell him about it, and to suggest that he put the palm of his hand on her belly to see if he could feel it, too. But the sensation was too feeble to be felt through her muscles and skin. The next day, when Jessie came over for a cup of tea, Bertha tried to describe it, but she couldn't find the right word. But Jessie had no trouble coming up with one that was perfect. "It's a *flutter*," she said, "like the wings of a small bird. A little bird that hasn't yet learned how to fly." Jessie had experienced the flutter four times. Her four children were all in school now, but the memory of that feeling was strong. "And just wait," she said, "until the little thing starts kicking. It's the loveliest sensation in the world." And it was. When that happened, Walter could feel the lurching movements, too, and he was as thrilled as Bertha was.

In fact, Walter was so pleased and proud about the baby that you would almost have thought that it was he who was going to give birth to this child. He strode off to school each morning — through rain, through mud, through deep snow — as though he was training (joyfully) for some major athletic event. No amount of after-school corrections or exam marking seemed to make him tired. He acted as though he was the first man who had ever been a father. And the more he loved the idea of fatherhood, the more he acted as if Bertha was the queen of the universe. Jessie still found these visible displays of affection too difficult to watch. She continued to see Bertha during the daytime, when Walter was away at school. He scarcely knew her, or she him.

The doctor had said that the baby would probably be born in mid-March. By Christmastime, Bertha was still feeling well and energetic. Therefore, when Jessie invited her and Walter to spend Christmas at her mother's home, with the huge army of Bolingbroke Gleesons and MacIntyres, they accepted. Bertha even made twelve jars of cranberry jelly for the dinner, and five mince pies, hoping that she'd chosen the right things to bring.

At eleven o'clock in the morning, six Gleesons and two Shirleys crowded into the huge rented sleigh, snuggled up beside the steaming turkey, the roasted potatoes, the plum puddings, the frosted gingerbread men, the gifts. They all sat on cushions and pillows, covered with blankets and afghans, while Mr. Gleeson was up on the driver's seat, urging his aging horses to move as quickly as they could, headed for the far side of the river. He had tied as many sleigh bells as he could find onto the horses, so that they made cheerful music as they raced over the snowy roads. Added to that were the slithers and squeaks that they could hear under the runners.

When they arrived at their destination, Bertha tried not to think about the lonely Christmases with her father, as she drank in the laughter and song, the children's shrieks, the babies' howls, the tables filled with good food, the tree with its strings of popcorn and real candles, the way everyone seemed to feel comfortable with one another.

Jessie's mother was exactly what Bertha would have expected — warm and welcoming, a little bit overweight, running the show, bossy. "George! You sit over here with your aunt Aggie, and stop pulling your ear. Jessie! Go find a comfortable seat for your friend. Arthur! After dinner, go show Walter your new horse. Somebody go look after that crying baby! No, Annabelle, you don't have to eat your carrots on Christmas Day! And Herbert, shove over a bit and make room for Uncle Joe! Alice! That cranberry's for everybody. Pass it along! Belinda — watch your petticoat don't catch fire on those candles!" There were five tables in two rooms, a turkey on every table, and more people than Bertha could count. She felt quiet and shy, but happy and comfortable in this warm and welcoming home. Walter was completely at ease, with a child on each knee before the meal was over, listening to what they had to say, laughing at their jokes. Bertha watched him, and decided that even though they'd never be able to afford it, they absolutely had to have at least six children. Jessie watched him, too, vowing that she would invite *both* Shirleys to dinner during the holidays. Maybe some of Walter's kindness would rub off on Gerald. But she also reminded herself that Gerald had, after all, remembered the sleigh bells, and had given her money for a new dress to wear on Christmas Day. He'd done it gruffly but he'd *done* it.

That night, when Bertha and Walter were in bed, she said to him, "Now I know what I want out of life."

"And what's that?"

"I want to fill this little house with children and laughter and *noise*. You can build a piece onto it when we need more space. Then I want there to be grandchildren and aunts and uncles and cousins so that we can have a huge party, exactly like the one we went to today."

"Whatever you want, my dear," said Walter, but the minute he'd spoken the last word, he was asleep.

*M*rs. Thomas Comes

New Year's Eve followed Christmas, and then came January.
Bertha got bigger and bigger, and the weather got colder and
colder. She discovered that she didn't want to take long walks
anymore — or even short ones. She felt tired by ten-thirty in
the morning. In early February, Dr. Bates came to see her, and
said that he thought she had some sort of prenatal condition
with a long name.

"It's a very common affliction during the last month," he
told Walter, "but it can be dangerous — for both her and the
baby. She shouldn't really be doing anything much except
resting." Then he paused, and frowned. "Would you be able
to ... do you think you could afford ... to hire a woman to come
in to help out with the meals and laundry and cleaning?" He
knew that schoolteachers made pitifully small salaries.

In spite of his anxiety about Bertha, Walter managed a
short laugh. "Well, no," he said, "we can't *afford* it, but yes, we'll
certainly do it." He wasn't sure *how* it could be done. But he
knew it *had* to be done. Maybe he could sell his father's watch.
It was old, but someone had once told him that it was worth
a lot of money. He wanted to keep it, but it wasn't as valuable
to him as Bertha and the baby.

"Could you suggest a woman who might help us?"
Walter asked the doctor. "If you do, I'd like her to come
right away."

"Yes," said Dr. Bates, "and I could probably arrange for her
to come tomorrow. The family she worked for moved to

Kingsport last week, and I happen to know that she needs the money. Her name is Mrs. Thomas."

Help arrived on the following afternoon. Joanna Thomas was thirty-two years old, tall and bony, with no soft corners. At sixteen, she'd been swept off her sensible feet by the strikingly handsome Bert Thomas, who'd been cheerful and attentive, a good dancer, a practical joker. Slender and graceful, she was as skillful a dancer as he was. She danced herself straight into Bert's heart, and believed that she would spend the rest of her life dancing. When she asked her parents if she could marry him, they disappeared into the parlour and closed the door.

"She'll be marrying beneath her," said Mrs. Harrigan. "I know what those Thomases are like. But the fact is that Joanna has the kind of looks that won't last. Right now, she's almost pretty. But she'll be skinny at thirty, scrawny at forty. We should maybe grab that young man while she's still halfway attractive."

Mr. Harrigan's mind was on other matters. "He's a handsome young man, and they're both tall. If they have two or three strong sons, they might inherit that big Thomas farm and become rich and important. The boy looks intelligent. He'll go far." He didn't know that Bert had dropped out of school in the winter term of the fourth class.

Mrs. Harrigan had sighed. "She'll be speaking like a Thomas before she's lived with him a year. Dropping all those *g*'s. That sort of talk rubs off on you. You'll see, soon enough. But never mind. We'll do it in July."

In the late summer, there was a house and barn raising, in the presence of much fiddle music, a lot of alcohol, and many cousins and brothers of Bert Thomas. The Harrigans gave this event a wide berth. "No way am I going to be part of that racket," said Mrs. Harrigan. "They'll have the shells of the buildings up by Sunday night. Let Bert Thomas do the fancy inside jobs in the winter." She sent over six blueberry pies.

Before the snows came, Joanna knew that her husband had a procrastination problem, a drinking problem, and unpredictable moods. Her house remained unfinished and drafty, with only the absolute essentials added. The barn was tiny, but big enough for a horse and a cow — and also large enough to accommodate Bert and his bottles. Joanna had morning sickness for four months, and a difficult labour. Nobody was doing any dancing.

By the time Mrs. Thomas turned up at the Shirley door, she had three children — all girls — as well as a husband who was unemployed more often than not. The daughters were thirteen, fourteen and fifteen, and all had inherited their father's physical beauty, thereby making Joanna look even more haggard and worn than she was. Eliza, the eldest, had received her mother's efficiency and quick ways, and looked after the cooking and cleaning when her mother was working away from home. She also kept an eye on the younger children to make sure they weren't playing hide-and-seek in the barn on days when her father was in there. When he was gripped by one of his frequent depressions and nursing a hangover, his temper could be pretty ferocious.

Joanna immediately took a liking to the Shirleys' small house, the atmosphere of calm, the loving couple who inhabited it. In her last job, she had had to clean a large three-storey house and feed five children and their two parents. This job was going to be like child's play for her. The house was so small; their meals were so simple, and no one was yelling or scolding or complaining.

Bertha and Joanna were Mrs. Shirley and Mrs. Thomas to each other. They kept their distance. But a real affection developed between them. In her own home, Joanna was often impatient and cross — because of the noise the girls sometimes made, Bert's bursts of anger, the times he would actually hit her, the way she felt defeated and unbeautiful. In the Shirley house, she became someone different — more in tune with her surroundings. When he was at home, Walter often sang as he chopped the firewood or shovelled the path to the road. Soon Joanna found herself singing — songs she'd not sung for sixteen years — as she scrubbed the small kitchen floor or kneaded the bread dough. She started offering to do things that weren't required of her — like mending a torn curtain or bringing Bertha an afternoon cup of tea. Once she made little heart-shaped sugar cookies, with sugar sprinkles on the top like drops of frost.

"Oh, Mrs. Thomas!" cried Bertha, when she saw them. "Those cookies make me want to cry." And then a few tears did slide down her cheeks. "My mother made cookies *exactly* like those! And they were my very, very favourites." Then she told Joanna about her mother's dying of consumption when she was only nine years old. After that, Joanna baked a small batch of those sugar cookies every Friday — not so many as to make the Shirleys tired of them, but as a special little treat for the weekend.

For Joanna, the little yellow house was an oasis in a thirty-two-year-old desert. She had gone from a cold, strict childhood, during which she had been scolded more often than thanked, straight into the brief dancing frenzy of Bert's courtship, and then into a shell of a house that was often cold of temperature and spirit. Bert's verbal and sometimes physical abuse made her feel unlovely and unlovable. She watched herself being as cross and strict with her own daughters as her mother had been with her.

But the Shirley home brought out everything that was good in her — good, but hidden. She worried about the small, pale figure huddled under the big afghan in the rocking chair, her swollen feet and ankles propped up on the footstool.

"What can I do for you, Mrs. Shirley?" she'd ask. "Tell me something I could do that might make you feel better."

"Oh, Mrs. Thomas!" Bertha would exclaim. "You're so thoughtful, so kind. Maybe a cup of tea, if the pot's on the back of the stove, and just one of your delicious sugar cookies. I'd love that."

Not once in living memory could Joanna remember anyone calling her thoughtful and kind. If Bertha had asked her to push the kitchen stove out into the back garden, she would have wanted to do it. Joanna loved it when the warm-hearted Jessie would come to call, loaded down with food and gifts and good cheer. Where had people like this been all her life?

It was a Friday, and Bertha had just asked Joanna if she'd mind very much bringing her the volume of Keats poems that was in the bookcase.

"It's red," said Bertha, "and small. It has gold letters. I feel that I need a poem or two today." It was unusually overcast and dark, even for March — a very gloomy day.

Joanna loved that bookcase, with its shiny glass doors (kept spotless by her own hands) and the way the books were lined up so straight behind the glass. Like a row of soldiers in colourful uniforms, she thought. But as she reached inside to get the book that Bertha wanted, she suddenly heard a sound from the front parlour — something between a groan and a shriek. She dropped the book and rushed into the parlour. Bertha was stretched back on the chair, her body in a contorted position.

"Quick, Joanna!" panted Bertha, forgetting the Mrs. Thomas title, "Get Walter! Get Jessie! Get the doctor! Get *somebody*! It's coming! I know it is! And oh! *Oh!* It's *terrible!*"

Joanna always vowed later that an angel had gone over to Jessie's house, picked her up, and dropped her on the Shirley doorstep at that very moment. There was a knock at the front door, and Jessie entered. Joanna rushed to greet her.

"Oh, thank the sweet heavens, Mrs. Gleeson! Her time has come! One of us got to go for Dr. Bates. Me or you. You decide. But hurry! She just started, but it looks like this could be a quick one. And bad things can happen. What if it comes feet first?"

"Oh!" There was a look of terror in Jessie's eyes. Then — suddenly — she became very businesslike and calm. "I'll go," she said. "Gerald's back from work for his noon dinner, and the horse is still hitched to the wagon. He'll go get Dr. Bates, and I'll come right back to help you. And Walter should be home from school early, because it's exam week. Don't let it come before the doctor comes! Tell her to take good breaths!" Then she was out the door.

But suddenly it opened again. "Boil a lot of water!" she yelled to Joanna. "And hold her hand tight."

Seven

Anne Shirley

Joanna had been right. It was a quick one. However, Dr. Bates got there in time to save Jessie and Joanna from acting as Bertha's midwives. Even Walter returned home from school before the baby actually arrived.

"Well!" exclaimed Jessie afterwards, in the kitchen. "I wish that just one of my four babies had arrived that quickly."

"Yes," agreed Joanna. "But y'know — I think Mrs. Shirley packed more pain into those two hours than I felt with all three of my girls put together. My, oh my! Such screaming! It scared the living daylights out of poor Mr. Shirley. I never saw such naked fear. Mrs. Shirley's always so quiet and sort of hauled in by her own nature. And there she was, sounding like a howling coyote." She walked over to the stove. "I've heated some clear soup for the new mother, and then I'll take these hot muffins in to the doctor and Mr. Shirley."

"I could use one of those muffins myself, Mrs. Thomas. I feel like someone had just squeezed me through one of those washing-wringers. Having a few babies yourself doesn't tell you what to do when someone *else* does." Jessie wiped the perspiration from her forehead with the back of her hand. "Did you get a good look at the baby when you were bathing her? Or was she too wrinkled and red to be able to tell what she really looked like?"

"Well, she wasn't all that wrinkled and red. But she was screeching so loud, with her mouth so wide open, that I couldn't tell much about her looks. I can only tell you that she's a skinny little thing and kind of long for a new baby. But she's been spared Mr. Shirley's nose. Even with the wide-open mouth I could see that she was lucky enough to get Mrs. Shirley's beautiful nose." Then she shook her head. "It was some strange," she said, "it being such a dark day and all, but just as Dr. Bates put that baby in Mrs. Shirley's arms, the western sun suddenly shot through those thick clouds and shone bang onto the window of the house next door — and then came pouring back into the Shirleys' east window. It was like a sunrise at four o'clock in the afternoon." She shook her head again. "That's how come I could see the baby so clearly."

"And her hair?"

"Well, it was hard to tell, it being so wet and all. Probably dark red, like Mr. Shirley's. And there's quite a bit of it — and wavy. But I'll have to say ..."

"What?"

" ... that she's not one of those chubby and cuddly kinds of babies. I hope Mrs. Shirley won't be disappointed."

Disappointed? With the sun streaming in the east window, Bertha looked at her new daughter, all wrapped up in a warm flannel blanket, and decided that she had never seen such a beautiful baby. After the confusion and agony of childbirth, she was convinced that Anne had been born at sunrise, and no one ever corrected her. Walter was just staring and staring at his child, stunned by an almost suffocating love.

"She has your perfect nose," he whispered, "and your sweet little chin. But have you had a good look at her eyes? They're enormous — *your eyes*." A large tear rolled down Walter's cheek.

"Look at her long fingers, Walter. Everything about her is long — even her little feet. She gets all that from you. But she's her own self, too. Look at her hair."

Walter looked. It had dried out by now, and it was clear that it was going to be a colour of red — orange, really — that was brighter than anything they'd ever seen on anyone's head. Walter's was a dark red — auburn, straight and almost spiky. His baby's was fine and had a distinct soft curl to it. He touched the tiny head with his long fingers and felt weak with the wonder of it all.

"Walter," said Bertha. "What's her name? We couldn't decide, beforehand. But suddenly, I want her to have a name *right now*."

"We thought of four names," he said, "Jean and Janet and Dorothy ... and *Anne*." He smiled. "I've looked at her and said the first three names. They don't fit. She's not Jean or Janet or Dorothy. But I knew right away that she was Anne. Not A-N-N. Anne with an *e*. She's our perfect, perfect Anne."

Then there was a knock on the door, and Joanna came in, carrying the chicken soup. Jessie followed with a tray of hot muffins and strong tea.

Bertha smiled at them, her face aglow with joy, her hair untidy and tangled for the first time in her adult life.

"I want you two ladies to meet our new daughter," she said. "Anne Shirley."

EIGHT

First Weeks

The first few weeks after Anne's birth passed quickly, with Bertha learning how to lift a baby, bathe a baby, change a baby. She loved all this, and wondered why she had missed her English classes so much. Last Christmas she had said she wanted six children, but surely having three — or even two — of these babies could fill your life so entirely that there'd be no space in your days for missing anything.

Anne was small, weighing six pounds at birth, and seemed to have a voracious appetite. She was fed, by the clock, every three hours, although Bertha worried that Anne's frantic wails between feedings might mean that she was hungry more often than she was fed. The baby gained weight quickly, but Bertha lost pounds with even more speed — from fatigue, from loss of sleep, from anxiety. There were rumours that a virulent illness was attacking the area around Bolingbroke. Bertha feared lest Walter might bring home the deadly germ from one of his students and pass it along to Anne. She knew that if anything mortal were to happen to Anne, she'd die herself on the following day.

Mrs. Thomas had left the Shirley household two weeks after Anne's birth. At that point, both Bertha and Walter felt well and strong. But as April passed, and the chilly winds of May brought no relief from Bertha's fatigue or from the fevers that were sweeping through the community, Walter sold his father's treasured watch and hired Mrs. Thomas again to help out in the Shirley household. Summer holidays

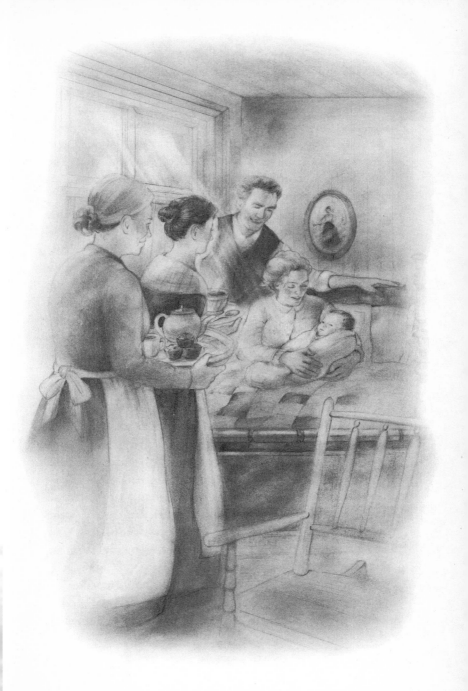

were still almost two months away for Walter, so he could only assist Bertha on weekends. Bertha was looking very pale and frail. He couldn't help thinking about the consumption that had gripped her own mother at such an early age.

Joanna was happy to be back in this amazing household. She was strong from many years of hard physical work, and found it easy to look after the laundry and cleaning, as well as much of the cooking.

"Oh, Joanna," said Bertha one day — having used her first name for the first time on the day that Anne was born, "I'll be grateful to you forever. I feel so much better now that you're helping me with the work. I'm able to *enjoy* Anne more now, instead of just *looking after* her. But I'm ashamed to have been so weak and wobbly. Some women seem to be able to care for six children without turning a hair."

"Well," said Joanna, "they may *survive*, but they're turning a lot of hairs. Most o' them are angry a lot o' the time, and they don't have enough energy left to be anything but cross with their children."

"*Really?*" exclaimed Bertha. "*Cross?*"

"Yes," said Joanna. "Cross. I've oftentimes seen it in myself, and I only have three. But Bert can't hold down a job, and he drinks both his own wages and mine. If he has to choose between a job or a bottle, the bottle always wins. So I get real angry. But he's a lot bigger and stronger than I am, and can't stand any arguing or complaints. So I take it out on the children. It's terrible unfair, and I hate myself for it, but your anger got to go somewheres. Some people get awful stomach pains and headaches. I get just plain *mean*."

"Oh, Joanna!" This was all that Bertha could think of to say. She hadn't felt that kind of anger for a long time, and she hoped she'd never have to feel it again. She tried to imagine

Walter being drunk and unkind, but her imagination wouldn't take her that far. She didn't even want to *try* imagining being cross at Anne.

"Stop sweeping that floor, Joanna," she said, "and come look at Anne for a minute. She's so *eager*, and so *alive*. Just look at those big green eyes, taking everything in. And *smart*. This morning I showed her a picture, and she laughed right out loud, in a ho-ho-ho kind of way. Like an *adult*. Not everyone has a sense of humour when they're only two and a half months old!"

Joanna came over and sat beside Bertha for a while, watching Anne. Well, she certainly was perky. No doubt about it. As if she understood everything she was looking at. Or else asking urgent questions with those huge eyes of hers. And that mass of curly orange hair was definitely ... *arresting*. But no matter how much weight the child gained, she was going to be thin until the day she died. And that wasn't going to be anytime soon. Joanna didn't know how she knew it, but she was certain that Anne was going to be able to stand up to whatever life threw at her. What was the word she was looking for? *Prevail*. That was the word. She was certain that this little person, this funny-looking little child, was going to *prevail*.

Joanna sighed. Of course if you had parents like Walter and Bertha, it might be pretty easy to prevail. Being surrounded by all that love could make almost *anyone* able to survive and flourish. But even for Anne, surely life wouldn't always be easy. There always the possibility that something awful might happen to her — a cruel friend, a bad accident, an illness, a disastrous marriage.

"But you'll survive it all," she said, and placed a tender hand on Anne's little red head.

"What do you mean by *but*, Joanna?" asked Bertha.

"I have no idea," said Joanna. But it didn't really matter. Bertha wasn't even listening. She was too busy admiring her baby.

NINE

*F*ever and Fears

"How come Mrs. Gleeson hasn't been in to see you?" asked Joanna, one Tuesday morning. "She always turns up on Mondays because she knows how much you hate saying goodbye to Mr. Shirley. And a couple of other times in the week. But not once this week, and it's three o'clock on Tuesday afternoon."

"You're absolutely right, Mrs. Thomas," said Bertha. She could never be sure which name to use. She slipped into the use of Joanna when she was passionate about something — extra delighted or extra shocked (or in *labour*) — but Joanna had only *once* called her anything but Mrs. Shirley, and that one time was only because she was terrified that Bertha was going to have her baby right there in the parlour, before they even had time to fetch the doctor. "I've been so busy with Anne that I actually didn't notice. Maybe we should contact her and make sure she's all right. I'd feel terrible if I discovered that she'd broken a leg or been ill, and I hadn't even sent over a note to cheer her up."

By "being busy with Anne," Bertha really meant watching Anne, talking to Anne, holding Anne, playing with Anne. She'd never been so happy in her entire life. And now the crocus plants had come and gone, and her little back garden was full of a crop of daffodils — which were so cheerful and so deeply *yellow* that Bertha could almost believe that this damp and windy May was actually *spring*. What's more, the next day was the first of June. They could leave that chilly month behind, and jump right into something like summer.

"I'll go right over," said Joanna, "as soon as the bread comes out of the oven."

But before that happened, Walter arrived home from school. When Bertha told him about her concerns about Jessie, he put his boots right back on, and set off for the Gleesons'. In half an hour he was back.

"Gerald's been in bed with a fever ever since Friday afternoon," reported Walter. "And now two of the girls seem to be coming down with it. Jessie's beside herself, she's so worried. I went in to get a list of the things she needs so that I can borrow Gerald's horse and wagon and pick them up for her tomorrow afternoon. Flour, sugar, potatoes, milk, ipecac — all sorts of things she's running out of. You can't believe the amount of sneezing and coughing that I could hear coming from the bedrooms. Of course I didn't go anywhere near them, and Jessie shooed me out of the house as soon as she made up the list. 'There's no way I'm going to let any of the Gleeson germs into that little yellow house,' she said."

When Walter returned from shopping for Jessie on the following day, and had delivered horse, wagon, and groceries to the Gleeson house, he entered the little kitchen with a frown on his face. Joanna had gone home, and Bertha was at the stove, testing the potatoes, stirring a pot of stew. Anne was gurgling in her basket, set up on the kitchen table.

"Walter!" she cried. "What's wrong?" He'd never come home like this. Even at exam time, when he was exhausted from staying up half the night marking papers, he always returned from school with a smile on his face.

"Jessie's youngest — Jenny — has a terrible fever," he said. "Jessie said that her little body is as hot as fire. Gerald got out of bed and went for Dr. Bates, but the doctor's so sick himself that his wife wouldn't even let Gerald speak to him. She said to give Jenny lots to drink and keep her warm. She said for her to gargle with salt and water. But Jenny's only six. She doesn't know how to gargle. Besides, she's too weak. She keeps swallowing it. Poor Jessie! She looks so full of fear. And I couldn't think of a single way to help her."

Bertha stopped stirring the stew, and sat down on one of the kitchen chairs. Her face was even paler than usual. She was twisting her apron strings together, round and round her index finger.

"Jenny could die," she whispered, "and there wouldn't be any way to stop it from happening. Oh, Walter, I want so much to go and comfort her and help her, but I don't dare enter that house." Bertha looked at Anne in her basket, so happy, so *healthy*, and her eyes filled with tears. She shut her eyes, and said, "Please, God. *Please.*"

On the following day, Bertha asked Mrs. Thomas to make another huge pot of stew. "Forget the laundry and the cleaning," she said, "and I'll look after supper for Walter and me. Fill the stew full of vegetables and meat, and pretend that you're making it for a family of fifteen. Walter will take it over to the Gleesons when he comes home. It's only food, but I can't think of anything else to do."

That evening, when Walter returned from delivering the stew to the Gleesons, Bertha met him at the door.

"Well?" she said.

"Jenny's worse. Her breathing's very bad. Jessie's afraid to go to sleep at night for fear she ..." He let the sentence dangle away. "Gerald and she are taking turns sleeping. He's better, and so is the other girl."

"Mary?"

"Yes."

"And Jessie isn't sick?"

"No. She hasn't got it yet. But I don't know why. She's been looking after all of them."

On the following afternoon, Walter delivered a plateful of muffins and two loaves of bread to the Gleesons. When he returned, there were the same questions.

"Jenny?"

"Bad. Very bad."

"And still no doctor?"

"No. But there's a rumour around the school that he may be ready to work by next week."

"But Jenny ..."

"Yes. I know."

"And Jessie. She's not sick yet?"

"It's hard to tell. She looks worse than sick from all the anxiety and loss of sleep. She said she had the start of a sore throat. But she's gargling with salt and water."

"Oh, my dear heavens!" breathed Bertha, and put both hands over her face. "I'm so frightened for them all."

And I'm frightened for us, he thought. He didn't tell her that he'd had a sore throat, too, ever since he'd awakened that morning. He pulled down his heavy sweater from the hook by the back door. It was June the third, and the afternoon sun was streaming in through the kitchen window. But he was feeling oddly chilly.

TEN

A Small World

Mrs. Thomas spent the weekends with her own family, so Walter and Bertha looked after their own small household together on Saturdays and Sundays. A combination of fatigue and anxiety had made Bertha's milk dry up, so Anne was now being bottle-fed. She wasn't too pleased with this change in her life, and did a lot of spirited crying in order to register the fact. However, the new regimen did mean that Walter could now get up in the middle of the night to feed her, and could take over some of her other nurturing needs during the day.

Nevertheless, Bertha felt so weak that she found it difficult to do the simplest of tasks — making a pot of soup, heating Anne's milk, boiling her bottles, making the bed, scraping the carrots for their own meal. Mrs. Hepworth, who dropped by to see how Anne had grown and to bring her a small toy rattle, was shocked by Bertha's appearance. She was paler and thinner than Mrs. Hepworth had ever seen her.

"I don't suppose," she said, settling into the kitchen rocker for a cup of tea, "that you have that fever that's going around. They say it just wears you down to nothing. And, Bertha, my dear, you don't look entirely ... you know ... *well.*"

Bertha managed what she hoped was a spirited smile. "Oh no, Mrs. Hepworth. Nothing like that. I don't have a single one of the symptoms. No headache. No sore throat. No aching bones. And how could I get it? I never see anyone who's sick."

"Well, then," prompted Mrs. Hepworth, better known for

her plain speech than her tact, "why on earth do you look so terrible? Even your beautiful hair looks limp and dry."

Bertha tried to keep the smile on her face and Mrs. Hepworth's words out of her mind. It was hard enough *feeling* dreadful without receiving the news that she *looked* that way. "I'm just worn down by lack of sleep," she said, "and by terrible anxiety." Bertha tried not to hear Anne's shrieks or the sound of Walter pacing the floor with her in the upstairs bedroom.

"Anxiety about what?" Mrs. Hepworth was sincerely concerned.

"Well, I'm afraid that the fever might get into this house and attack my Anne," Bertha said. "And I'm worried lest Jessie come down with it and be unable to nurse her family. But most of all, I'm frantic about little Jenny. She's *very* sick."

"Not any longer," said Mrs. Hepworth, without even a short preamble to soften the blow. "She died last night on the stroke of midnight. Just shut her eyes and stopped breathing. My Geoffrey went over to deliver some hot rolls, not an hour ago. Gerald told him. He had an apron on. And there was a terrible sound of everybody crying."

Bertha bent over, covering her face with her hands. Jenny *dead*! How do you survive having that happen to your child? She thought she would scream — right out loud — if Mrs. Hepworth didn't stop talking and *go away*. But she managed to ask, without removing her hands from her face, "Jessie — is she all right?" Bertha knew she wasn't all right, but she had to ask something.

"No," said Mrs. Hepworth. "She certainly isn't all right. She's in bed — so sick that she doesn't even have the strength to cry out loud. Gerald said she just lies there with the tears streaming down her face."

Bertha started to cry, and she felt as though she might never stop. Even Mrs. Hepworth could see that it might be time for her to leave. She rose from the chair and headed for the front door, calling out to Walter, "Mr. Shirley! I think perhaps Mrs. Shirley needs you." Then she was gone.

Upstairs, Walter had placed Anne in her crib and tucked the covers carefully around her. She'd stopped crying and was in a deep sleep. He went into the other bedroom and looked at himself in the mirror. He didn't look as sick as he felt. His throat was so sore that it was hard to swallow. His head was pounding with the rhythm of his own heartbeat.

But in general, Walter was extremely healthy. He was almost never sick. So although he felt ill, he still felt strong enough to cope. But Bertha. She could succumb to this fever very quickly and become extremely sick. And she had her mother's weak lungs. He shuddered.

But what should he do? He was determined not to let her know he was ill. Look at the way she was worrying so much about the Gleesons — particularly Jenny — that she could hardly walk across the kitchen without tiring. But how could he balance that thought with the possibility that he might pass along his sickness to her — and to Anne.

Then Mrs. Hepworth called him as she was leaving the house.

Walter raced down the stairs and into the small kitchen, where he found Bertha crying uncontrollably. However, amazingly, she stood up, held out her arms, and managed to say, "Jenny's dead, Walter. Jessie's too ill to cry out loud. Hold me, Walter. Keep me safe from all this. Make it not be true."

What could he do? This was not the time to talk to her about germs. He had kept his face averted from Anne when he was cuddling and comforting her, and he had heard that breastfeeding infants gave them an immunity from disease. He felt she was safe. He moved forward and gathered Bertha into his arms. He knew she wasn't at all safe. He buried his face in her tangled hair, stroked her neck, held her tight.

After a while Bertha's frantic crying stopped. Her face looked puffy and red — but calm.

"Thank you, Walter," she murmured, as she sank into the rocking chair. "You've comforted me in my grief, and swept away most of my fears. As usual, you've known how to rescue me."

Walter tried not to think. He shut his eyes briefly, and then went over to the stove to make her a cup of hot tea.

Walter needn't have worried about that warm and necessary hug infecting Bertha. She was already ill. The sore throat and blinding headache wouldn't strike her until early evening, but she felt weak and dizzy, and her mind was often confused as the day wore on. She put sugar in the boiling potatoes instead of salt; at one point she couldn't remember Jessie's name; her grief over Jenny's death took on a dreamlike quality. Walter cooked most of the Saturday meals, and she scarcely noticed. And some obscure part of her knew what lay ahead. When she went to say good-night to Anne, she didn't pick her up, didn't kiss her, didn't, in fact, even touch her.

"Anne," she said. "Thank you for being born. For being so beautiful and so smart and funny, even at three months of age. There is no one on earth so blessed as I am, to have received such a perfect gift. Be well. Be happy in your life."

Walter listened to this little speech with growing uneasiness. What did it mean? Why didn't Bertha touch her? He knew that sometimes she had little swiftly fading visions about tomorrow, or next week, or even next year. He didn't question her about this now. He didn't want to receive an answer.

By nightfall, Bertha's forehead was hot, her body shivering, her throat too sore to swallow the hot milk that Walter brought to her. She felt as though every bone in her body was an aching tooth. Her head was a drumbeat of pain; her eyes burned.

Walter knew that Dr. Bates was going to return to his duties on Monday, but he couldn't wait that long. Tomorrow was Sunday. In the morning, people would be getting out horses and buggies for their journeys to church. He would borrow one and go directly to Dr. Bates's home, begging him — if necessary on bended knee — to come to see Bertha.

When Walter arrived at Dr. Bates's house on the following day, the doctor himself answered the door. He looked thin and white, but his posture was erect and his eyes clear.

The doctor knew Walter well. He had, after all, delivered Anne, and had made calls on other occasions. Walter taught mathematics to two of his sons. Dr. Bates liked him. *Everyone* liked him, including the two sons.

"I know it's Sunday," began Walter, "and that you've been very ill yourself. But ..."

However, the doctor had already seen the anxiety on Walter's face, had recognized a face that was already flushed with fever. Before he finished his sentence, Dr. Bates was already reaching for his bag and his jacket.

Walter had been afraid to leave Bertha and Anne alone, but he had had no choice. It was too much to ask of a neighbour to come into that house and risk catching the dreaded illness. By the time he and the doctor returned, it was almost time for church. Walter hastily returned the horse and buggy while the doctor went into the house to examine Bertha.

When Walter arrived back at the house, the doctor was bent over Bertha, listening to her breathing. It was making a rough, rasping noise, and her eyes were restless and unfocused. Dr. Bates straightened up and faced Walter.

"I don't need to tell you, Mr. Shirley," he said, "that your wife is gravely ill. From what you've said, I gather that this fever is attacking a body that was already unwell. She's delirious. Her fever is appallingly high. I feel you need to know that her chances are not good. You may need to contact her family."

"We have no family, Dr. Bates. Neither she nor I. We're alone in the world. Except for Anne. She's our world."

"Then look after yourself, Mr. Shirley. She may be *your* world. But you are *hers*. Keep it safe for her. I know you have the fever yourself. I recognize the signs. Drink a lot of water. Drown yourself in tea and clear soup. Gargle with salt and water. Get a lot of rest. Take it easy."

Quietly, in her sleep, Bertha died at three o'clock on Monday morning. Walter sat in the room beside her for a long time, stroking her hair, memorizing each line of her face, grieving. He was scarcely aware of the disease that was ravaging his own body.

"This was too fast," he whispered. "The fever moved too quickly. It gave me no time to prepare my heart for this bitter blow."

Finally he stood up, just as the sun was rising over the far hills. He looked out the window at the flowers that Bertha had planted, at the lowlands reaching down to the river, at the road leading to the Gleesons' house. Slowly he walked into Anne's room. Oddly, she was awake, but not crying for either food or attention. She was smiling at him, reaching out with her small hands.

Walter went downstairs and washed his hands. After that, he put on a fresh clean shirt and carefully buttoned it. Then he went into Anne's room and picked her up, holding her close to his chest, letting his tears fall on her red head.

"Just you and me," he said softly. "Not a very large world."

ELEVEN

*F*our Days

Walter Shirley spent the next four days in a sort of physical and mental blur. This took the edge off his shock and grief at the loss of his beloved wife, but made it more difficult to cope with the other demands of his life. He had to arrange for Bertha's funeral and burial, oversee Anne's care at the hands of Mrs. Thomas, offer some kind of hospitality to the people who arrived at his door to offer their condolences, and try to figure out a way to pay the doctor's bills and look after the expenses in connection with the funeral. The casket, for instance: how on earth was he going to be able to pay for *that*? His mind reeled. His skin burned. His joints ached. He could hardly see out of his throbbing eyes. *This is not what Dr. Bates meant*, he mused, *by taking it easy*. He couldn't stop and sit down for one moment.

Walter actually went to teach his mathematics classes on Tuesday, attending Jenny's interment on his way home from school. Jessie wasn't there. Gerald stood beside the grave, his face a mask of despair, holding the hands of his two other daughters, with his son gripping his trousers, while the small casket was lowered into the ground. Mrs. Hepworth whispered to him, "The doctor wouldn't let Jessie come. She's too sick." Walter held tightly on to the nearest tombstone and tried not to think.

On the following day, Walter went to school once again. He had been up for much of the night trying to comfort Anne, who was weeping wildly — missing her mother's comforting arms. Walter didn't dare pick her up. His one remaining fear was that he might pass his illness to Anne and lose her as well as Bertha. He felt she was safer with Mrs. Thomas. When he fainted during school assembly on Thursday, the principal drove him home and told him to stay there until he had completely recovered. Walter staggered into the house and collapsed on the chesterfield, where Mrs. Thomas found him when she came downstairs from feeding Anne. She covered him with his grandmother's old afghan, and went into the kitchen to finish making dinner.

When Mrs. Thomas returned to the parlour to see if Walter would like a cup of tea, he appeared to be asleep. His breathing was shallow and laboured, and when she felt his forehead it was very hot. But he opened his eyes when he heard the rustling of her petticoats, and reached out his arm to catch her skirt.

"Joanna," he said, his voice barely above a whisper, "listen to me." He had never called her Joanna before. "You know the little blue enamel box that Bertha kept her brooches in. She loved it. Give it to Anne. Make sure she gets it. I'll keep Bertha's wedding ring. I need to keep *something*." It was a long speech, laboured and slow. After Joanna left the room, Walter Shirley closed his tired eyes. And died.

In the kitchen, Joanna suddenly stopped stirring the soup that she was preparing for Walter. Something was wrong. What was it? Well, for goodness' sake, she told herself, *of course* something was wrong. Bertha was dead — Bertha, who was the loveliest person she'd ever worked for. And now the little yellow house was no longer — and could never be again — the happiest home she had ever lived in. It was terrible witnessing Mr. Shirley's numbing grief — he who had been so lighthearted and full of laughter and warmth. Unlike so many others, he wasn't going to turn around and marry just any little snippet of a pretty girl who passed his way. No. That grief of his was going to last a very long time. And little Jenny was dead, too. Mrs. Thomas didn't know Jenny, but it was clear to her that she had been Jessie's favourite child. She had never said that, of course, but it was easy to read between the lines. Jessie had adored her.

And other things were wrong, too. Bert had been drinking ever since last Friday. When she'd been getting ready to return to the Shirleys' on Monday morning, he'd said, "So you're going to spend the day with that Shirley family that's so bloody perfect. You'll be workin' for them all week, while your own floor gets dirtier and dirtier, and the bellies of your own family are screamin' for a good meal." Then he had slapped her right across her face. She had hoped that Mr. Shirley wouldn't notice the black bruise just below her left eye. But she needn't have worried. Mr. Shirley hadn't been noticing anything at all.

So yes, there were a lot of things that were wrong. Dear Mrs. Shirley hadn't even been buried yet. Both the gravediggers were down with fever, and Mr. Shirley hadn't ordered the casket yet. Probably he could hardly bear to let her go. Joanna laid the wooden spoon on a saucer, and went into the parlour to see if Mr. Shirley was awake yet.

Walter had always had a ruddy complexion, and during the past week his face had been made an angry red by his burning fever. But now his face was white. "As white as death," she whispered. When she felt his forehead, she added, "And as cold."

Joanna sat down on one of the chairs and stared ahead of her at the blank north wall of the room. She stayed like that for a long time. Then she bent over and grasped her forehead with both hands. "What to do?" she asked out loud, over and over again. What to do about Mr. Shirley's body, about yet another casket, about the house, the furniture, the clothes, the books, the bills — for the doctor, for the new pile of wood at the back door, for the funeral, for *her*.

Upstairs, Anne was starting to cry.

Joanna looked at the ceiling and closed her eyes. "And most of all," she whispered, "what to do about Anne?"

TWELVE

What to Do?

Jessie looked out her parlour window at the dazzlingly beautiful June day. It seemed downright indecent, she felt, that this particular day would have the insensitivity to be sunny and warm, bright and cheerful with apple blossoms and dandelions, soft and fragrant with the scent of a dozen lilac bushes. She looked up the street to the little yellow house, and watched the trickle of people walking in and out the front door. Some were carrying baskets of food, bouquets of flowers, cards. For whom? Jessie guessed that they were for the other people who were doing the same thing. Mrs. Thomas was probably there — putting the food away, arranging flowers in pots and vases, reading the verses on the cards. And feeding Anne.

Jessie sighed. The beauty of the day was like a physical blow to her. At the moment, it seemed impossible to her that she would ever feel cheerful again. To lose your child and your best friend in the space of one week — and at a time when the fever was rushing through her like a torrent — this was far, far too much to bear. The fever had passed, but she felt as exhausted and weak, as if she was still gravely ill. She had had to miss Jenny's funeral, but she was going to attend this one, even if she had to crawl there on her hands and knees.

Jessie's mother, Mrs. MacIntyre, had left her big house on the other side of the river and come to help Jessie through her convalescence and bereavement. She entered the parlour as her daughter smoothed the curtains back in place, and spoke.

"Now, Jessie," she began, "I want you to show a little sense. You've only been out of your bed for one day. It's too soon for you to be out gallivanting around to someone's funeral. I don't want you to even *think* of leaving the house today."

Jessie sat down on the nearest chair in order to conserve the strength she needed to stand up to her mother. What she wanted to do was scream, but she knew from experience that screaming was a pointless strategy. Also, she didn't have the requisite energy for it.

"Mama," she said quietly, "I missed Jenny's funeral, but that's only because I was too sick to be able to resist what all the rest of you were making me do." Then she stopped talking and wept for a few minutes. Mrs. MacIntyre waited until her daughter had finished crying.

"Well," she went on, "I hope you'll listen to us this time, too. Your other children need you, and so does Gerald. You could slip right back into that fever if you overdo."

"Then I'll just slip," said Jessie fiercely. Although she was sitting down, her back was as straight as a board. "I'm going to that funeral this afternoon, Mama, and I'm going to take Anne with me. Bertha was the kindest friend I ever had, and Walter was a wonderful man. They were Anne's parents. She should be there. Besides" — and here Jessie choked back a sob — "she needs me, and what's more, I need *her*."

Jessie was thinking back to a conversation she'd had with Gerald yesterday afternoon: "Gerald," she'd said, out of the clear blue sky. "I want us to adopt Anne."

"*What?*"

"I want to take Anne. I want to keep her. I want to do that for Bertha and Walter. And to tell you the truth, I want to do it for *me*."

"You must be right out of your mind — clear *crazy!*" Gerald got out of his chair and started pacing around the room. "We've got three children left, and with what I make at my job, that's more than enough." When Gerald saw the tears starting to creep down Jessie's face, he knew he'd said the wrong thing.

"Oh, Jessie," he said, "I didn't mean that Jenny was one too many. Jenny was so sweet that I could have had six more like her." He stopped talking for a moment, because it was clearly hard for him to continue. When Jessie saw his grief, she almost forgave him for some of the things he did and didn't do. And almost saw his point of view. But not quite.

"It would help me," she said. "I know I'd get better faster. It'd be nice to have a tiny baby to care for and hold and love."

Then Gerald became his other self again. "If that Anne baby was an ordinary baby," he said sharply, "I might try to half listen to you. But that thing is so thin and scrawny and pinched-looking that it'd be easier for me to snuggle up to a fox terrier. And all that ugly orange hair! No, ma'am! If you think I'd let that pathetic excuse for a baby into this house to take the place of our beautiful Jenny, you got another think coming. Screeching and crying half the night, keeping everyone awake, and never anything you'd want to cuddle or love."

Then Gerald softened ever so little. "I'm sorry, Jessie, but I just can't. I know you need something to make you feel better. We all do. But taking in that little witch of a baby isn't going to help you one bit."

Jessie knew he was wrong. It *would* make her feel a lot better. But she'd lived with Gerald long enough to know when she'd hit a stone wall. She knew he'd never change his mind.

The funeral service was short, but moving, and there were a lot of tears. The high school was closed for the afternoon, and many teachers and students attended both the church ceremony and the interment. Bertha had been popular with her students in the preceding year, and many of them came to pay their respects, although few of them had any opinion as to how their attendance would benefit her. The rest of the church was crammed with a small army of Walter's students, who had looked on him as a hero, a mentor, a unique friend. Walter had been so vibrant and energetic that it was difficult for most of them to believe the body inside the casket was all that remained of their Mr. Shirley.

But the students and staff were not the only admirers of the Shirleys. A local cabinet maker, Mr. Hudson, whose three children had been taught by both teachers, had been in the final stage of making a casket for Bertha — a simple but beautifully fashioned pine box — as a gift to Walter. Suddenly his son had burst into the workroom and told him that Walter had died. Without a word, he had risen, gathered the necessary wood together, and begun to make the first cut in the wood that would become Walter's coffin.

At the graveside, everyone stood around the large double grave while the final service was performed. A chair had been provided for Jessie, because of her recent illness. Gerald stood beside her, as did her three children, and Anne Shirley lay in her lap, sleeping peacefully, unaware of the enormous tragedy that had befallen her.

Then, when the service was over, a number of people returned to the little yellow house to drink the tea that Joanna had prepared, and eat the many squares and cookies and sweet breads that had been provided by friends. They spoke quietly about Bertha and Walter, and talked of their good qualities and of how sadly they would be missed. They talked of the unusually early spring, and the loveliness of

Bertha's garden. They spoke of the price of sugar and the quality of the year's unusual crop of early strawberries. A member of the board of education made an announcement that the board would put up a memorial stone to mark the graves of two of the best teachers who had ever taught at Bolingbroke High School.

But what most of the people were thinking was, Who will pay the doctor's bills and the rent? How will Mrs. Thomas be paid? What will happen to all the furniture, all the books, all the clothes, all the little personal things that were on the shelves and in the bureau drawers? And most of all, what will happen to that little baby on Jessie Gleeson's lap?

THIRTEEN

*M*oving Out

That morning, Mr. Thomas — Bert — had sat on the edge of the bed, watching Joanna dress and fix her hair. She wore her best and prettiest dress. She had only three dresses that anyone could describe as pretty — but this was the one she loved best. If this wasn't an occasion worthy of wearing it, what was? Never mind that the last time she'd worn it — for cousin Minnie's wedding in Gary's River — Bert, who had been drinking for two days, had said, "It's like putting a queen's dress onto a slab of wood." Oddly enough, he remembered that comment as he watched her pin up her hair and pinch her cheeks to bring some colour into them. He wished he hadn't said that.

Bert hadn't had a drop to drink for three days. He'd had three days in which to look at that ugly bruise on her face. He knew that pinching her cheeks wasn't going to hide that big mark below her left eye. It had gone from black to blue, and now it was turning into a sickening shade of yellow. He'd like to take some of his boat paint and hide it. He felt *sorry*.

Bert could be kind, and he could bring warmth into the house on days when he was sober. Then he was often squeezed tight by regret at what he might have done when he'd been drunk. Sometimes he remembered, and sometimes he didn't. He didn't think he hit his three children, but he could often tell by the marks on Joanna's arms or face that he'd roughed her up. Then he'd go out to the barn and look for a bottle to ease his guilt.

But Joanna hadn't been bringing home any money from the Shirleys since the fever had hit them, and he'd been fired from his last job three weeks ago. So there'd been no bottles to comfort him in his aching despair, although he'd looked under and behind every single item in that little building.

"You look fine, Joanna," he said. He was lying, but it seemed the right thing to do. "I mind when we did all that dancin', before we was wed. You really knew good how to kick up those lace petticoats."

Joanna turned from the mirror and stared at him. This was a Bert she almost never saw, and each time it happened, she felt stunned by the wonder of it.

But as Joanna stared at him, she was also thinking. He was obviously feeling sorry about that blow to her face. And he knew she was grieving over the deaths of the Shirleys. He might be feeling something almost close to affection. Or a desire to *atone*. She decided to speak what was on her mind.

"Bert," she began, twisting her wedding ring round and round her finger. "I mightn't get any money from last month's work at the Shirleys'. I don't think there was much to give me, and I'm sure they owed some on the rent. And there's all that wood they just ordered for the kitchen stove. And doctor bills. But you know what? I don't care if I get none. I was happy in that house, and no one can take that away from me. But —"

"But what?"

"But everyone's near crazy with wondering what to do with that baby — with Anne. They might give me some of her stuff — Bertha's stuff — if I —"

"If you what?"

"If I took Anne. They might give us the furniture — and the clothes. They'd fit Eliza. She's right pretty and small, like

Bertha. She's fifteen, Bert. We don't want her to look like she came out of some orphanage. And she's old enough to look after Anne when I get another job. Bert?" She rubbed the bruise on her face.

"What?"

"Can I take Anne? Can I?"

Bert didn't answer. He was thinking. If they got the furniture, they could maybe sell it and get some money. He thought he was going to die if he didn't have a drink pretty soon, and you can't buy bottles with poker chips. It was clear that no one was going to find any money inside those two caskets. If he could get just one bottle, he'd drink it real slowly, and make it last. And maybe get a job. Things could get better. With more money he could make the house tighter for next winter. His brothers might help. God, but he needed a drink.

"Go ahead," he said. "Get her. Get that Anne baby. I saw her once. A weird-looking little thing. Skinny for a baby. Don't look like she'd eat much. Get her. Tell them right away when you go over this morning."

Tell who? Joanna wondered. Well, she'd just wait till the subject came up. She smiled at Bert, feeling some residue of affection for him. He was still handsome, and he'd passed his good looks on to his three children — something else to feel grateful for. She gave herself a quick look in the mirror. Even in her best dress, she was no great prize. But she'd have that nice furniture from the Shirleys' long-dead parents. And pretty dresses and petticoats for Eliza. And she'd have Anne. That might be like bringing a piece of that happy home into her own troubled one.

The warm and sunny day of the funeral passed, and with late afternoon came a gathering of clouds and a sharp wind. Joanna was dropped off at her house by the Gleesons. She was carrying Anne, and she was followed by a parade of boxes of baby clothes, bottles, a crib — all of it laid down in the front room by Gerald Gleeson.

"Well," said Bert, after Gerald had left. "So we got a new baby."

Anne looked toward Bert and gave him her wide, toothless smile. He found himself smiling back.

"When do we get the furniture?"

Joanna felt very frightened. But surely Bert wouldn't strike her while she was holding Anne.

"We don't," she said. Her voice was barely audible. "Reverend Anderson was in charge. He gave the furniture to Dr. Bates to cover his bills. I got all Bertha's clothes. They're in a big box in their little parlour. And a smaller box with more baby things. And the food that's left — not much. It's in another box. And some little things in a fourth box. They're marked. We can pick them up tomorrow. I got a key."

Then Joanna paused, looking shocked.

"Oh! And something I forgot!"

"What? For God's sake, woman, it'd better be good!"

"Something important that Mr. Shirley said I was to give Anne. A pretty little enamel box that Mrs. Shirley loved. It's blue. He said to be sure she got it — just a minute or so before he died. It's on the top of their bureau. I forgot to bring it. Oh, dear! I hope it's still there."

Bert looked at Joanna. His rage was visible, but he didn't touch her. "So," he rasped, "we got four boxes and one scrawny carrot-headed baby. That's what we got." He turned around and slammed his way out the back door.

Joanna handed Anne to Eliza, who held her and rocked her while her mother was preparing supper. Bert didn't return until nine o'clock, long after the dishes were washed.

"I got my horse outside," he announced when he came in, "and Marcus Hennigar's wagon hitched to her. I'm gettin' them boxes tonight. Gimme that key." Upstairs, Anne was crying. "Nice music," sneered Bert. "Fit to dance to." He gave Joanna a look full of hate, and left the house.

Bert drove up to the little yellow house and steered his horse and wagon over the lawn and Bertha's flowers into the back yard. There he tethered the horse and tried the key in the back door. It fitted. Good! He could do his work unnoticed by prying eyes.

Bert lit his torch and walked through the house. Yes, the furniture was nice. From Mr. Shirley's family in Upper Canada, they said. Lucky doctor. Dr. Bates had come to this house only five times. Joanna had been serving that family for months. Scrubbing floors, washing clothes, cooking a thousand meals. Sure, she got her money regular. He should know. She gave it to him, and he ... spent it. But nothing, not a cent, for the last two weeks.

He looked at the furniture carefully. What did he like best? What would make his house look like it was really ... what was the word his mother-in-law used? Oh yes. *Refined*. He'd show that woman. As soon as he saw it, he knew it was the piece of furniture that he was going to carry out of the house. It was a tall bookcase with elaborately carved frames around two glass doors. He opened it and threw all the books on the floor. Keats, Shakespeare, Matthew Arnold were piled higgledy-piggledy on top or beneath textbooks in mathematics. Bert kicked them aside and dragged the heavy bookcase over the hall floor, through the kitchen, and shoved and pulled it up onto the wagon. Then he collected the four boxes from the parlour and loaded them beside the bookcase.

Finally, he went upstairs to get the little blue enamel box. He found it on the bureau, picked it up quickly, and stuffed it in his pocket. He knew he needed to get away from that house fast, before someone came to inspect the flickering lights.

When Bert delivered the boxes and bookcase to his home, Joanna said almost nothing. She knew when it was wise not to speak. But with her heart pounding, she found the courage to say, "The little blue enamel box — did you find it?"

"It was gone." He said. "Somebody musta took it."

On the following day, Bert took the little enamel box and contents to the local pawn shop. It contained a ring, a small gold chain, and two brooches. He was pleased by the amount of money he got for it. Then he went to the bootlegger and bought five bottles. One to drink, and four to hide. He was drunk for three days.

Thus it was that Anne came to her second home.

FOURTEEN

*M*oving In

Right from the beginning, Eliza felt as though Anne was hers. Her own baby. She was fifteen years old, with a strong maternal instinct, and all she wanted out of life was to leave her troubled home, get married, and have babies. She hadn't done well at school. Bert said she didn't have to go back in the fall. She'd spent two years in the sixth class, and as far as Bert was concerned, that was more than enough schooling for anyone.

After all, it was three more years than he'd had. He knew you didn't have to be smart or have a lot of schooling to get a good job. He'd had good jobs often. Never mind that he lost them. That was because he kept turning up drunk. It didn't have anything to do with how good he was at those jobs.

Besides, Eliza wouldn't need a fancy job or money. With her milky skin and clouds of dark brown hair — curly, even — she'd be snapped up pretty quick by some handsome young man — a farmer, maybe, with twenty acres of fertile land and an itch for a pretty wife. She'd be wedded before she was eighteen. And with Bertha's pretty clothes, she could even snare some lucky buck by the time she was seventeen. Sure. No sense in any more schooling. That was just a waste of time. And he needed her at home when Joanna was out cleaning people's houses. Eliza might not have led her class at school, but she was good at everything else a man needs. She could cook better than Joanna, knew how to sew her own dresses, could mend his socks, and kept the other children out of the barn when he wanted to be alone. Yes. He needed Eliza.

Eliza gazed down at Anne, asleep in her warm blanket, and knew that she loved her. She was a girl who tended to protect their smallest chickens, cried over the calves that were sickly and had to be shot, kept wounded birds in old shoeboxes. This odd-looking little baby was exactly right for Eliza. She'd protect her from her quarrelsome (and beautiful) sisters, and would keep her in her own room. There were three bedrooms in the drafty Thomas house — one for her parents, one shared by her sisters and a tiny one she'd been given — for her *alone* — ever since she'd started having her monthlies. There was enough space to cram the crib into, and she could keep Anne's clothes in boxes, and stuff them under the bed. Eliza stroked Anne's soft curls, and knew that what she held in her arms was much more satisfying than any doll she'd ever owned. And she just bet that there wasn't even one other baby in Bolingbroke with hair that was that red — that *orange*. This baby, this Anne, was *special*.

Watching all this, Joanna nodded. Maybe it would all work out all right. Bert was already out in the barn drinking. She couldn't imagine where he'd found the money for the bottle that she saw sticking out of his back pocket, but he'd certainly found it. The three days of sobriety had been nice, but she'd known it couldn't last. She'd have to find another job. She'd heard that Jim Jamieson's old mother had moved in with them. She was a large woman, and she'd had a bad stroke. Jim's wife needed help with the lifting and bedpan and extra laundry. Joanna had thought she might have to pay more attention to Anne, who'd been doing a lot of screeching since her parents had died. But look at Eliza. She was acting like Anne was her very own child. And Anne was gurgling and smiling, holding out her tiny hands to touch Eliza's face. Good!

Joanna soon realized she didn't really want Anne for herself. Probably she just wanted something — someone — to remind her of her brief months of happiness in the Shirley home. And then there was all that furniture that she'd hoped she'd get. Well, she got the bookcase. She'd have liked to have the books, too — not to read, but just because she admired the way they looked, standing up so straight and colourful behind those glass doors. Bert must have dumped them all on the floor in his haste to get the bookcase out of the house. Oh, well. She could keep her dishes in there. Once they were behind the glass, it wouldn't be so easy to see how chipped and faded they looked. And she could pretend that the lovely piece of furniture had come from her grandparents. It would make any visitors think that once upon a time in her life — even if it was a long way back — her family had been some-bodies. She knew that her own mother had been stern and proud. But Joanna also knew — and so did everyone else in town — that her own family had been dirt poor. All that pride was just to fool people. Well, she could do that, too.

When Joanna returned after a day of exhausting work at the Jamiesons' (helping Ida to lift the old lady out of her bed, washing her soiled sheets every day, scrubbing those old pine floors, peeling potatoes, salting meat), she lacked the energy or interest to notice how quickly Anne was growing. But Eliza noticed. And talked about it all the time.

"Just look, Mama," she'd say. "See how long Anne's getting. She's going to be some tall. And her gurgles seem to *mean* something. Like 'I love you,' or 'Sing me a song,' or 'Give me my rattle.' Or even 'Thank you' when I do something she really likes — like bring her a bottle of sugar water."

Joanna would say, "Uh-huh" or "Is supper ready yet?" And Bert would say, "If you got nothing better to do than play with that damned baby, you could maybe try scrubbin' the dirt off this kitchen floor!" And her sisters would say something like, "Oh, hold your tongue! We're all sick of hearing about Anne, Anne, Anne!" or "Yeah. Long and tall. But funny-looking, too."

Eliza would go off to her cold little room with Anne, and sulk. By the time Joanna had cooked the supper that Eliza was supposed to cook, she didn't feel friendly toward anyone, especially Eliza or Anne. Up in her room, Eliza would think about how soon she could escape from this angry house. She'd get married as soon as she could find a nice man, and *leave*. Or get a job as a maid in some fancy house, where everyone was polite and kind and not yelling at one another. And wherever she went, she'd take Anne with her. Anyone would be happy to have Anne come too — Anne with her huge bright eyes, always so *interested* in everything, always smiling with her happy wide mouth if you did even the tiniest nice thing for her.

In spite of her weariness, Joanna couldn't help noticing a lot of things about Anne. She could see — without wanting to — that Anne did just about everything earlier than her own children had done. She could also see more and more of Bertha in her pert little nose, her pointed chin, her enormous grey eyes. And if the light was shining in a certain way, green eyes. Anne had a lot of Walter in her, too — her energy, her quick way of moving, her ready laughter. Anne sat up — all by herself — at an age when most babies would be lying down. Then she would often pull herself up on a chair leg, and walk around the chair, holding on to the seat.

One day Joanna heard a shriek from Eliza on the second floor. Before she got to the stairs, Joanna heard her yell, "She's *walking*! She's *walking*!"

"She can't be," said Joanna firmly, and somewhat crossly, as she climbed upstairs, "She's only eight months old." But there she was — Bertha and Walter's baby — walking with considerable steadiness across the bare boards of the upper hall. And laughing. Apparently even Anne could see that it was a funny thing for an eight-month-old baby to be doing. Then, one day, when Anne looked her right in the eye and said, "Mama!" as clear as could be, she looked back at Anne with something like awe. Her own children hadn't said a single word until they were two years old, and here was Anne speaking directly to her — at nine months. Maybe she'd been wise to take that baby, even without the furniture. It was clear that she was no ordinary child. She could feel a distinct glimmer of hope that Anne might be pleasant to have around the house after her own children had left home.

But by the time Anne was a year old, Joanna stopped having thoughts like that. She knew for a fact something that she'd suspected for some time. She was pregnant. It would be many years before all her children would have left home.

$\mathscr{D}$ifficult Times

It was a difficult pregnancy for Joanna. She was sick every single morning until her fifth month, and then she developed a sore back that made it difficult for her to bend or to lift heavy objects. Working at the Jamiesons' was what she called "pure torture" — helping to push and pull that old lady out of her bed, bending over the washboard to scrub the sheets, wringing them out with her tired hands, cooking over that stove in the hot kitchen. And then, if Eliza was out walking the roads with one of her young men instead of making supper, she'd have to turn right around and prepare another meal. Eliza's sisters, Trudy and Margaret, spent more time teasing and tormenting Anne than looking after her, so by the time Joanna arrived home, even Anne was sullen and cranky, pulling the faded tablecloth off the table, throwing cushions around, climbing up on a chair to reach the cookie tin — and spilling it. Sometimes Bert had a job, and sometimes not, depending on how many bottles he'd managed to stash away in his barn. By the end of the day, Joanna felt angry at the whole world, and spilled it all out on Anne.

"You wicked, wicked little girl!" she'd cry. "Look at the mess you've made with those cookies! Pick up that cushion and those papers! Stop looking so mad. You got it easy. You should be grateful that I took you in. You could at least behave yourself and be grateful." Then sometimes Joanna would slap her hand and Anne would cry. She was seventeen months old, but she looked as old as three years. And talked like a child of that age. It was easy for people to think that Anne was twice as old as she was. This could make things difficult for her, because everyone expected more of her than she was capable of.

Joanna worked until a week before the baby was born. As with all her children, her labour was quick, and she delivered the baby in her own bed. Bert was so delighted when he learned that it was a boy that he was sober for several months. "About time we got some more men around this place!" he declared. He got a job with the railway, and brought home his pay and gave it to Joanna. He went down to the lumberyard and bought enough wood to fill in some of the worst drafty places in the house. And did that work on his days off. He didn't want that baby to be cold. Joanna wondered if she had died and gone to heaven. The baby's name was Horace. Horace was strong and healthy, and slept a lot. Joanna adored him.

Eliza was now sixteen. It was true that the Thomas home had been almost a peaceful place ever since Horace was born. Most of the yelling had stopped. But Eliza's eyes were open. She knew it couldn't last. What she wanted was a husband — one who was tall and handsome, didn't drink except maybe on Saturday nights, had a job, and was a good dancer. And who would want Anne to live with them. Then she could just open the door and walk out.

Eliza loved Anne as much as ever — if not more. By the time Anne was two, Eliza thought Anne was the cleverest child she had ever seen. Sometimes she would read stories and poems to her out of her old readers before Anne went to bed. Often Anne would surprise and delight her the next day by repeating names of people and places in the stories, or asking questions about them. "Did the brook really sparkle?" or "Is the ship still on fire?" or "What's an 'empty dream'?"

But Bert eventually started drinking again, and Joanna had to return to work, in spite of not feeling well.

As time passed, Joanna wasn't just "not feeling well." She was pregnant again and knew it. Bert, who had been so thrilled by the arrival of a son, was not nearly as delighted by the delivery of a second boy, in November of that year.

One day, when Anne was almost three years old, Eliza took her for a walk in the woods. She told her about an old school friend of hers whose name was Katie Maurice. "Katie Maurice. Katie Maurice." Anne repeated the name over and over again. She seemed to be in love with the name, and with the sound that came out when she said it. "Katie!" she cried to Eliza. "It sounds like a little jump. Just listen! *Katie! Katie!*"

"And Maurice? You like Maurice, too?"

"Oh yes," said Anne. "It's like a smooth-running river." In the summer, Eliza had taken Anne down to watch the river. The tide from the bay was high, so the river was full of water, moving steadily along toward the sea. When Eliza took her there again in the fall, the tide was out, and the shiny banks of mud rose from a river that was almost empty. Anne would never forget that. A river — with and without water. She knew which she liked best.

"Eliza," Anne said. "Katie Maurice was your friend. What's a friend?"

Eliza laughed. Then she looked at Anne with a sad smile. *Poor little Anne,* she thought. *Five other children in this house, and you don't know what a friend is.*

"A friend," said Eliza, "is someone that's not in your family and who loves you. And who you love and play with every day. Friends tell each other secrets. They help you when you're sad."

Anne sat down on a rock and rested her pointed chin on her fist. "I guess I don't have a friend," she said. She spoke so softly that it was almost a whisper. "Can a very old person like you be a friend?"

Eliza grinned at Anne. "Not exactly," she said. "I'm more like a mother to you, but not quite. A real friend — a *bosom* friend — should be someone the same age as you."

Then Anne tried again. "Could the rocks and flowers out here be my friends?"

Eliza bit her lip. She thought she was really lying, but she couldn't bear seeing Anne look so sad. "Sure," she said. "You can make lots of things be your friends. Rocks and flowers would do fine. Or dogs or birds. And I changed my mind. I *can* be your friend. Of *course* I can, even if I'm sort of the wrong age. And you're *my* friend. A very special one."

"And your mama? Is she my mama too, or maybe a friend?"

Eliza was uncomfortable with that question. She couldn't think of a good answer.

"I don't know," she said. "Let's start back home. It's near suppertime."

One day when Joanna was preparing dinner for her family of eight, feeling particularly overwhelmed by the number of mouths to feed and the scarcity of food, Anne came up to her and said, "Mama, tomorrow's my birthday. I'm going to be four. Eliza told me."

Joanna looked down at the skinny little girl, and felt an annoyance that she couldn't control. What was this freckled little redhead doing in this family of handsome and beautiful brunettes? A distaste for Anne swept over her. "Don't you dare call me Mama!" she cried. "I'm not your mama, and I never will be. You're just a naughty orphan child that I was kind enough to take in when nobody else wanted you. And don't bother me with talk about birthdays. There's way too many births and birthdays in this house. Some folks have a party for a birthday. In this place, you're lucky to find enough potatoes to put in the pot."

Then Joanna left the stove and sat down on a kitchen chair. She leaned over to put her forehead in her hands. She couldn't stand the look on Anne's face. She reached out and touched her cheek. It was wet.

"I'm sorry, Anne," she said, speaking to her as though she was eighteen years old. "It's just that I don't want to even *think* about birthdays today. There's going to be a brand-new one, come August. And maybe you could call me Mrs. Thomas. There are just too many people calling me Mama right now."

Anne went upstairs and crawled into her crib, curling herself into a tight ball. The crib was too small for her, but there was no place else for her to sleep. Then she cried herself to sleep. She might have cried even harder if she had known that by the time she was five and a half, Mrs. Thomas would have produced a total of four babies — all of them sons. And by that time, the only girl left to help her look after those babies would be Anne.

Back in Bolingbroke, Jessie Gleeson looked out her window at what she would always refer to as "Bertha's house." It was still yellow, the lilacs still bloomed outside the door in early June, and the garden was well tended. But Jessie could hardly bear to look at it. She couldn't think of Bertha's death without thinking of Jenny's absence; the two tragedies were too bound up with each other. Even after all this time, the sorrow could descend upon her with its original intensity. And with it would come the old desire to see Anne, to look after Anne, to do something positive with her boundless grief. Jessie had tried not to look at the little yellow house or to think about Anne. When she could keep her mind closed from these reminders, sometimes she could forget her sorrow for hours at a time. But today — for some reason that she couldn't define — she was unable to make this happen.

Jessie had heard that Joanna's husband was often drunk. Some of the women for whom Joanna worked had seen bruises on her arms, her face. Was Anne safe? This uncertainty sometimes tortured Jessie. But she seemed to lack the courage to find out whether her fears were groundless. She had heard rumours that the oldest daughter — whose name, she thought, was Eliza — loved Anne and often looked after her. Jessie clung to that thought.

The children were at school. Gerald was at home because of some breakdown in machinery at the plant, but he had prepared the buggy for an errand later in the day. Here was Jessie's chance to visit the Thomas household and reassure herself. A quick trip to their home might give her back her peace of mind.

Jessie told Gerald she'd be gone less than an hour, and set off for the other side of the town. She felt brave and full of determination. Why had she waited so long to do this? She smiled at her foolish postponement of this obviously simple trip. Everything would be fine. And it would be lovely to see Anne.

But as Jessie rounded the bend and entered the part of the road leading to the house, she felt her courage falter. She could see a horse tethered to a post close to the front door, and she could also see that the door was open. She slowed her horse to a walk, and listened. Yes, she was right. She could hear a woman screaming. She was yelling, "Stop it! *Please!*" She could hear a baby crying. No. There was more than one. At least two. And she heard a crash — as of broken glass. She picked up speed, knowing that she would not be knocking at *that* door, and drove by the house just as Mr. Thomas stumbled down the driveway, swinging a bottle.

Back at home, Jessie attempted to convince herself that what she had seen wasn't significant. But from then on she once again avoided looking at the yellow house, tried not to think about Anne, and did all she could to erase from her memory the scene she had witnessed.

&liza's News

One day when Anne was five, she saw Eliza coming down the path with her head down. The last of that day's sun was touching her cheeks, and Anne could see that they were wet. Could Eliza be crying? Anne rushed out the door and ran to meet her, grabbing her hand.

"*Please*, Eliza," begged Anne. "*Stop crying*. You're my almost-mama, and it feels too terrible to see you cry. You're too old a lady to cry. It makes me feel not safe. I need you to be laughing, like *usual*."

Eliza sat down on the back stoop, and held Anne close to her. "I can't laugh right now," she said. "Nothing in my life is right."

"Why? *Why?*" prodded Anne.

"Listen, Anne," began Eliza. "Listen real carefully. Roger Emerson wants me to marry him."

Anne's face lit up. "Good!" she cried. "He's so handsome, and you already told me you love him. You told me that everything about him was *right*. And now you just said that nothing in your life is right. But he's perfect. Handsome. Good dancer. Good job. Doesn't drink except on Saturday nights. All those things you said you wanted. I don't understand."

Then Anne's large eyes opened extra wide, and she almost shouted, "And if you marry him, we can leave! You always promised me that! We can go where nobody's yelling, and where there's no babies crying. And nobody being drunk and angry. And Trudy can do all the work, instead of you and me."

Anne already knew about work. She folded the diapers, and collected the eggs, and stood on a box to wash dishes. When Anne stared off into space, with her thin arms dangling in the soapy water — often pretending that she was living in one of Eliza's stories — Mrs. Thomas would sometimes tell her she was wicked and lazy. She'd say things like "You lazy, ungrateful girl! I've brought you up by hand, even though you're not really my child! You should be ready to earn your keep! At the rate you're going, we'll be in the middle of the next meal before you finish those dishes."

"I'm tired," Anne might say. To which Joanna would reply, "Don't talk to *me* about being *tired*. You don't have three babies and another on the way. Try *that*, and then you'll *really* understand about being tired. Now, get moving!"

Anne, enfolded in Eliza's arms, shut her eyes and thought about life with Eliza and Roger. They'd be in a tiny little house — maybe like the yellow house she was born in. Mrs. Thomas told her about that once, and about how beautiful her mother thought she was, even though Mrs. Thomas said she was the homeliest baby she ever saw — which wasn't a nice thing for her to say, even if it was true. Maybe she didn't want to *lie*, and Anne supposed that was understandable, but she could have tried just saying *nothing*.

But life with Eliza and Roger would be so lovely. There'd be a pretty tablecloth on the table instead of oilcloth — maybe with roses embroidered on it by Eliza. She was so smart with a needle. And there'd always be lots of food, being as there'd only be three people. And maybe they'd get a kitten for her. She'd love that so much. Something alive and furry to hold and stroke — although Anne would be almost as happy if she could have a *doll*. Maybe a baby doll with its own little clothes. A baby with blue eyes and painted lashes, who wouldn't wet her pants or screech all night or smell bad. Roger had a good job, so he might even get her a doll for her birthday. She'd just like someone to *pay attention* to her birthday. And after a while, if Eliza and Roger got a baby, she'd help Eliza look after it and hold it and rock it. It was all going to be so wonderful.

"Can we plant daisies at the front door, Eliza? And a lilac bush would be nice. Could we have one? Hm? Would Roger like that?"

But Eliza was crying too hard to answer her.

Finally Eliza said, "Maybe I won't go. Maybe I'll stay. Maybe I won't marry him. I don't see how I can." Then she cried some more.

Anne squirmed out of her arms and drew away so that she could look at her.

Seeing Eliza's stricken face, Anne grabbed her arm and cried, "What's wrong Eliza? What's *wrong*? It all sounds so right to me."

Eliza stopped crying, and took a long deep breath. "No," she said. "I can't go." And ran into the house.

Inside, the chaos was even worse than usual. The dishes still weren't washed, and the evening meal was almost ready. Joanna was yelling for Trudy to come and wash them. But Trudy was hiding upstairs with her arithmetic homework. Arithmetic was better than what was going on downstairs. Bert came in from the barn — *lurched* in from the barn — and shouted, "How come supper's not on the table?"

When Joanna said, "Either get some work and buy some food, or stop tormenting me!" he slapped her face and hit the table with his fist. Two of the babies were crying. Margaret was absent, having left for the Jamiesons' that afternoon to be their full-time live-in maid, with her own room and Thursday afternoons off. There weren't enough hands in the Thomas house to do everything that needed to be done.

"Set the table, Anne!" shouted Joanna. "And you, Eliza, out gallivanting with Roger when I need your help! Get over here and finish washing these dishes." She picked up one of the babies and opened her bodice to feed him. The other baby continued to cry. Horace was racing around, banging the bottom of a pan with a metal spoon.

Bert shouted, "This place is a lunatic asylum! I'm sure gonna warn those sons of mine never to go dancing. This is what it leads to." He retreated to the barn, yelling, "Send someone out for me when there's food on the table!" He slammed the door behind him.

Eliza surveyed this scene before stationing herself at the dishpan. "I can't leave," she sobbed. "But I sure as hell can't stay."

"What's wrong, Eliza?" asked Joanna from her chair, "Roger jilt you? If so, be glad. Then you can maybe have some kind of a life."

"No, Mama," said Eliza, between sobs. "This afternoon, he asked me to marry him."

"Then what's wrong? Something bad you found out about him? Lost his job? Drinks? Hit you?"

Eliza turned around from her position at the dishpan. "No, Mama. None of those things. He's a nice man, and kind. With a good job. He wants me bad." Then Eliza paused. Her voice caught as she added, "But he just wants *me*. Not *Anne*. I begged and begged. But he said no." Eliza put her soapy hand across her face, and said, "Mama. I think my heart is breaking."

SEVENTEEN

Changes

Eliza wrestled with her decision for three days. When she found her mother actually *sitting down* one afternoon, she asked for her advice.

"Don't go," said Joanna. "You think Roger loves you, but just wait a bit. All that sweet stuff will fizzle away. Then the babies will come, one after another. Then it's just work, work, work."

Joanna discovered that images of Bertha and Walter were entering her mind — their warm loving faces, their tenderness with each other. Well, apparently it could happen sometimes — the loving stuff that could *last* — but mostly you found it only in the fairy tales that her mother had read to her when she was little. She pushed the memories of Bertha and Walter out of her head.

"And I need you here. Margaret's gone already, and I'm wondering if she's enjoying lifting and lugging old Mrs. Jamieson around more than she liked washing the Thomas dishes. And Trudy's going next week. The Archards want her to come and live in their house. She'll never come home. They have a big house and money and only two children. Mostly Mrs. Archard just wants her to clean silver and polish furniture, and mind the children when she's out playing whist. *Whist!* Trudy'll eat good, and she'll have a room of her own. She's one of the lucky ones. Margaret will be *so jealous. I'm* some jealous. Playing whist in the afternoons, or having little tea parties. Imagine a life like that!"

Eliza didn't care if her mother needed her. She didn't care that Trudy was getting a cushy job. But she did care about Anne. And she loved Roger. She'd waited so long for the absolutely right young man to turn up, that she was close to being an old maid. After all, she was almost twenty. If she let Roger slide through her fingers, she might never again get such a flawless husband. And she didn't believe for one moment that Roger would stop being kind and loving.

Eliza hadn't been smart in some subjects at school, but she was smart in other ways. In a small corner of her mind, she knew that if she gave up Roger for Anne's sake and because she loved her as though she was her own child, the time might come when she'd start to resent Anne. She knew this wasn't Anne's *fault*, but she also realized that she might feel that way.

"Life is so hard, Mama," she said to Joanna. "Nothing is simple."

Joanna found it impossible to find even a crumb of sympathy for Eliza. Joanna was only thirty-seven years old, but her own experience of life had hardened everything that had ever been soft and yielding. She'd stuffed away her own dreams for so long that she hardly knew what dreams were made of. Memories of her own youth were buried so deep that Joanna had forgotten the things she thought and felt at that time in her life. All she could find to say to Eliza was "I need you." Not even, *I love you, and want you to stay*. That wasn't what Joanna was thinking, so that's not what she said.

"Well, Mama, Roger needs me, too. And so does Anne. And I can't live your life for you. You're not helping me make my decision."

Bert had been sober for two days. He had a new job this time, loading cargo onto the trains and doing maintenance work. It was the kind of job that he liked. He'd try hard to keep it. The fourth baby would be coming soon, and in his sober moments — filled as they always were with regret and depression — he knew that he should be thinking about his paycheque as a means to supply food rather than rum.

For the first time in her life, Eliza went out to the barn and knocked on the door. She knew he wasn't drinking. There'd been no yelling or slapping for two days.

The door opened, and Bert stood there, mute with surprise. No one ever came to the barn when he was in it. It was an unspoken rule that visits were forbidden. But he was busy clearing out the stall and setting out fresh hay for the cow. He had nothing to hide or be ashamed of.

"Come in," he said, and opened the door wider.

"Papa," said Eliza, "I need your advice. Roger wants me to marry him. But he won't let Anne live with us. I love Anne like she was my own child. She *is* my own child. It will break her heart and my heart if I leave without her. But I love Roger, too. And something else, Papa ..."

"What else, Eliza?"

They were sitting on two milking stools, and Bert was absent-mindedly stroking the cow's flank.

"It's hard for me to say, Papa. But I got to say it. This isn't a nice home to live in. Winter will be coming soon, and it's awful cold in our house. And we often don't have near enough food. And there's too many crying babies and too much anger all the time. I want to leave — just like Margaret did, and like Trudy's doing next week. It's time. But Mama wants me to stay and help her. But Papa ..."

"Yeah. What?"

"It's not *her* life. It's *my* life. I know she has to work terrible hard. But that's not *my* fault. So ... what should I do?"

Bert stopped stroking the cow and looked at his beautiful

first-born daughter. He bit his lower lip, and thought about her question. He knew that Eliza had left a lot of things unsaid. Things about him. The bad things he did, and the good things he didn't do. Then he spoke.

"Go with Roger. If you stay here because of Anne, you'll begin hatin' her in a few years, when you start bein' a dried-up old maid and the young men stop callin' on you. If you stay behind because your mother needs you, you'll hate her even faster." He thought of saying, *And you hate me already, or if you don't, you should.* But he didn't say this. Instead, he said, "I'll try not to be drunk so much. I'll try to stop drinking. I know I said that before lotsa times, but I think we all got to try to believe that sometime it might happen. And something else ..."

"What?"

"That Anne. I'll try to keep an eye on her. When I can. There's something about her. She's got a real strong spirit. I admire that. I don't get mad at her like I get mad at my own children. She's only five years old, but I have this crazy feeling that she can see right through me. Like she knows what goes on inside. Like she understands how hard I struggle, and how bad I feel when I just can't make it. I know she hates the yellin' and the way I sometimes hit your mother. But I don't get the feelin' that she hates *me*. I tell you what, Eliza ..."

"What, Papa."

"When you go — when you leave us — tell her that she can sometimes knock on the barn door if she's got big troubles. No one's allowed to do that — like you did today. So this is a big secret. Just between you and me and Anne."

They rose from the stools and faced each other. Eliza reached up and touched his shoulder, his neck, his face. She hadn't done that since she'd been a tiny girl. Briefly, the thought slid across her mind that she'd never really known him. Maybe none of them had.

A tear slid down Eliza's cheek, and she smiled. "Thank you, Papa," she said.

$\mathcal{H}$eartbreak

And what was Anne doing while all this was going on — while all these conversations were taking place? She was hiding. And she was listening. As soon as she heard Eliza say to her mother, "But he just wants *me*. Not *Anne*," she felt as though she were made of a solid piece of ice. She felt *that stiff and that hard. That cold.* She knew — she just *knew*, without working it out in her head, that this was the end of everything. All the lovely things she experienced with Eliza — the hugs, the walks in the woods and over the lowlands, the flowers they found and picked and put in a little vase that Joanna kept in the china cabinet with the glass doors — all those things would be *over.* And the things Anne dreamed about — the embroidered tablecloth, the lilac bush (maybe a purple one), the kitten, the doll with the painted lashes — were all gone — dreams as blank and as empty as a blind fog.

Then, when Eliza had gone out to the barn to talk to her father, Anne crept out and stationed herself close to the ground, at a place where the boards were loose. She could hear things through that crack. She'd listened before. Once, after Mr. Thomas had been thundering around in the main house, yelling at all of them to stop the noise, and then slapping Mrs. Thomas when she told him that he was the noisiest of all, and then throwing Trudy's schoolbooks at the wall, one after the other, yelling, "Oh, you think you're so much smarter than the rest of us!" he'd then charged out of the door and pushed himself into the barn, slamming the barn door behind him. Anne had watched all this from a corner of the room, making herself as small as possible. The three boys were crying, shrieking, and Trudy was sobbing out loud as she picked up her schoolbooks, one by one. Anne had slipped out the back door so that she could escape from all that sorrow.

Then, suddenly she'd heard strange noises coming from the barn — a thumping, and a kind of moaning sound. She moved around to the side of the barn that had the missing board, squatted down on the grass, and listened. She also watched, because someone had kicked aside the loose board — Horace, probably — and now you could actually see into the barn. To Anne's astonishment, what she saw was Mr. Thomas hitting one of the milking stools with his fist — over and over again. And crying. Mr. Thomas was actually *crying*. Every once in a while, he'd stop pounding the stool, and would lean the side of his face against the cow's big belly, saying "Ohhh! Ohhh!" in a terrible low moan.

Anne was four years old at the time. She couldn't have put into words what she felt or thought as she watched this scene. But she at least understood that he was hurting. Somehow or other, doing his bad things *hurt him*. This was too complicated a thought to disentangle, but she stored it away in her small head to think about later. But she did know this: her feelings about Mr. Thomas had changed. Why, or in what way, she wasn't sure. But her mind slid away from the idea of hating him. Something was different.

On this terrible day when she discovered that Roger would marry Eliza only if she left Anne behind, she heard and watched the entire conversation between Eliza and her father. It didn't alter the intensity of Anne's grief. It didn't melt the ice she was feeling, even a little. But it told her two things:

she had a person to whom she could go for help if things got to be too terrible. She knew that if Mr. Thomas was drunk, he'd probably be unable to help her at all. But she wouldn't have to worry about him hitting her. The other revelation was that Mr. Thomas liked her. Anne wasn't used to being liked. Maybe Mrs. Thomas did like her — maybe a *little*. But she never said so, and seldom behaved as though she did. Trudy and Margaret mostly acted as though she wasn't there, and had never shown her any affection. Horace and Harry and Edward hit her when they felt like it, and Mrs. Thomas was apparently too busy to notice or care.

But Eliza loved her, and that had made everything else bearable. In fact, in spite of the misery and violence with which she was surrounded, Anne had been a cheerful, happy person, as long as Eliza was nearby to protect her. She enjoyed the opening-up of spring, the sun on her skin in the summer, the dandelions and buttercups that grew wild in the fields, the warm and gentle old cow, the wild winds bending the trees in the late fall, the huge snowdrifts in the winter, the million shapes of the starry snowflakes, the pictures in Eliza's old readers of birds and animals and ladies in fine dresses. There was so much to enjoy and love when she was with Eliza — or even on the rare occasions when she was alone. Eliza was always there to come back to.

But now, everything was changed. It was the end of Anne's life as she had known it, and in some intuitive way she was aware of it. But the intuitive knowledge led her nowhere. All that was there was the heavy block of ice. In a week's time, she would go off into the nearby woods all by herself, and scream and cry so loudly and for so long that she scared the birds away, and the grass at her feet moved as though a wind was blowing. But on this day, when the news of Eliza's going was new, she felt like someone who had suddenly gone blind. There was no colour or shape to anything, and no way to know where she was going or how to get there.

NINETEEN

*E*liza's Wedding Day

There was no wedding celebration for Eliza and Roger — no new dress or flowers, no music playing softly in the background. And no party afterwards, with special little cakes and fizzy pink drinks and everybody laughing. How could there be? Those things cost money, and there was barely enough of that to feed the growing Thomas family, even with Mr. Thomas working on the railway. No. Eliza and Roger just went to the home of Rev. Martin MacLeod, the Presbyterian minister, and he married them in his own best parlour. Mrs. MacLeod stood up for them, and was the required witness. She had brought in a small bouquet of late field flowers and put them on the table that held the Bible. Then she lit a candle and put it beside the flowers, in her best brass candlestick. No one else was there. Roger's family all lived in St. George, in New Brunswick, on the Bay of Fundy. They couldn't make that long trip in one day, and there was no place for them to stay overnight.

Mrs. Thomas had planned to come, but her waters had broken that morning, and she had to send Bert off to fetch the doctor. At the very moment when the Reverend MacLeod pronounced Eliza and Roger man and wife, Eliza's fourth brother, Noah, was being born, back at her own house.

Right up to the last moment, Eliza had hoped that Anne would come to her wedding — *could* come. But ever since Eliza had decided to leave Anne and marry Roger, Anne had seemed to withdraw to a place in her own head that Eliza couldn't reach. Mostly, Anne had just gone about her many chores in silence — heating bottles, fetching milk, washing diapers on the scrub board in a low tub that Joanna had set up for her, digging up fall carrots from the back garden. But in the rare moments when she wasn't working, she didn't answer when Eliza spoke to her, held herself rigid from Eliza's hugs, and acted as though they weren't in the same room.

"This is hard for me, too," Eliza had pleaded on the morning of her wedding. "Please, Anne. Speak to me, or smile, or touch me, or *something*. Don't make me be sad on my wedding day!" Anne didn't care if she was sad on her wedding day. What was the wedding, anyway? It was the thing that would make Eliza go away to be Roger's wife, so Anne certainly wasn't going to be happy about *that*. So why should Eliza not be sad? Anne's grief hadn't caught up with her yet. What she was feeling was mostly shock. But she did feel a lot of anger — anger at Roger for not wanting Eliza to bring her into their new home; anger at Eliza for choosing Roger over her, and for leaving her in this cold and noisy house. And anger at Mrs. Thomas for having so many babies.

By noon of the wedding day, Eliza knew that there was no way Anne could come. Mrs. Thomas was in labour, and her husband had raced off to get the doctor or a midwife — *anyone* who knew how to deliver a baby. Anne would have to stay home and look after the little boys. Eliza put a large pot of water on the stove to boil. Then, with a sad heart, she went upstairs to put on her best dress — a rose-coloured chiffon one that had belonged to Anne's mother, with a tight lace bodice and high neck. She put up her hair in a style suitable for a bride, and pinned a small artificial rose behind her ear. Standing in front of the Thomases' one small mirror, she pinched her cheeks to make them pink. She looked very pretty. Surely when she went downstairs, Anne would rush to her as she'd always done, and give her a big hug. Eliza wouldn't even care if her hands were sticky or if milk spilled on her lovely dress. But when she came into the kitchen, Anne was sitting on the rocker, feeding one-year-old Harry with a bottle. She looked up briefly, and her eyes widened when she saw Eliza in all her wedding loveliness. Then she looked down and centred her meagre attention on the baby. Knowing what it signified, Anne could hardly bear to see Eliza looking so beautiful. Horace stomped by and hit her on the leg with a toy wagon. Anne hardly felt it. Horace was four. Anne was five and a half.

Then the front door opened, and Mr. Thomas came in, followed by Dr. Bates. After that, everything happened very quickly. Eliza kissed her mother on her damp cheek, and wished her an easy birth. Joanna managed to say, "I'm glad you're leaving Anne behind, Eliza. I need her bad to help me with my four babies." Then a large pain hit her, and her groans became more like screams. Dr. Bates pushed Eliza aside and bent to examine Joanna. Roger arrived, his arms full of flowers; Bert stood by the stove, waiting for the water to boil; Horace and Edward ran around pretending to be fire trucks with their bells ringing; Anne sat, silent and stiff, feeding the baby. Eliza bent and kissed Anne on the cheek. Anne's eyes stayed fixed on Harry.

"Forgive me, Anne," said Eliza. And walked out the door with Roger.

TWENTY

*K*atie Maurice

One day, about a month after Eliza's wedding day, and about three weeks after Anne had screamed out her grief in the woods, Anne was putting some dishes away in the old glassed-in bookcase that had once belonged to her own family. It was kept in a corner of the house that received very little light. When Anne closed the door, after depositing the dishes, she saw her own reflection in the glass door. She stared and stared at it. In the dimness of the reflection, her freckles had disappeared and her hair looked almost brown. For a moment or two, she thought it was another person. Even after she realized that this was not the case, she clung to the idea. "A friend! A friend!" she kept muttering under her breath.

The house was unusually quiet. All four babies and Mrs. Thomas were asleep. Mr. Thomas (who had not had a drink for many weeks) was at work. During this period, Anne was starting to get used to Eliza's absence, although still deeply sad about it. And she rather liked the new baby. He didn't cry as much as the other ones did, and he was much less beautiful than all the bigger Thomas children. In fact, he was quite odd-looking, with an oversized nose and a slight cast in one eye. He wasn't exactly cross-eyed, but he wasn't as oppressively handsome as the older little boys. Anne had always regarded herself as an unattractive-looking person. She was used to people mentioning her multitude of freckles, her excessively red hair, her skinny legs. She had always admired the beauty of the Thomas children — because Anne did

admire beautiful things and people — but still, it was hard. It made her feel more than ever as though she didn't belong. She felt an odd sort of kinship with this new baby — this Noah — and liked holding him and feeding him more than she liked looking after the other boys. Furthermore, with Mr. Thomas working again and not drinking, there was food in the house. Anne's ice was starting to thaw ever so little.

And here was this phantom person, this magic *friend*, behind one of the glass doors of the cupboard that contained the family's dishes and preserves. With Eliza gone, there was no one to whom Anne could confide her thoughts, her dreams, her secrets. But maybe she could do this with her new friend in the cupboard. It wasn't in a part of the house where people gathered. The boys seldom even played there. Maybe she could *talk* to this person when no one else was around. *Yes.* She *could.* But she needed a name. At the very moment when Anne had that thought, the name was on her lips. "Katie Maurice!" she said out loud, but in a soft voice. "You're a jumping, happy person, and a smooth-running, gentle friend, just like I told Eliza about the name of her own friend *Katie Maurice.*" The little girl in the glass was speaking. Her lips were moving. And when Anne heard one of the babies crying, and knew that she'd have to leave, Katie Maurice raised her hand in farewell at the exact moment that Anne did.

For the first time in three weeks, Anne entered the kitchen — the social centre of the drafty house — with a light heart. She could hardly wait for tomorrow. Ever since Eliza had started reading to her, Anne had wanted to make up her own stories — about her dreams and fantasies. And when life became sadder for her — after Eliza's departure — she longed to tell the history of her own life. But how could she do that when there was no one to tell it all to? If she knew how to write, she could do it that way; but she didn't know how. But now, suddenly, there was a friend to whom she could recount her own tales. There was so much she wanted to tell Katie Maurice, so many secrets, so many sad and happy thoughts. This would be almost as good as being able to write them down. But she wouldn't be able to do that for *years*. She could learn how to do that in school, but that was a long way off. She had four whole months before she'd be six.

So school seemed very far away to Anne. But that was all right. In the meantime she could talk to Katie Maurice. Anne knew she'd listen without interrupting, and she'd never tell her to shut up. All these wonderful things could start happening tomorrow afternoon. That's when the boys took their naps and Mrs. Thomas went to lie down. No one would hear her. No one except Katie. And *she'd* hear *everything*.

Anne could hardly sleep that night. She was too busy thinking about tomorrow's meeting with Katie Maurice. Her new friend would be dressed in a beautiful dark green dress, with at least three petticoats — maybe four — all of them with lace on the bottom. It was so dark in the hall that she wouldn't be able to see all those petticoats, even if Katie lifted her skirt. But she'd know they were there. She'd have brown hair and pale, creamy skin, and a beautiful smile.

What would she tell her first? Anne decided that she'd tell her about her own parents, and the little yellow house. She'd tell her about how beautiful her mother thought she was when she was a baby, and how kind her father was — never angry and never drunk. She'd tell her that there was a lilac bush beside the front door, and lots of flowers in the back garden — yellow, red, blue, mauve, every colour you could think of. And Katie would want to know that her mother had bought her a doll — maybe *made* her a doll with her loving and skillful hands — even though she was too little to know what to do with it yet. She'd tell her that it was always nice and warm in that house, and that there was wonderful food to eat — *every day*, not just on payday — molasses cookies and big slices of crusty bread, with wild strawberry jam on top. Katie Maurice would be so interested to hear about all those things.

On the following day, when naptime came, Anne suddenly wondered — just for a moment — if she could make herself believe that Katie Maurice was the real person she wanted her to be — her first friend who was the same age as she was. But she thought she could do it. After all, she often pretended that she was back in the little yellow house, living with her own parents — who would *of course* not have died at all — helping her mother make cookies and knead bread dough, loving the smells coming out of the oven, looking forward to her father's arrival home from his school. It was all so wonderful — the sound of her mother's gentle voice, the feeling of the hugs — that Anne had no difficulty in believing that all of it was real. Surely the same thing would happen with Katie Maurice.

Anne stood in front of the china cabinet in the dim back hall and closed her eyes. In the background, she could hear various gurgles and snores — the sounds of sleep. She felt safe. She raised her hand and opened her eyes.

Behind the glass door, Katie was waving her hand in greeting and smiling broadly. Anne felt her heart skip a beat or two.

"Hello, Katie Maurice," she whispered. "I'm so glad you've come to be my friend. My name is Anne, Anne Shirley, Anne, spelled with an *e*." Eliza had always said that, so it must be important, even though she had no idea what it meant.

Then Anne paused. Katie Maurice was standing very still and smiling quietly. It was clear that she was eager to hear anything that Anne might choose to tell her.

"I was born about five and a half years ago. Mrs. Thomas says that I was a very homely baby, but my mother was sure I was the most beautiful baby in the whole world. I expect that my mother was right, don't you?"

Already Anne was feeling a warmth inside her whole self that was new to her. Here was someone to whom she could tell all her private thoughts — even the ones she'd been unable to tell Eliza — like about how sad she felt when Mrs. Thomas called her lazy or wicked, when all she was doing was stopping work for a few minutes so that she could pretend she was a princess — like in the story Eliza read to her from one of her readers — or a brave knight killing a dragon. Already Anne was starting to tell Katie about that.

"When you're doing something boring like scrubbing diapers, those pretend things just happen, and when they happen, you have to just stop whatever you're doing, to look at what the princess is wearing or what colour the dragon is. It's not really being *lazy* or *wicked*, is it, Katie?"

Anne looked hard at Katie. She was definitely shaking her head.

Anne sighed with relief. "Oh, Katie Maurice!" she said. "I *knew* you'd understand. So now I'll tell you all about my own wonderful parents."

Anne was still talking when the first baby started to cry, one and a half hours later.

TWENTY-ONE

*K*atie and Anne

During the next week, Anne had a conversation with Katie Maurice every day, and every day Anne felt a small bit better about the absence of Eliza. Sometimes after she had gone to bed at night, she even let herself feel sad that she hadn't been able to look at Eliza when she went out the door with Roger on her wedding day, that she hadn't run after her to give her one last kiss, one last hug — that she hadn't told her that she loved her. And now Eliza was in faraway New Brunswick, where Anne would never be able to do or say any of those things. But when she told Katie Maurice about her regrets, she seemed to understand exactly how Anne felt.

"I feel so bad," said Anne to her friend behind the glass door, "that I didn't do one single nice thing for Eliza on the day she left. In fact, Katie Maurice, my dear, I really spent the whole week before that day being as nasty as I could possibly be."

Then Anne stopped talking, and looked hard at her new friend. "I see you are frowning," she said. "You probably think I'm just as wicked as Mrs. Thomas says I am. But what else could I do? I felt that my heart was a chunk of ice, and that my tongue was glued to the roof of my mouth. I was that angry. How could she choose Roger over me? She only knew him for half a year. She'd known me for years and years. And how could Roger take away the lovely life I was going to have in their new little house? — probably yellow, like my own mother's house. With a new doll and maybe a kitten. And perhaps even *books*. Eliza even took her school readers away with her — those Royal Readers with their pictures and the poems she read to me. Couldn't she even have left them behind for me?"

Katie Maurice stared back at her, with her head on one side, looking sad, but not at all like someone who was thinking she was wicked. Anne felt she could say a lot more.

"Eliza often said I was like her own child. So how could she leave me? You can't believe how angry I was. It was as though she took Mr. Thomas's axe and chopped my heart up into a hundred pieces. I can't count to a hundred yet, because I'm not old enough to go to school. But everyone says that a hundred is a whole lot. So if your heart has been cut up into a hundred pieces, it's not easy to act loving to the person who's been doing the chopping. How could I have hugged her — or even told her that she looked beautiful *in my mother's dress* (Mrs. Thomas told me *that*) — when I was so angry that I couldn't even *move*? But ... Katie Maurice?"

Anne was sure that she nodded.

"Well, now I'm sorry I didn't do those things. I wish I could have sprung loose from the rope that seemed to be tying me to the chair, and chased after her. I lie in bed at night and think of the things I might have done, and then what might have happened. I might have reached her before she got in the buggy, and given her a big hug. Then she would have bent down — when Roger wasn't looking — and pushed me up into the buggy and under the seat. When they went into the minister's house, I would have crept in, too — *ever so silently* — and hidden in a far corner of the room where they were going to get married."

Anne looked at Katie Maurice. She was smiling. Anne was certain that she was thinking — or even *saying* — Go on! Then what happened?

"Then," continued Anne, "when the wedding was over, Roger would have turned around and seen me — sitting so sad in the corner, with tears dribbling down my face — and would have said, 'Eliza! Look! There's your Anne! Your own Anne. I was wicked to take you away from her. Let's bring her along with us. To the little house with the lilac bush and the daisies. It would be fun to have a little red-headed girl in our home, and maybe we could get her a doll with painted eyelashes for her birthday. She looks so sad and lonesome in that corner. Eliza — go get her. Bring her over to me so that I can give her a hug. Then she'll know I really mean it when I say that all three of us will be going to New Brunswick together.'"

This was such a happy pretend thing that Anne could feel tears of happiness sliding down her freckled cheeks. And she could see that Katie Maurice was crying, too.

"Then I'd rush over to them," continued Anne, "and hug him. And I'd stop hating him. I'd just know that he'd get me a kitten as well as a doll. And Eliza would be with me forever, wearing my own mother's dresses and being like a real mother to me."

Then Anne sighed.

"But I didn't do any of those things. I just sat there feeding Harry. And Eliza and Roger didn't do anything, either. Well, I guess Eliza tried. But then they just *went*. And I stayed."

Two rooms away, Noah was crying. Horace was stomping around the kitchen, hitting things with a metal spoon. The other boys were fighting. Mrs. Thomas was yelling at all of them to be quiet. Then she was shouting, "Anne! *Anne!* Get in here and help me! Stop lazing around!"

Anne waved to Katie Maurice, who waved right back. "I'll see you tomorrow," she said. "Thank you for listening to me."

Thank you weren't words that were spoken in the Thomas household. But Anne had heard Roger and Eliza use them. She liked the sound of those two words, and the feeling that seemed to go along with them. And she thought she knew what they meant. They sort of meant, *I'm pleased that you did that for me.*

Anne loved words. She wished she had more of them. Sometimes she had very complicated thoughts, but didn't know how to talk about them — even to herself. If Eliza hadn't taken those books away, maybe she could have learned a whole lot of new words — even long and fancy ones. But they were gone, and so was Eliza. And she couldn't have read them, anyway. But she could have looked at the pictures and told the stories to herself.

"Coming!" Anne yelled, and raced down the hall to the kitchen.

$\mathcal{M}$r. Thomas and Anne

Every day, from Monday until Friday, Anne had a conversation with Katie Maurice. Sometimes it was long. On other days it might be very short. It could just be a quick, whispered, "Hello, Katie Maurice. I can't talk to you. It's washday, and I have to help Mrs. Thomas on the scrub board and carrying water. And wringing out the diapers. I hate that. Afterwards, my hands hurt. I'll talk to you tomorrow."

Or even just "Sorry, Katie Maurice. I can't visit with you today."

But they talked often and long enough that Anne was able to tell her about the things she feared and loved, the sad things that had happened in her life, and the wonderful things she pretended or hoped for. Having Katie Maurice wasn't as good as having Eliza, but it was very, very good. Eliza had taught her about volcanoes, and how they erupted. Those were two wonderful words, and they made pictures come into her mind. But she'd never had a chance to use them. Mrs. Thomas wouldn't even know what they meant. If Anne said that Noah was "erupting his breakfast," no one would know what on earth she was talking about. But now she could say — at least to herself — "Katie Maurice lets me be a volcano. She doesn't mind it a bit that I do a lot of erupting. In fact, she seems to be interested in every single thing I tell her."

So Anne was able to tell Katie Maurice about Mr. Thomas's rages, and how he hit his wife; about the way Mrs. Thomas was impatient — and often angry — if Anne took time from her work to dream she was a princess, or a beautiful white racehorse, or even just a little girl who had no freckles but a lot of toys and a loving mother. And she told her about Eliza's stories from the Royal Readers, and could even recite some of the poems to her from those books. She described to Katie Maurice her long walks with Eliza and everything they saw — huge herons poised like statues at the edges of ponds; hundreds — *hundreds* — of wildflowers; huge brown cows with kind eyes; even people walking on the streets of Bolingbroke in dresses with bustles and wide skirts and lace petticoats that showed when they lifted their skirts to go up a set of steps; trees that turned orange and yellow and red in the autumn. But Anne reminded Katie Maurice that although those things had been wonderful, she — Katie Maurice — lived in an even more beautiful place. Behind the doors of that china cabinet was a whole world of fairies and queens and kings and castles and high bridges, and every other possible thing that Eliza had told Anne about — things she had learned in school or read about in a book, or seen in pictures in her old classroom. Every wonderful thing in the whole world was behind those glass doors, and Katie Maurice was in the middle of it. There was no limit to the wonders that were there.

It had been a long time since Mr. Thomas had had a drink. The noise that the boys made irritated him, but his wild, black rages were a thing of the past, and he often treated Mrs. Thomas in a manner that was almost courteous and kind. He had long ago stopped loving her, but now he no longer acted as though he hated her.

He was never angry at Anne, and often watched her with a puzzled and interested expression. Sometimes if he was alone with her, he would engage her in conversation. One day when the kitchen was particularly noisy, with the little boys racing around yelling and sometimes wrestling or hitting one another, and with Mrs. Thomas shouting at them to stop whatever they were doing, Mr. Thomas took a kitchen chair and put it down beside Anne. She was sitting in the rocking chair with Noah, feeding him his bottle of milk.

"Hello, Anne," said Mr. Thomas.

"Hello, Mr. Thomas," she said. "How are you?"

"Well, Anne," he replied, "to tell the truth, I feel kind o' frantic. Listenin' to this racket and all. Watchin' my sons batter one another. I like things peaceful. A war zone has got to be a lot like this. How come it don't seem to bother you?"

"Well," said Anne, "I'll tell you why. In the old days when you were drunk and angry so often, pretty much everything bothered me. Your voice was louder than all the others, and there was all that hitting you did. When you stopped drinking and yelling and hitting, I liked life so much better that I didn't much care about the other racket that was going on. I just sort of let it happen, and thought my own thoughts. Besides, feeding a baby is a very peaceful thing — if you happen to like the baby. And I like Noah. He's funny-looking. But he likes me, and sometimes I pretend he's mine. Pretending things can make a whole lot of bad things seem not so awful. You could maybe try doing that sometime." She looked up at him with her enormous eyes. They were green today. Sometimes they were grey.

Mr. Thomas looked hard at Anne, and did some thinking. There, beside him, was this odd-looking child — freckly and skinny — sitting so calmly in the big rocking chair, feeding his small, scrawny baby. She appeared to be serene and content in the middle of all the crying and banging and shouting. And here he was, a big, handsome man — the father of seven children, a husband, a railway employee — wishing he could be more like her.

He grinned at her. What a funny little person she was. "How do you do the pretend thing?" he asked.

"Well," she said, "it's easiest if you stop what you're doing. When I'm scrubbing diapers or washing the kitchen floor, it's hard to believe that I'm a princess who's playing with her five beautiful dolls in a big castle beside a smoothly flowing river. So I stop for a few minutes and pretend really hard that I'm that princess. Pretty soon I can see the river and all the candles in the castle windows; and the first thing you know I'm in one of the castle rooms, sitting on a huge canopy bed playing with my dolls. Little girls, even princesses, like dolls. I know that, even though I've never had one. And I know about canopy beds, because Eliza told me about them. There are wonderful heavy brocade curtains above and around the bed, so if you're on it, you feel like you're in your own little secret house. Eliza told me about brocade, too."

Mr. Thomas frowned. "I don't think I'd know how to do that."

"It's not hard," said Anne. "First you have to think about something you really love doing, or maybe wish you had or wish you were. I loved walking in the woods with Eliza. I can pretend I'm doing that, and all of a sudden I can see the trees in my head, and all the flowers — like mayflowers or strawberry blossoms — and little spotted ladybugs and sweet little toads. I can see the birds on the tree branches, and if I try hard enough I can even hear them sing. It's easy, but perhaps you'd have to practise a bit. Or maybe you're too old."

Anne took Noah and put him against her shoulder, patting his back until he burped. Then she added, "Of course Mrs. Thomas doesn't like it when I do a lot of pretending when

I'm supposed to be working. Because of having to stop what I'm doing until I can really feel myself being who I want to be, and doing things I want to do. That can mean that the washing doesn't get done as fast."

"Don't it bother you when she gets mad about those things?" Mr. Thomas wondered what her answer would be to *that*.

"Oh, yes," said Anne. "Sometimes it even makes me *very* angry. Because she's getting in the way of my beautiful dreams. But getting angry makes me almost more upset than the thing that *makes* me angry. But if there are seven people in a house and four of them are useless little boys, there's an awful lot of work to do. And it's just me that helps her. So I guess it makes sense that she doesn't like me standing around dreaming. But I still feel angry.

"Mind you," Anne continued, "when I was Horace's age, and even Edward's, I did a lot of work. And they don't do *anything* useful. But they're *hers*. I'm *not*. I'm just the mother-less and fatherless child that she saved from the orphan asylum. So I try like anything to be grateful. But sometimes I can only manage to do that by pretending I'm somewhere else. And by pretending I'm not me."

Mr. Thomas looked in puzzlement at Anne. "Tell me more about your pretend thing. How do you start?"

"You think about something you love to do or else someone you'd like to be."

"Well," said Mr. Thomas, "I reckon I'd like to be Mr. Archard, with all that money and his big fancy house. You know — the place where Trudy works. But then I'd have to do the kind o' work he does, and I don't know how to be a mill owner —"

"Oh," interrupted Anne, "you don't have to know how to

be the person you pretend to be. I don't know how to be a princess with a little golden crown and dresses with brocade skirts and handmade lace bodices. But it's easy to pretend it anyway."

"Not for me," said Mr. Thomas. "So I guess I'd have to think about something I like to *do*. I used to love dancing. So did Mrs. Thomas. She was good at it. It was the thing she did best. I thought we'd spend our whole life dancing ..." His voice trailed off. "But that's not what our life turned out to be."

"Fine!" declared Anne. "Think hard about dancing. About how you did it. About the music. About the clothes you wore."

Well, he'd try. He closed his eyes and thought about the fiddles tuning up and then starting a reel. He saw himself beginning to step-dance in a corner, and then moving onto the centre of the floor. He could smell the tobacco and the beer, and he saw pretty girls standing in a row against the wall in their full skirts and high lace collars, pretending to talk among themselves, but really longing to be asked to dance. He saw all that, and heard and smelled it, before Mrs. Thomas's voice split open his dream. "Anne!" she was yelling. "Put that baby in his crib and get over here and start cutting up the carrots for supper. It seems like all you got time to do is dream and talk. And, Bert! I could use some more wood for the fire. You may have a day off from work, but I sure don't know what that'd feel like. Sunday's the same as any other day for me."

That evening, Bert put on a clean shirt, his best trousers, and a pair of shoes that he used to wear for dancing. Then he saddled his horse and rode over to the MacIntoshes' barn. He knew that Sid MacIntosh was having a big dance in the barn to celebrate his brother's marriage, with three fiddles from the nearby village of Corkery. If Bert couldn't learn to *pretend* to dance, he'd do the real thing. He'd dance his feet off, and get rid of some of the poisons that were piled up inside him.

And that's what he did. His feet still knew what to do, and his tall good looks still captivated the pretty young girls he danced with. He felt happier than he'd felt in years. This would be a good dance to pretend about when he was waiting for his trains to arrive, or when he was wanting to block out the noise in his own kitchen. It wouldn't be hard to think back to the catchy music, the stomping of feet, or the swirling skirts of the young girls.

Then one of his neighbours noticed that Mr. Thomas was attending a dance without his wife. This angered him. He poured six ounces of rum into a glass of fruit punch, and then offered it to Bert. Bert was tired, happy, hot, and thirsty. He drank the whole thing down before he realized what he'd done. He didn't leave the party until four o'clock in the morning, and on the way home, he stopped at the bootlegger's.

$\mathcal{D}$isaster

At four-fifteen in the morning, Anne awoke to the sound of loud singing. She slept in what was really a closet, so there was no window in her "room." In spite of the cold winter air, she crept downstairs and looked out the kitchen window just in time to see Mr. Thomas ride into the back yard, waving his hat in the air and singing "Down By the River Liv'd a Maiden" at the top of his lungs. There was a full moon overhead, so she could make out the large bag of bottles hanging from his saddle; there seemed to be about five of them, and they were large. Anne's hand flew to her throat, as she dared to hope that the moon was playing tricks with her eyesight, and that she was mistaken in what she was seeing. But no. The bag was familiar, and so were the tops of the bottles, even though she hadn't seen this sight for over six months.

"Oh, *please*," whispered Anne, having no idea to whom she spoke. "Let me be wrong. Don't let this be what I think it is."

Anne watched Bert lurch into the barn, swinging the bag, with the horse walking along behind. Then she heard a crashing sound when he bumped into the butter churn and sent it banging into a pile of metal pails. Then his singing changed into a lot of noisy swearing as he struggled to unharness the horse and put him away for the night, followed by a long period of silence, while Anne stood at the window, chewing on her knuckles. She needed to know whether or not Mr. Thomas had fallen asleep in the barn. She knew he was drunk, and this idea scared her. But she also knew that it was a cold January night, and that he might freeze to death in the barn.

Finally, after ten minutes with no movement or sound, Anne pulled on her boots and felt around in the back porch for a coat she could put on. Then she opened the door and struggled through the snow to the barn. She found Bert on the floor of his own private end of the shed, sound asleep, hugging his bag of bottles.

What to do? Would he swing one of those bottles at her if she woke him up? He was drunk enough that Anne felt sure he would have forgotten his promises to Eliza about protecting her from his rages. He could easily hit her with one of those bottles — one had fallen out of the bag, and she could see how huge it was. The winter wind was whistling through the cracks of the barn door, and Mr. Thomas's lantern — which had mercifully landed right side up on the barn floor — was flickering with an eerie and unfriendly light. Anne was very frightened. She knew if she went back to the house to get Mrs. Thomas, his rage — on wakening — could be really terrible. There were too many dangerous weapons in this barn — shovels, pitchforks, milking stools, large pieces of metal machinery, the bottles of rum.

But if she did nothing, Mr. Thomas could be dead by first light. She couldn't just *leave* him. And he seemed to be the only member of the Thomas family — except Noah — who really *liked her*. He had talked to her so nicely last night. She was trembling with cold and with fear, but she reached down and shook his shoulder — *hard*. "Wake up!" she said, in the loudest voice she could manage.

He opened his eyes and stared at her in the lantern's unfriendly light. "So!" he said, his voice fuzzy and low. "The witch girl! Here to rescue me."

He rose slowly and unsteadily to his feet. "And I don't happen to want to be rescued. Get outta my way, and fast, before I do something we'll both be sorry for." He kicked the bottles into a corner of the shed and then stumbled out the door. At his own back entrance, he tripped on the top step and fell against the garbage barrel. Swearing, he picked up the large snow-shovel and broke it in two over the top of the barrel. Holding one end of it, he lurched into the house, banging the handle against the stove, the sink, the armchair, the table. Then he took a sudden turn into the back hall and — just as Anne arrived in the house — took a swing at the china cabinet and smashed the glass in one of the doors.

Anne heard the sound of breaking glass, and knew — without seeing it — what had happened. She sank to the floor on her knees, as though it had been her he had struck. *Katie Maurice!* She rose from her knees and fled to her bed-closet, locking the door behind her, and pulling the covers over her shivering body — still in her coat, still in her boots. Then she cried, as silently as she could, until, at six o'clock, Mrs. Thomas pounded on her door, shouting, "Get up, Anne! Get up! Come down and help me clear up the biggest mess you ever saw!"

When Anne opened the door, she could see the bruise forming on the side of Mrs. Thomas's face, and it was easy to see that she'd been crying. On a sudden impulse, Anne moved toward her and hugged her. Mrs. Thomas, startled by the gesture, laid her hand briefly on Anne's head, and then hugged her back. It was like two adults sharing their grief, and it was a consoling moment. But it was brief. Then Mrs. Thomas said, "Why on earth do you have your coat on?" and then, "Get downstairs fast. There's a mountain of broken glass to clean up. If the boys get into it, they'll be cut to ribbons. How they could sleep through all that racket I can't figure out. Now *hurry!*"

All Anne could think of was *Katie Maurice! My poor Katie Maurice.*

However, when Anne reached the back hall, she could see at once that the panel of glass that had been destroyed was the left-hand one. It wasn't the home of Katie Maurice. In fact, there she was, staring back at Anne with red and swollen eyes. Anne gave her a small and secret wave. Katie Maurice would understand that this was not a time when she could talk to her. But she was still there, still in her enchanted world of fairies and turreted castles and canopied beds and beautiful cornflower blue dresses. Anne hadn't lost quite everything.

Mr. Thomas stayed in the shed for four days, keeping the fire going all day and night, sleeping on the hay under a pile of blankets. On the fifth day he turned up at his job in the railway station at 11:30 a.m., smelling of rum. His boss, Mr. Haley, said he was sorry, and that he'd told the head office that Bert had done perfect work for six months. But word had come back that you have to be able to trust your employees *absolutely* if you are dealing with trains. There can be delays, accidents, collisions, injuries, death. Mr. Haley said that there was a position open in Marysville that didn't involve safety precautions. Bert could have that. There was also a house that was provided as part of the job, and a small barn. But this job at the Bolingbroke station — the one that Bert had liked so much — didn't belong to him any longer. He was fired.

TWENTY-FOUR

The Fruits of Disaster

Mr. Thomas came home, went into the barn, and rested his forehead on the side of the cow. He stayed like that for a long time. Then he went back into the part of the building that was his private place and drank one-third of the remaining bottle of rum. After that, he put a cork in the bottle and set it on the floor. Then he sat bolt upright on the milking stool, staring at the wall of the barn, thinking. He thought back to the first time he had danced with Joanna, remembering the swift and skillful movement of her feet, the delight it gave him to dance with her. He recollected the wedding, the barn raising, the building of the drafty house, the start of his heavy drinking, the coming of his first family of beautiful girls, and then his second family of three handsome boys and one homely one. Somewhere in the middle of those memories came the arrival of Anne, and his shattered hopes of inheriting her parents' furniture.

Bert had almost no clear picture of his physical abuse of Joanna, but he knew it happened; there were so many bruises to prove it. He thought about how his quick infatuation with Joanna had evaporated as soon as the dancing stopped, as soon as morning sickness dampened her spirits, as soon as she was too busy with babies and cleaning jobs to pay much attention to him. He thought about the times when she either voiced her anger or lapsed into grim silences when he took the money she'd earned and bought liquor with it instead of food. And how she stopped fixing her hair in the attractive way she had done it when they'd first gone dancing.

Bert also thought about how much he'd loved the job he'd just lost, and how boring the new one would be, and how lonesome he would feel for his old railway buddies. He worried about how they could get all their furniture and clothes and pots and pans — or even themselves — to Marysville, and whether the house would be big enough for two adults and five children. He thought about Anne, and wondered if this might be the thing that would finally break her spirit. He wondered if his own was already broken. He leaned forward and buried his head in his two hands. He stayed like that for over half an hour. Then he rose, saddled his horse, picked up his last bottle of rum, and rode over to the riverbank. He dismounted, took aim, and hurled the bottle into the exact centre of the river.

That afternoon, after Bert had returned home, three of his friends from his railway job called at the house. They stood at the doorway of the kitchen, without taking off their boots, each standing on one foot and then the other foot, rocking back and forth — embarrassed.

"Bert — we're some sorry about you getting fired from your job. Word got around pretty quick about that party at the MacIntosh barn — about how that Albert McClinty spiked your drink. It was like he wrecked your life with one drink. We're all some mad about that." Then he turned to the man beside him. "Your turn, Ned," he said.

Ned cleared his throat and spoke. "We bin busy — today and all last night. We took up a little collection. That's for moving expenses, and food for when you get there. It ain't exactly in the middle of New York City. Jerry Boland?"

Then Jerry spoke up. "I have a big wagon what I got from my father when he died in November o' consumption. I also got another horse. The wagon is some big. Couldn't figure out what I'd ever use it for. Same with the extra horse. I got no place to keep either one, and it costs a bunch to feed a horse." He looked down at the floor, and spoke in a quiet voice, stuttering a bit as he went along. "You'd be doin' me a big favour if you took that c-confounded wagon and the h-horse. It takes two horses to drag that bloody big thing, and y-you only got one. You could use them fer movin' yer stuff, and then maybe fer gettin' extra work in M-Marysville." Finally, he looked up at Bert and said, "I'd be much obliged if you'd take both o' them off my hands."

There were tears in Bert's eyes, but he took great care to keep them from falling.

"I'm some grateful, boys," he said, and then repeated it. "Right grateful. Maybe it's true what they say about Nova Scotians — that they're the most generous people in North America. And I sure got proof that when disaster strikes, they knows right well how to empty their pockets. I thank you most kindly."

Then the men said, almost in unison — as if they'd maybe planned ahead what they would say — "We bid you good day, Mrs. Thomas, and we wish you well for future times."

After the men had gone, Mrs. Thomas sat down in the kitchen rocker and cried into her apron — whether from grief or gratitude, no one would ever know. Bert gave her a small pat on her back, as he went outside to the barn. Even the little boys were quiet. They'd sat down in a row on the floor when the men had arrived and continued to sit there after they'd gone — frowning, trying to make some sense out of what they were watching.

Anne sat on one of the kitchen chairs, her eyes wide and grey today, her mind busy with thoughts. With one hand, she rocked Noah in his cradle, which was on the kitchen table. Her other hand lay in her lap in a position that looked almost serene. But had you looked closely, you would have noticed that her index finger was slowly but rhythmically scratching the fabric of her skirt. She was feeling anything but serene.

Mrs. Thomas had stopped crying and suddenly spoke.

"We got two or three awful busy days ahead of us. And right now, we're clear wore out. You boys — off to bed with you for a nap. Not one squeak out of you, or you're in big trouble. Noah's already asleep, and I'm ready to take to my bed for an hour, as soon as you all get outta the kitchen. Go! All o' you — scat!"

Katie Maurice! Here was Anne's chance. She left the kitchen, and no one knew or cared where she was going.

"Katie Maurice," she whispered, as soon as she reached the back hall, "Oh, Katie! Our life is upside down. My fears are eating me alive." She looked in the remaining glass panel of the china cabinet and saw that her friend was looking as sad as she was. "Let me erupt my fears. I need to get all of them out before my volcano bursts out the sides. No one's ever seen a volcano do this, but I feel that mine could do it any minute.

"Oh! My biggest fear is that this china cabinet — holding all your favourite fairies and princesses and castles and dragons and brave knights — will be too big to fit on that wagon. After all, we have to bring all our beds and dishes and pots and clothes and chairs and *people*. But maybe Mr. Thomas can make two trips. And I'm almost old enough to go to school. What if there's no school in Marysville? I think I will die until I'm completely dead if such a thing happens. I cannot continue on with life if I'm not able to go to school. I've looked forward to it too long. It seems like forever.

"And what if Mr. Thomas goes right on drinking all the time, even though I think — and *almost* know — that he won't hit *me*, I'm still scared as anything when he gets wild like that. What if? What if? I can hardly bear to live with all those ifs.

"And do you know what, Katie Maurice? It's all my fault that these terrible things are happening. It was me that tried to get Mr. Thomas to pretend about dancing, being as it used to be something he loved to do. He got real close, I think, to being able to do it; but Mrs. Thomas broke into his dream and woke him out of it. So off he went on that very night to a real dance. And look what happened! It was the end of everything. My fault! My fault!" Anne burst into tears in the back hall, and Katie Maurice cried right along with her.

TWENTY-FIVE

*P*reparing to Leave

The next three days were, as Mrs. Thomas had predicted, "awful busy days." They were also days that were confusing, sad, exciting, dispiriting, exhausting, and full of unexpected interruptions. Large though the wagon was, it couldn't accommodate every single person and every single thing in that house. Some things had to be left behind, given away, or sent to the dump.

Although Anne worked very hard during this period, it was fear that exhausted her, not the work. The fear filled her with a sort of crazed energy, and she was hardly aware of the loads she was lifting, the furniture she was pushing, the little boys she was carrying around. For once in her life, she wasn't tempted to stop her work and weave her dreams together. Temporarily, at least, she had no dreams. Her thoughts were centred on two things: Katie Maurice's china cupboard and herself. The china cabinet was broken now. It was no longer a piece of beautiful antique furniture. They might decide to give it away or to use it for firewood. And Anne certainly wondered if she might be as disposable as the cabinet. The prospect of the orphanage loomed on the edge of her brain like an ugly preying monster. Everything, she felt, would depend on the size of their Marysville house.

On the second day, Mr. Thomas, overwhelmed by the mountain of clothes and pots and pans and boxes and bags of food and personal treasures that were piled up in the back hall, decided to make one trip to Marysville with that pile of belongings and a lot of his tools and other barn necessities. It was clearly going to require three trips — today's journey, tomorrow's with the beds and people, and on the third day an unspecified number of leftovers, and the cow. He would return the next day with information about the size and condition of the house, the general location, the state of the barn.

In the meantime, in the midst of the confusion, many people arrived to say goodbye — or so they said. Anne saw people on that day whom she'd not laid her eyes upon before. But they'd heard that the Thomases were throwing away and giving away things. Therefore, neighbours who had never entered the house to say a friendly word to Mrs. Thomas felt that this would be a good time to make a call and to offer warm wishes for a happy future. It is only fair to add that most of them arrived with plates of biscuits, pots of soups, or warm loaves of bread. Someone even brought a whole cooked ham. They left with an uncomfortable ladderback chair that no one ever sat on, a cracked stool, a number of pieces of metal cookware, a lot of broken toys, as well as an assortment of outgrown baby clothes that Mrs. Thomas was determined never to need again. The women were not pleased by the exchanges. They had never been drawn to Joanna when she moved in, and it was clearly too late to reverse their attitudes.

In the background of these bizarre social scenes, the little boys wailed as they watched their broken toys disappear. Horace even rushed forward at one point to snatch a one-armed teddy bear from the arms of a startled woman. Anne stood at the doorway to the back hall, terrified lest the china cabinet disappear into someone's wagon.

A big surprise was the arrival of Jessie Gleeson. She had never returned to the Thomas house after witnessing the violent scene of two years earlier. But she had had a new baby since that time, and some of the wounds of Jenny's death had healed. She was still troubled by feelings of guilt in connection with Anne's fate, and continued to think of her friendship with Bertha as one of the happiest times of her life. Gerald was making more money now. Their older daughter had left home and gone into service, so the house was less crowded. Gerald had also become gentler and more considerate since Jenny had died. Grief sometimes does that to people. He was now willing to receive Anne into the family if such a thing seemed to be desirable or possible. Jessie continued to be haunted by what she had seen and heard during her one abortive visit to the Thomas house. She wanted — if she could — to make amends. It might be far too late. Anne might be damaged beyond any help Jessie might give. But she had to try one last time before the Thomas family disappeared into Marysville.

Jessie approached the house as another buggy moved away. Mrs. Thomas was just closing the door, but left it open when she saw Jessie coming up the walkway. She recognized her; and a flood of memories left her speechless. Here was a woman who belonged to that short period in her life, almost six years ago, when she had been happy — when she had spent time in a home where a man and a wife clearly loved each other — when she had been part of that household, and had experienced what it was like to have kindness and consideration rub off on you. All of this rushed over her as she watched Jessie approach. She even remembered the love with which she made Bertha the special sugar cookies that gave the ailing woman such pleasure. Since then, had there been a single person to show Mrs. Thomas that sort of kindness and appreciation? And for whom had she made sugar cookies or any other special thing? Regret, sorrow, anger, guilt all engulfed her as — incredibly — she moved forward to embrace Jessie. Both of them dabbed their eyes as they moved into the house, Jessie with a handkerchief, Joanna with the hem of her apron.

Jessie was shocked by Joanna's appearance. It would have been easy not to recognize her if they had met on a Bolingbroke street. Joanna had never been very pretty, but all aspects of her attractiveness were gone. She looked fifteen years older, and she had made no effort to fix her hair in any way that was either becoming to her long face or even neat. Two permanent lines were etched between her eyebrows, and her general appearance was one of sadness.

In the background was a scene of domestic chaos. Horace was chasing Edward around the kitchen table, and Harry was yelling for them to let him play. Pillowslips full of clothes were piled in the hall, and everywhere you looked there were cartons of food, towels, curtains, afghans. Anne was standing at the kitchen table, changing Noah's diaper, her mouth full of safety pins.

"Hello, Anne," said Jessie.

Anne looked up warily. This woman was better dressed than most of the other women who had come to call. Maybe she had come to buy the china cabinet and Katie Maurice — a woman who might have enough money to replace the glass door. Anne took the pins out of her mouth and frowned.

"Hello," she said.

The frown wilted Jessie's spirit somewhat, but she pressed on.

"I knew your mother," she said. "She was my favourite friend."

"My *mother!*" said Anne, her voice barely audible. Suddenly, her face was lit up with joy. Her smile was like something that Joanna had never seen before.

"Yes," said Jessie, taking in the untidy red hair in long braids, the nose and chin exactly like Bertha's, Walter's wide and radiant smile, the freckles, the sad little dress, the busy hands, the way she handled Noah with such gentleness.

She took Joanna's hand and drew her into the back hall, where they would not be heard. "Mrs. Thomas ... Joanna," she said. "I don't have much time. Gerald needs the buggy by three o'clock, so I got to be quick. You seem to have four more children than when I knew you six years ago. I know that you're having hard times and got to move. If it could help you any, I'd be willing to take Anne. I'd give her a good home."

Anne heard none of this. She had gone upstairs with Noah, fearful lest Jessie's retreat to the back hall meant that she was about to buy the china cabinet. Even if that woman had known her mother, Anne couldn't bear to see that piece of furniture leave the house.

Joanna stood in silence beside Jessie — thinking. And struggling with a part of herself that she barely recognized. Ringing in her ears were the words, "I'd give her a good home." She knew that these were true words. She also knew, in a secret part of herself, that the Thomases had *not* given Anne a good home, even though she had told Anne so often about how lucky she was to have been rescued from life in an orphanage. Something soft and unfamiliar in Mrs. Thomas wanted to say, *Yes. Take her. Give her a childhood while there's still time.* She almost said it.

Then — sweeping across Joanna's mind's eye, in one swift instant of painful knowing — she visualized the move into the new and probably dirty and mouse-ridden house; Bert in a new drinking spell; the need for her to find work in order to feed six hungry people; the unending cycle of work, even if she stayed home. Then she saw Anne carrying water, scrubbing diapers, caring for Noah, shushing the boys, washing the endless dishes. She didn't even reply to Jessie with any civility or thanks.

"No," she said. "I've had her for almost six years. I need her. She has to earn her keep. This is home enough for her."

After Jessie had gone, Anne came slowly down the stairs with Noah in her arms. She had wanted to talk to the woman who had known her mother, but she had disappeared too swiftly into the back hall — the back hall where Katie Maurice lived. Maybe she had somehow removed the china cabinet — with Mrs. Thomas's help — while Anne had been hiding upstairs. Anne approached the entrance to the back hall uneasily, slowly. She hardly dared look.

It was still there! Anne's relief was so huge that for a few minutes she forgot Jessie's stunning words: "She was my favourite friend." Then she remembered. But it was too late — too late to ask her the thousand questions that were ready to spill out now that she knew that Katie Maurice was safe. Her feeling of regret was so enormous that she felt swamped by it. She put Noah in his crib, and then sat down beside it, on Harry's bed, her head in her hands. Everything suddenly seemed far too awful. The past and the future were full of unanswered questions, and she didn't want to even think about the present — the uncertainties, the endless work, the fears about Katie Maurice, the longing for things that she couldn't even define. Mrs. Thomas found her there, in the same position, an hour later. With an absence of her usual sharpness, she said, "I'd like you to come along now and help me, Anne. It's time we started to get supper ready."

Without a word, Anne rose from the bed and followed her downstairs. She would never learn what passed between Mrs. Thomas and Jessie on that afternoon. She would never know that this had been a pivotal day in her life.

TWENTY-SIX

Leaving and Arriving

Mr. Thomas arrived home at eleven o'clock the next day. It was bitterly cold outside, so everyone waited in the kitchen until he put the horses and wagon inside the barn and cleaned out the cow's stall. He gave the horses some oats and water, but he left the wagon attached to both animals. He'd be making another trip to Marysville that afternoon, so he wanted to make his work as simple as possible. He would take two of his boys and Mrs. Thomas and the cow, as well as their mattresses and enough food to eat until he made his final trip. He would tell them of those changed plans as soon as he joined them in the kitchen. It wasn't the way they'd agreed to do the move, but it had suddenly seemed to him to be the best way. Whatever way you looked at it, it wasn't simple. The cow was the main problem. Everything revolved around her. She had to be milked twice a day, and there had to be someone who knew how to milk her.

When he entered the back porch and stomped the extra snow from his boots, a sudden hush fell over the kitchen. You could hear the wood crackling in the kitchen stove, and the pipes making popping noises in the cold. But no one spoke. They waited while he took off his cap, coat, and heavy boots. Finally he entered the kitchen. Even after over twenty years of a difficult marriage, Mrs. Thomas took note of how handsome he looked, with his thick black hair tousled from his cap, and his cheeks red from the cold and the wind.

"Well?" said Mrs. Thomas.

"It's all right," he said. "The house, I mean. It's big enough. Bigger than this one. It's got three bedrooms. One for me and you, and a big one for the four boys, with lots of room for four beds. And a small one under the eves for Anne."

Anne's eyes were large and alive with excitement and hope. A real *room*. *All her own*. She couldn't wait to ask, "Does my room have a window?"

"Yes," Mr. Thomas answered.

"Oh!" Anne exclaimed, almost as though she were in pain. And again: "Oh!" Then, "What can you see out the window?"

Mr. Thomas scratched his head. "Dunno," he said. "Trees, maybe." Then he continued speaking.

"There's a big kitchen stove — not rigged up yet, but I can do that tomorrow. There's some furniture left from the last people who had it. Three chairs. An old sofa in the parlour — yes, there's a parlour — and a couple of torn cushions. A few old hooked rugs — but you probably won't want them."

"Oh!" Anne spoke without meaning to. She wanted one of those rugs for her bedroom.

"Anything else?" This was Mrs. Thomas speaking.

"A few dishes, a vase or two, in a sort of china cupboard. Other small stuff."

Anne held her breath. If they didn't need Katie Maurice's home for the dishes, they might leave it behind. Or smash it up.

"What else?" Horace asked. He hoped there'd be some toys.

"A big child's wagon, an old stuffed bear, other toys, mostly broken, I think. I can't remember. A couple o' small cots. A chest with drawers into it."

"Clean?" asked Mrs. Thomas. "Is the place clean?"

"No," said Mr. Thomas. "One o' the windows is broken,

and animals has got in. There's mouse and squirrel droppings everywheres. And mouse nests. We got to get a cat. Maybe two. We can keep them in the barn at night."

A cat! Anne's eyes looked too big for her small face. *Maybe two. And one could sleep in my room, right on my bed. It would be better than a doll.*

"Now listen," said Mr. Thomas. "We got to do it this way, and we got to hurry. It'll be comin' on fer dark before we know it. The cow got to go today, and you, Joanna, and two o' the boys. I had to change my mind about how we're gonna do it. Never mind why. It just got to be done this way. It's because o' the cow. Get yourself ready fast, Joanna, and two boys. And enough food for two days. I'll come back and get Anne and the littlest ones tomorrow. I need to get goin' *in an hour* because I need to hook up the pipe to the stove before nightfall. Dress up warm. It's terrible cold out there, and it's a long drive. While you're gettin' you and the boys and the food packed, I'll load some furniture and the blankets onto the wagon. If we move real smart, we can get there before the dark comes down." He stopped talking for a moment. "And I need some food for my belly before we start."

"*An hour!*" Mrs. Thomas threw her eyes to heaven. It was one whole day less than she'd counted on. But she told herself not to make a fuss. All of this was bad enough without having Mr. Thomas's itchy temper thrown into the mix. Well, at least he wasn't drinking. She'd gone out to his shed while he'd been gone and searched over and under everything. She'd not found one single bottle. But then, he could have taken some rum with him. She went off to pack clothes, fill boxes with food, collect blankets — trying not to think.

Anne put some pieces of cold ham on the plates and got the potatoes ready, cutting them into small chunks so that they'd cook faster. Then she cut the bread into large slices. She might not be much of a cook yet, but if there were things to boil or to slice, she could get a meal ready for seven people. And there were two pies left from their visitors.

As Mrs. Thomas rushed to and fro, muttering to herself (" ...Sweaters, socks, hats, nightshirts, pillowslips, pillows, bread, cheese, the left-over ham, potatoes, carrots, apples ..."), Anne continued to work. She wondered if she'd be scared in the house, all by herself with the two boys. *What if someone knocks at the door? Should I let them in? Or pretend we've left? But the boys might cry. What if I see a face at the window? If that happens, I'll die — right there, on the other side of the window. I'll have to keep the fire going in the stove so we won't freeze. What if I fall asleep and the house burns down? What if Mr. Thomas has an accident on the way back, and doesn't get here for two days? What'll we eat? And the wood's almost gone. How'll we keep warm?*

And then, all of a sudden, supper was ready, and Horace and his brothers and Mr. and Mrs. Thomas were sitting down to eat it. Anne took a few minutes to dash into the back hall to speak to Katie Maurice.

"Listen, Katie Maurice," she whispered. "Maybe you'll be going on the wagon tonight. Or maybe left behind forever. Thank you for being my friend. Thank you for listening to my very sad stories. Thank you for believing that my dreams will come true. Thank you for being my one and only true friend.

"But listen again, Katie Maurice. There's a lot of mice and squirrels in the new house. We'll have to have a cat. Maybe *two*. Have you ever heard anything more wonderful? Maybe one of them — my favourite one, perhaps a grey one — can sleep on my bed. He'll snuggle up really close to me, and I'll hug him with my free arm so he'll feel warm and loved. And

I'll feel warm and loved right back. *In my own room*. With a window. You have to come, Katie Maurice, so I can tell you about my room and hold up the cats for you to see."

Anne could hear Mrs. Thomas calling for her to come back to the kitchen. They'd finished their meal, and were already carrying boxes and pillows and mattresses out to the wagon.

"Anne," she said, when Anne returned, "go on out to the china cabinet and take the dishes out of it. Wrap them among these two sheets and put them carefully in this box. I think we'll have room to put the cabinet on the wagon tonight, so hurry up and get those dishes out of it. And carefully, mind. I don't want any of them broken."

For a moment, Anne just stood in front of her with her mouth open, a look of wonderment and bliss lighting up her thin little face. "Oh, thank you! Thank you!" cried Anne, as she rushed off to pack the dishes.

As Bert came in for another load, Mrs. Thomas shook her head and said, "That Anne happens to be the strangest child I ever knew in my life. I just gave her a big job to do, and she thanked me!"

Eventually, the wagon left with its two horses and four people, a china cabinet, a lot of boxes, and a cow. They all disappeared behind a grove of spruce trees at a bend in the road, and were gone.

Instead of letting her imagination run wild, Anne squashed it right down. She concentrated hard on not thinking. She locked the door and got to work. The sun was still shining down on the snowy fields outside the house, and Anne felt entirely safe while it was still light. She heated water and washed up the dishes. She put some fresh wood on the fire, and as she fed it, it spoke back with a friendly crackle. She got the two small boys ready for bed, but let them stay up later than usual so that she'd have company in the house. She went out into the back hall and looked at the blank place where Katie Maurice used to live. "Thank you," she said out loud to the ceiling.

As it got darker, Anne avoided looking out the windows, and chased out of her mind the idea of faces looking in at her. She made up two whole stories about a princess in a corn-flower blue gown and a handsome prince and a pair of white horses with bells tied to their tails. She sat Harry down on a stool beside the warm stove, and put Noah in his old crib. Then she told them two stories by the light of the kitchen lantern. Before it became completely dark, she went upstairs and dragged down the two thin mattresses from Harry's bed and her own, and made two more trips upstairs to bring down a mountain of blankets. By the time darkness truly fell, Anne was too tired to be frightened. Leaving the lantern burning, all three of them fell asleep on the kitchen floor, beside the warm wood stove, which continued to make friendly chortling sounds throughout the night. Anne put fresh wood in the stove from time to time, but was able to fall asleep again immediately. Her imagination was at rest, and so was she.

TWENTY-SEVEN

Marysville

By the time the wagon reached Marysville on the following morning, with Harry and Noah and Anne, Mrs. Thomas had swept the house free of animal droppings and washed most of the floors with hot water boiled on the stove. Mr. Thomas had hooked it up on the previous evening. Not many of the boxes had been unpacked, but there were a few chairs scattered among the rooms, and three of the beds were assembled, with the pillows and covers in place. Anne and the boys ran through the house, inspecting every room, every hall, every corner. Anne had been afraid that the china cabinet might have been placed in a central part of the home, but Mr. Thomas was still ashamed of having smashed the glass out of the left-hand door and had placed the cabinet in a secluded spot, close to the cellar entry. Beside the back entrance Anne spied a pile of filthy hooked mats and some broken furniture, obviously placed there to be thrown away. She rushed out to the kitchen. "Mrs. Thomas. *Please.* Please, can I have one of those mats? *Please?* For my new room."

Mrs. Thomas had to stop to figure out what she was talking about. Then she said, "Oh! Those grimy little hooked rugs. Yes, take one. Or more, if you want. But carry them out later and try to wash them off with the snow. They're so dirty that you can't even see the patterns on them." Then, "*Later,* I said!" as Anne raced to the door. "We got a ton of work to do before we get to the end of this day. I need your help bad. C'mon. Get started unpacking some of those big boxes, while I get the food put away."

"Would you maybe like me to start with the dishes? So we'll have something to eat off?" Anne looked cheerful and helpful. She wasn't too young to be devious if she wanted something badly.

"Go ahead," said Mrs. Thomas absently, "but be careful of them dishes. And watch you don't scratch the glass on the door. It's bad enough one of them is gone, without doin' damage to the other."

Anne smiled as she took the dishes out of their newspaper wrappings. Imagine thinking she'd put so much as a finger smudge on the door of Katie Maurice's house. And here was her chance to have a little stolen conversation with her.

"Katie Maurice," said Anne after she'd placed the dishes swiftly and carefully in their proper places, "do you like being here?" Katie Maurice smiled back at her. "Oh, I'm so glad," continued Anne, "because I love it already. I wish you could see my room — my *very own room*. It has a window, and outside the window you can see five birch trees with snow piled up on their bare branches. Their trunks are white with black lines on them. Behind that is a flat place. It could be a tiny field, but I want to think that it might be a little pond. I'm going to try so hard to wish for that. Than maybe it will really happen. I want a little pond so badly. But my room looks almost perfect to me. The wallpaper on the walls is torn in places, but not everywhere. It has green leaves on it and small round things that look like cherries. There's a little rickety chair in the corner that belonged to the people who lived here before. You'd probably break your back if you sat on it, because I'm sure it would just fall down in a hundred pieces. But I'll use it for putting my clothes on when I go to bed. I always had to just pile them up on the floor. There's six hooks in the wall for hanging up things, and there's a tiny mirror on the wall so that I can keep a count of my freckles, and for checking if my hair's getting any darker. Mrs. Thomas told me my father's hair was auburn, so I'm waiting for that to happen. The mirror is just the right height for me, so a child must have lived in this room before me. I'm almost six, so the child must have been eight or nine. One of the ladies who brought us food before we left our last house said I was 'abnormally tall' for my age, and that I looked two or three years older than I am. She also said my hair was 'abnormally red.' She must really love that word. I think it must mean something like 'extra much.' Or 'more than most people.' Just like I'll be abnormally happy when we get our cat.

"I wish I had more words to use. I want some long ones that sound important, and ones that say more exactly what I mean. But I'll learn all that if I go to school. If I do go. If there's a school near enough to go to. If Mrs. Thomas will *let* me go. My life is so full of questions that I can't answer. But now that I know you're in Marysville and that your house hasn't been chopped up into firewood, and now that I have a little room of my own with cherries on the wallpaper and birches and *maybe a pond* out my window, I can stand not knowing about a lot of other things."

"Anne! Hurry up and get back in the kitchen! I need you to feed Noah while I cook supper. And there are some diapers that need washing. Hurry! You must have unpacked those dishes by now." Mrs. Thomas's voice had a frantic note to it. Anne waved goodbye to Katie Maurice and raced back to the kitchen.

That evening, after dinner was eaten, the dishes washed, the cow milked, the little boys readied for bed, Anne climbed up the stairs to her new room. Earlier, she'd taken up a big box to put her clothes in, a smaller box for her treasures (just in case she might ever have a few special things to put in it), and a wooden crate to sit on while she looked out the window at the five birch trees and the field of flat ground that she hoped was a frozen pond.

The room looked like a palace chamber to Anne. The large box was a high chest of drawers with handles made of intricately embossed gold; the small box was a little wooden treasure chest, with metal edges and a key for locking it — in which she kept her diamond rings, her silver necklaces, her shiny metal belts. Her wooden crate was a stool with curved legs and a green satin cushion with yellow tassels. And her bed was, of course, a canopy bed, with purple brocade curtains and deep flounces on top and around the bottom. It was a room fit for a princess, or even a queen. And it was hers.

Anne put on her flannel nightie quickly and blew out her candle. It was cold in the room, and her nightie was thread-bare and too small for her, so she dived under her covers and drew them around her. Light from the moon — blue on the snow outside but warm on the wooden floor — shone through her window. She shivered — not with cold but with delight. She was going to love Marysville.

TWENTY-EIGHT

Mats, Education, and Eggs

So many things happened on the following day that Anne wished she could just sit on a chair and think about them. Or lean against the wall and do the same thing. Or maybe even put on her boots and coat and hat and wade through the deep snow to the five birch trees and do her thinking out there. Thinking about some of the things that were going on in the Thomas house was every bit as exciting as her pretending thoughts. But she couldn't do that. There were too many things to be *done* to permit her the luxury of *thinking*. Well, she could wait until the afternoon. Then maybe Mrs. Thomas would be tired enough to collapse on her bed after she'd shut the three older boys in their bedroom. If so, Anne would warm up a bottle of water and put a little bit of sugar in it. Then she'd give it to Noah and put him in the old crib — that same old crib that had once held her three-month-old self. She knew he'd go right off into a deep sleep.

Noah was over a year old now, and could walk and say a few words. But he still loved his bottle, and Anne counted on that bottle to keep him happy and quiet if she had something special and private that she wanted to do — like talk to Katie Maurice or just sit and dream about being a princess in a glittering jewelled gown, dancing with a prince in a red waistcoat with jet black buttons and a lace ruff at his neck. Anne didn't have enough words to describe that scene, nor did she know if she was dressing her princess and prince in the right clothes. But she didn't need words to construct her dancing couple,

137

and she didn't care one whit if they were dressed in the clothes that real royal people actually wore. If the picture in her dream was beautiful, that was all that mattered to her.

There was a small room off the kitchen, which was supposed to be a pantry or a storeroom. But after the first night, when the three older boys kept Noah awake half the night with their talk and noisy games, Mr. Thomas brought Noah's crib downstairs and put it in the tiny pantry. There was room for his clothes and his diapers and his few toys on the shelves, while still leaving space in the cupboards for food in boxes and bags, and the potatoes and root vegetables like carrots and turnips.

Anne put Noah down in his crib, with a hug and a kiss on the top of his small head. "Thank you for being you, Noah," she whispered. "You're the nicest of them all." Then she rushed to get the vegetable brush, two of the dirty hooked mats, and her outdoor clothes. Out in the deep snow of the back yard, she scrubbed those mats for a full hour. While she worked on them, she talked — to the birch trees, to the mysterious flat space behind the trees, to the sky with its scudding white clouds, to herself. She was perfectly at ease and happy talking to herself or to trees or fields. Since Eliza's departure, she had had no one to talk to, and sometimes she felt as though she might burst wide open — *erupt* — if she didn't speak. Talking to Katie Maurice was best, but at the moment she had a job to do that couldn't be done in the cellar hallway. Maybe she'd talk to the mats today and urge them to become beautiful.

"My dear little mats," she began, "please let me get you so clean that pictures will suddenly show through the dirt. Or maybe just one picture. That would be enough to make me happy."

Anne worked the snow into the crevices of the hooking and spread it over the surface. Then she attacked the rugs with the vegetable brush. She did this *ferociously* — with all her strength poured into her thin fists. And one picture did, indeed, seem to be trying to appear. As this began to happen, with vague, indistinct colours starting to emerge through the grey surface, the bristles of the brush became shorter and shorter and dirtier and dirtier. But Anne didn't give this fact a single thought. The urgency of her task engulfed her. Besides, she was talking.

"Oh, such a morning!" she exclaimed. "We put up the curtains, with me standing on a ladder, and Mrs. Thomas handing me the curtain rods hung with curtains from our old house. They didn't quite fit, so they reminded me of my too-short nightgown, and we had nothing left to put up on the last window, but oh! What a difference they made! The kitchen looked cozy and bright with their yellowness, and the parlour looked to me almost like a palace room, with those pale green flannelette drapes with the little roses all over them.

"Then a man came. He seemed to be very important. He stood so straight and tall — like a policeman or a soldier, even though he had on ordinary men's clothes. He asked if there was anyone in the house who was old enough to go to *school*. You can imagine that I almost fell off the ladder! Then I came down off it and stood close to him so that he'd see how tall I was and maybe think I was eight years old, and that it would be *absolutely necessary* for me to go to school. I got those words from him. Mrs. Thomas said that soon I'd be six. He said he was surprised I wasn't older, and I smiled at him and sort of curtsied the way Eliza told me you do if a queen happens to come into your room, so that he'd think I was a pleasant person, and not just a skinny little girl with red hair and too many freckles.

"So this important man said that it wouldn't be 'absolutely necessary' for me to go to school when I was six, and my heart flopped right down like a heavy stone. But he said the school was small, and there weren't many students, and that the teacher was young and *energetic* (another nice new word, but I'm not sure what it means), and hoped she could find more pupils to teach. So that if I wanted to go, and if Mrs. Thomas thought I could walk the mile through the woods to get there, I should go! I'd be happy to walk five miles through the woods in a raging blizzard to get to school, so I bit my lip so hard that it even bled a little bit while I waited for Mrs. Thomas's answer.

"She took a long time to answer, but finally she said, 'I guess she can go if she wants to, just so long as she won't need fancy clothes — or anything special that costs money. My husband just lost his *good* job, and the new one don't pay as much. There's no space here for chickens, and we got three animals and five children to feed, besides him and me. I sure hate to lose her help, but she can work extra hard for me on the weekends.'

"The man looked around the place while he was talking, and I saw he was frowning. Maybe he didn't like the way the three older boys were chasing around and yelling while they were talking. Noah started to cry, so I picked him up and held him in my lap while I fed him his bottle. I figured I'd better try to keep everything quiet if this man didn't like noise.

"Then he said, 'It's our duty to see that Nova Scotians are educated people. So if it's not absolutely necessary for this child to stay home, I'd be in favour of her starting school on March fifteenth. I'll leave the first two Royal Readers for her so she can become familiar with the pictures, even though she won't be able to read them. Then she'll not be so shy and frightened when she starts school.'

"'I don't expect to be frightened when I go to school,' I said, standing up so quickly to take the readers that I almost dropped Noah. 'I may be a small bit shy at first, but when you want anything as badly as I want school, you don't mind being shy.'

"The man said, 'Good! Then it's fixed. I'll tell the teacher to expect you. Her name's Miss Henderson. So what's the little girl's name, Mrs. Thomas?'

"I answered for her. 'My name's Anne Shirley. Anne spelled with an *e*. I'm not Mrs. Thomas's real child. I'm an orphan whose two dead parents were schoolteachers.' I thought if he knew my mother and father were schoolteachers, he'd be less likely to change his mind. And he didn't. He just gave me the two Royal Readers and also a very big smile.

"Then he turned to Mrs. Thomas and said, 'I wish you good day, Mrs. Thomas. Someone will bring you directions about how to reach the school and what time Anne should arrive. Maybe you'd like to accompany her on her first day.'

"I just looked at him very firmly and said, 'That won't be absolutely necessary. In fact, it won't be necessary at all. I'm used to doing things on my own.' I didn't want the boys trailing along and yelling and spoiling the most beautiful day of my life.

"The man looked as though he wanted to smile but knew he shouldn't. 'I can see that,' he said, and then turned back from the door. 'Mrs. Thomas, there's a man who sells eggs about a mile down the road in the other direction. And they're a good price. You might ask your husband to pick up a dozen or so, if he's riding his horse in that direction.' Then he went away."

Anne stopped talking at that point. A picture of a little pink house and a tree had emerged from the surface of the hooked rug. She jumped up, clapped her hands together, and actually danced around the mat.

"One is enough," she said gleefully. "Besides, I'm tired of scrubbing." As soon as the picture was clear, she hung the little mat over the back stoop railing to dry, and hugged herself with the joy of the day's events.

But her delight was short-lived. Mrs. Thomas appeared at the back door — as angry as Anne had ever seen her.

"You *wicked, wicked girl!*" she was shouting. "Just look what you've done to my vegetable brush! You've scrubbed its bristles right down to nothing, and it's too black with dirt to ever use again, anyway. Get in here and start working for your keep. I should have given you away to Mrs. Gleeson when I had the chance!"

Anne had no idea what she meant, nor would she ever find out.

TWENTY-NINE

A Long Walk

Soon it was February, and Mrs. Thomas was suddenly aware of the fact that in just six weeks she wouldn't be able to call on Anne for any little or big job she wanted done. She'd be in school. As Mrs. Thomas couldn't think of a single way in which she'd benefited from her six years in school, she regarded Anne's schooling as a waste of valuable time. But she also knew that children in Nova Scotia were required to attend school, and she didn't want to break the law. It was humiliating enough to have a husband who kept losing jobs because of his drinking, but it would be worse if she herself ended up in jail for failing to send her children to school — or whatever else they might do to parents who kept their children at home during the school year. She'd hoped that Marysville might be so far from a school that it would be impossible for Anne to reach it. But it was clear that this was not the case. Still, even in late March and early April, there might be enough snow or freezing rain to keep a child home from school from time to time. She could hope for that.

But Mrs. Thomas wasn't very good at hoping. So she determined to get as much work out of Anne as she could while she was still at home all day. Besides, she continued to be angry about the vegetable brush. It was totally useless, and she knew of no stores nearby where she could hope to buy a new one. It was no help that Anne had converted a horrible dirty little hooked rug into a rather charming little mat for her *own room*. It wasn't as though anyone else could benefit from looking at it. Selfish. That's what it was — *selfish*. It was hard for her to believe that the dearly-remembered Bertha Shirley could have produced such a self-centred child. Forever standing around and dreaming when there was work to be done. Completely wrecking her only vegetable brush, not giving a moment's thought to the consequences. Without precisely knowing she was doing it, Mrs. Thomas thought of a way to punish Anne. Eggs! She would make Anne walk the mile to bring back eggs — at least once a week, no matter what the weather was doing. The road was largely untravelled, so the snow would often be deep. It would be a hard walk. And the eggs — depending on how they were packaged — might be heavy. *Well*, thought Mrs. Thomas, *she brought it on herself. It's her own fault.*

Anne set off on the following day for the eggs. She had clear instructions on how to get there, and what to expect when she reached the home of the Egg Man. Apparently that's what everyone called him. But his real name was Mr. Johnson. Mr. Thomas — who had picked up bits and pieces of local gossip in the course of his work — told Anne that the Egg Man was tall and thin, wore torn and messy clothes, had a cross and unfriendly manner, but never hurt anybody.

Anne was not afraid of the deep snow, the long walk, or Mr. Johnson. As she set off from home, all she could think of was that she had a free morning to be by herself and to enjoy whatever the long walk might reveal to her; and there would be *no work*. No diapers to wash. No floors to scrub. No food to prepare. Maybe — if she was gone long enough — no dishes to wash. She knew that there would be two houses on the road, and that after she reached them the snow might be more broken up and flattened down — from horses and sled marks and general travel. But in the meantime, she'd have trees to look at, maybe a crow or two, and there might be a big white field. This, she was sure, would make up for her tired legs.

And tired they became — very quickly. Anyone who has plodded through deep snow can imagine how difficult this would be for a six-year-old child — not quite six years old — no matter how tall she was for her age. "A mile," she mused, as she trudged along, "is a long way. Our old house was only a couple of miles from the main part of Bolingbroke, and we almost never went there. Too far." She was panting by now, and hoping that the houses would hurry up and appear, so that the road would get easier from there on. Maybe around the next curve in the road. Or the next.

Then she saw the rabbit. From then on, the snow didn't seem so deep, nor her weariness so acute. The rabbit was large and pure white. He looked at her with a serene and steady gaze, and she was enchanted. What other wonders might she not see? She raised her eyes from the road as she walked along, her mind no longer focused on her tired legs. She looked at the branches of the spruce trees and the enormous pines, laden with snow, and marvelled at their beauty. Other trees almost joined together above her, like a giant archway. The morning was cold but sunny, and the snow glistened in the intense light. Anne saw a scarlet grosbeak on one of the branches, a bluejay on another.

Long before she reached the houses, Anne even spied a deer in a small clearing, nuzzling through the snow in search of maple bark and reaching up for birch buds. Anne stopped walking and watched the deer for a long time. She forgot that she was tired, no longer noticed the cold. It was the first deer she had ever seen, and she was stunned by its beauty. She would see many more in the course of her walks to school and to Mr. Johnson's; but this was her *first deer*, and the image would remain branded on her brain — its slender neck, its large soft eyes when it raised its head to look around, the markings on its coat, the small white clearing where it stood, the wall of the surrounding trees. She would never forget that scene or the depth of her joy as she watched it.

But she knew she couldn't stay there forever. Reluctantly she trudged on, and then suddenly, as she rounded an abrupt curve, she saw the two houses. As she came abreast of one of them — an orange house, bright against the snow — a woman came to the door, and called out to her. "Little girl! Hello! What are you doing here?"

"I'm going to the Egg Man!" Anne shouted back. And then, unnecessarily, "For eggs." She held up a cloth bag — now sodden from the snow.

"Would you like a cookie? Or a cup of hot tea?"

"Yes!"

"C'mon, then. Hurry! I'm letting in the cold."

Her name was Mrs. Archibald. She introduced herself as soon as Anne came in the door. She had a nice warm kitchen that smelled of cinnamon and chocolate, and she urged Anne to take off her coat and rest for fifteen minutes. The cookie was delicious. The tea was warm and sweet. Anne felt as though she'd like to stay in that kitchen forever.

"My!" said Mrs. Archibald, when Anne took off her hat. "What beautiful hair!" Anne stared at the woman with gratitude and wonderment. *Beautiful hair!* She'd really said that. Could she have ... *meant* it? Could this be happening? *This* and the *rabbit* and the *deer*, all in one day!

"I'm Anne Shirley. I'm the orphan child who lives with the Thomases down the road a piece, close to the railway line. You're supposed to spell my name with an *e*. I saw a rabbit and a deer on the way, and a red bird and a blue one. I'm very tired, but so many nice things are happening to me that I can hardly wait for the next time. The snow is all full of sparkles in the sun."

"I used to have a little girl," said Mrs. Archibald.

"Don't you have her anymore?" asked Anne. "Did she die? Did she run away? Oh! I'm sorry. She must have been very nice if you're her mother."

Mrs. Archibald laughed. "No," she said, "she didn't die or run away. She grew up. She got married and moved to Kingsport."

"Oh," said Anne. "Just like Eliza. Away. So I'm still sorry."

"Who's Eliza?" Mrs. Archibald passed her another cookie. The first one had disappeared very quickly.

"She was the Thomases' oldest daughter. She was the person in the family who loved me. But not enough. Because she married Roger and went away to New Brunswick. I thought I would die from sadness when she left. But I didn't. She wanted to take me with her, but Roger wouldn't let me go to their house with maybe a doll or even a kitten."

Mrs. Archibald reached over and squeezed Anne's hand. "Who's left in the house now that Eliza's gone?"

"Well, Margaret left to go work at the Jamiesons' to lift old Mrs. Jamieson in and out of bed. Mrs. Thomas says it's hard work. Trudy works for Mrs. Archard, but she has an easy job. She wears a black dress with a tiny lace apron, and opens doors and passes sandwiches to ladies in beautiful gowns. I'd love to have a job that easy."

"A job that easy?" said Mrs. Archibald. "What do you mean?"

"Well, I guess I mean that I wish my work was that easy."

"Work? What work?"

"Like scrubbing diapers and cleaning floors and bringing buckets of water to Mrs. Thomas and chopping up vegetables for dinner and washing dishes. I think opening the door in a lace apron would be a whole lot easier."

"Who's left at home?"

"Mrs. Thomas has three bad little boys and a nice baby called Noah. And Mr. Thomas. Right now he's not drinking. Not since he lost his job in Bolingbroke after the dance."

"How old are you, Anne? Eight?"

"I'll be six next month. Then my whole life will change. I'll be going to *school*. I'll learn about all those wonderful long words I want to use, and I'll learn how to read. The man who came to our house last week gave me two Royal Readers, and because Eliza read me stories from them I know some of them by heart, and I feel like I'm reading them when I open to the right page. I know it's the right page because of the pictures. I can't count to a hundred yet, and I suppose it would be nice to be able to do that, but I don't really care. I'd rather be able to read. What's your daughter's name?"

"Isabella."

"Oh!" breathed Anne. "What a beautiful, beautiful, name! I love the name Isabella. I hope she's happy in Kingsport. I try to hope that Eliza is happy, but I'm still angry with her for choosing Roger instead of me, so it's hard to hope that. I try not to hate Roger, because hating is so exhausting, but it's difficult not to. I know the word *exhausting*, because that's what Mrs. Thomas says her life is. But I like the sound of it much better than plain old *tiring*, don't you?"

"Oh, absolutely!" said Mrs. Archibald, looking nonetheless troubled.

"Absolutely. What does that mean? The man who came about the school used it. And I use it now, too. But I'm not really sure exactly what it means."

Mrs. Archibald thought for a moment. "Well," she said, "it's something like a strong yes or *very*. If I say I'm absolutely certain that it's going to rain, I pretty well know it's going to happen."

"Well," said Anne, pulling on her boots and struggling into her coat, "I absolutely know I should leave. I really only have the morning free for this trip to the Egg Man, but by the time I get back to Marysville it's going to be close to suppertime. If I'm very late, Mrs. Thomas will be ... oh, never mind. I'd just better hurry. Those were lovely cookies, and the tea made me warm again."

"Anne," said Mrs. Archibald, "come and visit me again when you come for eggs. I miss having a little girl around. And here," she went on, "take this bag of cookies. You'll be hungry before you get home, and you can't eat the eggs."

Suddenly Anne remembered about Eliza and hugs. She stepped forward onto the clean floor in her snowy boots and hugged Mrs. Archibald. "Bye!" she said, and moved toward the door.

"Mr. Johnson's place is a bit beyond the next bend in the road. He seems gruff and cross, but it's just his way. He's not dangerous. He won't hurt you. And his eggs are good."

Back on the road, Anne felt as strong as a giant. That warm kitchen. That bag of cookies. The words of Mrs. Archibald about her "beautiful hair." The hot tea. The rabbit. And absolutely the deer. Anne didn't care one bit if Mr. Johnson was cross and gruff. She felt ready for anything.

THIRTY

The Egg Man

Mr. Johnson's house — if you could call it a house — was more than "a bit" beyond the next bend in the road. But the walking was easier than it had been before Anne reached Mrs. Archibald's house. She was out of breath when she reached her destination, but not as tired as she'd been earlier.

Before knocking, she looked very carefully at the house. When she had even the smallest adventure, she liked to pay close attention to all aspects of it so that she could think about it when she got to bed at night, or so that she could tell Katie Maurice all the details when she had a chance.

First, Anne took note of the size of the house. It was small, very small. It had to be all one room, because there was no way you could fit two rooms into that tiny space. The outside was unpainted, and was the kind of weathered grey that she had noticed on old shacks and barns that had never seen paint or whitewash. With just a little itch of apprehension, Anne knocked on the door. There was no response. She took off her mittens and knocked harder.

The door opened about three inches, and a low voice said, "Whaddaya want?" Anne could see only a small part of the face on the other side of the door. It seemed to be composed largely of black beard.

"Eggs," said Anne, holding up the damp bag.

"Come in for a second," he said, and opened the door.

On the following day, at nap time, Anne had a chance to talk to Katie Maurice about Mr. Johnson.

"Oh, Katie Maurice," said Anne, "it's so lovely to have something new to talk about. You must get tired of hearing about dishes and diapers. Well, the Egg Man is worth talking about.

"When he opened the door, it was very warm inside. There was an oil lamp on a shelf or table across the room. But I could hardly see a single thing. It had been so bright and sunny outside that I almost felt blind when I got in that house. But because of the lamp, I could see that Mr. Johnson was very tall and that he had a big bristly beard. I felt a little bit scared, but not very. He said, 'How many?' I said, 'Sixteen. Four for Mr. Thomas, and two each for the rest of us. That makes sixteen. I can't count to a hundred, but I can do it to sixteen.'

"'All right, all right,' he said, sounding very cross, 'I don't need an arithmetic lesson. I'll get your eggs.' He pushed by me and went out the front door, slamming it behind him. Then, Katie Maurice, I was alone in that room. When I got a little bit used to the dim light, I could see that there was a table under the lamp, and one small window. There seemed to be some books on the table, and a cup and a teapot. I wanted like anything to see what was in those books, but I didn't dare cross the dark floor. I might trip over a chair or a jug of water or a *dog*.

"I could see Mr. Johnson quite well in the doorway when he went outside to get the eggs from the henhouse — or wherever he keeps them. The beard wasn't as black as I'd thought, but he looked old and dirty. As though he slept in his clothes. I was glad that people had told me that he wasn't dangerous, because he looked absolutely dangerous to me. I got two new words today, and you just heard them. Mrs. Archibald taught me both of them. I hope she asks me in for tea and cookies every time I go to the Egg Man, because it would make me strong and brave for when I have to knock on Mr. Johnson's door. But the only way she can know I'm there is if she's looking out the window. And a woman who keeps such a lovely clean, warm kitchen and makes beautiful cookies can't be spending much time looking out the window. She has a daughter, but she's grown up instead of dead. I'm glad she's not dead, because I'd hate anything awful to happen to Mrs. Archibald, and having a daughter die must be the most awful thing in the world — maybe awfuller than having two dead parents. Her daughter's name is Isabella. Did you ever in your life hear such an absolutely beautiful name? I wish she was still a little girl so that we could play together. But she's not, and I can't. But never mind. I have you.

"And next month I'll be in school. The man who came here about me going to school said there weren't many children in the school, but surely there might be *someone* for me to talk to and play with. Not that you're not the most perfect friend in the world, Katie Maurice, but you can't play in the snow with me or go down and float sticks in the pond in the springtime — if there's really a pond out there behind the five birch trees."

One day, shortly after her sixth birthday, Anne made a journey to Mr. Johnson's house on a sunny March day. She'd seen Mrs. Archibald only twice since her first trip to the old Egg Man, but each time she invited Anne into her warm kitchen and gave her cookies and tea. The last time this had happened, she looked carefully at Anne as they sat there together, sipping their tea. "I don't know whether I should tell you this," she said. "Maybe you're too young to take it in. But there's something I'd like to tell you about Mr. Johnson. It might help you to understand him better. Or it might worry you. Or *bother* you."

"Oh, Mrs. Archibald," said Anne. "I hope you'll tell me. I'm not too young. I'm six now. It happened on Friday of last week. Mrs. Thomas told me it was my birthday, but I knew anyway. I'd been counting the days. I wanted so badly to be six. Five doesn't sound like much more than a baby. Even Horace will be five in August."

"So what happened then?" asked Mrs. Archibald.

"When?"

"When she told you that it was your birthday?"

"Oh, I don't know. It's almost a week ago. Probably I washed the diapers, because I remember that it was sunny. So it was a good drying day. I like hanging them out. Seeing them dance along the clothesline in the wind. That's a lovely thing to watch. I can pretend that the diapers are dancers and I try to hear the music they're dancing to. Mr. Thomas made me a nice little ledge thing so that I can reach the line easier. I love hanging them out. But I hate taking them in when they're frozen like boards and hard to pry off that bristly rope. You feel like your cold fingers are going to fall right off."

"That's what you did on your birthday?"

"Probably. I can't remember for sure. I know that sometimes wonderful things happen on people's birthdays. I've heard about them. Birthday cakes with candles and maybe a present. Or even two. A doll. Or beautiful blue ribbons for my awful hair, to make it look almost pretty. I'd like that, of course, but orphans who've been taken in and kept for years and years can't expect special treats. Specially when they've been brought up 'by hand.' That's what Mrs.

Thomas calls it, but I don't know what it means. There are seven people to feed in our house, and I'm not even a member of the family."

Then Anne stopped talking for a moment, and said to Mrs. Archibald, "I know a present you could give me for my birthday."

Mrs. Archibald leaned across the table and took Anne's hand. "*Tell me!*" she said. "I'd *love* to give you a present."

Anne grinned. "Here's what the present is: tell me the secret about Mr. Johnson. I'm six now, so I'm old enough to understand. And I won't worry. Or be *bothered.* I've been worried and bothered lots of times, and it didn't *kill* me."

Mrs. Archibald wasn't sure if that last statement of Anne's made her want to laugh or cry. But she didn't do either. "All right," she said. "Here's your present. Once, long ago, Mr. Johnson was engaged to be married to a beautiful woman. He loved her a whole lot. But on the morning of the day they were to be married, she sent him a note telling him that she didn't love him anymore, and that she was leaving from their city on that very morning — with another man. And the man she was leaving with was his best friend."

Anne stared fixedly at Mrs. Archibald with her large eyes — grey today, and suddenly full of tears. Then she laid her head down on the table and cried out loud for a long time.

Mrs. Archibald was beside herself with distress. "Oh, Anne!" she said, coming around to the other side of the table and stroking her hair, rubbing her back. "I'm so sorry. I thought it might make you feel better about Mr. Johnson's crossness."

"Oh, Mrs. Archibald!" stuttered Anne, between sobs and hiccups, "it does, oh it *does!* It's a beautiful and terrible story. I'll never be scared of Mr. Johnson again. I'll just think of him as a poor wounded bird, and be extra polite to him and careful never to make him unhappy. Oh! I can see him all dressed up in his fine clothes, ready to go to the wedding, and then suddenly hearing the awful news. Reading the cruel letter. Oh, I know exactly what he felt like. It's like when Eliza left me to marry terrible Roger. But Roger wasn't my best friend, and at least I didn't find out about it *at the very last minute*."

Anne had been sitting up as she spoke these words to Mrs. Archibald. Now she put her red head on the table again, groaning, "Oh! Oh! Oh!" Then she stopped all of a sudden and looked up. "Is that why he lives in that shack and never washes his clothes?"

"Well ... yes," said Mrs. Archibald, afraid of a fresh outburst of tears from Anne, but realizing that she needed the end of the story. "He gave away — or threw away — all his possessions except for one change of clothes and a few bits of furniture and pots and pans and the like, and moved into these woods, living in a tent until the cold weather came on. At the time, there were no other people nearby. Then he built his little shack and moved into it. He'd been a schoolteacher, and he brought several crates of books and a few pictures. That's what he *does*. He reads books and looks after his hens."

"He was a *schoolteacher*!" breathed Anne. "Just like my own two parents. I won't tell him I know the whole sad story of his life, but I feel that I will love him forever! It's been a beautiful birthday present for me!"

Mrs. Archibald gave a sigh of relief. While Anne was preparing to leave, she went upstairs, and soon returned with a little parcel wrapped in pink paper with a white bow on it.

"For you," she said to Anne. "Happy birthday."

With shaking fingers, Anne opened the gift. It was a long, curled-up roll of pale blue ribbons.

Anne's eyes shone as she took out the ribbons and held them to her face.

"For your beautiful hair," said Mrs. Archibald.

Although people seldom said thank-you in the Thomas household — it was simply an expression that nobody used —on this occasion it wasn't necessary. The joy on Anne's face was so vivid that Mrs. Archibald spent the rest of the day in a sort of happy trance, and made her husband a lemon meringue pie for his supper.

THIRTY-ONE

*W*ords

Shortly after rounding the bend in the road that led to the Egg Man's house, Anne spied a strange object on the snowy road. Even at a distance, she could see that it was moving. When she reached it, she could tell that it was a hen — a large one — and she could see that its leg was broken. Her heart went out to the injured bird, but she was also frightened of it. It had that beak, and those feet didn't look very friendly. Oddly, she thought about Mrs. Thomas. She could be almost serene and friendly when she wasn't tired and when her husband was going through a dry period. But she was nearly always tired, and even when Mr. Thomas wasn't drinking, she had frequent memories of his past anger and physical abuse, all of which she found hard to forgive. And certainly forgetting was out of the question. So, even during her easier times, she was often moody and unpredictable in her responses. What a strange thing for Anne to be thinking as she stared down at the suffering hen. What might it do if she tried to pick it up? On the other hand, she shouldn't leave it to freeze to death in a snowbank. She couldn't do this to either the bird or the Egg Man — a person for whom she had recently developed so much empathy and concern.

She dropped her canvas bag on the road and bent down to look at the broken leg. It, at least, was lying limp. So she had only the one foot and the beak to worry about. Clamping her teeth together and screwing up her face, she reached down and picked up the hen. To her astonishment it didn't struggle or thrash around. Maybe it was close to freezing. Maybe even a hen can welcome being in the safety and relatively warm embrace of a pair of arms. Anne could feel the sturdiness of its body and the softness of its feathers. Almost against her will, she found herself loving the bird. Not as good as a kitten, but better than a doll. But she'd better hurry. It might be dying. Why was it so *quiet*? Shouldn't it be struggling just a little bit? Forgetting her cloth bag, leaving it lying on the road, she walked quickly on to Mr. Johnson's house, saying soothing words of comfort to the hen, stroking its feathers.

When Anne reached Mr. Johnson's shack, she kicked the door with her foot because she had no hand free to do the knocking. He approached the door, gruffer then ever. "No need to kick the door down!" he yelled.

When he opened the door, Anne was astonished to hear herself say, "And there's no need to yell at me, either. Your hen has a broken leg, and he's probably half frozen. He'd like to have it nice and quiet and warm so that he can get better."

When Mr. Johnson saw the skinny little girl with her arms full of hen, his mood changed. "Come in, come in. I thank you. You're probably cold, too. I'll make you some hot cocoa. Here" — and he reached out — "I'll take the hen." Then he looked at her kindly. "A hen's a she, you know, not a he. She lays the eggs. The rooster is the he. Please sit down." He drew a straight wooden chair up to the table. "Now, wait a bit. I'll just shove the kettle to the hot part of the stove, and then I'll put the hen someplace where she'll be safe. Maybe in this box here, until she heals." He placed her tenderly inside the box.

Then, while he busied himself lighting two more lamps and making the cocoa, she drew a couple of his books toward her and flipped through the pages. There were pictures in one, and they showed people with wings. Maybe they were very big fairies. They didn't look like the kinds of fairies *she* thought about. Hers were tiny, in flowing garments, their hair — garlanded with flowers — blowing in the wind. With sparkly wands and magic powers. In size, somewhere between an insect and a chickadee.

Mr. Johnson approached her with two steaming cups. "It should be made with milk. But maybe cocoa made with water is better than no cocoa at all."

"Oh," said Anne. "I've never had cocoa at all, so I'm sure that what you just said is true." Then she pointed to the picture in the book. "Why do these people have wings? They're too big to be fairies. Or *I* think so. And in another picture everyone looks like they're so unhappy. Why?"

"They're angels. But they've been bad, so God chased them out of heaven. That's why they look so sad. And you're absolutely right. They're not fairies."

Anne looked at him with a wide-open, delighted smile. "Oh!" she said, "You know that word, too! *Absolutely*. Isn't it a wonderful word? It says so much more than smaller words. Like *very*. But *angels*. I don't know anything about angels. Or heaven. But you said something about fairies. Do you believe there are fairies too? And are angels real?"

The Egg Man produced a rumbly laugh behind his bushy beard. "Well," he said, "it depends on what you mean by *real*. Maybe they're real and maybe they're not. But if people apply their imaginations to them, they can become very real inside our heads, and surely that's a valid kind of reality."

Anne's eyes were open very wide, and were green in the lamplight. "I don't understand half of what you're saying, but it sounds so lovely. I think it means that it's not sinful to think about things that other people don't really think are there. Mrs. Thomas thinks it's very wicked of me to be dreaming about princesses and fairies and people dancing in beautiful clothes and music playing and all. I can really *hear* the music if I dream hard enough. Do you think that's wicked?"

"What would you be doing if you weren't dreaming? Reading? Playing with your friends?"

"I'd be washing diapers or carrying water for Mrs. Thomas or cutting up carrots for dinner. And no. Not reading. I don't know how. And I don't have any books. Eliza took her books with her when she went away with awful Roger. And I live in the woods. I don't have any friends. You live in the woods, too. Do you have any friends? I hope so. Mrs. Archibald lives around the bend, and she has a wonderful kitchen with cookies and tea, and she just gave me a lot of blue ribbons for my terrible hair. She thinks it's beautiful. My hair, I mean. But I've heard lots of people say it's horrible. Mrs. Archibald would be a nice friend for you. Sometimes having no friends makes you feel lonesome."

Mr. Johnson's eyes were focused on Anne's face, with its lively expression as she talked. He looked at her thin arms, her long delicate fingers with their chipped and broken nails.

"How old are you, Anne?" he asked.

"I'm six," said Anne, sitting a little straighter. "Last Friday was my birthday."

"And before that, you were five," he murmured, shaking his head.

"But I'm tall," said Anne. "Lots of people think I'm really old. Like eight. Or even nine. But never mind that. Please tell me if you think that dreaming is wicked. You seem to know a lot of things, so maybe you know the answer to that."

Mr. Johnson cleared his throat. "What you're talking about is imagination."

"Is *what?*"

"Imagination. Imagining things. It's one of the most important qualities that human beings possess."

"I don't know what *imagining* means. I'm not sure, either, about *qualities* or *human beings*, or what *possess* means." She didn't know the meanings of the words, but she had accurately memorized them when he spoke them. "Are you saying that it's not wicked to be dreaming things? Is that what all those words mean that you've strung together?"

"Yes," said Mr. Johnson. "*Yes!* What's more, it's far more important than washing diapers or carrying water."

Anne laughed right out loud. "Now that's a pretty silly thing to say! What would babies do without diapers? And how could we wash them without water? I *do* those things, but sometimes Mrs. Thomas gets kind of frantic. That's a word I learned from her. She's frantic a lot of the time, and if I stand in front of the dishpan staring at the wall and thinking about *fairies*, it makes her *crazy*. It wasn't hard to learn that one, because she uses it almost every day. I love words so much, but I need a lot more of them. I'd like to have some really long ones for telling things I see and things I think."

"Anne," Mr. Johnson said quietly and firmly, "listen to me. Imagining things is *not wicked*. It's *good*. It's what makes people write books and paint pictures and compose music. It means *pretending* things. Go on doing it. Don't for heaven's sake stop, even if Mrs. Thomas gets cross. It can often rescue you from the depths of sadness."

"What's *rescue* and what's *depths*?" said Anne.

"If I pull you out of a river when you're drowning, I *rescue* you. Sometimes life can seem like drowning, so it's very useful. Depths means ... what? ... oh, it means *deep*. The way a well or a hole in the ground is deep. And the ocean is very deep. The bottom is far, far away."

"I have often felt the depths of sadness," said Anne, "but it feels a lot better, just because I know how to say it. And now I also know that talking to Katie Maurice isn't a wicked thing."

"Katie Maurice?"

Anne told him about Katie Maurice, and about her conversations with her. She told him about Mr. Thomas smashing one of the doors of the china cabinet when he was drunk, but she also said she liked him and he liked her and that she wasn't afraid of him. She told him about being an orphan and that her parents taught school in Bolingbroke.

"It seems like an unhappy story," said Anne, "but I had Eliza for a long time, and now I have Mrs. Archibald." She was silent for a moment. "And you. You've taught me about seven new words today, and I'm going to practise them all on the way home."

Mr. Johnson cleared his throat. "I tell you what, Anne," he said. "Each week when you come, I'll teach you five new words. I'll even write them down so that you can try writing them. I'll have five especially nice ones ready for you. And I'll give you a small notebook and a pencil for writing them."

Then, of course, they had to search for Anne's canvas egg bag, which she'd dropped on the road. It was soaking wet, but she didn't care. The eggs were heavy and the snow was quite deep, but she hardly noticed that she was walking. She felt more as though she was flying.

THIRTY-TWO

*A*nger and Fear

On Anne's return journey to the Thomas house that afternoon, she could hardly wait to talk to Katie Maurice about the many adventures she'd had that day. But a lot of things would work against the possibility of that happening. On the way home, Anne had already taken note of the fact that there was beauty on all sides of her. Behind her, the white snowy road wound its way between tall stands of spruce and pine. She could easily pretend — *imagine* — that it led to a magnificent palace, composed of snow and sparkling icicles. The trees were heavy with last night's snowfall, and some of the lower branches were bent over so far that they were nearly touching the ground. In the west, the sun was just disappearing behind the hill that hid the railway track from the house. In the east, the afternoon was painting the clouds orange, rose, yellow. Anne looked around her, and decided that everything in her life was perfect. The end of that road led to Mrs. Archibald and Mr. Johnson. Surely they were even more important than any crystal palace. And they were real. She smiled as she looked in the direction of the house.

The door opened, and Mrs. Thomas appeared. Her straight brown hair had come loose from its pins in several places, and the rest of it was drawn tightly back from her face. The loose strands hung down along the sides of her sallow cheeks and neck, and her eyes looked unusually bright — bright with anger.

"Where in heaven's name have you been? Don't give a

thought to *me* back in the house with four noisy boys and no help *at all*, while you're out playing in the woods. I need two of those eggs right this minute, and I need you inside to feed Noah his porridge and to cut up the potatoes for supper — not that we have a proper brush to wash them with. So get a move on!"

Anne made an effort to be quick, but the snow was deep at this end of the road, and it was hard to make her legs go faster. She looked at Mrs. Thomas, and thought of the way Mrs. Archibald's mouth turned up at the corners. Mrs. Thomas's turned down. As she struggled through the drifts, Anne thought about Mrs. Thomas dancing. Mr. Thomas had said she was really good at it. Anne put her in a dress with a wide pink skirt and lacy petticoats. She turned the music on in her head, and tried to see Mrs. Thomas whirling around the floor with flying feet. But it seemed that her imagination wasn't strong enough for that. Mrs. Thomas was firmly rooted on the back porch, and she was frowning. Anne rapidly replaced her with her own mother, always beautiful, always smiling, holding out her arms in welcome, exclaiming, "You must be so cold! And your feet must be so wet! Quickly! Come into the kitchen and rest beside the fire. I'll bring a ginger biscuit and a hot cup of tea. And then you can tell me all about your wonderful day." A tear squeezed out of one of Anne's eyes, and rolled down her cheek. *There must be children all over the world who come home every day and have that happen*. Anne could hardly bear to think that thought. As she struggled up the steps in her slippery boots, she muttered, "Sorry I'm late."

Mrs. Thomas moved aside to let Anne in, slamming the door behind her. "Five more days," she growled, "and you'll be in school. Then we'll all be in a fine pickle." And she added, "Mr. Thomas is drinking again."

Anne was torn between those two pieces of information. *School!* In five days' time! And then, almost before she'd had a half second to welcome that thought into her mind came another: *Mr. Thomas is drinking again.* She removed her outdoor clothes quickly, stripping her wet socks off her cold feet and pulling up a pair of stockings that were on a hook in the back porch. Then she quickly moved into the kitchen, filled a bowl from the porridge pot at the back of the stove, and went in search of Noah. The house was full of the sound of crying children, so it took her a few moments to find him. But there he was, the only one not crying, sitting on the floor in a corner of the kitchen, looking small and frightened.

Anne picked him up and hugged him. She could feel his tense little body relax, and whispered to him, "What's wrong?"

He replied in a small voice. "Papa hit."

Anne held him away from her body and looked him full in the face. "You? Papa hit Noah?" He was the smallest. Anne hardly dared think that thought.

"No," said Noah, in a louder voice. "Mama. And Horace."

Anne carried Noah over to the rocking chair and sat down on it with him. When they were settled, she fed him his porridge. After he was finished, and had gone to sleep in her arms, she moved him into his little sleeping space beside the kitchen and put him in his crib. Then she went over to the table and started to cut up the potatoes. In the background was the sound of three crying boys, with their mother period-ically shouting, "*Stop* it! Be *quiet!*"

Mr. Thomas entered the kitchen — slowly, carefully, testing his balance. His head looked as though it were only loosely attached to his neck, and his eyes were heavy-lidded and unfocused. He slammed his fist on the table, and several pieces of potato jumped onto the floor. He held a hammer in his other hand.

"*Stop that infernal racket!*" he yelled, louder than anyone else. There was a sudden silence in the kitchen. "I work all day," he continued, "at a stupid, boring, lonely job, just to put bread on your table! So let's have it quiet when I get home! Let's have a little peace!" He slammed the table again. "Where's supper?"

Anne could feel something unfamiliar rising in her chest. Something inside her seemed to give a little *snap*. She stood up. "Some of the rest of us," she said, "have stupid, boring work to do, too. And we're not the only ones who make a racket. You scared Noah this afternoon. He's not much more than a baby. *And supper's not ready yet.*" Then she turned her back on him, and continued to cut up the potatoes.

Anne's heart was beating hard and fast. Her back was to him. Would he take that hammer that he was holding and strike her with it? She knew that he'd told Eliza that he wouldn't hurt her. But Eliza hadn't been around for a long time. And when he was drunk, he sometimes did things that he didn't remember later — things he was sorry he'd done. She kept chopping and chopping the potatoes, trying not to think about what might be going on behind her. And then, suddenly, she heard the kitchen door close — *softly*. When she turned around, he was no longer in the room.

Later that evening, when everyone else was in bed, Anne took her lamp and walked quietly down the stairs and into the cellar hallway. She wouldn't be able to sleep if she didn't tell Katie Maurice at least a few things about Mrs. Archibald and Mr. Johnson. Just a few things. She felt she would explode if she wasn't able to tell her *something*.

Anne didn't have any difficulty getting Katie Maurice's

attention. She was right there waiting, eyes bright and eager in the lamplight. First, Anne told her about her time with Mrs. Archibald, and the gift of the blue ribbons. She'd even brought them downstairs to show her. "Maybe," said Anne, "my hair will look as beautiful as Mrs. Archibald says it is when I decorate it with these birthday ribbons."

After that, Katie Maurice heard the sad tale of old Mr. Johnson's cruel bride, who ran away on the morning of his wedding day. Anne thought she could spy a tear slithering down Katie's cheek. Certainly she could feel that her own cheek was wet. Then she told about the wounded hen.

"Oh Katie Maurice — there he was in the middle of the road, not moving. And hens are always busy walking around, you know, except when they're doing something lazy, like laying eggs. This one was just *there*, like a big lump of dough in the cold snow. Then, when I went up to him — no ... *her*, because Mr. Johnson says that all hens are shes — I could see that her leg was broken. I felt that I must *rescue* her (that's a new word straight from Mr. Johnson) because she might freeze to death if I didn't; but I was scared — *absolutely* scared — because of his — her — sharp beak and claws. But I did pick her up, and she lay in my arms without even the smallest wiggle."

Then Anne told Katie Maurice about Mr. Johnson's angels and the cocoa, and about the five new words he was going to teach her every week. And about Mr. Thomas and the things she said to him, and the hammer, and how frightened she was. Then she said, "Now I'm tired. Going for the eggs is wonderful, but it makes me tired. So good night, dear Katie Maurice. Tomorrow's washday, so I'm going to bed this very minute. Have a nice sleep."

Anne picked up the lantern from the floor and made her way down the hall and up the stairs. She took time to blow a kiss to the five birch trees outside her window — to the "Five Sisters," as she now called them — and then dived under the covers. She wished that Mr. Thomas would hurry up and get that cat. He'd promised he would. It would be lovely to be able to snuggle up to it in bed. But right now wasn't a good time to ask him. However, Anne was asleep almost before her head hit the pillow. So it must have been in her sleep that she murmured, "School in five days."

THIRTY-THREE

New Directions

Somehow or other, Anne managed to live through the next five days. In her dreams and in her waking hours, her mind was full of thoughts of school. Whenever she had a free moment, she opened one or the other of her Royal Readers and pretended to read the stories and poems. She recited the words to "Mary's Little Lamb," and looked at the pictures of the wreck in "The Storm," and the woman in the shoe with all her children. Soon all those things would be part of her life.

Mr. Johnson had taught her five new words this past week; they might be useful for her in school. He had even recorded them in the little notebook he'd given her. He'd written them with a real pen, so he must have brought paper and pens and ink when he'd left his home so long ago, in order to live in the woods. Or did he use his egg money to buy those things? Maybe there'd be stores for such things in Marysville. If so, Anne would love to go into one of them and pretend she had money to buy something. She'd never, ever, in her whole life been in a store. That thought was almost as exciting as the thought of school.

During those five days before she left for school, Anne scarcely noticed the diapers she was washing, or the floors she was scrubbing, or the carrots she was cutting up. And she was working hard. Mrs. Thomas was determined to get as much work as she could out of Anne before she was left all alone to cope with the meals, the cleaning, the boys' noise and fights — and Mr. Thomas's rages. But Anne didn't mind the extra work. In her mind, she wasn't even in the house. The work didn't matter.

Besides, other things had happened during that time to make Anne feel more contented. Two days after she had actually *scolded* Mr. Thomas for yelling and for scaring Noah, he arrived home with a large bag. He placed it on the rocking chair in the kitchen, and said to everyone in the room, "Gather 'round! I brought something!" His eyes swept the room as he spoke, but he seemed to be looking most often at Anne. Then he reached down and opened the bag. The western sun was streaming into one of the kitchen windows as he did this, so when a very large orange cat walked out of the bag, he was framed by a particularly vivid sunset.

Mrs. Thomas was pleased. Already she could foresee a decline in the mouse population. The three older boys, awed by the hugeness of the animal and unfamiliar with cats, stepped backwards a few paces, uneasy about this new visitor. Noah was holding Anne's hand when the cat appeared, and might have been able to sense Anne's reaction. In any case, he reached forward to touch the soft fur. For her part, Anne felt an intensity of joy that was new to her. As she was later to describe how she felt to Katie Maurice, "My heart within my chest felt squeezed with ecstasy." To Mr. Thomas, all she could say was a long-drawn-out "Ohhhhhh!," which was almost like a groan. She went over and picked up the heavy cat, loving his weight, his softness, his loud purr, his tiger stripes, the fact that he was almost the same colour as her own hair. Why had she ever thought she wanted a grey one? With him in her arms, she felt comfort for a thousand sorrows.

"He came out of the sunset," said Anne from behind the huge mound of fur. "Out of the west. I'm going to call him Lochinvar. Eliza taught me a poem that started out with the

words, 'O young Lochinvar is come out of the West.' It's such a beautiful poem. The real Lochinvar is handsome and brave, and he tosses the fair maiden up onto his horse and rides off with her. I couldn't imagine a more perfect name for my cat."

My cat. No one voiced any objections to this announcement. The boys were too scared. Mrs. Thomas didn't care. And Mr. Thomas was clearly pleased.

Anne had never before travelled along the mile-long stretch of road that led to the school. She knew how to get there and what to do when she arrived, because the School Man had visited the house and given her all the necessary information.

She'd been on her knees when he arrived, with scrub brush and pail beside her, but Mrs. Thomas told her to get up and listen to what he had to say. So she dried her hands and went to sit on a chair beside him at the kitchen table. He had prepared a little map for her, with marks and arrows to explain exactly how she would find the school; and he laid it on the kitchen table and told her how to read it. "Go this way, and around this bend," he said, pointing to the map, "and then follow this arrow until you reach the store. Then turn left and go up a short hill. The school's on the right. It's not very big. But there's a bell on the roof. You'll know it's a school. And there'll be children in the yard, playing. Walk right in, even before the bell rings, and Miss Henderson will explain things and tell you what to do."

Anne took the map from him and folded it very carefully, smoothing it between her hands, as though it was a treasure — which of course it was. After the man left, she took it upstairs to her room and put it in an envelope that Mr. Johnson had given her, along with her five new words. She couldn't read them, but she knew what they were and what they meant: They were *curious, delighted* (and *delightful*), *disappointing, alarming, amazing*. She said them aloud to Lochinvar, who was stationed on her pillow. She tucked the envelope in an old school satchel of Trudy's, beside the two Royal Readers. What else could she put in the bag? A handkerchief might be a useful thing. If her nose started to run, or if she heard a poem so beautiful that it made her cry, she'd need one. She wished that her only clean handkerchief didn't look so dingy, so grey. And it had a tiny hole in one corner. But never mind. It was better than nothing. She didn't want to use her sleeve. She stuffed it way down into the bottom of the satchel. No one would see it unless she really needed it.

"Anne!" It was Mrs. Thomas's voice. "What on earth are you doing up there? Come down this minute!"

Oh! She was supposed to be washing the dishes. She hung the satchel over the door handle by its long strap and rushed downstairs.

The rest of that week passed, and the morning of Anne's first day of school finally arrived. It was a sunny March day, with a strong promise of spring in the air. Real spring in Nova Scotia arrives late, and it was still a long way off. But even in February, there can be days that are so sunny and bright, so deceptively warm, so *promising*, that even native Nova Scotians — who should know better — find themselves thinking that spring must be just around the corner. Today was just such a day. Anne rose and dressed, made up her bed, blew a special kiss to the Five Sisters, and then raced downstairs. She wouldn't have to wash the dishes this morning. Or even feed Noah or slice the bread. There wouldn't be enough time to do those things. Anne felt as though her insides were a big cave, packed full of more excitement than she could possibly hold. She didn't know how she could eat one single bite of the bread that she'd just finished spreading with jam. Someone else would have to eat it. And the porridge on the stove looked even more impossible. Eating anything was out of the question. Anne looked at Mrs. Thomas, her eyes huge and bright with joy, and said, "I'm so happy that I feel like I might just fall off this chair and die!"

For a moment, Mrs. Thomas saw the beloved Bertha Shirley in that radiant face. She remembered how she had looked when the eastern sun had shone in on her newborn baby's face. She smiled, and to Anne's astonishment, she put her arms around her and hugged her hard. Then, instead of scolding her for not eating her breakfast, she folded the large slice of bread and jam into a sandwich and put it in a small paper bag. "You'll be hungry later, come noon. There's one of last fall's apples in there, too. And a molasses cookie. And now," she continued more briskly, giving Anne a gentle push from the table, "be off with you, or you'll be late."

Anne rushed upstairs, collected the satchel, and returned. She kissed Noah on the top of his head, ran the palm of her hand down Lochinvar's soft back, waved to the three boys, and touched Mrs. Thomas gently on the arm as she swept out the door. Mr. Thomas had left for work an hour earlier, hung over and depressed, but still capable of working at his job.

The journey to school was the same distance as the long trip to Mr. Johnson's, but the road was well travelled and easy to walk on. The countryside was more open, less fenced in by dense trees. Anne felt released, as though, like angels and fairies, she'd been newly equipped with wings. After the first bend in the road, a field stretched out to her right, with a barn and a small farmhouse off in the distance. To the left, the trees gave way to a small treeless hill, with a group of tall poplars at the top. Anne recalled her walks with Eliza over the marshy grasslands outside Bolingbroke, and revelled in the way the sky was more accessible here than it was in the woods. And the sky was worth looking at that day — intensely blue, with a few isolated white clouds moving lazily across it. Then she entered a short section bordered by bare maple trees, with the slow drip of melting snow falling off their branches. As she continued along the road, more wonders were opened up for her — a small stream, chuckling over the rocks, where the sudden warmth of the day had broken away the ice; a lone chestnut tree in the middle of a small field, with a house and barn close to the road; a large grey cat sitting solemnly on top of a broad fence post; a little red house with a small pond beside it, obviously cleared off for children's skating, because she could see the marks of the blades on the ice.

And then, suddenly, Anne was in the main village community of Marysville. There, in front of her, was the store, where she'd have to turn left. But she didn't do this right away. She looked in the store windows, and marvelled at all the items on display — an egg beater, a small bucket, a blue china bowl with daisies on it, a *doll* with painted-on shoes and a dress made of fabric with small roses on it, a lady's hat with feathers and a bouquet of cherries, *and a vegetable brush*. How Anne longed to have enough money to buy that brush! — to banish Mrs. Thomas's still-simmering anger, and to squelch her own uncomfortable feelings of guilt. She looked at it for so long that she almost forgot to turn left and climb the hill to the school. If she had it to give to Mrs. Thomas, she could completely enjoy the little mat that had destroyed the old brush, instead of only half enjoying it. And this brush was even nicer than the first one. She wanted it so badly that there wasn't even any room in her head to yearn for the doll.

At last Anne pried herself away from the window and started up the hill. There, at the top, on the right-hand side, was the school. Already she could see the bell. And outside, in the schoolyard, there was a group of children playing. Anne's steps slowed. Maybe, after all, it wasn't going to be so easy to enter that building — or so wonderful, either. Apart from the wild Thomas boys, she wasn't used to being with children, and there must have been at least fifteen of them milling about in that yard. Would her clothes be the same as theirs? Would they laugh at her red hair? Or would the blue ribbons — carefully tied to the ends of her braids when she got up this morning — make it all right? Would they all know more than she did? *Would they like her?*

The chatter and movement of the children stopped as she entered the yard and moved toward the school door, and all eyes turned to watch her as she walked into the school.

Inside, double desks were lined up in rows behind a larger desk and a blackboard. Small slates — some framed with wood and some not — lay helter-skelter on the desks, and slate pencils had been supplied too. At the back of the room, quietly chugging away, a small wood stove was doing its best to keep the room warm.

"I'm Anne Shirley," said Anne to the back of the woman who was busy writing something on the blackboard — words that she couldn't read, and numbers that she didn't recognize. "Anne. Spelled with an *e*."

THIRTY-FOUR

*F*irst Day at School

Anne was standing very straight as she made her announcement to the teacher's back. She didn't want her terror to be visible when the teacher finally turned around to look at her. And she *was* terrified. All her school dreams had been beautiful ones. She'd seen herself seated at a desk beside a pretty little girl with golden curls, who would almost certainly become a close and loving friend. She'd visualized a scene in which she was happily working on her slate, writing new words, spelling them perfectly. She'd looked forward to laughter and games in the playground outside the school. And now it was as though she'd written all those lovely dreams on a slate and some evil hand had wiped them off.

So Anne's fear was real. She'd actually seen a little girl in the schoolyard who had a pretty face and golden curls. But she'd been watching Anne's ascent up the hill with a frown on her face, her brows drawn together with either curiosity or distaste. Was the girl looking at her long red braids and hating them? Was she thinking Anne was too tall, too skinny? And what were those words that the teacher had written on the board? What did that collection of letters add up to? Would the teacher expect her to know all those things? Would every single child in the room understand more than she did? Would they make fun of her — the way Trudy used to do when she had lived at home, calling her dumb because she didn't know her alphabet? *Alphabet!* What was *that*? Was that something everybody was supposed to know and understand before entering school for the first time?

As for the laughter and games in the school playground — well, that was almost the worst disappointment of all, and perhaps the source of Anne's worst worries. The schoolyard wasn't much bigger than the little square back yard of houses she'd seen in Bolingbroke. And it wasn't all grassy, ringed with flowers, the way it had been when she imagined it. Of course it wasn't. There was just tramped-down snow, with little patches of dirt showing here and there. It had a wire fence around it so that you couldn't get out. Suddenly the woods seemed more free to her than this place, even when they were thick, shutting off the sun. She longed for her lovely birch trees, standing guard over something that she was sure had to be a pond. In the springtime, a duck might come. Or even two.

Anne thought all those things while she waited for the teacher to turn around. The thoughts flew through her mind like a flash of lightning, but like lightning they were very vivid.

Then, suddenly, the teacher was facing her. Smiling, she came forward and held out her hand. "And my name is Miss Henderson," she said, now holding Anne's hand in both of hers. "I'm so happy that you've come to our school. I was told that you'd just turned six. That's a bit early to be starting school, but I'm sure you'll be fine. I can tell by looking at your eyes that you're just crammed full of brains. And motivation. And that can be even more important. Mr. Summers said that you were very eager to start school."

Anne had no idea what motivation was, but she could tell that it was good, and apparently she had it. And Mr. Summers was probably the School Man. She was still standing very straight, and she was determined not to show her fear. Besides, she was feeling much less frightened. This Miss Henderson was more beautiful than any woman she had ever seen — even in Bolingbroke. She had lovely honey-coloured hair piled high on her head, with small curls escaping around her cheeks and forehead, framing them. Her face was soft and kind, with pale, clear skin and a smile so warm that ...

" ...it could melt icicles" said Anne out loud, before she realized that she was going to say it. Then she said, quickly, "Mr. Summers must be the School Man. He's absolutely right. I *am* eager to start school. How fast can you teach me to read? When I can do that, I think I'll be as happy as an angel with wings."

Miss Henderson looked at the thin little girl in front of her and shook her head ever so slightly. Mr. Summers had described Anne as a child who was being very overworked by a grim foster mother; and everyone in Marysville already knew about Mr. Thomas's drinking binges. Miss Henderson hadn't known what to expect of the new pupil. Would she be frightened, depressed, difficult to teach? But *absolutely right ... an angel with wings*"! Where did those words and thoughts come from?

Miss Henderson felt her heart quicken. Every teacher feels this with the arrival of an unusual student. "I'll teach you how to read as quickly as I can, Anne. We'll move along at whatever speed feels right to you. But I don't want you to feel pushed or hurried."

"Oh, Miss Henderson," said Anne, "I'm used to feeling pushed and hurried. So don't worry about *that*." She looked at the tangle of letters and numbers on the blackboard and pointed to it. "Will I have to understand all that before I leave today?"

Miss Henderson laughed. "Anne," she said. "There are only sixteen children in this school, but I teach every class from primer to the senior class. That work on the board is for the sixth class."

Anne breathed a noisy sigh of relief. Her rigid stance relaxed somewhat. But she had to pay attention. She might miss something important.

"I'll be starting you off today with the alphabet. That's the very first step to take if you want to learn to read." Miss Henderson pointed to a long strip of letters that was affixed to the wall above the blackboard. I'll teach you how to *say* the letters, and then, if you want to, you can try to *write* them on your slate. We'll start with the first five or six letters today." Then she added, "As soon as you learn the alphabet, you'll be able to use a dictionary."

"A dictionary? What's that?"

"Randolph has one," said Miss Henderson. "His grandmother gave it to him." She pulled it out of his desk. It was a big book, heavy and fat. "It's full of words. And when you learn to read, you can look up any word to find out what it means."

Anne had to sit down on the nearest chair. "A book of *words!*" she whispered. "Randolph must be the happiest boy in the world to possess such a book!"

"*To possess such a book.*" Miss Henderson stared at Anne with puzzled fascination. What collection of elements had come together to form this surprising child?

As though in answer to this question, Anne said, "My mother and father were teachers. I just bet they had a dictionary. But when they died, everything was sold. To pay the doctor — who didn't even cure them. Someone must have bought their dictionary. I wish it was mine."

So her parents were teachers. Her odd vocabulary must have come from them. "How old were you when they died, Anne? I'm so sorry."

"Well, I'm very sorry, too, Miss Henderson. They died of

fever when I was three months old. But I didn't die. As you can see, I'm still here." Then she added, "That's a long time ago. Six years ago on the fifth of March I was born. That's my birthday. Mrs. Archibald gave me these blue ribbons. So I got a gift this year, after all. But sometimes I fall into the depths of sadness when I think about my dead parents."

Miss Henderson was feeling on the brink of a well of sadness herself. She was also greatly mystified. Where did Anne get her long words and her manner of speaking, if not from her parents? Briskly she said, "I've enjoyed talking to you so much, Anne, that I forgot the time. I have to ring the bell. We're ten minutes late."

With the ringing of the bell, all sixteen children started to stream into the classroom. Some were small, some tall. Some handsome, some plain. Some dirty, some clean. Some cheerful, some cross. But all of them were staring at Anne as they entered the room.

Anne was seated beside a little girl called Sadie Brown. They smiled shyly at each other, but classes had started, so they didn't speak. Sadie was short, unbeautiful of face, uncoordinated, and *kind*. She was also six years old. The only other child in the first class was Mildred Plimson — the child with the golden hair and sapphire blue eyes; but Miss Henderson knew that she couldn't count on her for kindness. Both Sadie and Mildred had been in the primer class since September. Anne was six months behind them. Mildred was smart. Sadie was not. That was another reason for placing Sadie beside Anne.

As soon as she was free — as soon as all sixteen children had something specific to read or write or study — Miss Henderson brought Anne up to her desk, and quietly taught her everything she needed to know about the first six letters of the alphabet. Anne chewed her lower lip as she concentrated on learning how to say A, B, C, D, E, and F, and then how to write them. She went back to her desk and wrote the letters over and over again, muttering their names to herself as she wrote. In the past, she had memorized whole poems that Eliza had read to her. So it was easy to remember the names of six letters — and not very hard to write them, although her printing was wobbly and inconsistent. She watched Miss Henderson as she swiftly wrote whole sentences on the blackboard. Anne marvelled at this skill. Would she ever — even if she lived to be a hundred years old — be able to do that?

Then Miss Henderson took Anne up to her own desk again, and taught her the different sounds that the letters could make. After that, she made four words out of the set of six letters:

CAB
FACE
BAD
BED

"Those are all real words," she said. "And they'll show you the different sounds that the same letter can make. After recess and after lunch, I'll teach you how to do that. If you work hard and think hard, you'll be able to read four words before you go home."

Anne remembered Miss Henderson saying that as soon as she learned the alphabet, she'd be able to use a dictionary. Well, she'd work hard and think hard. She looked over at Randolph. He was very tall. He was in the sixth class for the third time, and he was drawing absently on his slate and looking out the window. Sticking out from the shelf below the surface of his desk was his dictionary. Yes, she wanted to *possess* it. The school had few books and no dictionaries. Anne stared hard at Randolph. He looked bored and cross. He was also fourteen years old. He wasn't likely to become her friend. But she'd better remember to be *nice* to him, no matter what he was like. She knew that she was going to want to borrow that dictionary.

After what seemed like a few minutes — and had really been two hours — Miss Henderson stood up and pulled the rope on the school's bell. The rope reached up through a hole in the ceiling to a little peaked structure that held the bell.

"Recess!" she announced. She took Sadie aside. "Sadie," she said, "please look after Anne in the schoolyard. Make sure that she learns how to play your games, and that no one is mean to her."

So far, Anne loved school. And she adored Miss Henderson. She'd already memorized the six letters, and she could write them all down without even checking. She'd also carefully printed CAB, FACE, BAD, BED. She just knew that by the time she left the school this afternoon, she'd be able to read four words. She'd be able to *read*! School was every bit as wonderful as she'd hoped it would be.

By the time recess was over, she wasn't at all sure that this was true.

THIRTY-FIVE

Recess

Sadie took Anne's hand and led her out into the tiny school-yard. Anne looked at Sadie's face. It was broad and pock-marked, with eyes that were small and too close together. But she had a sweet and gentle smile, and she looked across (and up) at Anne with total acceptance. Anne, who admired all beautiful things, wished that she'd been placed in the care of the little golden-haired girl, but she'd have to make do with what she had. But at least Sadie was making her feel *safe*. Her clothes were just as shabby as her own, and beside her Anne felt tall and strong. The Thomas daughters had never made her feel that way. Their beauty — although she admired it — was part of what made her feel so ugly. And how could she possibly have thought that the schoolyard would be full of grass and flowers — in *March*. It wasn't perfect, but Anne should surely have learned by now that life had a lot of cracks on its surface. Everything would be fine.

Or would it be? Later on that day — in the night, in fact — when everyone else in her house was fast asleep, Anne crept downstairs with her lantern to tell Katie Maurice about her day.

"Katie Maurice," she said, "I have to tell you about my first day in school, because I'm sure that it was the most important day of my life. Except for the day I was born, of course. Because before that day I was nothing. Then, suddenly, I was a real live *human being*. Katie, what do you suppose I was before that happened? Was I *really* nothing? What are you when you're *not*? That's even harder to figure out than what you are after you die. Oh, life is so full of questions that are too hard to answer. But interesting.

"Now that I've started school, I know that there are answers to a whole lot of questions. I just have to learn what they are. And I know I can do that. Miss Henderson told me I was a 'quick learner.' Just as well, because I'm six months behind the other girls in my class."

Then Anne told Katie Maurice all about the first six letters of the alphabet, and how you could make real words out of those letters and even write them down.

"At first, I thought that nothing in the whole world could be a happier thing than school. Miss Henderson is so beautiful and kind, with little silver buttons all up and down her bodice, and long sleeves with lace around her wrists. And she taught me how to read those words, all in one day. And Sadie is my new friend — my *only* friend. The only one I ever had. I was sorry she wasn't beautiful until we went out into the schoolyard. That was at recess time.

"We all put on our boots and coats and things and went outside. Sadie held my hand. At first I wasn't sure I liked that. But she must have known I'd need it.

"Randolph was out there, the one who possesses the dictionary. He's very tall and also handsome, but he's mean and also dumb, so today I learned that being beautiful isn't everything. I'm sure I knew that *before*, and I guess I'll forget it *again*, but *today* I possessed the thought. He was standing in the middle of the yard with two other big boys, and beautiful and clever Mildred was beside them. Even in just one day in school, you can learn who's smart and who isn't. Mildred's so smart that it scares me. She can even do *sums*. Sums are what you do with numbers. Like 1, 2, 3. I haven't learned how to do sums yet. But I watched and listened. I think it's hard. I'd rather work with letters. I'll never catch up to Mildred. She can print a whole sentence with wonderful neat letters. Miss Henderson is going to teach me six new letters tomorrow, because she says I learn so fast. Mildred looked really *mad* when she said that.

"Like I said, Randolph was in the middle of the schoolyard — much taller than anyone else. He had his hands on his hips, and as soon as Sadie and I came out the door, he yelled, 'There's the two stupidest-looking girls in the school!' I gave Sadie's hand a little squeeze, because I knew he was talking about both of us — what we looked like. I knew who was stupid, and it wasn't me. It wasn't *me* who stayed in the sixth class for three years. Mildred was just standing there looking up at him and smiling. Then he said, 'That Anne girl's got her orange hair hid by her hat, but we can still see all her freckles.' It was Sadie's turn to give *my* hand a little squeeze.

"I looked at that fence then, Katie Maurice. I thought about how I wanted to run, as fast as I could, all the way home. But that fence held me in. I didn't know where to look, because all those fifteen pairs of eyes seemed to be staring at me. So I dragged Sadie over to the fence, and we just stood there looking at it, looking *through* it, until the bell rang for the end of recess. But all the time we were looking through the fence, we could hear them all laughing. So my lovely dreams about laughter in the schoolyard turned out to be laughter of a different kind. I didn't know that laughter could be so ugly. I felt very sad, and I cried a little, but not out loud. But I felt mad, too, and might have said some nasty things back to Randolph. But I couldn't do that. Because of the dictionary."

Then Anne smiled at Katie Maurice, who smiled back. "But so many good things happened, too. By the end of the day I could sound out those four words and read them. *I learned to read today.* That's why it was just about the most important day in my life, except for the morning I was born. Today I felt like I got born all over again. And I feel like Miss Henderson is my brand-new mother.

"After school was out, Sadie asked me to come over to her house in Marysville to play. I wanted so much to go. Oh, *so* much. She said we could play house. I asked her what that was. She said it was pretending you were a grown-up family and that we could be the mother and father and her dolls could be our children. So she knows how to pretend things, too. But she lives half a mile away on the *other* side of the school. I could never go all the way there and play house and then get home in time to do the diapers and cut up vegetables for supper. I was surprised that Marysville could be so big. I thought it was just where *we* were. But it stretches all up and down the road on each side of the main part. I felt as though my heart would break in two. *Dolls.* More than *one!* And she said that her mother would give us molasses cookies and tea. Oh! Oh! Oh! They have a cow, too. I'd love to pat that cow. I feel in the depths of sadness about that and about horrible Randolph, but it still was the second most important day of my life."

Anne yawned. "So now, Katie Maurice," she said, "I have to go to sleep so that I won't be too sleepy tomorrow to be a quick learner." She blew a good-night kiss to her friend, who blew one back, at exactly the same moment.

When she went up to her room, Lochinvar was waiting for her on the bed. Very early on, he had decided where he was going to spend all his nights.

THIRTY-SIX

A Talk with Mr. Johnson

On the Saturday after she started school, Anne went to Mr. Johnson's to collect eggs. He opened the door and invited her in.

"*Well?*" he said.

"Well, what?" asked Anne, puzzled.

"School. How was it?"

"Oh, Mr. Johnson! It was wonderful."

"Shall I make tea instead, this week?" He motioned for her to sit down.

"Yes."

"Yes, please. Does no one say *please* in your house?"

"No. But Miss Henderson does."

"Tell me about her," he said, measuring out the tea, and bringing the kettle closer to the front of the stove.

"She knows everything. There is not one thing in the whole world that she doesn't know. It's not just the alphabet she knows. I listen a lot when she's teaching the other grades. She talks about other countries — things like *pyramids* and real castles, and big huge churches called *cathedrals*, and real lions and tigers. She knows about numbers, too, but I shut up my ears when she talks about them. And she reads long poems out loud that are just like music. She's very kind to me, and spends a lot of time helping me catch up. I'm six months behind Sadie and Mildred.

"She's very beautiful. Her hair is piled on top of her head. It's the colour of honey. I would gladly risk my life in a cage of lions if I could have her hair. Today she told the fifth class about Daniel risking his life in a lion's den or cage or something."

"Den. But why risk your life to have honey-coloured hair? Lots of people have hair that colour. Yours is special."

"Well, I don't want to be that kind of special. Randolph says it's orange and ugly. He hates my freckles, too."

"What do you do when he says that?"

"I want to yell at him that he's dumb and mean, but I have to just smile and say nothing."

"Why?"

"Because he's almost as big as you, and could squash me dead. And because I might want to borrow his dictionary. So I have to pretend to like him. In my dreams I tie him to a chair and yell mean things at him. Once, when my imagination was feeling almost crazy, I drove a knight's sword right through him. It came out the other side."

"You know about knights?"

"Yes. Eliza told me stories from things she learned in school. Knights ride around on white horses and kill dragons. I call one of our horses the white charger. But I feel myself that Randolph is more dangerous than any dragon."

"If he's so big," said Mr. Johnson, passing her a cup of tea, "why is he in your school?"

"Because he can't seem to finish the sixth class. He just sits there and looks out the window. He hates school. And he never, ever, reads his wonderful dictionary."

"I feel sorry for him. Some people — often big boys who'd be happy being farmers or hunters — would learn more *outside* a school than *inside*. Sometimes they must feel as though they're in jail."

"Maybe that's the way Eliza felt when she left school," said

Anne. "She was in the sixth class. But she just wanted to get married and have babies. She loved the stories and the poems. But she didn't want to learn the other stuff. She was no good at arithmetic. And Mrs. Thomas wanted her to stay home and help with all her babies. But then I think Eliza got to thinking that living in that house was like being in another kind of jail. So she went away and married awful Roger." Anne sighed and put down her cup. "And left me behind." Then she added, "And took her books with her."

Then there were a few moments while Anne didn't talk and didn't drink her tea. She just looked ahead of her, as though she could see things that nobody else could see. Mr. Johnson didn't interrupt her thoughts. He just waited. But he could see that her eyes were full of unshed tears. He felt that they might spill over at any moment. And that was perfectly fine with him. There'd been times in his own life — once in particular — when it would have been satisfying to feel free to cry. But he did pass Anne a plate of cookies.

Anne shook herself out of her sad dream and looked at the cookies. She wiped her sleeve across her eyes. "From Mrs. Archibald, I just bet," she said. "I've seen those cookies before. Last week in her own kitchen."

"Yes," he said. "Yesterday, after she collected her eggs, she left them outside the door on the stoop. She knows I like to be alone, and respects that."

Anne frowned as she looked at him over the rim of her cup. "You're not alone when I'm here," she said.

"No," he said.

"But is that all right?"

"Yes," he replied, but didn't explain why this was so.

"Good!" she said. "Because I love coming to see you. It's almost as good as being in school. And there's no Randolph here. I've borrowed his dictionary three times, and he always manages to say something mean, every single time. You always give me your words so —" Anne frowned. "I need a word that means that you're happy to give them."

"Cheerfully?"

"Well, that's a nice word, but it's not exactly what I mean. If I had five cents and I gave it to you, what would that be?"

"I think it would be very *generous* of you. It was also generous of Mrs. Archibald to leave the cookies."

"I think that's *it*!" Anne exclaimed. "You give me my new words in such a generous way.... But if I had five cents I wouldn't be generous enough to give it to you."

"No?"

"No. I'd buy that little vegetable brush in the Marysville store."

"*A vegetable brush? Why?*"

"To give to Mrs. Thomas. I wore down her vegetable brush cleaning the little hooked mat that I found in our house. It was so dirty that you couldn't see the pattern on it. So I took the mat and the brush — *without even asking* — out into the snow and scrubbed it and scrubbed it and *scrubbed it* till the little pink house and the tree just *came*. Then I hung it on the porch railing until it was dry."

"And then what?"

"I put it in my room. When it was dirty and all just grey, Mrs. Thomas said I could have it."

"But the vegetable brush ..."

"Oh yes. *Ruined.* She was as angry as a ferocious animal. I don't think she will ever forgive me. But if I had five cents, I'd buy a new one. And maybe buy something else in that wonderful store, in case the brush didn't cost that much. Maybe *candy*. Sadie says that candy is even better than cookies."

Mr. Johnson looked as if he was thinking hard. His brows were drawn together above his very blue eyes. At last he spoke.

"Well," he said, "she must really need that brush badly. Seven people eat a lot of potatoes. But I just had a good idea. If you help me sweep up the henhouse and collect the eggs each time you come, for three visits, I'll give you five cents. Would that work? We can start today and make it Visit Number One. In two weeks, you'll be ready to buy that brush."

Anne had to control herself to keep from rushing over and hugging Mr. Johnson. "I'm so happy!" she cried. "I'll have a *job*! And I'll be on the heights of joy. I'll make money! I never had any before. Mrs. Thomas is almost sure to forgive me. I hope so, anyway. This is so ... generous. I'll work very hard. That little henhouse will be the cleanest in our county. And I won't break any eggs. I promise."

They spent the next half-hour working on the henhouse. Mr. Johnson sawed the top off an old broom and made it a perfect length for Anne. She wished she could take it home. Working with Mrs. Thomas's long broom wasn't easy. Anne was tall for her age — but not *that* tall. She enjoyed collecting the eggs. She loved being so close to the warm, soft hens. And while they worked, Mr. Johnson taught her another word. He asked her what kind of word she'd like.

"Let me see," she said, leaning on her broom, making its bottom even more crooked than it already was. "I want something to describe the jewels that the princess wears in Katie Maurice's house. I say they're pretty and beautiful over and over again. Katie Maurice must be tired of hearing those words."

"I know the very word. Try *exquisite*, which means delicately and deliciously beautiful. I know that the princess's jewels would be exactly like that." Mr. Johnson grinned.

As they walked back to Mr. Johnson's house, the day was much warmer than yesterday had been, and all around them they could hear the drip, drip, drip of melting snow. Suddenly Anne stopped walking, and pointed to a row of icicles on the edge of the roof, blazingly bright in the late afternoon sun. "Look!" she cried, "Exquisite icicles!"

"Now, one more. You already have enough. Let's try for one more. Tell me what you'd like."

Anne stopped walking again, and did some thinking. Finally she said, "I'm sad quite often, and I get tired of using the same word when I tell Katie Maurice about it."

"Well," he said, "if you're about as sad as you can possibly get, you feel *despair*. The depths of despair are at the very bottom of the well."

"I like *despair* a lot," said Anne. "And I'll keep repeating the new words all the way home."

Fifteen minutes later, Mrs. Archibald looked out her window and saw Anne trudging along on the snowy road. Her lips were moving, and she was flinging her arms around the way she always did when she was talking. This wasn't the first time she'd seen Anne do this, and it was always when Anne was on the way home from Mr. Johnson's house — not when she was on her way there. Mrs. Archibald was puzzled. Maybe she'd ask her to explain this sometime. Meanwhile, it remained a mystery.

THIRTY-SEVEN

*A*nne Receives a Dictionary

It was April, and there was a real feeling of hopeful anticipation in the air. The snow had disappeared on the previous Wednesday when a warm, drenching rain had melted all the remains of it. The ground was still sodden and brown, and the trees bare, but there was a softness in the wind that was unlike the shrill gusts of March.

The evening before, when Mrs. Thomas was busy with some mending, Mr. Thomas sat down beside Anne at the kitchen table, where she was muttering to herself as she moved her fingers slowly along one of the lines of her Royal Reader.

"How's school, Anne?" asked Mr. Thomas. "Tell me about it."

Anne looked up from her book and grinned. "It's too wonderful to explain," she said. "Miss Henderson treats me like I'm her own child, and teaches me things so fast that maybe I can catch up to Sadie and Mildred before the summer comes. Look! See? I'm *reading*. Do you want to hear what it says?"

"Yes," he said, "read it to me."

Anne spoke very slowly, as her thin little index finger slid across the page.

" 'I have been milking the cow. You can see her on the grass in the field.' Of course I don't know how to milk a cow, but it's fun to pretend I'm a little milkmaid. I like it about the cow, but later on, when I'm in the third class, I'll like it much better, because the stories are more *exciting*. Mr. Johnson taught me that word, last week. The cow story isn't exciting, but when I listen to the third class reading, I find some of their stories so exciting that I can hardly pay attention to my own work. There's a story about a shipwreck, and a beautiful picture of the ship with all its sails up, and it tells how the poor sailors were saved from drowning. There are also stories about people dying. I find these stories sad, but I like them, too. I don't know why.

"Listen to this one that Eliza taught me:

'He will not come,' said the gentle child
As she patted the poor dog's head.

The dog's master has died, and he can't bear it. But I love the poem. And it also gave me the word *anguish*. I know about anguish, so it's nice to have a word to describe it.

"And the pictures! There's one of a little boy riding along on an ostrich. An ostrich is a very big bird with long legs. I don't know if they can fly. But they can run exceedingly fast. And dogs called Saint Bernards rescue starving people from the snow. One dog saved forty-two people! Just imagine! But those exciting stories are in the later readers. I'm still with the cows. But I can hardly wait to be in third and fourth so I can read about those other things."

Mr. Thomas hadn't been drinking for three days. He was hanging on tight, trying to stop for good, but right now he felt as though he'd not be able to make it. He'd kept his job, because he drank his rum only in the evening and on days off — like Sunday. But he didn't feel well, and the itch to drink never left him.

"How do you do it, Anne?" he suddenly said.

"Do what?"

"Stay happy about life when you got so much ... *anguish*. I seem to feel anguish most o' the time. And I know I do real bad things when I'm drunk, even when I don't know I'm doin' them. My life just don't add up. I got seven beautiful children. Well, I suppose Noah isn't beautiful, but I know he's your favourite. And he's sure a nice child. And Joanna cooks good and keeps things clean. But somehow it don't add up."

"You mean like when you get your sums wrong? Miss Henderson is trying to teach me arithmetic, but I'm not very good at it. I can add two and two and get four, but often Miss Henderson says that I've added three or four numbers *incorrectly*. That's her word for when I get it wrong. Is that what you're saying?"

Mr. Thomas produced a small, sad chuckle. "I suppose it's almost exactly what I'm tryin' to say. Seems like I got it wrong — way back when there was some hope o' gettin' it right. Sometimes I can still *almost* get it right. Then I do something stupid or bad, and first thing you know it's not addin' up again. It's not workin' for me — or for anyone else. But *you* — you often get the right answer, even when all the numbers seem to be wrong. You're only six, but I oftentimes envy you. But then I can feel real mad that I'm envying a six-year-old child; and having that feeling can make me add things up wrong again." He sighed.

Anne just sat and looked at Mr. Thomas, trying to think of something to say. She could see he was hurting again, but she felt as though anything she said would be the wrong thing. After a while, he rose.

"Well," he said, in a louder voice, "g'night. Guess I'll go out to the barn for a bit. I done the milkin', but I got two horses what need some attention."

After Mr. Thomas had left the room, Mrs. Thomas and Anne raised their heads and looked at each other. Both of them knew that the barn contained two horses and a cow — but also several bottles of rum. No words passed between them. Then Anne went upstairs and climbed into bed. Lochinvar was already there — waiting. As soon as she pulled up the covers, he nuzzled up against her knees, purring loudly. Anne loved him almost as much as she loved Noah.

On Monday, Anne enjoyed walking on a road that had no snow, even though puddles and mud were often making it just as difficult to walk. She stopped to watch a group of fourteen cows standing like statues in their brown field — their first outing for many weeks. Anne loved cows, but she found herself feeling impatient with them today. "Why aren't you looking more *pleased*?" she said right out loud, although the cows were much too far away to hear her. "Why are you just *standing* there, instead of moving around and stretching your poor stiff legs? Can't you tell that spring is coming?" She saw her first robin that day, puffing out his red breast on the branch of an apple tree — a breast that was almost the same colour as Anne's hair. She had a little conversation with him, too. In fact, there were so many things to stop and look at that she was almost late for school. She was at the bottom of the hill when the bell started to ring, and she had to run all the way to the top. She was still panting when she sat down on her seat beside Sadie.

"Oh, good!" whispered Sadie. "I was so scared you were home sick or something. Mama gave me an extra molasses cookie to give to you, and I knew you'd want to have it."

One of Sadie's mother's molasses cookies? Anne could hardly wait for recess. It was almost as good as going home with Sadie and playing house with her dolls. Almost, but not quite. No. *Absolutely* not quite.

Never mind. At least she had someone to sit beside her who *liked* her. Supposing it had been Mildred! Mildred did *not* like Anne, and she had a devious way of dragging others over to her way of thinking.

"Just look at her!" Mildred whispered to her own seatmate, Hanna, who was in second primer. "She thinks she's *so smart*. Sitting up so straight and proud, listening to the third class reading — so that she'll be the best in the class by the time she gets that far. Teacher's pet, too. Miss Henderson's so busy teaching her special things that she has no time for the rest of us. It makes me sick!"

Hanna nodded as though in agreement. She was afraid of Mildred and her sharp tongue. She didn't want to be on the bad side of *her*. But secretly she was intrigued by Anne, by her wild red hair and freckled face, by her fast-moving brain, by her strange way of speaking. She envied Sadie for being lucky enough to sit beside her. She wished that Mildred would keep her nasty comments for people like Randolph, who certainly deserved them. But Mildred was the only girl in the school that Randolph wasn't mean to.

Miss Henderson came over to Anne's desk and handed her two sheets of paper, on which she had written sums for her to do, and some spellings to learn. "You made a hundred in your spelling yesterday, Anne," she said. "See if you can do as well with these harder words." Then she turned her attention to the sixth class.

For the sixth class she had a new reading lesson to assign. But first she handed out the results from their own spelling test. The other two people in his class got scores of ninety-two and ninety-six. Randolph got twelve. He folded up the paper quickly and stuffed it in his desk. Then he stood up. He shook his fist at Miss Henderson.

He had a speech to make, and he yelled it so loud that anyone passing by on the road could have heard it.

"You're a damnable mean teacher! You wear stupid clothes and you give all them hundreds to a dumb orphan girl what got a face full o' ugly freckles and thinks she's smarter than the Queen! She don't deserve it! She's only bin here a month, and you act like she's your *baby*. I bin here almost eight years, and you act like I'm *nuthin'*!"

Anne heard all this, and sat frozen in her seat. She hated Randolph; she also feared him. And she needed to use his dictionary. But certain of his words hammered in her head: *damnable; stupid clothes; ugly freckles.*

Then Randolph said one last thing. "That stupid carrot-top keeps tryin' to steal my dictionary!"

That did it. Anne stood up and faced him, two rows over, in the middle of the room. In a voice almost as loud as his, she yelled, "I hate you! You're dirty and smelly and dumb, and meaner than a rabid dog, and Miss Henderson wears *exceedingly* beautiful dresses, with high necks made of *real lace*, and puffed sleeves and real pearl buttons, and you only said that because your mother never wears anything but dresses full of holes, and aprons with gravy all down the front! You don't *deserve* that dictionary!"

Anne, of course, had no idea what his mother wore, but her imagination kicked in with a lot of detail. Nor was he dirty and smelly. But she knew it was the worst thing she could possibly say.

With that last bit of rhetoric, Randolph climbed up and stood on his desk, took aim, and threw the dictionary at Anne, shouting, "Here it is! Keep it! I hope it breaks your snooty head!"

But Randolph didn't know that Anne was as well coordi-nated as she was smart. She caught the dictionary in full flight, hugged it to her chest, stroked it softly, and said — in a voice both quiet and tender — "Thank you very much, Randolph, for your generous gift."

That day, after school was over and Anne had stayed behind to clean the blackboard, Miss Henderson asked, "Anne, where do you get your big words? How did you know about that word, *generous*?" Miss Henderson knew enough about Anne's foster family to be pretty sure that she didn't learn that particular word at home.

"From Mr. Johnson. He's my very good friend who lives a mile from our house. He keeps hens and sells eggs. He's an old man with a big beard, and every week he gives me five new words to have as my very own. He says that to pretend things isn't a bit wicked. He told me that pretending is using your imagination. He said that if people didn't have good imagina-tions, there'd be no pictures or stories or music. He also said that he felt sorry for Randolph. But I don't. I've *tried,* but so far it seems like it's something I can't manage to do." Then Anne looked thoughtful for a moment. "Maybe," she went on, "it may be easier to do now that I possess his dictionary."

Miss Henderson took the board eraser and put it in a drawer beside the chalk box. "Sometime," she said, "I hope I'll be lucky enough to meet that kind and wise old man."

THIRTY-EIGHT

A Blizzard of Surprises

The lovely warm weather of that week in April didn't last long. When the snow returned, it came with such violence and speed that it caught up with Anne on the road between the Thomases' house and Mr. Johnson's grey shack. All she was wearing over her dress was a short spring jacket, and her head was bare. She had no heavy boots on; and the snow was soon very deep. How could the sun have disappeared so quickly, and where was all that bitter wind coming from? Anne plodded on, head down against the driving snow, slipping and sliding on the icy road. She walked like a drunken person, or someone afflicted with dementia. It was difficult for her to see where she was going, and only the wall of tall trees on each side of the road kept her moving in the right direction.

Although Anne didn't realize it, she was close to Mrs. Archibald's house. As she approached the gate, she could see a ghostly form opening it and stepping out onto the road. When she came abreast of the form, she could tell that it was all bundled up in a heavy coat and warm scarf.

Suddenly, the form spoke. "Anne! What in the name of heaven are you doing here?"

It was Miss Henderson! Anne couldn't have been more surprised if the form had turned out to be one of Mr. Johnson's angels, sporting a pair of giant wings.

Miss Henderson didn't wait to hear Anne's reply. She took her by the hand and dragged her back to Mrs. Archibald's house, up the slithery steps, and in the front door. Mrs. Archibald was as shocked and concerned as Miss Henderson. "Anne!" she cried. "You must be almost frozen solid. Like Janie here, you've come out with your spring clothes on. Don't the two of you realize that April in Nova Scotia is never really *spring*? It tried to fool us this past week, but you should have known better."

All the time Mrs. Archibald was talking, she was drying Anne's face, arms, hair, with a warm towel, undoing her thin boots, wrapping her in a soft blanket. Anne was still too cold and shocked to speak, so Mrs. Archibald continued on.

"Janie here says she's your teacher. She's also my niece, and she wasn't any smarter than you about the weather. I've given her a warm coat and boots for her trip back to her uncle's place where she's spending the weekend. He's my brother, and lives about a quarter mile beyond Mr. Johnson's. Oh! The world is some small! Here *you* are, in the middle of a blizzard — her pupil for goodness' sake — half frozen and wet to the skin. Sit down now and hold that blanket around you while I get you some hot tea and an oatmeal cookie. Then I'll go upstairs and dig around in my big trunk. I bet I'll be able to find some of Isabella's old clothes that might fit you. Going for eggs, no doubt. Well, you can't go by yourself. Janie will take you."

"I agree absolutely," said Miss Henderson, "and I can hardly wait to meet that Mr. Johnson of yours."

When Miss Henderson and Anne reached Mr. Johnson's house, Anne banged very hard on the door. The wind was whistling and roaring through the trees, and she was afraid he mightn't be able to hear the knock. Just as had happened at the time of her first visit, the door opened just a crack, and he peered out. But when he saw Anne, he opened it wide. "Anne!" he exclaimed. "What on earth are you doing here *today?*" Then he saw Miss Henderson, bundled up and barely visible under her hat and scarves.

"Oh!" he said.

"It's all right, Mr. Johnson," said Anne. "You can let her in, too. She's Miss Henderson, my teacher, and a very nice lady. She rescued me from almost certain death when she found me on the road, all bent over and staggering along. She took me to Mrs. Archibald's, who's her aunt, and we had tea and oatmeal cookies. So you don't have to make tea for me today. But if you want to make cocoa, that would be very nice."

They were still standing outside the door.

Mr. Johnson actually stamped his foot, and almost yelled. "Anne! For heaven's sake, stop talking and come in! The snow's blowing all over my floor. Bring your teacher, too. I can't very well leave her standing out on the stoop while you settle yourself down to drink cocoa and collect your weekly eggs and words. Come in. *Come in!*"

They shuffled in, stamped the snow from their boots, and took off their hats and coats and scarves. Anne saw to her delight that he was lighting two extra lamps. Usually there was a lamp lit on the table where the angel book was, and sometimes two other small ones in the kitchen end of his small home. This was the first time she'd been able to see the three large pictures on the wall. She could also see the disarray — the widespread *mess* — that surrounded them. But the *pictures!* Anne stood, shocked into stillness, by those pictures. The first was of the Taj Mahal. That there could be such a structure, such *exquisite beauty*, in all the world, was beyond even Anne's powers of imagination. Then, beside it, was a print of Botticelli's *Birth of Venus*. It was a picture of a beautiful young woman who seemed to be rising out of a giant shell, with her long, honey-coloured hair streaming down around her body.

Once again, Anne found the word *exquisite* rising in her mind. What's more, she was thinking that this beautiful woman — this Venus — looked very much like Miss Henderson. Mr. Johnson, who was trying to look as though his mind was on the cocoa, was thinking exactly the same thing.

The third picture was a painting by Vermeer, and depicted a woman standing in a room — probably a kitchen — that was so tidy, so clean, so shiny with a sense of orderliness that Miss Henderson was wondering how you could live with that picture on your wall and still continue to inhabit a place so dreary, so chaotic, so ... *dirty*. But she knew that Mr. Johnson was a giver of words, and someone who knew how to make Anne happy. She could also see the row upon row of books lined up — remarkably neatly — on a wall full of homemade bookshelves. She was ready to like this old man, in spite of his dismal shack, his own appearance. She also knew the story of his lost love and humiliation. Mrs. Archibald had told her. How many decades had that poor man been carrying around that awful memory?

"I'm sorry to intrude on your privacy," she said. "It's my understanding that you prefer to be left alone. I can understand that with all those books to read, you might have no need of people. Tell me, who are some of your favourite authors?"

"Yes," said Mr. Johnson, ignoring her last question, "you're right. I normally do not welcome visitors. However, a blizzard has created a special occasion. In fine weather, I open the door to almost no one."

"Except Anne," she said, watching him closely. Also, listening carefully. His was not the voice of an old man.

"Yes," he said. "Except Anne." He looked at the floor while he was speaking.

"And why is that?" she asked.

Then there was a silence. Miss Henderson wondered if he had decided not to reply. But finally he spoke. "I used to be a schoolteacher myself. In Kingsport, at the Academy. I even enjoyed it. Anne resurrects in me the pleasure it used to give me. She also has a unique mind. Would you agree?"

"Yes, I would."

Again there was a very long pause. Then Mr. Johnson looked directly at Miss Henderson and said, "But some time ago, I discovered that I hated the world and everyone in it. Or, as you might point out, *almost* everyone. Something happened to me that removed both trust and affection from my life. It was as though someone had put both of them in a box and slammed down the lid. Now I take great care that it not be opened."

Anne sat quietly in a corner, sipping her hot cocoa, listening to every word. She didn't understand everything she heard, but there was a way that the meaning of it soaked into her mind through a process she would have been at a loss to describe. But she knew she was happy. She watched her two favourite people talking, and felt the rightness of it. She revelled in the four bright lamps and in the three beautiful pictures. She stared at the hundreds of books, and wondered what it would be like to be able to read all of them. She thought about the angels in Mr. Johnson's book, remembering the size of their wings. Today, she almost felt as though she had wings herself. She whispered, "Thank you for the blizzard," not knowing to whom or to what she was speaking.

On their way back to Mrs. Archibald's house, bundled up once more against the storm, Miss Henderson said, "I wish I could get the lid off that box."

"Maybe you've pried it a little bit loose already," said Anne. "I heard him asking you — *inviting* you — to visit him again sometime."

THIRTY-NINE

An Expedition

Time passed, and spring finally arrived. Not just the irritatingly mock spring of April, but the real spring, with mayflowers and clintonea and Indian pipes and cherry blossoms.

One day, not long after the blizzard, Anne went into the little store in Marysville to buy the vegetable brush. She had her money, and the brush was still there. She took time to look at the doll, and to feel the fabric of her dress, but her main focus was on the brush. She was so excited that her hand was trembling as she handed the storekeeper her five cents. The man wrapped up the brush in a square of brown paper that he unrolled from the ceiling, and handed her back one cent.

"Would this be enough for a candy?" she asked.

"Enough for five candies," he said. "Take your pick."

It took Anne so long to choose that she was almost late for school. With such a wealth of candy at her disposal, she gave one to Sadie at recess. They took up their station at the fence, sat down in the snow, and chewed quietly, with a look of deep satisfaction on each of their faces.

When Anne presented Mrs. Thomas with the brush, and after she had explained how she got the money, Mrs. Thomas's eyes filled with tears.

"I love it," she said. "It's better than the other one. I'm sorry, Anne. I'm sorry I'm not nicer." Then she held Anne close to her for a moment, and the tears spilled out of her eyes and down her face. Anne knew she was forgiven.

Then spring, too, passed, and summer came to the woods

and fields around Marysville. There was no school, of course, and Anne was sad about that. But she loved the warmth, the lush fields, the wildflowers and trees. Sometimes she was able to steal time away from her work in order to walk along the road leading to the centre of Marysville, and to soak up all that summer beauty. Often, Lochinvar would come with her — as though he were a dog. Or she'd pick him up and carry him, not caring how heavy he was. In the evening she'd talk about her day to Katie Maurice.

"Katie Maurice, my dear, I'm sorry you have to stay in that dark cupboard all day, now that summer is here. I know you have kings and queens and fairies to keep you company, but I don't think that's enough. You should be allowed to walk in the woods with me. Or to sit on the fence and watch the cows. I love them so much. The cows, I mean. They have such gentle brown eyes and smooth coats and swishy tails. I think the tails swish to keep the flies away. I sit on the fence and watch them whenever I can escape from the house.

"Today a cow came so close to the fence that I was able to put my hand on her lovely body, and let her lick my fingers just like Lochinvar does with his own prickly tongue. I think the cow likes me. I always feel that if an animal likes you, it must mean that you're not a *completely* wicked person. When my work is done, Mrs. Thomas often wants me to look after the boys. I hate doing that, unless it's just Noah I'm taking care of. The other boys like to torment me by calling me a 'stupid orphan girl' or an 'orange-headed witch.' They also throw sticks at me — sometimes even stones — and jump out from behind bushes or corners or doors and shriek at me. I pretend not to be scared by this, but while I'm smiling and acting like I'm just fine, my insides are doing flip-flops and I hold my hands tight at my sides so the boys won't see them trembling.

"But sometimes I escape. I run out the back door and race down the hill to the Five Sisters. There's a big rhododendron bush down there that I can hide behind. Then I just sit on the grass and look at our lovely little pond. I remember so well the day — it was April fifteenth — when the flat place behind the birches stopped being a small field of snow and ice and started being *water* — the day it became the Pool of Mirrors. It was the answer to one of my biggest dreams. And I can see it from my bedroom window. Often I can even watch it at night, if the sky is clear and the moon is shining down into it. But even when I *can't* see it, I know it's *there*. And every so often I run as fast as I can up the grassy hill on the other side of the pond and then throw myself on the ground at the top — panting. After I lie there awhile, staring up at the sky and making pictures out of the clouds, I hop up and race *down* the hill, and it's so much easier than running *up* the hill that I feel like I'm flying."

Mr. Thomas hadn't been drinking for two and a half weeks. Everything was calmer and happier in the Thomas home. Sometimes he took a ball out in the back yard and played catch with the boys. Once he was heard to say, upon rising from the table, "That meal was some nice, Joanna." Mrs. Thomas was smiling more often, and had started arranging her hair less severely around her face. Horace stopped hitting his brothers so often; after all, his father hadn't hit anyone for almost three weeks. And sometimes Mr. Thomas would go down behind the rhododendron bush and sit beside Anne, and tell her about what life was like when he was a little boy, so many years ago.

But the best was to come. One warm August day Mr. Thomas rigged the two horses up to an express wagon he'd rented, and took the whole family on an all-day picnic. Mrs. Thomas prepared enough food for two meals, and Anne helped her to pile blankets and pillows into the rough old wagon. The wagon had been used for cartage purposes; but he swept it clean the day before and sloshed buckets of water over it. By nightfall it was dry and ready for the expedition.

They left home early the next day, directly after breakfast. Everyone was excited by the prospect of this trip, but for Anne it seemed like a large miracle. Mr. Johnson had taught her that word last week, and this amazing outing seemed to be fitting its definition. She knew that other people — in the past or in the stories she'd read in her readers — went on journeys, sometimes to very far places. The longest trip she'd ever been on was the drive from their old home in Boling-broke to their present one in Marysville. But that one had only taken a few hours, and had been through dense forests — and to the accompaniment of a fair amount of anxiety. This one, she knew, was going to be very different from that journey. For one thing, it would probably be long. Otherwise, why would she and Mrs. Thomas have prepared so much food? And why all the pillows and blankets? After all, it was a warm day. Those must have been put into the cart in order to let the children go to bed when it started to get dark. Dark! So they were almost certainly going to be gone *all day*.

Anne had to keep an eye on Noah to make sure he didn't climb up over the sides of the wagon and fall off. He was at the age when most children want to climb over everything and investigate new territory. And this was certainly new territory. But while she was watching him, Anne was also making sure that she didn't miss a single thing or person or place that they were passing. And everything she was experiencing was stored away in her red head for future revelation to Katie

Maurice. On the following day, she would find time to tell her all about it.

"Katie Maurice," she would begin, "I don't know where to start. I felt like I had three eyes. One for watching my Noah, and two for looking at all the wonderful pieces of the world that I was seeing on both sides of the wagon. For that, I almost needed *five* eyes. And up ahead, too. It made me happy enough just to be able to watch those horses — jogging along, flipping their tails from side to side, making deep throaty sounds, taking us to places I had never seen before in my whole life. I thought I might die from being so happy.

"And to right and to left there were a hundred things to watch. I saw a huge bird swoop down and land on the *very top of a tree*. Mr. Thomas shouted back that it was an *eagle*. I'm pretty sure I saw a picture of one of them in one of the readers. So big and proud-looking, like he thought he was the king of the birds. And more cows than I could count. Sheep, too, all white and very woolly. Even above the clatter of the wagon, I could hear the loud, harsh 'baaaa' sound that they make. Wouldn't you think that an animal that's so gentle-looking — that looks exactly like something you'd like to hug — would have a softer voice? I wish so much that you could have seen them.

"We saw lots of trees, of course. After all, Nova Scotia is just *full* of them. The people who came to this country first — Miss Henderson told the fifth class all about them — must have taken one look at Nova Scotia and wanted to turn their ships around and go back home. All those huge trees to cut down before they could even start to build their houses. And where would they find grass for their poor cows? So we saw lots of trees — all kinds of them, not just the Christmas tree with needles. I saw some with leaves way bigger than my hand. Or yours, Katie Maurice. Mrs. Thomas sometimes knew their names, and would tell me when I asked her. I only remember three, but they were wonderful: oak, chestnut, and big huge floppy maple trees.

"But I liked it best when the world opened out into fields — with hills full of grass, and cows bending their necks down to munch their dinners, and fences made out of big tree roots, and yellow goldenrod in the ditches. And when the fields came, the sky came, too, with some big interesting clouds that you could make pictures out of. Mostly it was just blue, blue, blue forever, because there were no trees in the way. I remember all that sky when Eliza used to take me for walks over the flatlands near the river. Then there was so much sky that there was hardly any room left for the earth.

"But then, Katie Maurice," continued Anne, "try to imagine what came next!" She stopped talking for a moment or two so that Katie could absorb the suspense. And very quietly, she began to speak again.

"After we drove for a long while, we climbed a hill at a place where there were both fields and trees, and when we reached the top, Mr. Thomas yelled, 'Whoa!' and the horses stopped. You can't guess what we saw! We saw *water*, starting at the bottom of the hill and reaching out to where the sky began — water so blue that the sky above it looked almost white. If I live to be two hundred years old, I'll never, ever forget that sight. Even the three boys stopped fighting and fooling around and just stood up in the cart with their mouths open. I took a minute to look at Mrs. Thomas, and her face was so lit up that she looked almost pretty. If my own hair had turned from red to yellow in that moment, I wouldn't have been one bit surprised. I was that shocked by the glory of it. *Glory* is another of the words that Mr. Johnson gave me last week. Isn't it lucky that I got a chance to use it so soon? It's not like we're face to face with glory every day of our lives.

"When I was able to speak, I actually yelled, 'What is it?' and Mr. Thomas said, 'The sea.' So now I know something for absolutely sure. The sea is the most beautiful thing in the world. I love most trees (not alders) and all flowers and fields and cows and sheep and especially kittens, and I love our own little pond behind the five birches, but I also know that the sea is the best of all those things. And guess what?"

Anne stopped talking, as though certain of receiving some sort of reply. Then she answered her own question. "Nova Scotia is only attached to Canada by a little bit of land. Miss Henderson says that the edge of the rest of it is right on the sea. It's a tiny province, but she says it has 3728.4 miles of coastline. Coastline means parts that are *right on the sea*. I learned all that by listening to her lesson with the fifth class. Sometimes I get my own work wrong because I'm not paying attention to it, but I learn lots of *other* things by just *listening*. Just think about Nova Scotia being so full of the sea, and yet I never saw one drop of it till I was almost six and a half years old."

Anne had to stop talking then because she was too sleepy to continue. But when she slept that night, she dreamed of their day at the beach, with its long stretches of sand, the breakers booming onto the shore, the whitecaps racing out to the horizon, the swoop of the seagulls, the little sandpipers skittering across the tide line. It had been the single happiest day of her entire life.

FORTY

A Terrible Shock

The summer passed, and by the last week in August there was a distinct chill in the air. But the end of summer meant more than the end of heat and roses and rolling down the hill behind the birches. It meant autumn, and people often say that September and October are Nova Scotia's loveliest months. The air is brilliantly clear, and if you happen to live beside the sea, you can look at islands that are seven miles away and see houses on them as clearly as if they were across the road. Everywhere the leaves begin to turn from their summer green into colours that never cease to be amazing. The birches can become a luminous yellow, almost blindingly bright in direct sunlight. The giant oaks turn a very sober and majestic bronze. The maples can vary in colour from a warm orange to a blazing vermillion. And in most places, this colourful garden of giant foliage blooms against a background of evergreen trees — which look almost black beside the bright hardwood growth. Increasingly, the air has a frosty bite to it, and when the wind comes from the north, it's no longer soft. But anyone with a taste for beauty knows to put on a warm sweater and go outside to welcome this annual miracle. They need to do it *now*, and as often as possible, before the savage winds of November strip the leaves off the trees and leave them bare.

September would also bring *school*, and the long walk to Marysville in the clear, sunny air. Anne looked out her window on the last day of August and thought about the coming school year. She could hardly wait to sling Trudy's old school bag over her shoulder and start the long walk to the village of Marysville. She didn't need to shut her eyes to see the store at the bottom of the hill, the long slope up to the schoolhouse, the small building with its bell tower. And Miss Henderson would still be inside, ready to serve up her feast of knowledge and skills and *poetry* to Anne's willing ears. She'd see Sadie again, and her heart warmed to that thought. They weren't what Eliza used to call "bosom friends," because they could never meet or play outside of school. And Sadie fell short of Anne's greedy hunger for beauty. But she was loving, and comfortable, and safe. Mildred was *not* safe, nor was Randolph. But maybe Randolph wouldn't be there. Once again he hadn't passed the sixth class, and perhaps his ambitious father would have given up his dream of Randolph as a rich and prominent lawyer, and set him free to find a job on a neighbouring farm. Then Mr. Johnson wouldn't have to feel sorry for him anymore, and Anne wouldn't have to feel afraid of him.

Holding Lochinvar, scratching him gently behind his left ear, Anne took one last look out her window before she went downstairs to help Mrs. Thomas prepare supper. The hill beyond the Five Sisters — the one she so loved to run up and run or roll down — had lost the most brilliant of its green, and was already preparing to fade into its winter shade of beige. The little pond was as smooth as the glass in her tiny mirror, and the birch trees were motionless in the still air — looking limp and faded, not yet equipped with their bright yellow leaves. If it was very cold tonight — if she woke up tomorrow to grass that was tinged with a light coating of frost —the leaves might start to "turn." Sometimes this happened at the end of August, but those times were rare.

The sun suddenly disappeared behind a large cloud — white at the centre but rimmed with grey. A storm coming?

Why were the leaves and the pond so motionless? Anne had an uneasy sense of foreboding. But she shoved it to the back of her mind and went downstairs.

Anne had been happy all day. In fact, she'd been happy during most of the two weeks that had passed since the wonderful trip to the sea. "I have two big pieces of thought that are keeping me contented," she had said one night to Katie Maurice. "One is the extreme glory of our trip to the sea. That, all on its own, could keep me feeling very happy for a long time. In fact, exceedingly happy. The other piece of thought is knowing that before very long I'll be returning to school — which is a kind of heaven for me. I know more about heaven now than I used to. That's because Mr. Johnson and Miss Henderson have told me a lot about it. Not that they've seen it or been there or anything like that. It seems to be something that people think about in many different ways. Mr. Johnson says he thinks about the heaven he reads about in all his books. It always seems to be a perfect place in his books — but different kinds of perfect places. That's hard for me to understand, but Mr. Johnson is a very *complicated* (new word) person. Miss Henderson says it's a perfect place, too, or even a *state of mind*. I don't have one single idea what she means by that. I asked, when I met them out walking together—sort of strolling, like they weren't going anywhere special—whether sitting on the fence beside that exquisite field and stroking the cow's coat could be a kind of heaven, and they both said it probably could. In fact, Mr. Johnson said, 'Absolutely.'

"Mr. Johnson has clipped his big shaggy beard and seems also to have washed his clothes. And do you know what? This is even more of a miracle. He isn't really an *old* man. He's twenty-eight. He told me, after I asked. He said that many people might be cross if I asked how old they were, but I can't see why. It's nothing to be ashamed of. Although maybe being old might be a bit like having red hair and freckles. Anyway, he didn't mind, and answered me *immediately*. That is also a new word, and very useful. Miss Henderson, of course, being so exceedingly beautiful, is very young. Mrs. Thomas told me that she heard she was just out of high school, and only nineteen years old. Does that mean that if I stay in school for every single class, I'll know as much as she does?"

But that conversation took place the previous week. Anne had no time right now to talk to Katie Maurice, or even to think about her. There were potatoes to wash with the lovely vegetable brush, and then she'd need to cut them up for fried potatoes. She loved fried potatoes. But as Anne entered the kitchen, she knew immediately that something was wrong. Mrs. Thomas was sitting on one of the kitchen chairs, twisting the end of her apron into rolls, and then twisting it back again in the other direction. She was staring straight ahead of her — at a blank wall. Even the boys were quiet, looking at her.

Anne grabbed her arm. "What's *wrong*?" she exclaimed. "What *is* it?"

Mrs. Thomas looked at Anne, her eyes dull, listless. "He's drunk again. He did it in the daytime. He got in a fight at work in Marysville and lost his job. All he'll have now will be the money he gets from work with his wagon. We can't live on *that*. I'll have to go back to work. And if I do that, you can't go back to school. I'll need you here to mind the boys and get their meals. I've found out already that we're allowed to stay in the house. I don't know why. Maybe the new person in the job has a house in the town. I don't know, and I don't even care. I'm just relieved. But we got to *eat*. And have clothes.

The boys are growing fast. You seem to have stalled in your growth spurt. You're getting on for seven, but you only look about eight. Your clothes will fit. I've heard tell already that there are women in Marysville who'll pay me to clean and cook for them. So that's what I got to do."

Anne had no pity for Mrs. Thomas. She felt as though her own life were just one big gaping wound. She walked over to the potato bin and started to remove the potatoes she'd need. *No school!* She'd only been in school for about two and a half months. That was so little that it didn't even *count* as going to school. It was just as if all she'd had was a *taste* of school. But the taste had been so delicious. As she cut up the potatoes, her tears streamed down her cheeks and onto the table.

The door slammed, and suddenly Mr. Thomas was in the kitchen. "Stop that crying, you red-headed witch!" he yelled. "*I'm* the one who should be crying! There ain't nothin' left in my life! Nothin'! You got your whole life ahead of you. I'm only forty-two, but I'm *finished!* So *shut up!*"

Mr. Thomas had never spoken to Anne like that before. She dropped the knife she was working with and stared at him, her eyes wide with fear and with pain. Then she turned around and raced upstairs, slamming the door of her bedroom behind her, and threw herself on the bed to cry out her despair and her rage. Downstairs, she heard the kitchen door slam, and she knew that he was gone. Then she could hear the chop-chop-chop sounds of Mrs. Thomas cutting up the potatoes.

FORTY-ONE

A Hardened Heart

On the following afternoon, Anne escaped from the house and ran down to her secret hiding place behind the rhododendron bush. Beside it, the drooping branches of a small weeping willow tree created a private little room for her. Then she sat down by her beloved pond — her Pool of Mirrors — and thought about her life. She also did a lot of crying. If it was *absolutely necessary* — if, for instance, she could hear Mr. Thomas coming with his cart — she could stop. But later on — when she looked back at the two weeks that followed Mrs. Thomas's terrible announcement — it seemed to Anne that she cried almost continuously. She hadn't known that she had that many tears inside her.

So she could stop — and last night she did stop — when she knew that Mr. Thomas would soon be in the kitchen. When he arrived, she made a point of not even *looking* at him. He had promised to be kind to her. He'd made that long speech to Eliza about how he would treat her. And look what he'd done. He'd yelled at her and called her a "red-headed witch." She couldn't forgive that. No, she could *not*. He had broken his promise to Eliza, and his cruel words hurt her especially deeply because she was used to trusting him. And by losing his job, he had taken school away from her. This was an injury for which there was no bandage big enough. Anne had tried hard to understand his need to drink all that expensive rum. Maybe, she had so often argued to herself, it was like her need to dream, to talk, to *imagine*. But she didn't hurt other people when she gave in to those needs. Well, she supposed that maybe it hurt Mrs. Thomas a little. But Mr. Thomas hurt people a *lot*. That made it much harder to feel sorry for him. Right now she didn't feel sorry for him *at all*. He could bend down in the new barn and cry his eyes out for all she cared. Her sadness was *way* bigger than his. And it wasn't her *fault*. In a tiny little corner of her mind, Anne knew that maybe, just *maybe*, it wasn't totally *his* fault, either. But she turned away from that thought. She wasn't going to look at that possibility any more than she was going to look at *him*. She would never look at him again. Not *ever*.

As her tears dripped into a very small stream that fed her pond, Anne concentrated on everything awful that she could think of about her life. Orphaned at three months. A poor little freckle-faced baby with no mother, no father (her trickling tears became sobs). Eliza deserting her, in order to marry that cruel Roger. Mr. Thomas smashing in half of Katie Maurice's house. The way Mrs. Thomas called her wicked when all she was doing was stopping her work long enough to imagine something nicer. Her work: all those diapers; all those dirty floors to be scrubbed; all those potatoes to be chopped up; all that water to carry. And Horace to put up with. It was hard, hard, *hard*.

September was even more beautiful than ever that year. But Anne hardened her heart against all that loveliness — the bright sun, the clear air, the very blue sky. She refused to let anything intrude on her sadness. Mrs. Thomas, who often found Anne's ceaseless chatter tiring, found herself wishing that she'd *talk*. Mr. Thomas was genuinely cowed by the way she turned around in the opposite direction every time he entered a room. He had enjoyed his little talks with her. Now he was uneasy about even saying hello to the back of her head. She was still attentive to Noah's needs, and made sure that he had a lot of hugs, and took special care to say "I love you" to him at least once a day. But he wished she didn't look so *sad* all the time. Even Horace stopped tormenting her. It was clear even to his meagre intelligence that she was angry at the whole world. He didn't want to get in the way of anything physical she might do about it. He was already as tall as she was, and very strong. But he knew that Anne's skinny arms could easily throw a bottle or pick up a chair and heave it across the room. She'd never done such a thing, but he knew all about those violent feelings. And he was made nervous by the silence that she was maintaining.

Mrs. Thomas went off to her first of four jobs on September fifth. Horace departed for his first day at school on the sixth. Anne was glad to see him go, but she was consumed by intense envy. He was big. He was strong. Why couldn't *he* do some of the work that she was doing? Why was he granted the joy of learning the alphabet and listening to the older children be taught about faraway lands and long-ago times and the kind of poetry that made Anne ache with pleasure? She was very angry, and decided to stay that way forever. She almost never talked to Katie Maurice. *I cannot talk to her,* she said silently and to herself, as she stared at the serene surface of her pond behind the birch trees. *She doesn't want to hear that I'm in the deep, cold, dark pit of despair.*

But she was running out of eggs. If there wasn't enough money for meat or fish, she could at least hard-boil a lot of eggs and make a meal out of them and carrots and potatoes. Hard-boiling eggs was about as far as her cooking skills went. They were cheap. She'd leave Edward in charge of the two younger children and walk to Mr. Johnson's in search of eggs.

On the way to Mr. Johnson's, Anne paid no attention to the bright glitter of the sun on the damp evergreens. A cat crossed the road — a particularly beautiful grey one — and she didn't speak to him or approach him to stroke him under the chin. An enormous crow flew down and stared at her from its position on a fence post. Normally its size would have set her to wondering if it might possibly be a raven. But she scarcely noticed it. As she approached Mrs. Archibald's house, she didn't even look in the direction of the front door.

However, the front door opened, and Mrs. Archibald appeared. "Anne!" she called, and when she received no answer, "*Anne!*"

Anne stopped walking and waved, her face a mask of sadness.

"Come in!" called Mrs. Archibald. "Why aren't you in school? Come quickly! I have a batch of molasses cookies that are still warm from the oven. Hurry — before they cool down!"

Anne came. She had a mug of tea and two cookies. It was the first time she'd felt hungry in two weeks. She told Mrs. Archibald her sad story.

"I'll tell Janie," she said to Anne, as she left the house. "She'll be wondering where you are."

When Anne knocked at Mr. Johnson's door, she was met by the same question. "Anne! Why aren't you in school?" Anne went in, sat down beside the Botticelli painting, and burst into a stormy fit of weeping. When she finally stopped, she said, "I know *exactly* how you felt when your beautiful bride left you and went away with your horrible best friend. I hate everybody, and I'd like to run away and live in the woods, too. *Forever.*" Then she told him the whole story. After that, she banged her fist on the table and declared, "No school! No books! No learning wonderful new things! No Sadie! And Oh! Oh! Oh! No Miss Henderson! Mr. Thomas drunk and mean to me! Work! Work! Work! I'll never ever be happy again. *Never!*" Then she succumbed to a new fit of crying.

Mr. Johnson took her two hands in his and held them until she stopped weeping. Then, in a voice so quiet that she had to strain to hear him, he said, "Listen, Anne. I know you feel like this now. I'm sure I'd feel the same way. You're aware that I've walked down the same road. Now answer me this question." He paused, and she looked up at him. "Have I ever told you a lie?"

"No." She was still now, and quiet.

"Then listen carefully. *It will get better*. Probably not today. Maybe not tomorrow or next week. Or even next month. Look at how long it took me to crawl out of the hole I was in. *But I'm out.* I thought I never would be, but it happened. And what's more —"

"Yes?"

"You've got twice the spirit I ever had. It will happen to you more quickly than it did for me. So you just remember this, and believe it: *It will get better*."

Anne took a long, deep breath. She even summoned up a small smile. Then she actually gave a small chuckle. "I find I'm feeling hungry this morning. Do you have any of those oatmeal cookies you had the last time I was here? I sort of haven't been eating very much. Too sad. I couldn't swallow."

"I just happen to have one left," he said. "It's yours."

"B-But ..." stammered Anne. "Your last cookie? No, I don't think —"

Mr. Johnson reached into his cookie tin and held out the cookie. "*Eat!*" he ordered. "Now," he said, as she sat there, hungrily eating it, "I think I'll just heat up some soup that's on the back of the stove, and you'll have some of that. After that we'll go out and get the eggs. Then I'll teach you your five new words. Then you'll go home and look after those boys and cut up the potatoes. Make one of them bring in a bucket of water for you. Say please. It makes all the difference. If Mr. Thomas comes in for supper, look at him. You don't need to smile, but see if you can manage to *just look at him*. You're the only person in that house that he really *likes*. Give him some hope."

"But he said I was a red-headed witch."

"Yes. I know. But he didn't mean it."

"But he *must* have meant it! How could he say something if it wasn't even in his head? He must have *thought* it."

"You're often right, Anne. But you're wrong here. People who are drunk often say things they don't mean. And do things they'd never do if they were sober. I don't understand this any better than you do, but it's a fact. I'm not asking you to *forgive* him. Forgiving is the hardest thing in the world. I haven't managed that yet myself. But could you maybe just *look* at him?"

"I can't promise for sure, Mr. Johnson," said Anne. "But I'll think about it on the way home."

Then they collected the eggs, after which they went back to the shack while Mr. Johnson taught Anne her five new words. He wrote them down in the little book he had given her, and she put it carefully in the bag with the eggs. The words were *grief, hope, courage, confidence* and *mercy*.

FORTY-TWO

A Surprise Visit

By October, Anne and Mr. Thomas had made an uneasy kind of peace with each other. She had started to look at him again, and sometimes even smiled at him if he did something nice — as on the morning when he brought in two buckets of water for her to wash with, or when he took the three boys with him one day when he was delivering some gravel with his wagon. "To give you a break," he said sheepishly, obviously feeling shy about doing this good deed.

Mr. Thomas wasn't drunk every single day. If he could find no work to do with his wagon, he had no money. And with no money, you can't buy any rum. Mrs. Thomas now hid her money from him. He delivered her to her work in the morning and brought her back in late afternoon. But she didn't let him know when she'd received money. She hid it inside her corset, and later, when Mr. Thomas dug around in her bag in search of money, he couldn't find any. This could make him frantic — and often angry — but during this period he hit no one. He knew Anne hated violence, and he didn't think he could stand it if she started turning her back on him again.

As the family moved into the second week of October, the intense autumn colours were blazing all around them. The maples were particularly brilliant this year, and the Five Sisters were as warmly yellow as Anne had ever seen them. The beauty lifted her out of her gloom from time to time, but her delight was muted; it was also mixed with resentment and longing and a deep sense of injustice.

Then, on one fine Saturday when the bright fall sun was shining especially brilliantly on the five birches and on the wild red maples on the other side of the house, Anne heard a knock on the door. As so often happened on Saturdays as well as on weekdays, Mrs. Thomas was working in the town, and Mr. Thomas had taken his horses and wagon to pick up a load of gravel for a local road builder. Anne had just finished hanging out the wash, and she was already very tired, although it wasn't yet noon. She had on one of Mrs. Thomas's aprons that came down below her knees. She hadn't taken the time to braid her hair that morning, and it was escaping from two scraggly pigtails. Her hands were red and wrinkled from two hours spent in soapy water. She had just picked up one of Edward's muddy shoes from the middle of the kitchen floor, and then scratched an itchy spot on her face with a dirty finger. She had never looked worse.

Who could this be at the door? Mr. Thomas had told her never to open the door to a stranger. But how could she know whether it was a stranger if she didn't open the door to find out? She opened it.

It was Miss Henderson. She was looking more beautiful than ever, her honey-coloured hair piled high on her head, with little curls coming loose around her face. Her wine-coloured dress was long and full, and she wore a small black velvet jacket over it, with the little buttons fastened tightly against the bright but chilly October day. She was carrying a canvas bag over one shoulder. It would be hard to say which was the more surprised — Miss Henderson, to see Anne looking so pathetic and woebegone; or Anne, to witness the arrival at the door of this miracle woman. Anne had almost forgotten that wonderful things could sometimes happen, but here was one unfolding before her very eyes.

Surely she had to be dreaming. She shut her eyes for a moment, and then opened them again, just to be sure. Yes. Miss Henderson was still there. And she was speaking.

"Anne," she was saying. "How lovely to see you! May I come in?"

Anne opened the door wide. But it would still be a few moments before she could find her voice.

"I'm so sorry not to have come before," Mrs. Henderson was saying. "I thought you were probably ill. But I missed you. The little schoolhouse wasn't the same without my Anne. Then — last night — I discovered the reason for your absence. Oh, Anne! I'm so sorry!"

Anne hadn't cried for at least two weeks. She'd made her heart stiff and cold so that she could somehow survive the life she was leading. Now, suddenly, everything felt melted and soft, and the tears came. Miss Henderson held her skinny little body close, and Anne felt a warmth and a comfort that she hadn't felt since Eliza's departure. When she finally stopped crying, Miss Henderson said, "I brought you some presents, Anne. Blow your nose hard, and then come and have a look." She handed Anne a pretty little mauve handkerchief with crocheting around the edge, and then walked over to the table to put her bag down beside a bowl of carrots and a pile of dirty breakfast dishes.

Anne blew her nose hard with the beautiful handkerchief and wiped her wet face with her apron. Then she approached the table.

"Look, Anne," said Miss Henderson, reaching into the big bag. "I've brought you a slate and some chalk, and a soft cloth for wiping it clean. I've also brought you the reader for the class you would be in if you were at school — and *two more*. I've brought you the readers for the next two classes. I know you always liked to listen in to my lessons with the older classes. The books will be too hard for you, but I think you may already know some of the stories and poems by heart. And you can look at the pictures and make up your own stories to go with them."

If Miss Henderson had brought her three big bags full of diamonds, Anne wouldn't have looked half as thrilled as she did now. She picked up the books — one by one — patting them, smoothing them, leafing through the pages, hugging them to her chest.

"Oh, Miss Henderson!" she gasped. "I think I'm maybe going to die from too much happiness. Ever since I learned that I wouldn't be able to go to school, I almost never smile. Certainly not on purpose. If you do it on purpose, that means that you care what other people think. I don't care anymore what people think. I don't try — no, not for one single moment — to make Mrs. Thomas think that I'm happy. And I don't smile to make Mr. Thomas feel less guilty about drinking up the food money and losing another job and having a life that he says doesn't add up. No. I want him to feel bad. I love Noah, and of course I smile at him a lot. And hug him and all that. And of course Lochinvar. Katie Maurice never does anything wrong, so you'd think I might spend a lot of time smiling at her. But mostly when I talk to her, I'm telling her why I'm so unhappy. And that's not a smiling matter. So it's usually only Noah and Mr. Johnson who get any smiles from me. But you came to see me this morning and brought all those presents. Today I feel like smiling at the whole world."

Anne did, indeed, look as though her face might crack wide open. In spite of the scraggly hair, the long wrinkled apron, the dirty face, she looked very beautiful to Miss Henderson.

Anne's joy had transformed everything about her. Suddenly, any onlooker — possibly even Horace — would find it easy to notice her perfect little nose, her pert and proud chin, her huge expressive grey-green eyes.

"I used to feel great fondness and pity for Mr. Thomas, too," continued Anne. "But *he ruined my life*, so I don't feel like that anymore. He made it so I can't go to school, so my anger is very, very huge. Mr. Johnson says that forgiving is exceedingly hard, so if it's hard for him, I don't expect that I'll be able to manage it at all. I don't feel the tiniest bit of mercy."

"Maybe you will," said Miss Henderson. "*Sometime*."

"Well," said Anne, "I might just be able to do it sooner than I thought. Because of today. Because of you coming. I'm not allowed to go to school. But you brought the school to *me*."

Miss Henderson laughed. "Yes, and I didn't just bring the things you love best. I brought the arithmetic book, too. I don't know how much you can teach yourself, but you can try. You can add numbers a little bit already. But if you get stuck on the subtractions, I'm sure Mr. Johnson will give you a little help."

When Miss Henderson brought it out of the canvas bag, even the arithmetic book looked good to Anne.

Suddenly there was the sound of loud voices coming from down the road.

"The children?" asked Miss Henderson.

"Yes."

"Anne," said Miss Henderson, "quickly — put the school things in the bag and take it upstairs to find a hiding place for it. You can keep the bag. I've had Horace in my school long enough to know what he might do with your presents. Make them all disappear before they all arrive."

Later, as Anne watched Miss Henderson walk down the road toward the homes of Mrs. Archibald and Mr. Johnson, Anne thought about miracles. She felt she knew all about them.

FORTY-THREE

A Magic Day

On one of the Saturdays when Miss Henderson came, Mrs. Thomas was home. She was uneasy in the presence of this beautiful young woman — cowed by her gentle ways, her quiet and formal way of speaking, the fact that she was a *schoolteacher*. Therefore, when Miss Henderson suggested that she and Anne go up to her room to talk about arithmetic, she just smiled stiffly, offered two terse words, and let it happen. It was time for Anne to start washing the dishes, but Mrs. Thomas turned sharply around, walked over to the counter, and washed them herself — noisily.

Later that day Anne found a free half-hour in which to talk to Katie Maurice.

"Hello, dear Katie Maurice. I can see by your face that you're feeling happy. Yesterday you looked so terrible. But not today. No. You look as though a great big miracle has dropped out of this sky and landed in your arms.

"And do you know what the miracle was, Katie Maurice — the miracle that arrived in our house today? It was Miss Henderson. She came *again*. She came right up the front steps and knocked at the door. I never know when she's going to come, so each day is changed for me. That's because I can say to myself *every morning*, 'Anne. Maybe this will be the day when she'll come!' And that thought changes my entire day. But today was special, *absolutely special*, because Mrs. Thomas was here. That meant I didn't have to keep bobbing up and down to look out the window and make sure that the boys weren't doing anything ferociously bad. But there was something even better than *that*." Anne paused here, to make sure that Katie Maurice was paying close attention to everything she was saying. She certainly was. Her head was cocked a little to one side, and her big eyes looked very eager.

"Well," continued Anne, "she asked Mrs. Thomas if it would be all right if she and I went upstairs to my room to work on some arithmetic. And it was exactly the time when I was supposed to be washing the dishes. The hot water was in the pan, and everything was steaming and ready. I held my breath till I thought my face had to be purple. I was that afraid she'd say no. But you should have seen Miss Henderson when she asked that question. She talked as if Mrs. Thomas was the Queen, and as if we were all standing in the middle of a huge entrance hall to the biggest castle in the world, instead of in the Thomas kitchen beside a steaming dishpan. So Mrs. Thomas couldn't really say no to anyone who was asking for something in such an exceedingly polite way. I think she said something like this: 'Oh, Mrs. Thomas! How lovely to see you! I'd appreciate it so much if you'd permit me to go upstairs with Anne so that we can work on her arithmetic.' How could Mrs. Thomas say no? Well, she couldn't, but she didn't sound one bit like a queen when she said, 'Go ahead,' and then started washing the dishes and making loud clattery noises.

"So up we went. Miss Henderson and I sat side by side on the bed and did arithmetic for a while — but not for very long. Then she reached into her bag and brought out a book with a story and a lot of wonderful pictures in it. She read the *whole story* to me, very slowly, so that I could watch the words as well as look at the pictures. She pointed her finger at each word so that I'd know *exactly* what the word was. That way I could maybe — just *maybe* — remember the word and work out the letters later on.

"Then she reached in her bag again and took out a flat box. It was full of pictures. Pictures of boats on wonderful stormy seas. Of women in dresses so beautiful that if you imagined them for a hundred years you'd never be able to pretend anything that amazing. There was one of a boy in a blue suit — such a blue as you've never, ever seen — with a feathered hat in his hand. He's called *The Blue Boy*. There were pictures of *angels*, but prettier than Mr. Johnson's angry angels. She said I could keep them until she comes the next time. Then she'll bring me some more, and take these ones back home. I showed her the place under the mattress where I keep all the treasures she has brought. I wish I could keep them in the box that I call my Treasure Box, but I know I can never put real treasures in it, because Horace, or maybe even Edward, would steal them. Or worse still, break them or tear them on purpose. She laughed when she saw where I keep the books and slate and pictures, and asked if they made the bed lumpy. I told her yes, but that I didn't care. She gave me a hug, and then she went away.

"Now I can take those things out from under my mattress when I'm all alone. I look and look and look at them, and I try hard to read the words in the books. Sometimes I can do it — even the hard ones. I keep hearing Miss Henderson in my head, telling me that she's sure I can keep up with Sadie and Mildred. That she knows I can do it. Remembering her saying these things makes me almost believe I can do it, too."

Anne turned away from the china cabinet and made her way to the back hall. She could hear voices in the distance, and she knew that what she was hearing was Mrs. Thomas and the four boys returning from picking up fallen apples from the neighbouring orchard. Anne had somehow avoided that expedition, and now she escaped again, sliding out a side door before the Thomases came spilling into the kitchen. Swiftly she raced down to the rhododendron bush and crouched on the other side of it. She was determined to make this as perfect a day as she could, and staring at her beloved pond — her Pool of Mirrors — was the best way she could think of to make that happen.

It was a warm Indian summer day, and although most of the bright autumn leaves had been blown off the trees in last week's windstorm, there was still much to watch and wonder at. The crows remained in Nova Scotia all winter, and Anne loved to see their black silhouettes against the blue sky. A few late goldenrod blooms lingered on, and were grouped at intervals around the pond. There were also one or two large but limp butterflies that had come out to test their tired wings in the unusual warmth. A small breeze blew through the long grasses and dried weeds, but it was comforting rather than cold.

Anne thought about Indian summer, and decided it was another of life's miracles. Here it was almost time for the first snow, and she was sitting in the grass without even a sweater on. If she closed her eyes, it would be easy to believe that it was the middle of July. Two miracles in one day! And Anne was determined to enjoy them both. Even if Mrs. Thomas was angry at her for disappearing, even if she called Anne wicked and Horace called her an ugly orphan girl, even if Mr. Thomas turned up for supper silent and gloomy and complained about the soup, she knew she'd be able to keep the magic of this day close to her heart.

She returned to a house and to a kitchen that was full of noisy strife. The boys were punching one another, and at least one of them was crying. Mrs. Thomas was telling the whole world that Anne was both wicked and *lazy*. Where on earth had she *been* all day? How dared she repay Mrs. Thomas for her seven years of care — bringing her into her house as though she was her own child — by disappearing for *four whole hours*. Horace was sticking his tongue out at her. Mr. Thomas was sitting at the kitchen table with his head in his hands. He wanted, he *needed*, a drink, and after one full hour of searching, he'd been unable to find a single piece of money. Not even a *penny*. And why wasn't supper ready? If he could eat something, maybe he wouldn't feel so awful. And how could that Anne girl stand there, in the middle of all this unholy noise, cutting up carrots and looking so *serene*? And her lips were moving. He moved his chair up closer to her.

"You're doin' it again," he said, talking above the background of family noise. "You're pretendin' things. And why are your lips movin'? Are you *prayin'*?" This made him nervous.

Anne turned her head and looked at him. Because Mr. Johnson had said she should do that, she did it. She even managed a smile. She was working on forgiveness, but so far it hadn't quite happened. Anne's angers were ferocious and deep. After all, he'd taken school away from her. And she didn't see *him* washing any dishes or scrubbing any floors. Sitting out in the barn with his three animals didn't look like very hard work to *her*. But she could see the torment in his face, and felt some hidden need to answer him.

"I'm not pretending," she said. "I just had a very beautiful day, and what I'm doing is *remembering* it. If you've had an exceedingly happy day, remembering is just as nice as pretending."

"So," he said, offering a scornful rejoinder to this unwelcome catalogue of joys, "what was so wonderful about this day? And why all the silent mutterin'?"

"Well," she said, scooping up the chopped carrots and dumping them into a pot, "first of all, Miss Henderson came. She's my teacher. As you know" — she just couldn't resist saying this — "I can't go to school anymore, because I have to stay home and *look after your children*. I love school. And I just happen to be a child, too. My life — like yours — *doesn't add up*."

Mr. Thomas frowned. He came very close to leaving the kitchen and going back to the barn. But it was very cold out there. So he stayed. "How come you got all this *happiness* t' remember?"

"As I already said, Miss Henderson came. She's my teacher. *She came to see me*. I love her a lot. She's like a mother to me, and you may have noticed that I don't have one of my own." Anne lined up the potatoes in a row and started to scrub them with the new brush. "She came up to my room, and she taught me how to do sums. I don't like arithmetic very much, but it might be useful if I ever get a job. Then she read me a beautiful story out loud and showed me the letters in the words, and then we looked at the pictures in the book. I don't know which I liked best — the words she spoke or the pictures. I loved all of it so much. She was bringing school *right into my bedroom*. It was like a miracle."

Anne started to cut up the potatoes. The background noise was ferocious. No one could possibly have overheard their conversation. But she whispered the next part.

"She also," she said, "brought a box of pictures that were so wonderful that I can't even find a word to describe how I felt. They had been painted by *artists*. That's what artists do. That's their *job*. I'd love to do that job, but I can't draw well enough to do it. But I'd like even better to write stories. And I don't think that would be so hard. You need to be able to write and spell, but sometime I'll learn how to do those things — when I go back to *school*."

Mr. Thomas winced. But he stayed where he was. "And your movin' lips. What did that mean?" Then he asked again, "Were you prayin'?"

Anne stopped chopping for a moment and looked again at Mr. Thomas. "I don't know what praying is," she said. "No one ever taught me how to do it. What I was doing was trying to remember the words of the story that Miss Henderson read to me today. I thought if I could get it exactly right, I could tell it to Noah when he gets a bit older. The other boys don't like sitting still long enough to listen to stories. I've tried. I know some stories from Eliza. But they don't want to listen to them. Sometimes I do tell them to —" She stopped abruptly, and a shadow of fear crossed her face.

"To who?"

"Oh, no one in particular. I just tell them."

"To *who*?" Mr. Thomas was insistent.

Anne felt cornered. Frantic. Finally, she said, "To *me*. To *myself*."

Mr. Thomas sighed. "And what else was so wonderful about this *magic day*?"

Anne took a deep breath and crammed everything into one sentence. "It was Indian summer today and very warm until the sun went down, and now it's cold again, but it was just like July, and when they went out to collect apples *I didn't go*, and when they came back *I escaped again*, and ran down to sit beside the Pool of Mirrors and watched the crows and butterflies and listened to the wind, and during all that time I wasn't *working*. Wouldn't *you* call that a magic day? A day of real miracles?"

Mr. Thomas got up from his seat. "Anne," he said, "sometimes I want so much to get inside your head and *be you* that I can hardly stand it. Sometimes it makes me so mad at you because *you can do it*, and *I can't*, that it makes me nearly crazy." He yelled at Mrs. Thomas, "I'm going out to the barn. Send Horace out to get me when dinner's ready." She just nodded. She was too busy to reply.

FORTY-FOUR

A Long Fall

For Anne, there weren't many miracles or magic days during the next eleven months. Looking back on it in later years, she would sometimes think that there'd been nothing but work, work, work — as well as a lot of noise and anger. Everyone seemed to have a reason for feeling angry: Mrs. Thomas because she had a rum-drinking husband who didn't love her; Mr. Thomas because he kept creating catastrophes for himself and everyone else, and because he couldn't seem to stop doing it, and because his boys were too noisy, and because his wife never combed her hair, and because there was nothing even a little bit like *dancing* in his life. Horace was angry because everyone else was, and because he just seemed to have been born that way. Edward and Harry were angry because Horace had been mean to them so often that they'd started to be mean to each other. Anne was angry because she couldn't go to school. She was *sad* about other things, but the fact that she had been deprived of school was the main source of her anger. But that particular anger spilled over in many directions — at Mr. Thomas for causing it all; at Mrs. Thomas for having to go out to make money — thus leaving Anne to look after the house, the meals and the children; at Horace because he hit her and insulted her, and then was able to trot off so jauntily to school each morning.

Noah was the one small oasis of calm in the midst of the unhappy house. He was loved by Anne, and he loved her back. She protected him from the violence that surrounded him, and as a result he felt safe. He was used to noise and the background scene of sadness and anger. He hardly noticed them. He listened to the stories that Anne told him, and then sat down on the floor in his favourite corner and thought about them. He liked being quiet, and he didn't mind being alone. He liked spending time with Lochinvar, and the big orange cat seemed to love him right back. On the whole, no one paid much attention to Noah. It was almost as though he wasn't there.

The foliage finally fell from all the trees, and gradually the colour seeped out of the grass, leaving the grassy hills and pastures a dispiriting beige. On nearby farms, the men had plowed the crops under, and the fields were brown, with awkward little sticks poking through the stiff soil. The evergreens kept the land from looking stripped bare, and continued to provide colour against the blue of the autumn sky. But the whole landscape had a waiting look. *Waiting for what?* Anne wondered about that, as she looked out the window. Probably waiting for something better. Often there would be strong winds, and Anne thought about the family's one day at the seashore, and wondered if the waves were high and scary now — and exciting. But that was far away, and she couldn't see it. She loved to see the trees flouncing around and bending in the windstorms, but she longed to see what that wind might be doing to the sea. What was the point of Nova Scotia having 3728.4 miles of coastline when she lived in the middle of the province and never saw it? Besides, on stormy days, she knew that Miss Henderson wouldn't come. And she wondered if she would *ever* come when the snow arrived.

Snow! That's what the landscape was waiting for. As the first two weeks of December passed, there were a few sparse flurries, but nothing that you could pile up and roll into a snowman. The hill beyond the Pool of Mirrors remained beige, with no hope of sliding down it on an old burlap potato bag. And it wasn't even quite cold enough for the ice on the pond to be safe to slide on. No. The world was just *waiting*. For snow, for Miss Henderson, for Christmas, for something that might make some kind of change in any of their lives.

But then, early in the third week of December, Miss Henderson came. There was still no snow, but it wasn't easy to walk over that frozen roadbed, with its hard chunks of congealed mud and dirt, and its few slippery puddles. It must have been a difficult journey for her. But she came. It was Sunday, and Mr. Thomas was home. Therefore, she and Anne could go upstairs to Anne's room, where Miss Henderson read aloud two wonderful stories, showed her the new batch of pictures, and told Anne about what was going on at school. She said that Sadie missed Anne, and often spoke about her. Mildred was doing well with her arithmetic, but Anne was ahead of her in reading.

Randolph had finally left school and Marysville in November and was working in Kingsport down by the waterfront, loading and unloading vessels. Miss Henderson had seen him on a street in Kingsport, and she told Anne that he was happy, and that she wondered if being happy had leached all the meanness out of him. She said that he'd even asked, "Is that Anne girl enjoying my dictionary?" Then Miss Henderson added, "I don't remember his liking *anyone* in that school except Mildred, but he sounded as though he actually *hoped* you were enjoying it. He certainly didn't like *me*. He thought I was his jailer."

"Well," said Anne, "if you see him again, you can tell him that I still love his dictionary. It's the biggest lump under my mattress, but I look at it every single day — just before I go to bed at night. I try to find one new word that looks especially interesting. I write it down on my slate, learn all the letters, and then ask Mr. Johnson what it means, when I go for eggs." Then Anne added, "I deeply love Mr. Johnson."

She was looking directly at Miss Henderson when she said that, and was able to see that her teacher blushed a glowing shade of dark pink. Anne looked quickly down at the picture she was holding and pretended not to notice. *Why did she turn so red? Why did she look so ... strange?* Kings and queens. Princes and princesses. Knights and maidens. She'd been told a lot of stories by Eliza. Was it like *that?* With Miss Henderson and Mr. Johnson? Could anything that wonderful really happen?

Before Miss Henderson left, she exchanged the new pictures for the old ones, gave Anne a few sheets of rough paper and a new pencil, and a flat present wrapped in red tissue paper. "The pencil and the red present are your Christmas gifts." She said. "But I'd like you to be able to use the pencil right now. They're our secret. I don't have enough money to buy gifts for the whole family, but I want *you* to have one. Sometime on Christmas Day, you can come up here and unwrap the red one. Then you can think about me thinking about you on that special day."

Then she gave Anne a small bottle containing a dark liquid. "You have four little boys to look after," she said. "Often children get croup in the winter. This is a bottle of ipecac. You may need it." Then Miss Henderson told Anne exactly what croup was, and exactly how to use the medicine. "This can save a child's life if he's very sick with the croup. I'd like you to repeat what I just told you about how to use it." Anne did so, using almost exactly the same words that Miss Henderson had used. Then she gave Anne a big, warm hug, and was down the stairs and out of the front door before Anne had a chance to tell her how happy she had made her. But that was all right. Miss Henderson knew.

FORTY-FIVE

*W*inter

On the twentieth of December, the snow came. And it was deep. The boys spilled out of the house and were so happy that they forgot to be angry with one another. They made snowmen, slid down the hill on the far side of the pond, made forts, and had snowball fights — which had nothing whatsoever to do with anger. Mr. Thomas got a lot of work clearing snow away from essential roads and driveways, thereby increasing his meagre income. Mr. Boland had given Bert runners when he'd given him the horse and wagon after he lost his job in Bolingbroke. Once those runners had been affixed to the wagon, he could go many places that the other buggies and wagons couldn't reach. With money coming into his pockets, Bert could have seen life as one long binge. But something in the general excitement over Christmas seemed to have reached him. Everywhere he went to do his shovelling and hauling, people wished him "a very Merry Christmas," and often gave him a little extra money. They seemed to like him. He dug in his heels and resolved to stop drinking until at least the New Year. If he drank his way through the whole holiday season, he wouldn't be the only one who thought his life didn't add up. And if he could make it right through New Year's Eve and New Year's Day, maybe — just *maybe* — that dry period might last a whole lot longer.

While Bert was in the village of Marysville clearing a lot of the roads to houses and barns, he spent some time in the little store. He bought a tin soldier for each of the boys, and a small stuffed bear for Anne. It took him a long time to choose something for Mrs. Thomas, for Joanna. A pair of gloves? Where would she wear them? A parasol? In December? No. A small fur muff, made locally from soft rabbit's fur? Hmm. Would she *like* it? He couldn't be sure. She'd never owned anything that luxurious. When she used it, would she feel ... *silly*? Maybe. Maybe not. But in any case, it would keep her hands warm on the daily trip to Marysville. He bought it. Plus seven oranges — a rare treat. He pictured himself bringing them into the kitchen, piled up in his mother's wedding present bowl, and laying one of them in front of each person's place at the table — including his own. As he stood there in the store, he could see the look of joy in each face, particularly Anne's. And even more specially, Joanna's. Hers would be looking astonished as well as joyful. He was smiling as he handed over the money for all these special things. This must be what Anne meant when she said she was *imagining* things.

On the twenty-third of December, Mrs. Thomas ran out of eggs. Horace had thrown one at Edward on the previous day, and he enjoyed that experience so much that he'd thrown two more. Now there were none left.

She'd planned to make a pudding for Christmas dinner from some ingredients she had on hand, but without eggs she could do nothing. She had some spiced homemade sausage set aside for Christmas dinner, and maybe she and Anne could mash the potatoes to make the meal seem more special. But she wanted to make that pudding. Well, she'd have to send Anne to the Egg Man to get more eggs.

Then, for the first time that day, Mrs. Thomas looked out the window. She could see nothing except a white cloud moving sideways with great speed. This was snow, blowing horizontally in a fierce wind. "A ferocious wind!" exclaimed Anne, who was standing beside her.

"Yes," sighed Mrs. Thomas, who was used to hearing Anne use that word. "Too ferocious to send you out in. You'd never make it to the Egg Man. You'd be dead before you'd gone a quarter of a mile." Then she started to cry.

Anne grabbed her arm. "What's wrong?" she said, feeling an unusual compassion for this discouraged and beaten-down woman. "Is it anything I did? I'm sorry. What is it?"

All Mrs. Thomas could get out between sobs were the words "No eggs. No pudding."

Mr. Thomas was sitting beside the kitchen stove. He'd heard everything. His Christmas wish to be a good person was still with him. "I'll go," he said. "The horses is still hitched up. I can get there easy. I was just restin' between jobs. I didn't notice how bad it's got."

"I don't know, Bert," said Mrs. Thomas, who had regained her ability to speak, although her voice was not yet steady, "it's blowing some hard. Maybe you couldn't see where you're going." Lately, Bert had been of more use to her alive than dead. She didn't want to lose him in this blizzard.

"There's trees on both sides o' the road, Joanna. Besides, them horses know. They're way smarter than people. And strong. It's only a mile." He was already buttoning his coat and winding a scarf around his neck. "How many you want?" he asked, as he laced up his boots.

"Two dozen," she said. And then, "Be careful. And ..."
"And what?"
"Thank you."

It wasn't all that easy after all. It took a lot of manoeuvring to get those horses and their wagon through the driving snow to Mr. Johnson's shack, with the wind slamming into his face.

But, wet and cold though he was, Mr. Thomas was still seized by strong waves of goodwill. He was thinking about the muff he'd bought for Joanna. He felt more and more sure she was going to love it. When Mr. Thomas finally reached his destination, he asked Mr. Johnson for three dozen eggs instead of two. And he said, "Do y' have any good fat capons on hand? I'd like two for Christmas dinner, if y' got them." Mr. Johnson did. He'd killed two hens that morning for a customer who cancelled her order an hour later. Someone had brought her a turkey.

After Bert collected his three dozen eggs and two capons, and when he'd turned his horses and wagon around, he set out for his own house. On the return trip, the wind was at his back, and the journey was easier. He felt like a warrior on his way home from a fearsome battle. He couldn't remember when he'd felt this great.

Bert stopped the horses at one point and climbed off the wagon to cut down a small spruce tree. Maybe they'd all like to have a Christmas tree. They had no ornaments, but perhaps the children could think of some way to dress it up. He'd make a stand for it tomorrow. Christmas was still two days off. There was lots of time. If the weather cleared up a bit, he could ride one of the horses into the Marysville store tomorrow and see if he could buy a star or an angel or something to put on the top. And they might have some sleigh bells in that store. There was still a lot of winter left, and he'd kind of like to hear that jingling music as he drove around. He thought about Christmas Day. He could almost smell those capons cooking. Maybe he'd put the tin soldiers on the tree after the boys went to bed on Christmas Eve. He thought some more about the muff. Joanna was sure to like it. And the bear. If Anne loved the bear, maybe she'd be nice to him again. She'd stopped turning her back to him, and once in a while she smiled at him. But it wasn't the same. It wasn't the way it used to be. He knew that a doll would have been better than a bear. And there'd been one in the store when he'd been in there last week. But when he went to buy the tin soldiers, it was gone. He hoped so badly that she'd like the bear.

Christmas Day was when Anne forgave Mr. Thomas. She still couldn't go to school, and she also knew that there was an *exceedingly* good chance that he would stop being cheerful and kind as soon as his wild Christmas spirit drained out of his new self. And she'd almost given up hoping that when he stopped drinking he would never start again.

But how could you fail to forgive someone who took your upside-down life and turned it right side up — all within three days. She told Katie Maurice about it as soon as she got a chance on the day after Boxing Day — December twenty-seventh.

"I'm sorry, Katie Maurice, to have been away from you for so long. But so many things have happened to keep me away — *good* things this time. First there was the day Mr. Thomas drove through the blizzard to get *three* dozen eggs instead of two, and *also* two whole capons from dear Mr. Johnson. I don't always call him the Egg Man anymore — even though everyone else does. I often call him the Word Man. Then Mr. Thomas stopped the horses — right in the middle of the storm — to cut down a tree for us. I'd have been happy enough if he'd just taken the darling little tree and stuck it in the snow outside our kitchen window. But no. He went out to the barn and made a little stand for it. Then he put it up in the parlour. We didn't have any ornaments for it, but the boys stuck some of their toys among the branches, and

Mrs. Thomas had two necklaces that she hung from it. It looked *exquisite* to me, and even the three noisy boys stopped running around and yelling, and sat right down on the old torn chesterfield and just *stared* at it. Noah sat up on the old armchair looking like he was seeing a *vision*, with Lochinvar snuggled up to him, purring. It smelled exactly like being in the depths of the forest on a wet day.

"*Then*, the next day, Mr. Thomas drove one of his horses — the white one, which I always think looks like a white charger — and bought a tinsel *angel* to put on the top. Not like the Word Man's angels, who look so upset and angry. A dainty one with a filmy skirt. And he bought bells for his horses, but he didn't put them on their harnesses yet. He hung them on our tree. I could hardly hold in my joy. I felt like either dancing around the room or falling to the floor in what's called 'a dead faint.' I didn't do either one, but I felt like it.

"But Christmas Day was best of all. We all got a present. The boys each got a tin soldier, which Mr. Thomas hid on the tree on Christmas Eve. They had to hunt for them. They were so excited that they nearly knocked down the tree, but they didn't. Then he gave me the most wonderful present I ever could imagine he'd give me. It's a little bear. It's just like a real bear — brown, with a round, kind face — but small. But big enough to be very, very satisfying to hug. I can take him to bed and sleep with him as well as with Lochinvar. Lochinvar likes to push in against my knees, so there'll be no need for him to be jealous.

"But almost best of all was Mrs. Thomas and the muff. When Mr. Thomas gave it to her, he looked very, very worried. I could tell he was scared she wouldn't like it. It was made of soft fur, so it must have cost a whole lot. He could have bought rum with that money, but he didn't. That was

one of the biggest miracles. Then, when Mrs. Thomas saw the muff, she took it and stroked it and stroked it, and held it against her face, and hugged it close to her chest. Then she started to cry, and I think that everyone — even the boys — knew that they were tears of joy. Then — and here was the second miracle — she stood up and went over and *hugged* Mr. Thomas. I never even knew she *liked* him, and there she was hugging him! And he looked very surprised, but also exceedingly pleased. It was clear that it was a satisfying moment for him.

"I have to go to bed now, Katie Maurice, but I'll just tell you before I go that we had a most wonderful feast. We had roasted chickens and mashed potatoes, and Mrs. Thomas made *gravy*, which we poured all over everything. After that, we had the pudding, which was full of a lot of raisins, and of course eggs. And *then* Mr. Thomas came marching in like a soldier or knight or something, with a big bowl of *oranges*. We each got one. You cannot even begin to imagine how beautiful it tasted. Then Mrs. Thomas and I washed the dishes, and she looked so happy and talked so nicely to me — even while washing the dishes — that I could see that inside of her there is a really kind and gentle person. That secret and sort of *squashed* woman doesn't know how to get out very often, but it made me think that maybe my mother might have made that happen. Mrs. Thomas told me once that she was happy when she worked for my mother. But I never saw much sign of her being happy until Christmas Day. But it happened then, so now I know about the other person inside her. And also about this other new man inside Mr. Thomas. It's like living with four people instead of two! This is very confusing. But I'll have to admit that it's also very interesting.

"Good night, dear Katie Maurice. I'm off to bed now, with my cat and my bear."

But Anne had one more gift to open. When she went up-stairs, she opened it up. It was the picture of *The Blue Boy* that Miss Henderson had lent her. But now it was in a small, em-bossed, gold-coloured frame. Anne kissed it, hugged it very carefully, and then tucked it in under her bear. She gave *The Blue Boy* a name — Bernard. The bear was named Boris. And Lochinvar was Lochinvar.

FORTY-SIX

*A*nother Surprise Visit

New Year's Eve passed, and so did New Year's Day, but Mr. Thomas was still not drinking. Anne took note of all this, and she felt nudged by a small finger of hope. Would Mrs. Thomas now stop working for other people and come home? Could she go back to school? With Randolph gone and only Mildred to worry about, school had become like a kind of heaven in Anne's mind. Like the angels in Mr. Johnson's big book, she'd been chased out of heaven, and her desire to return grew stronger with each passing day.

But Mrs. Thomas wasn't going to be in a big hurry to give up those jobs. She had seen Mr. Thomas stop drinking before, and had tricked herself into feeling a lot of optimism. But time after time — she couldn't even begin to count how many times — he had started up again. And then the yelling and hitting had begun anew. Sometimes she tried to figure out what it was that made him want it, made him *need* it. But all her figuring came to nothing. However, she did know one thing for sure: she would never feel completely safe. So — no. She would not give up those jobs. If she did, the chances were good that within three weeks she'd need them back.

The winter that year was cold, with many snowfalls, so it was true, as Mrs. Thomas had to admit, that Mr. Thomas found a lot of work with his wagon and horses. Over a large area on both sides of Marysville, people became familiar with the jingling bells of his rig. He was getting to know a lot of people. And they liked him. His life was starting to add up.

But he had loved his job in Bolingbroke, and had had a lot of friends. However, one spiked drink had wrecked all that. Mr. Thomas was doomed to walk a tightrope. He could never be sure that he wouldn't fall off. And when he did, he took the whole family with him. Mrs. Thomas didn't want to do anything that might jiggle that wire. Anne's longing for school remained strong, but it wasn't until November of the following year that the longing turned into something different.

One Saturday morning of that particular fall, there was a rap at the front door. Mrs. Thomas was home, and she was seated in the kitchen rocking chair shelling some late peas. Anne was on her knees, scrubbing the floor. She sat back on her heels, full of eagerness. Miss Henderson was almost the only person who ever came to the front entrance. But when Mrs. Thomas opened the door, it wasn't Miss Henderson. It was Mr. Summers. The School Man.

Mr. Summers followed Mrs. Thomas into the kitchen. It was a cold day with no snow. The boys were upstairs, making a great deal of noise. He looked at Anne as she knelt on the floor, her face at first eager and then sad, the scrub brush in her hand, the bucket of water beside her. He said, "Hello, Anne," and then frowned. He didn't waste any time.

"Mrs. Thomas," he began, "according to our records Anne is eight years old, and has only attended school for a little less than three months. This is already November of the new school year. And it is my understanding that she has not yet appeared in the Marysville school. The teacher there — Miss Henderson — has indicated that she has an unusually quick mind — a *superior* mind, she said. Nova Scotia needs superior minds, Mrs. Thomas. Superior *educated* minds. Is there any good reason why Anne is not attending school?"

Mrs. Thomas sat down and took an uneasy refuge in the shelling of her peas. She needed a moment to decide what she was going to say, and how to say it. How to sound *educated*. Finally she spoke.

"Anne is an orphan," she said. "She is not a part of the Thomas family. We took her in when she was a mere baby, after her parents died. We've been caring for her and feeding and clothing her ever since. We are not rich people, so this has not always been easy. School supplies cost money. So do new shoes and other clothes. I work for five women in the town. I need her here. I have three little boys at home and one in school. His name is Horace."

"I know about Horace," said Mr. Summers. "He started school when he was underage. We checked on that but let it pass. Miss Henderson said she was willing to take him. Anne is *over*age. She should be in school." He hadn't smiled since he entered the house.

"She's not really my responsibility," said Mrs. Thomas. "She's not *mine*. She's not even adopted. We need the money."

"We've been aware that sometimes there have been — uh — *difficulties* with your husband's — er — *work*. But it's our understanding that at the present time, he has a rather successful cartage and odd-job business."

"But still ..." Mrs. Thomas was thinking about how many times Bert had lost jobs, or used his earnings for rum. It could happen again.

But Mr. Summers had very little mercy. "Miss Henderson has told me that Anne can use some of the books and other materials that belong to the school, if you agree to send her. And possibly we could start with three days a week. Could you keep two of your jobs and let three go? Or do one on Saturday?"

Anne sat on the floor, looking from Mr. Summers to Mrs. Thomas, and back again, as in a tennis match. She was scarcely breathing, and her heart was thumping in her chest like a broken drum.

"I'll have to think," stammered Mrs. Thomas. "I'll need to ask my husband. And speak to the ladies I work for. This is *hard. Very* hard."

Mr. Summer's frown was deeper, his mouth turned down, his forehead creased. "What would you be doing if you didn't have Anne?"

"*What?* What do you mean?"

"Who would be doing the work and looking after the boys while you were in Marysville working — if you didn't have Anne?"

Mrs. Thomas laid down the peapod she was working on. To her dismay, her hands were shaking. "Well ... I don't ... I guess ... I'm not sure ..." She stumbled along, and gave him no clear answer. Twenty-three years with Bert Thomas had roughed up her good diction. But she could usually speak well if she spoke slowly enough. But her careful language was deserting her. "We done good by her. Her clothes ... my girls had some nice dresses. They fit her fine. Shoes, too. We feed her lots. Her parents was thin."

Mr. Summers buttoned up his coat and prepared to leave. "I haven't required five days a week, Mrs. Thomas. Miss Henderson says she can do the work in three. I'll tell her that Anne will be at school three days a week from now on. Starting right away on Monday. If there are stormy days in the winter, she'll be expected on the fine ones. I'm afraid you'll have to arrange all that with your ladies."

He let himself out. Mrs. Thomas found herself incapable of rising. And also incapable of speaking to Anne. But that wasn't worrying Anne. Scrubbing hard at the mud spots on the floor, she was already on wings, preparing to fly. In her mind, she was packing her school bag, setting off through the woods and fields a half-hour before Horace so that she could be alone with the kind of joy she was already feeling. And she had two whole days in which to look forward to it.

$\mathscr{S}$chool and Other Things

Anne had risen from her bed one hour before anyone else in the family, dressing carefully and quickly, affixing Mrs. Archibald's blue ribbons to her meticulously braided pigtails. Then, although she had packed and repacked her book bag at least three times during the weekend, she checked it carefully — item by item — to make sure it contained everything she might need. Yes, it did.

Eating breakfast was difficult, because Anne was almost too excited to swallow. But she knew she needed strength for the long walk and for a day in which she was determined to do the best work she had ever done. She wanted to prove Miss Henderson absolutely right when she'd told Mr. Summers that she could do five days' work in three. She'd have to work really hard on her sums, but she was ready to do that. But she needed to have at least a little food before starting such a demanding day. She had to be sure that she wouldn't disappoint Miss Henderson. Because Miss Henderson — she was sure — was the person who had made all this happen. She cut a piece of cheese from a slab in the cold room beside the back door, and sliced through the big loaf of homemade bread that was on the kitchen counter. Lochinvar had followed her down from her bedroom, and was rubbing his head against her legs. She cut him a small cube of cheese, and fed it to him as she stroked his head. "Don't be lonely without me," she whispered, as she collected her own bread and cheese and wrapped it up for her journey. "I'm going to eat my breakfast on the way to school, because right now I'm in too big a hurry to eat. I'm scared Horace might come down and want to walk to school with me. I couldn't stand such a terrible thing happening on my very first day back at school. I want to be thinking happy thoughts all the time I'm walking. And I almost never think happy thoughts when I'm with Horace."

She put on her coat and hat and mittens, and gave Lochinvar a last, long pat. Then she closed the door quietly, and was gone.

The landscape was basically barren and cheerless, the November trees stripped of their leaves, the grazing fields full of beaten-down beige grass, the friendly cows shut away behind closed barn doors — without even any crows to enliven the grey fall skies. But none of that would trouble Anne.

The scenery didn't look bleak and colourless to her. She imagined things into what she saw — planting flowers that were still in her mind from last summer, making the grass green, putting a cover of bright red leaves on the maple trees. It had never looked more beautiful to her. She ate her bread and cheese with one bare hand, not even noticing how stiff and cold her fingers were. It tasted wonderful, and by now she was hungry and it was almost easy to swallow.

Anne walked along, remembering her very first day at school — the way it had been one of the most important days of her life, but one of the scariest. Mildred and Randolph had made fun of her, and most of the other children had followed their lead. She remembered standing by the fence with Sadie, trying to imagine that the laughter was the friendly kind — but knowing that it wasn't. However she also recalled — with a rush of happiness — how she'd learned to read four words on that very first day. She was all alone on that road, but Anne laughed right *out loud* when she thought about that.

But she wasn't scared of anything today. Randolph wouldn't be at the school, and she didn't *care* if any of the other children were mean to her. It didn't matter one bit. Sadie was there, and they could protect each other in the schoolyard. And inside the school, Miss Henderson would be at the front of the room, as strong as ten tigers, ready to save her from every disaster that might come her way.

And that was what the day was like. Mildred did try to make things difficult for Anne — making fun of her freckles, pulling nasty faces at her, telling everyone that Anne was making mistakes with her arithmetic. But Anne just held up her pointy little chin and pretended that she hadn't noticed what Mildred was trying to do. So it wasn't fun for Mildred anymore. Besides, she didn't have Randolph there to back her up. And when she saw how well Anne could read, Mildred started acting more worried than mean. For the rest of the day, her blond curls were bent low over her reader and over her slate, as she tried to make sure that the freckle-faced witch didn't become smarter than she was.

Sadie, of course, was wonderful. She knew that Anne might arrive on Monday morning, and her plain little face lit up with joy and excitement as soon as she saw Anne climbing the hill to the school. She ran down the hill to meet her, yelling, "Anne! Anne!" and then gave Anne the best hug that she'd had in a very long time.

"I brought you two molasses cookies!" exclaimed Sadie. "Mama gave me an extra one so you could have one for your long walk home. And Miss Henderson says we can sit together again. I've been sitting with Mildred for a whole year, and it made me hate coming to school. She keeps telling me how dumb I am. And how smart she is. You're smart, too, but you're not mean. So I don't mind. I know I'm dumb, but

Mama says that being nice is more important. But when you have to sit beside Mildred all day, you're not so sure. I don't have to do that anymore."

Anne's eyes filled with tears, but they didn't spill over. She wasn't sure if Sadie would understand that they were tears of joy, so she just swiped her sleeve across her face and held on to them.

She grabbed Sadie's hand and they walked up the hill together. "How are your dolls?" asked Anne, taking a bite out of one of the molasses cookies. She wasn't having any difficulty swallowing. Not even a little bit.

Going to school three days a week was so much better than never going to school *at all* that Anne felt only the smallest regret at having to miss the other two. She brought her books home with her, and as her reading improved more and more, she picked out poems from the readers and memorized them.

"Some of the other children call me a 'teacher's pet,'" confided Anne to Katie Maurice, "and say that she loves me best of all the others. They don't like that. But I don't care if they do or they don't. Maybe she does love me best. Well, I don't have anyone else to love me best — like a mother or a father or a twin sister, or the old Eliza before she started liking Roger best. So it's lovely if she loves me best. But, Katie Maurice, I'll tell you a secret. I think Miss Henderson loves me best of all the *children*, but she doesn't love me best of *everyone* in the world. I think she loves Mr. Johnson truly the *very* best. Every time I mention his name, she *blushes*. I asked Mrs. Thomas what you call it when people get red in the face. She told me that it's called *blushing*, and you do it when you're embarrassed about something or when you secretly *love* someone. I'm sure I don't embarrass her when I mention his name.

So she must *love* him. Isn't that romantic? I know what *roman-tic* means now, even though I haven't seen many romantic things in this house. The princes and princesses in your house are always doing romantic things, but that's what those princes and princesses are *for*. I thought it was very romantic when Mrs. Thomas cried over getting her fur muff at Christmas and then hugged Mr. Thomas. I just *loved* that. But beautiful things like that almost never happen around here. I love Noah and Lochinvar very deeply, but that's not what I mean by romantic. Romantic is things like bouquets of flowers to the loved one, and music playing, and exquisite garments (that's a romantic word meaning *clothes*), and strolling along in the moonlight, hand in hand, on a windy path below the castle's highest tower.

"But we were talking about Miss Henderson and the Word Man. Now, that *is* romantic. He's not an old man like I thought he was, so they can get married and have babies. It would be two schoolteachers getting married, just like my own mother and father. They'd never have terrible children like Horace and Edward, so I'd go to her house and help her with the diapers and tell them stories so she could have a little rest. I can hardly wait."

In January, the snow came, and in the third week the winds were so strong and the drifts so deep that no one in the Thomas household could get into Marysville. Mr. Thomas managed to shovel a path between the house and the barn so that he could get out there to milk the cow and clean up the floor in the stalls. Apart from that, no one went anywhere. The boys couldn't even get out to play in the snow. It was that deep.

With seven people in the house, it was noisy. But it was a peaceful noise — busy but without strife. Anne and Mrs.

Thomas went about their business of cleaning and cooking, and Mr. Thomas often fell asleep on the old sofa in the parlour, glad of a few days off from his work. Elsewhere in the house, the boys played games, running from room to room and doing a lot of yelling. But there was very little fighting. Even Horace seemed to be subdued by the snow — so deep that it came halfway up some of the windows. Sometimes Anne would read to them, and the four of them actually sat down on the floor and listened. Anne felt full of wonder. *This is what a family is supposed to be like.* It was hard for her to believe that she was so happy at home that she didn't even mind missing school for a few days.

That was before Friday of that week, when it was discovered that no one knew where Noah was. He was missing.

FORTY-EIGHT

*T*error

On Friday, just before the noon meal, Harry and Edward and Horace came bounding down the stairs. "Where's Noah?" Horace yelled. "We need a fourth person for our game, and we can't find him up here."

Anne left the table where she'd been kneading some bread dough for Mrs. Thomas, and wandered around the main floor, calling, "Noah! C'mon out! Stop hiding! The boys want you for a game." There was no answer.

Mr. Thomas left his position on the sofa and looked in all the corners and under the furniture. Noah was so small, and he loved crawling into things and under things. Bert checked the cellar door, trying not to think about those treacherous stairs into the basement. But the door was locked. The sooner the boys returned upstairs for their games, the better. So he hoped they'd hurry up and find him.

"Look in all the closets and under the beds upstairs," he told the boys.

But not under my mattress. Anne followed them upstairs to make sure that none of her treasures would be discovered. The four of them looked everywhere — in large boxes, in cupboards, in the biggest bureau drawers, under every chair, table and bed.

Anne was aware of a small nudge of fear in the centre of her chest. "He must be downstairs," she said, with a small frantic edge in her voice. "He must be hiding, trying to trick us."

There wasn't an inch of the downstairs that Anne didn't

cover. Mrs. Thomas went on with her cooking, so used to noise and games that she had no sense of urgency or fear. Mr. Thomas stood by — too tall to fit into the small spaces the children were climbing into, but searching every surface and corner with his eyes. He frowned. He hadn't realized that he cared all that much about Noah. He was so funny-looking, with the odd cast in his left eye and his broad nose. His hair was light brown and straight, always falling over his forehead. And so small. All his other children were so sturdy, and either beautiful or handsome. The boy must have inherited all his mother's background and none of his. Maybe he hadn't paid enough attention to him because he was so homely and weak. Suddenly, all those negative qualities made him seem extra endearing. Where *was* he? Well, thank heavens they didn't have to worry about him being outside.

Outside! Mr. Thomas rushed to the side door, where a little outside porch was always locked against possible trespassers or burglars. The key wasn't in the lock. He opened it. The door of the little porch opened inward, and it was ajar. Yanking it open through the snow that had drifted in, he looked outside. The sun was in his eyes, and at first it blinded him. Everything was so *white*, so terrifyingly bright. But finally, as his eyes adjusted to the light, he saw a small figure crouched against the lower porch step, almost covered with snow. It was Noah, surrounded by drifts of snow so high that there was no way he could have got through them. He must have fallen from the top step. And then waited. And waited. Mr. Thomas jumped down off the stoop and picked him up. He didn't dare look closely at him. He was afraid of what he might see. Noah wasn't crying or speaking. Oh, why hadn't he played with him more often, or even talked to him? He didn't even really *know* him. He slithered up the steps with Noah in his arms, twice almost falling. Once inside, ignoring the outside door, but closing the inside one against the cold and snow, he yelled, "Blankets! Blankets! Hurry!" He brought the little bundle into the kitchen, where Mrs. Thomas was standing, surprised and stricken in the centre of the room, her hand on her throat. Anne was rushing down the stairs, with two blankets trailing behind her. Snatching Noah from Mr. Thomas, she brushed the snow off him and laid him on the kitchen table. With lightning speed, she stripped the cold, wet clothes off his little body, and then wrapped him up in fold after fold of the first wool blanket. Then she picked him up and sat down in the big rocker, hauling up the second blanket to cover him on her lap. Then she started rocking.

Back and forth she rocked, murmuring over and over again, "Be alive! Be alive! Be alive!" His eyes were closed. Mrs. Thomas approached cautiously, and asked, in a raspy voice, "Is he *breathing*?"

Anne snapped back, "I don't know! I don't *want* to know!" Then, continuing to rock, she started to sob, the tears streaming down her contorted face. But she managed to speak, between convulsive breaths, "Why didn't we notice he was *gone*? What's *wrong* with all of us? Don't we realize he's *special*? Why wasn't I *watching*? Oh! I'll be angry at myself about this *forever*. Noah! *Do* something! *Say* something! Don't you *dare* die!"

Anne suddenly looked up at Mrs. Thomas. "Do you want to hold him? He's not *my* baby. He's *yours*."

"No," said Mrs. Thomas sadly. "He loves you best of everybody, and if you hold him maybe he'll feel something through your arms."

So Anne continued rocking the small bundle. After a while, there was a tiny sound — not much more than "Uh," and then Noah started to cough. Anne had never heard such a beautiful sound. Soon afterwards, he opened his strange eyes, gazed up at Anne, and produced a very weak smile. Everyone laughed with relief — even Horace — and decided that their worries were over.

But they weren't. Noah's coughing heralded a bad case of bronchitis, and his throat also became raw and sore. Mr. Thomas brought his crib out from his "room," and placed it in the big kitchen, close to the stove so that he'd be warm. Anne slept on the old sofa in the parlour so that she'd be nearby if he needed her. And he needed her often. He had frequent coughing fits, and whimpered, and each time Anne heard that sad little cry, she leapt off the sofa and rushed into the kitchen to make sure he was all right. And it seemed to her that his small forehead was hotter and hotter each time she felt it. *So he has a fever. A big fever. This is how my mother and father died.*

"He's so hot," Anne said to Mrs. Thomas in the morning. "And so *dry*. Why isn't he sweating?"

"Because that's how a fever is," said Mrs. Thomas. "The other boys are right healthy, but I seen my girls be sick like this oftentimes. If they started to sweat, I knew they'd be fine. But it can make you some scared when your child's skin is so hot."

Anne thought about her parents, and shut her eyes. After all, they *died*. And Noah was so *little*.

"Anne, dearie," said Mrs. Thomas, "you go on upstairs and try to get some sleep. I'll keep an eye on him."

Dearie. Anne looked at Mrs. Thomas in amazement. That was her other self leaking out of her again. But she only had room in her head for one thought right now. "Oh, Mrs. Thomas," she said. "That's right nice of you, but I know I'd never shut my eyes if I went up there. I'd be too far away in case ... anything ... happened. I'll go and try to sleep a bit on the sofa."

When Anne woke up it was four o'clock. She rose quickly and went into the kitchen. Mrs. Thomas was sitting on a straight kitchen chair beside Noah's crib, looking at him.

"He's still terrible hot," she said, "and his breathing sounds awful. Listen to it."

Anne was already listening. It sounded bubbly and thick, and the lids were low over his eyes. He didn't seem to be looking at anything.

"Oh, Mrs. Thomas," said Anne. "I feel so bad about being so deep in the pit of despair just because I couldn't go to school. I didn't know that the only important thing in the whole world was that my Noah — *your* Noah — was alive and well."

"I feel bad, too," said Mrs. Thomas, her eyes never leaving Noah's face. "Bert and I both feel bad. It was like we hardly knew Noah was *there*. He never made a fuss about anything, and he was so quiet. And he's so — oh, I don't know — almost *ugly*. I didn't even know I liked him. And now I'm close to thinking he's my favourite child. That's so crazy." Then she added, "And so awful."

"Where's Mr. Thomas?"

"He's out in the barn, cleaning out the stalls. He's too scared to stay in the kitchen. He's afraid Noah's gonna die before his very eyes. He says if that happens, he don't see how he can keep off the bottle any longer. He says he's been finding it terrible hard, even before this happened."

Suddenly Noah started to cough again — at first weakly, and then with an alarming force. It had a harsh, barking sound, and Mrs. Thomas put her hand to her forehead, exclaiming, "*Croup!* I'd recognize that sound anywhere. They say that a barking seal sounds exactly the same. Trudy had it when she was two when we lived in Bolingbroke. Bert had to hitch up the horse and fetch the doctor. He got there and made things right before she choked to death. But no one could get through to a doctor in this snow. Oh my God, Anne! What a terrible sound!"

But Anne didn't hear her. She was already halfway up the stairs. Croup! Ipecac! She repeated in her mind all the things she had to do. By the time she got back, even the other little boys were standing around Noah's crib, looking frightened. The cough was louder, stronger than ever. It was hard to believe he wasn't choking. Anne reached down and picked him up out of the crib, holding the blanket around him. Then she gave him the medicine in the exact way that Miss Henderson had instructed her to do. After that, she took him over to the rocking chair and — holding him close — rocked him back and forth until he was quiet.

That evening — long after everyone else was in bed, Anne got up from the sofa and went into the kitchen to check on Noah. An oil lamp had been left on, and a kettle of water was humming softly on the back of the stove, to keep the air moist. She could see that Noah was sleeping peacefully — his eyes closed, his little chest rising and falling. She felt his forehead. It was cool and damp.

Anne went back to the sofa, pulled the afghan up tight around her, closed her eyes, and slept until morning.

FORTY-NINE

ℬirthday Presents

Noah slowly recovered from his fever and was back to his usual good health by March. That had been a perfect ninth birthday present for Anne, and for the first time in several years, she didn't spend the week before her birthday wishing and wishing that someone would pay some attention to it. She had long ago given up reminding Mrs. Thomas that the day was coming. Anne had discovered that this either brought forth discouraging responses ("There are already too many birthdays in this house," or "We need to use our money for food, not parties," or "Getting a year older is nothing to celebrate") or was ignored. This year, however, Anne received three gifts. Mrs. Archibald gave her a set of new ribbons for her "beautiful hair" — bright green and very shiny. Anne wasn't sure which she loved more, the ribbons or the compliment. Miss Henderson and Mr. Johnson came to the Thomas house on the Sunday after her birthday, and brought two gifts. Miss Henderson's was a tiny little homemade purse containing two five-cent pieces. It was made of a soft pink fabric, and had two little pink buttons to keep it closed. Anne had told Miss Henderson how much she loved pink, and how sad it made her feel that she could never have a pink dress. "It would just make my red hair look all the awfuller," she had once said to her, "but it grieves my heart that this is so. Sometimes my longing for pinkness is so strong that I can feel a tightness in my chest." Well, Miss Henderson felt that a little pink purse — no bigger than Noah's hand — would be safe. She could keep it in her pocket if she wished, far away from her hair.

Anne thought that the purse was better than perfect, but Mr. Johnson's gift was even more amazing. He had extracted the insides from an egg, and had painted the shell with intricate designs and many colours. "I learned how to do this while I was in Europe, when I was younger. Maybe sometime I'll teach you how to do it."

No big celebration could have made Anne happier than she was with her three presents. They were really five gifts when you counted the two five-cent pieces. *Two*. She was *rich*. After Miss Henderson and Mr. Johnson left, Anne put on warm clothes and went down to her favourite spot behind the bare rhododendron bush, and sat by the frozen Pool of Mirrors. She needed to be alone so that she could think about how happy she was. Too much noise and too many people sometimes cluttered up Anne's thinking. She stayed down there for a long time, staring at the hill beyond the pond, gazing up at the Five Sisters, thinking how April and May would change everything she was looking at. Then she started up the hill to the house, in order to start preparing vegetables for the soup that Mrs. Thomas was going to make for supper.

Mr. Thomas looked out the window and saw Anne slowly walking up toward the back door. "We should of bought her a doll," he said to Mrs. Thomas.

Mrs. Thomas frowned. "Whatever would she do with a doll?"

"She wouldn't need to *do* anything with the doll. She could just *love* it. Look at the way she loves that bear I gave her. She even has a name for it. Girls like dolls. I feel bad that we never gave her one."

"Well, she's got the bear. I never cared much for dolls myself."

Or children, either. Mr. Thomas looked troubled, and fidgeted with the button on his shirt. *And Joanna sure got enough o' them. I wonder what she really does care for. Dancin', maybe. We could both do with more o' that. But it's too late now. No music. And besides, our feet and our hearts has got real slow and heavy. Well, she used to think Horace was perfect, all the while he was drivin' her crazy with his noise and mean ways. Now she seems to fancy Noah, ever since he did his dyin' act and then got hisself well. That's good. She got somethin'. And I got him, too. But I'm not sure what else I got. And I sure wish I'd bought Anne a doll for her birthday.*

Mr. Thomas got up and walked up and down the large kitchen, up and down the hall. Mrs. Thomas watched him, her eyes troubled. What was happening was familiar to her. Gloom. Guilty feelings. Restlessness. She knew what the next step might be. And he had the money for it.

"Maybe you'd like a strawberry pie for supper," she said. "With the soup."

"That would be some nice, Joanna. Thank you." Then he put on his hat and coat.

"I'll maybe go for a ride on Blackbird after supper. It'll still be light. I'll saddle her up. I need some air."

Blackbird was the black mare. Anne had named her. Mrs. Thomas watched him through the window as he went out to the barn. He was walking slowly, and his shoulders were hunched. Her thoughts were busy and her face uneasy as she mixed the pie dough and rolled it out. She was using her last jar of strawberry preserves, but if the strawberry pie did its work, it'd be worth it. *He said, "That would be some nice, Joanna. Thank you." That's new language for Bert. And all that rattling on about the doll. Anne never said she wanted a doll. How come he thinks he knows what she's hankering for? But he's got that look on. What's that fancy new word that Anne used last week — melancholy. Yes, that was it. She said that the teacher told her that some poets were melancholy. Then she told me what it meant. That's what he is right now. Doing all that silent thinking. And none of the thoughts good. All of them gloomy. And staring at the wall. He shouldn't of ever taken off his dancing shoes. He shouldn't of got married. Not to me, anyways. He's still some handsome. I like that. But he shoulda married some perky little piece of fluff that would prance around the kitchen and the bed and sing songs. But me — I was never a prancer, or a singer of songs, for that matter. I thought he'd turned a corner when he was so worried about Noah dying. And when he was so happy when he didn't. He plays with the boys a little bit now. But not much. And the light's gone right out of his eyes. Even his lids droop. Oh, I know the signs, I do. I don't like to think where he's going with that horse tonight. He says he needs some air. You can't fool me. Air isn't what he's wanting or needing right now.*

Anne was so happy with her ribbons and her purse and her money and her egg that she was attacking each carrot and potato with joy. She was unaware that the air around her was stirring.

Everyone enjoyed the pie. It was probably the best pie that Joanna had ever made. She poured the whole jar of strawberries into the shell, covered it with the second circle of dough, made the necessary slits, and frilled the edges with her thumb and index finger. She knew that before the week was out, she'd be needing those extra strawberries — for muffins, to top a pudding, or as a special treat on newly baked bread. But she just dumped the whole jarful in, without a moment's hesitation or thought. She was that desperate. When it came out of the oven, it looked like a huge golden flower. With a sudden unfamiliar trickle of tenderness, Mrs. Thomas said, "If I had a couple of candles, Anne, I'd stick them in and light them, even though your birthday was last week." Anne didn't care about the candles. She was perfectly happy the way she was. Mrs. Thomas didn't cut a piece of pie for herself. She wanted to be sure that Bert had an extra-large piece.

"You don't have any pie," said Anne.

"No," said Mrs. Thomas. "I'm not very hungry tonight." Which was perfectly true. When some people are worried, they eat an extra large amount, in order to feel better. When Mrs. Thomas was worried, her appetite deserted her entirely.

It was a long evening for Mrs. Thomas. Bert and his mare took off in the direction of Marysville directly after supper. The boys went to bed earlier than usual, and Anne disappeared into her own room soon afterwards. She'd given her gifts hurried and temporary hiding places as soon as Miss Henderson and Mr. Johnson had left, but she wanted to find places that were safer and more permanent. The ribbons and the little purse went under her mattress with her books and her precious pencil and her picture of *The Blue Boy*. But where could she put the egg — so fragile and so beautiful? She knew that Horace could demolish it with his thumb and index finger — and would very likely want to do exactly that. She certainly couldn't put *it* under the mattress. Or in her Treasure Box — which held no other treasures and had no lid. The windowsill was unthinkable. Nothing would be safe from the boys in her dresser drawer. Where? Where? She went downstairs and looked around the large back porch, where coats and hats and boots were hanging or stacked against the walls. Finally her eye hit on a pair of her old boots — far too small for her now, but definitely made for a girl. They weren't things that the boys would ever wear. She snatched them quickly and ran upstairs with them while Mrs. Thomas was looking out the front window.

Up in her room, Anne took the egg from out of her bureau drawer and put it carefully inside one of the boots. Then
she put the boots in a low cupboard that was built in the side
of the north wall, under the eaves. The egg would be safe
there. She knew it. She wished that she could put it out on
her dresser or on the windowsill so that she could look at it
anytime she wanted. But she knew that this could mean a
short life for the egg. She intended to keep it until she was an
old, old woman. Therefore, safety was her biggest concern.
And she was sure she'd achieved that. She picked up Lochinvar and gave him a particularly long hug. Then she went to
bed, sighing with pleasure over the perfection of this particular day. Tomorrow she'd tell Katie Maurice all about it.

FIFTY

*T*ragedy

Downstairs, Mrs. Thomas waited. She was in her night-clothes, and when Bert returned, she would race up the stairs, jump into bed, and pretend to be asleep. He wouldn't want to see her waiting up for him. It could make him angry if he'd been drinking. But she was determined to witness his return. In the bright moonlight, she'd be able to see if he was unsteady on his feet. Then she'd know if she needed to brace herself for the days ahead. She'd done this so many times. She knew the ground rules. But it was never easy.

This time it was harder. It had been a long time since Bert had had a drink. She'd grown almost used to a life that contained little anger or violence. She'd even been feeling *affection* for him. He seemed kinder, softer. He almost seemed to *like* her a little. As a result, she noticed something in herself changing. She'd been harbouring a sort of nervous hope. Maybe there could be a life ahead that was good. After the children all grew up and they were alone again — when there was less need for a lot of food to buy and cook, when there was less *work* — they might be like those old couples who sit on rocking chairs on their front verandas, rocking, rocking, and watching the world go by.

But she'd seen the signs. Sometimes she almost felt as though she were inside his head. She'd travelled this road so many, many times before. It was too familiar. It wasn't difficult for her to imagine where it might lead.

However, uneasy though she was, Mrs. Thomas was also tired. Against her better judgment, she fell asleep on the old sofa in the front parlour. At a quarter after three in the morning, she awoke to the sound of loud knocking on the front door.

The front door! The only people who ever came to the front door were Miss Henderson and Mr. Summers. But at this hour! Who could it be? And why? If it was Bert, he had to be very drunk indeed. Wide awake now, she approached the door cautiously and checked that it was securely locked. Then she stood there in her bare feet on the cold floor, waiting. Whoever it was would surely knock again or speak. Or go away. There was nothing in this house worth stealing. Surely everyone would know that. Or could it be that ...? Her fist flew to her mouth.

The knocking — the *banging* — started again, much louder than before. "Open up! Mrs. Thomas! Are you there? Wake up! Let me in!"

He knew her name — whoever he was.

"Who is it?" she asked, in as loud a voice as she could muster.

"Jackson Higgins. A friend of Bert's," came the reply. "Please! Open the door! I have bad news!"

Even at this point Joanna was conscious of Bert's warning that she must never open the door to a stranger. He'd be very angry if she did. But she opened it. And the man — someone she had never seen before — walked in, stomped the snow from his boots, and walked past her to the kitchen, where two oil lamps were burning brightly.

"Come in here where it's warm," he ordered. "And sit down."

Joanna went slowly into the kitchen, her heart thundering in her chest. Whatever this man was going to tell her, it wasn't just about a wild drinking spree. Bert must have done something really terrible this time. Maybe damaged some property — or even a *person*. Joanna wasn't worried about his losing jobs anymore. She was thinking about *jail*. Or worse. He'd hit her often enough when he'd been drinking. Suppose he'd done that to someone, and — She closed her mind off. She dared not think of such a thing. She sat down in the rocker and clasped her hands together. With a small corner of her mind, she noticed that her knuckles were white.

"Yes," she said. "Tell me."

He was sitting on one of the straight kitchen chairs.

"Mrs. Thomas," he said. "I'm sorry. I have real sad news to tell you."

"*What?*" she said, her voice rising. "What are you trying to tell me? *What?*"

He drew the chair closer to her, and sat down again. "There was an accident. The train. Carrying logs to the Bolingbroke mills."

She was almost screaming now. "I don't *care* what the train was carrying. What happened? What did Bert *do?*"

The man cleared his throat. This wasn't easy. He wished they'd sent somebody else. "He didn't *do* anything. Well, yes, I suppose ... No, he didn't do anything. He was crossing the tracks. Sort of dancing. The train hit him."

Joanna covered her mouth with the flat of her hand. She thought she might throw up. "Is he ...? Was he ...? Is he *all right?*" *No.* He said this was sad news. Bert couldn't be all right.

The man sighed. "No," he said in a very low, soft voice. "He's not all right, Mrs. Thomas ... Like I said, I'm terrible sorry. He's ... dead. He didn't have no chance. The train was coming some fast. Around a bend, too."

Joanna laid her head on the back of the rocker, her eyes closed. In her mind were shock, confusion, horror, and yes, *fear*. Already she was thinking, *What now? What now? What will become of us? There are seven of us. No. Six, now. What will happen to us? Today? Tomorrow? Who will look after us?*

Almost in a whisper, she said, "What will become of us?"

Mr. Higgins was relieved to hear her speak. He'd been alarmed by her inert stance, her head thrown back on the chair, her eyes closed. "There was people there what knew yer husband. A man what used to work with him in Bolingbroke. He's acquainted with all yer folks. As soon as the offices are open, he'll send telegrams. To both families. Yours and his. They'll find out fast."

Joanna closed her eyes again. Her hands were no longer clenched together with their white knuckles. They lay in her lap, limp, lifeless. *I can't cope. I can't even think about breakfast. The boys had best go to school. That'll just leave Noah here. Then what? Do I start packing stuff? This isn't our house. It belongs to the railway. Where do six people go when they have no home and no money? And Bert. Where will they bury him? Will there be a funeral? Who looks after those things?*

Without opening her eyes, she said, "Where is he?"

Mr. Higgins sighed. He'd been waiting for this question. "He's in Marysville. Down by the tracks. In the maintenance shed."

Suddenly Joanna could see his dark curly hair, his handsome face, his sturdy build. She felt dizzy. She opened her eyes.

"Mr. Higgins," she said. "There's a teapot on the back of the stove. From last night. It'll be extra strong. There's a cup on the table. And a bowl of sugar. I'd be much obliged if you'd bring me a cup of tea. With a lot of sugar. I have a feeling I might faint. And I got no time for that kind of foolishness today. The boys wake up at about six-thirty."

After he'd brought the tea, she said, "Will they bring him here?"

Another awful question. Mr. Higgins cleared his throat again. "No. No, I fancy not. It was ... a bad accident. Best not to bring him here. With the children and all. I reckon Bert'd like to be buried close to his own family. All of us — his friends from Marysville — has agreed to get a coffin made. A box. We'll pay. We talked this out down by the tracks. All of us that was at the party."

"The *party*?"

"Yes. We was close by and saw it all. He was still dancing when he tripped on the tracks. The other men send their respects. We're all right sorry for your troubles. And Mrs. Thomas ..."

"Yes. What?"

"Is there someone else in the house who can take care of you? I got to go. My wife will be half crazy with worry. But it frets me to leave you alone. You sure don't look too good."

Someone to take care of me?

Anne. She'd forgotten about Anne. Joanna sat up a little straighter. "Yes," she said. "There's someone here who can help me. You go. Your horse shouldn't be standing around in the cold. Tell the men I'm much obliged. For ... you know ... the box and all. I'm right grateful."

After Mr. Higgins had gone, Joanna continued to sit in the rocking chair. Waiting. Waiting for Anne to get up.

FIFTY-ONE

The Downside of Death

Anne always rose from her bed long before the rest of the family — even before Mr. Thomas, who needed to leave the barn by eight. Anne got up this early in order to avoid having to walk to school with the boys. She loved that walk through the forest and beside the fields and barns. She could do so much thinking and imagining when she was alone, with no noise or activity to interfere with her thoughts. She could even talk out loud. Horace wasn't the only problem anymore. Edward and Harry went to school now, too. With them along, there was no way for her to dream her dreams. Even *enjoying* was impossible. Enjoying the few birds that had returned from the south, the drip-drip of melting snow, the closed barn door. It was easy to imagine the cacophony of birdsong, the instant arrival of green grass and blossoming crocuses, the barn door wide open, the big field full of cows. In her mind she could mount one of the cows from the top of the fence and ride her bareback all over that luscious hill, stroking her warm side, leaning forward to nuzzle her beautiful head. There might be that grey cat, stalking mice, jumping through the grass, walking between the cows' legs. The boys even threw stones at the cows; they clapped their hands to scare the birds. No. She refused to walk with them. Better to rise a whole hour early and do the walk on her own.

So, shortly after five-thirty, Anne rose from her bed. It was Monday — her favourite morning. Three whole days of school stretched ahead of her. And it was March. Spring was coming. Well, not *soon*. But it was on its way. What's more, yesterday had been an almost perfect day. She could think about it and relive it during her long walk to Marysville — the visit from Miss Henderson and Mr. Johnson, the beautiful egg, the little pink purse, the strawberry pie for supper, hiding the egg in her boot, feeling that all her treasures were safe. They had been given a poem to memorize last Wednesday. She had read it and reread it on the weekend, and she had learned it completely "by heart." She hoped Miss Henderson would ask her to recite it. She'd practise that during her walk to school, too. It was called "The Wreck of the Hesperus," and like so many of the poems in the readers, it was about dying. But somehow or other, the poets had a way of making death both awful and beautiful. Mr. Longfellow, who wrote this poem, certainly knew how to do that. Anne recited the first verse as she put on her warm clothes for her journey to Marysville.

Last week, Anne had read part of the poem to Katie Maurice. Before she started to read it, she explained it all. "This is so sad but so romantic," she said. "A big storm comes up, and the little daughter is very frightened. But her father says not to worry. He'll lash her — which means tie her — to the mast to keep her safe, because it would be very easy for a tiny child to slide off the wet decks and be drowned. He wraps her in his own coat and fastens her tight to the mast. Then, of course, the ferocious storm gets worse and worse, and the whole crew is swept off the ship into the sea. Listen to this, Katie Maurice:

> The breakers were right beneath her bows,
> She drifted a dreary wreck,
> And a whooping billow swept the crew
> Like icicles from her deck.

Imagine, Katie Maurice! '*Like icicles.*' Frozen and stiff. And of course the small maiden perishes when the ship is blown up on the shore, and a fisherman finds her the next day. I cried when Miss Henderson first read this poem to us. But now I'm overwhelmed by the beauty of it all. Mr. Johnson taught me the word *overwhelmed* last week, because he said I seem to be constantly overwhelmed by both joy and sorrow. But he did say that it was a good way to be if it happened to be joy that was overwhelming me."

Anne was now ready for the day. She came down the stairs, carrying her school bag. She was quietly whispering the last verse of the poem.

Mrs. Thomas was in the kitchen! She was never there when Anne came down on school mornings to prepare her breakfast. And she was just *sitting there*, watching her.

"Anne," said Mrs. Thomas. "Sit down. And put your school bag on the hall table. You won't be needing it today."

Anne held on extra tight to her school bag. What did she mean? The School Man had said she *had* to go to school. Three days a week. And Mrs. Thomas had to do her work in Marysville on other days.

Anne stood very still. She did *not* sit down.

"Why?" she said.

Mrs. Thomas didn't approach her reply with any mercy. "Because Mr. Thomas is dead. He was killed last night by a train."

Anne had actually dropped to the floor, and was staring now at Mrs. Thomas, her eyes large and stricken. Then she started to cry — slowly and quietly at first, but then with wild sobs and moans.

Mrs. Thomas sat silently for a while, letting Anne cry. Then she started to speak. Anne held in her sobs and listened.

"I'm awful weak, Anne. I feel like if I stood up I'd fall right over. Like you did. I don't know what to do. A man came and told me about it all, banging on the front door. There was a party, so lots of people saw it. Some men will build a box and put him in it. So he can be buried near his own home. In Bolingbroke. It's best the boys go back to school. We need them out of the way, 'cause we got lots to do. Packing. Getting ready to move."

"*Packing? Moving?*"

"Yes. It's not our house. Trouble is, we got no place to go. I'm right frantic. I got no idea what to do. I feel limp like a damp rag."

"I liked him," said Anne. "After I got over hating him for taking school away from me, I almost loved him. Maybe I did. That Christmas when he did all the wonderful things. My bear. The oranges."

Then Anne started to cry again — quietly this time, with long agonized sobs and tears streaming down her face. But Mrs. Thomas continued to speak.

"They're telling people. The men who were at the party are doing that. They'll come. Then we'll know what to do. But no matter what, we got to pack."

Anne stopped crying. "*Who*'ll come?"

"Our families. *My* family. *Bert*'s family."

"It's not like the poems in the Royal Readers," said Anne slowly.

"What?"

"The readers are full of stories about dying. Dying children. Dying dogs. Dying sailors. The writers are in love with shipwrecks and terrible *disasters*. And they make it sound very tragic ... but also ... wonderful. I don't know how they do it. Or *why* they do it. They don't talk about being an unwanted orphan, or having red hair, or not being able to go to school, or not knowing where you're going to live after the man gets killed by a train. They make death sound beautiful, just because the lines rhyme and the poet puts his words together right. But it's not *really* like that. What's so beautiful about being put in a box and sent to Bolingbroke? And what will happen to Blackbird and the white charger and to our cow? How do we pack when we don't even know where we're going? And Lochinvar? Will he come with us? Will he be all right? Oh, Mrs. Thomas. I feel like I want to be one of those sailors in the poem — swept off the boat into the raging ocean — to die forevermore."

Anne remained on the floor, her face buried in her hands. "I'm mad, too. Why did he go to that *party*? He must have known when the trains come and go in the nighttime. Why did he have to do anything that *stupid*? I can't *stand* it!"

Mrs. Thomas sighed. She felt neither compassion nor irritation. She just felt a kind of hollow emptiness. "You *have* to stand it," she said wearily. "I can hear the boys stirring. They'll need some breakfast. Then I got to tell them about Bert. After that, I hope they go to school. I can't have them underfoot while we're packing. I told Mr. Higgins that you'd help me. Anne, you got to do that. I feel like I can't even stand up."

Anne wasn't crying any longer. "I don't feel so good about standing up myself, Mrs. Thomas. I'd like someone to be helping *me*. Yes, I'll help you. But sometime I hope I get a chance to be young before I get too old to enjoy it."

But Anne didn't have a chance to say anything else. All four boys were suddenly in the kitchen, and Anne discovered that she was making breakfast for them. Mrs. Thomas continued sitting in the rocker, staring at the wall, wondering what to say to the boys about their father's death.

FIFTY-TWO

A Sad Conversation

Monday passed, and so did the following day. On Tuesday evening, after the four boys and an exhausted Mrs. Thomas had gone to bed, Anne crept downstairs to the place where the china cabinet stood, and had a long conversation with Katie Maurice.

"Oh, my dear, dear friend," she began. "There have been many sad nights in my life, but this one may be the very saddest of them all. Mr. Thomas killed! And Mrs. Thomas getting around like she was walking in her sleep. But not crying. Didn't she like him even a little? I know he hit her and yelled at her when he was drunk. But other times I could see him trying so hard to be good. He was a sad and suffering man. And he liked me. So now there's no one left to love except you and Noah and dear soft Lochinvar. Maybe Mrs. Thomas *likes* me a little. I suppose that's *something*, but not much use to me now. Besides, she never *says* she likes me.

"Let me tell you about today. They all came. Mrs. Thomas's parents, the Harrigans, came first. Her mother said bad things and made Mrs. Thomas cry — at *last*. Mrs. Harrigan said, 'We knew that Bert was no good from the very day of your wedding. Dancing with other women, and drinking too much. And never fixed that freezing shell of a house. That's why we never came calling. Liquor and yelling every time we came. And the children all taking after him. Too handsome and beautiful for their own good, but low class and selfish. Eliza was nice enough, but the rest were trash. Didn't even know how to speak right. For certain those boys are going to be carbon copies of his own self. And there he goes and gets himself killed on the railway tracks — *dancing* onto the tracks, if what I hear is correct — of all the dumb things. After he'd worked for the railway for the most of his life, you'd think he'd have the sense to keep off the tracks when a train is coming. But no. Brains were never his strong point. So he leaves his wife and sons with no home and no money. It makes me some sick to think about it.'

"Katie Maurice, she went on and on, and said other mean things. It was awful to listen to. Then she said, 'If you think me and your father are going to step forward and take you all in, you can think again. I'm only fifty-nine and I got some living still to do. I sure got no intentions of spending that time looking after someone else's family.' After that, she and her husband got up from the parlour sofa and went back to Bolingbroke.

"Then the other family came. Mr. Thomas's mother and father and three of his brothers. The men all sat around and stared at their feet, but the mother had lots to say. She started right in by saying, 'We heard right quick yesterday that that woman won't take even one of your sons into her cheerless, tidy house. And we was told that she said things about Bert that was altogether terrible — and him not dead for even six hours when she said them. Shame on her! And it's not like he got any great prize hisself when he was wed. Forgive me for sayin' it, but Joanna didn't exactly set the male population o' Bolingbroke afire at that time. Never mind, we ain't mean, like some. We knows our duty. Havin' five extra mouths to feed don't fill me with any tremblin' shivers of joy. But you can come. It ain't fancy, but we got a big house. I had a lot o' children, and they's all grown up and gone. We got space.

Joanna, you can do scrubbin' 'n' such in the town to bring some cash for us, and you can work for me on the weekends. There'll be lots o' cleanin' 'n' cookin' for you t' do.' "

Anne stopped talking and sat down on the floor. Katie Maurice sat down, too. "Now listen hard to the next part. I have to sit down while I tell it. It makes me shocked and sad and scared. She said, "We'll take the horses and the cow and all the furniture. The boys took some of ours when they got married, so the house could use some extra stuff. It's kinda sparse. I saw that china cabinet in the hall. It will look real nice in the parlour. We'll take everything. What we don't use, we'll burn. My boys brought a big wagon. And we can use yours. It won't take more 'n two trips.'"

Anne shot Katie Maurice an agonized look. "So look where you're going. You're going to live with that awful woman who didn't say one single kind word about her dead son."

Anne put her head in her hands. With her head still bowed, she continued to speak. "But there's much more awful news to come. You maybe thought that I could walk through that terrible woman's parlour from time to time and have a little talk with you. Listen carefully, Katie Maurice. I have worse things to tell you. Worse, worse, worse."

Anne was now crying, and it was hard for her to get the words out. "Then that woman, that Bert's mother person, said, 'Yes, I'll be real generous and take in Bert's widow and his four sons — even the one that don't look like he belongs t' him — but I'm sure not goin' t' give house space t' that witchy red-headed girl you been feedin' for nine years. No, siree! Someone else can jump forward and offer t' take her in. She ain't no prize, but Joanna says she can clean good, and help with the cookin'. One o' the ladies around here might find her useful. I don't care if she's useful. She weren't Bert's child, so she ain't gonna be no child o' mine. I don't want her and I won't take her.'

"Those were her very words, Katie Maurice. They are deeply engraved on my mind. It would be torture to live with that woman, and you'll have to do it. But it still would have been nice to hear that she wanted me.

"By then, there were quite a few other people there — men who knew Mr. Thomas, or their wives. Not one of them asked if they could have me. Finally, a woman spoke up. 'I know a woman from up river — name of Hammond — who could maybe use her. She's got two sets of twins and is often tired. No wonder.' She turned to Joanna. 'You still got two days here. I'll see if someone's going up her way. Maybe her husband could come get the Anne girl. It's a bit of a long ways off for any of us to take her. Otherwise, I guess we could try to get her in at the orphanage.' "

Anne choked on the last word. For her entire orphaned life, this had been her biggest fear — to be sent to an orphan asylum. She had so often asked herself what went on in those scary places, with all those children squashed together under one roof. She was thinking about that right now, as she sat on the floor. *Imagine not having even a closet of your own to sleep in. With nowhere to go to be alone to talk to yourself and think and imagine. Washing dishes for maybe seventy-five grown-ups and children. And probably lots of mean orphans who would be like Randolph and Mildred. Fifty beds all lined up in rows, in the biggest room that anyone has ever seen. And no place at all to keep your treasures. Where would I put my Blue Boy picture, my bear, my little pink purse, my beautiful egg. Oh, my fear of all of this is overwhelming. Please let that Mrs. Hammond woman come and take me away before some stern orphan asylum person scoops me up and drags me away to the orphanage.*

Please? Who was she talking to? Katie Maurice couldn't

save her. So Anne had to ask herself who she was talking to. Then she remembered. One of the women who had come to the house today — a kind-faced lady — had said to her, "I'd take you, but I got too small a house. My own children fills the rooms right up. And uses all the beds. You look right scared. Try praying that everything will be lovely for you."

"Praying?" Anne had asked. "Who to?"

"To God, of course," said the lady.

"God?"

"Yes. Your Heavenly Father."

Oh. The big person who had chased all of Mr. Johnson's angels out of heaven. There was talk about that in the reader, too. The God person. All right, she'd try.

The kindly woman added one more thing. "Don't forget to say please."

So Anne tried out her first prayer. She did it right there on the floor, in front of Katie Maurice. She said, "Good evening, God, whoever you are. Life is hard for me right now. If you're smart enough to fix things for me, you must know about the orphanage. And how they are going to make me go there if the lady with the twins doesn't come to collect me. The twins are all little, even though there are two sets, so I might like them. They couldn't — even if they tried — be as bad as Horace and Edward and Harry. It's too late to save Katie Maurice for me, and anyway, try as I will, I can't imagine how you'd do it. It will be hard enough trying to figure out how to save *The Blue Boy* and my pink purse and the beautiful egg and Lochinvar and the bear called Boris that poor dead Mr. Thomas gave me. But maybe you could try to do that for me. I forgot to say please, so here I am saying it. *Please*. But most of all, please make Mrs. Hammond come and take me away. Or Mr. Hammond. Maybe his wife can't leave the twins, there being so many of them. And please make it nicer than living here. *Easier*. Maybe you may think that's too much to ask, but I'm asking it anyway. Please make Mrs. Hammond cheerful and kind, and see if you can maybe even make her love me a little. And being as my dear Lochinvar will be gone from me, it would be nice, also, if the Hammonds could have a cat. I could talk to him or her, and I'll need that now that Katie Maurice is going to leave me. I hope that's not too much to ask. I probably should be careful how much I ask for. You did chase all those angels out of heaven, so I do know that there are things you just absolutely won't put up with. So I hope this prayer suits you fine, and doesn't make you cross. Please and thank you and good night."

Then Anne rose, and pressed her face against the glass door of the china cabinet. "Goodbye, Katie Maurice. Thank you for being here for me to talk to and love for all the years of my life." But no one who was looking on could have heard what Anne was saying. She was crying too hard. However, she knew that Katie Maurice heard and understood every single word.

$\mathcal{M}$rs. Hammond Comes

Mr. Hammond didn't come to the Thomas house. Mrs. Hammond came herself. She left twenty-four bottles of milk for Mr. Hammond to use in case she got held up by anything. After all, it was still only March. A big windstorm could push the buggy right off the road; or there could be a blizzard. In March, you just never knew. But she wanted to see this girl child who they told her was good at working in the kitchen and at the scrub board. Either one would be nice. She wanted to see her with her own eyes before she moved into her house and became another mouth to feed. And she had to hear with her own ears what Mrs. Thomas might say about her. A woman needed to do those things herself. Besides, it would be almost a full day off. Maybe more, if she got held up. Well, twenty-four bottles would be enough.

A full day off! Mrs. Hammond hadn't had even a quarter of a day off since that first set of twins had been born. Or a full night's sleep. She didn't think that anyone could be as tired as she felt most of the time. A day of sitting behind that horse might even make her feel a little bit *rested*. She could just look at the trees and fields, and maybe doze off from time to time. The horse would know what to do. A road was a road, no matter how bumpy or rough. No way would that horse just up and walk into the woods. Yes, she might be able to do quite a lot of sleeping. Then there'd be tea and cake at the Thomas house. There was always tea and sweet things at houses of mourning. That poor woman. Four boys and a dead husband.

And she'd heard he was very handsome. But a drunk. Well, her own husband wasn't handsome — straight hair, and not very tall — but he was quiet and steady. And didn't drink. He wouldn't be one to dance onto the railway tracks and into the path of an oncoming train.

Mrs. Hammond thought about Kendrick as she drove along. *He's even kind. But a little bit boring.* She thought back to when she met him at her cousin's wedding — in Maine, where she used to live. He'd danced so many dances with her and seemed to love her curly hair so much. Until then, she'd always thought that her hair was just extreme back luck. But — and she had to chuckle a bit to think of it — if someone pays that much attention to you, it sort of turns your head. And when he said he was a *lumberman*, and then asked her to marry him, she said yes so quickly that she surprised even herself. There'd be tea parties and a fine house and a life that would be much more exciting than her own. Her parents prided themselves on being well educated, but they never had any money. Not for anything you'd call a luxury. And it wouldn't be far from home. New England and Nova Scotia had always been like first cousins. There'd be a lot of travelling back and forth. And Nova Scotia looked intriguing on the map. So much sea all around it, with nothing but a little neck tying it to the mainland of Canada.

Then Kendrick brought her up to Nova Scotia, and put her in the middle of a dense forest, twenty miles from even a whiff of the sea. Their house looked like a barn, with windows.

"I made it," he'd announced proudly.

"It's so big," she said.

He smiled and squeezed her arm. "We'll fill it."

"With what?" she asked.

"You'll see," he said.

She'd been doing so much thinking and remembering that she didn't realize how far she'd travelled. Just before the last bend in the road, she thought about Kendrick's work as a "lumberman." He cut down trees, and made logs and boards in his small mill on the edge of a nearby river. He was good at making things with wood — chairs, tables, cupboards — and liked doing it. But mostly all he did was saw and chop. That's all he had time for.

She recognized the Thomas house from the directions she'd received. She was sorry she'd arrived so quickly. The ride had been so peaceful. No crying babies. No diapers to wash. She even had a nice little sleep. Now she'd have to meet this nine-year-old girl and decide if she'd be useful, or if she'd be more trouble than she was worth. Decisions! She hated them. Even this small one was making her feel anxious again. She'd been prone to worries and fears ever since her first child had been born. That happened to some women, and the doctor — who'd come for the last birthing time — said there wasn't a thing you could do about it. "Try to get out more," he'd said. *Out? Where? Walk a mile in both directions, and you wouldn't find anything but trees. I can look at them just as well from the kitchen window. And what do I do with all those children and babies when I'm out?*

Mrs. Hammond knocked on the door. A thin little girl answered. The first thing she saw was brilliantly red hair and pigtails, and a lot of freckles. But when the little girl's face lit up with joy, all Mrs. Hammond could see was her dazzling smile. "You *came!*" exclaimed the child.

Mrs. Thomas came to the door, looking even more wilted than usual. "Mrs. Hammond?" she asked.

"Yes, I'm Charlotte Hammond." In her girlhood, her friends had called her Lottie, but there was no one close enough to her house to call her anything at all. And even

Kendrick hadn't called her anything but Mother, ever since the moment his first child had been put in his arms.

"Excuse me," said Anne. "I think the potatoes are boiling over." And she rushed to the stove to do something about it. Charlotte Hammond watched all this with great interest. When Anne took a cup out of the dishpan, dried it, filled it with tea, and brought it to her, she was even more interested. "Do your twins look alike?" asked Anne carefully.

"Two do, and two don't," said Mrs. Hammond, settling into the rocking chair.

"Is it hard to tell the difference with the ones that do?"

"Yes. It is. They're both boys. One has a small mole behind his left ear. Sometimes I have to look."

"Maybe you could cut their hair differently, to make it easier," said Anne, as she spooned out some soup for Noah, and kissed him on the forehead.

"Well, at the moment, they don't have enough hair to cut." Mrs. Hammond found herself smiling.

Anne couldn't wait any longer. "Have you come for me?" she asked.

Mrs. Hammond's decision about this was as swift as the one that followed Kendrick's proposal. "Yes," she said. Gratefully, she sipped her tea.

Anne hugged herself. The china cabinet and Katie Maurice had departed that morning with the first load. Anne had been a bundle of jittery nerves ever since. She'd tried not to think about either Mrs. Hammond or the orphanage, but it was impossible not to think of either one or the other. One spelled *hope*. The other one — *doom*. Now Mrs. Hammond was here, and she'd been rescued. She felt almost calm.

It was also a comfort to know that Lochinvar was going to a good home. The previous evening, a farm lady from up the road had arrived and said, "I don't know if I should ask, but if nobody wants that big orange cat I sure would like to have him. I been admirin' him ever since he first started prowlin' around my woods a few years back. Oftentimes I fed him real cream from my cow. I could pick him up tomorrow afternoon in the buggy." Anne's feelings had been a mixture of sorrow and relief.

It didn't take Anne long to get ready. The day before, Mrs. Thomas had given her an old battered tin suitcase to put her things in, and she had done most of her packing last night. The bag was roomier that she'd expected, and she was even able to put in the little boot with the egg in its toe. She had very few clothes, but she put in an old dress of Trudy's, just in case it might fit her next year. She'd found it one day in an old trunk, when Mrs. Thomas had sent her up to find a cook-book she thought she'd brought from Bolingbroke. She told Anne she could keep it until she was big enough for it to fit her. It was prettier than her own drab clothes — a deep blue, with three small metal buttons below the little lace collar, and with a bit of a flounce around the hem. She could hardly wait to be the right size for it. She often shut her eyes and imag-ined herself in that dress, going to visit the Queen. She would look deep into her eyes, pick up the edges of the wide skirt, and curtsy deeply. The Queen would smile at her, adjusting her jewelled crown ever so slightly, and say, "My! What a beautiful dress!"

Last evening, Anne had placed her books, including her precious dictionary, among the folds of the dress, and positioned *The Blue Boy* and her slate very carefully among the other pieces of clothing so that nothing would break. She now put her bear in an empty corner of the case, giving him a little pat as she did so, and placed the small pink purse inside one of the sleeves of Trudy's dress. She looked around the room carefully and lifted the mattress one more time. She had left nothing behind. She took one last look out the window at her beloved Five Sisters and the Pool of Mirrors, the hill and the bare rhododendron bush. Lochinvar had followed her upstairs. She picked him up and held him close, burying her face in his fur. She felt a constriction in her throat and a burning sensation behind her eyes. But she was determined not to cry. She still had Noah to say goodbye to, and if she started to cry before she did that, she felt as though she would never stop. She had to cling to the one good thing that had happened. *Mrs. Hammond had come. There would be no orphanage.*

FIFTY-FOUR

*G*oodbyes

So as Anne came down the stairs, she was actually able to smile. Perhaps she'd be able to give Noah his goodbye hug without howling with grief. But before any of that happened, there was a rap at the front door. There had been many calls since Mr. Thomas's death, most of them from people that Mrs. Thomas was meeting for the first time. But today the callers were Miss Henderson and Mr. Johnson. Miss Henderson knew how much Anne loved pretty clothes. So she had been careful to wear a lovely mauve hat, trimmed with a crown of velvet violets, and a purple taffeta gown under her warm black coat. On the front placket of her dress was a long row of small pearl buttons, as well as a single one on the cuff of each sleeve. The purple dress and black coat were suitable for a house of mourning, but the hat was definitely for Anne. Mr. Johnson looked handsome and protective in a brown coat and gloves, his beard neatly trimmed, his expression tender.

Miss Henderson spoke first, "Mrs. Thomas, we're sorry about all your troubles. But we heard Anne might not be joining you in Bolingbroke. We've come to say goodbye to her."

Then it was that Anne knew it would be impossible not to cry. There was no hope of saying her goodbye to Noah with dry eyes. She'd tried to keep even one thought about school or Miss Henderson or Mr. Johnson from entering her head. But there they both were, right in front of her. Tears were already streaming down her face. But she was doing her crying quietly. Miss Henderson was able to talk to her. And Anne was able to hear.

"I'm sad you're leaving, Anne," she said. "I don't ever again expect to have a pupil quite like you — not ever. If I'm one day lucky enough to have a daughter, I don't know how I could manage to love her more than I love you." Then one of Miss Henderson's tears plopped down on Anne's nose, and she knew she couldn't talk anymore.

So it was Mr. Johnson's turn. "Anne, thank you for showing me again that words are important. Also that teaching is fun. And that forgiving is possible. You showed me all those things."

Mr. Johnson stopped talking long enough to clear his throat and to blow his nose. Then he continued.

"So this is a sad time for us. We don't want to see you go. But we have something we'd like to tell you — Miss Henderson and I. We hope you'll think it's good news. It's something we wanted you to know before you left."

Good news? Anne took a deep breath, wiped her eyes and face on her apron, and was able to stop crying.

"What?" said Anne. "What is the good news?"

Miss Henderson was smiling again. "Mr. Johnson and I are engaged to be married."

Anne shut her eyes and clasped her hands. "Oh!" she exclaimed. "That is almost the most exceedingly beautiful news I have ever heard. My two such favourite people in all the world — *married*! I could never hope for anything so perfect to happen. But *oh*!" Suddenly Anne's hand came up to her mouth, and her eyes filled with tears again.

"What's wrong, Anne?" Mr. Johnson held both her shoulders and looked into her eyes, waiting for her response.

"But I won't be here. I won't see the wedding. I won't be able to hold your babies. I won't have anywhere to go for eggs or words or hugs or lessons about Egypt and the pyramids. *I won't be here.*" Anne wept noisily into the palms of her hands.

Miss Henderson moved over and held her close. "Listen, Anne. Listen carefully. *We won't be here, either.* We're not getting married until July of next year. In the fall — *this year* — I'm going to the Normal School in Bolingbroke to take my teacher training and get a real teaching licence. Mr. Johnson will be teaching high school again — this time in Bolingbroke. He wouldn't be here to give you either eggs or words. And I wouldn't be here to teach school. If you were still here in the fall, we'd be gone. So dry your eyes, Anne." She took a small embroidered handkerchief out of her bag and wiped away Anne's tears. Then she slipped the hankie into a pocket in Anne's dress. "So it's not so terrible after all," she said. "And who knows but that sometime in the future, we may all live in the same place again. It could happen. And —"

"What? And *what?*" Anne was no longer crying.

"And I know — I just *know* — that whatever is ahead for you, you're going to have a wonderful life. I don't know how I know that, but I do. Maybe it's just that I have confidence that you'll *make* it happen."

Anne had always believed everything that Miss Henderson told her. She wasn't going to stop doing that *now*. She could feel most of her jitters and sorrows subsiding. Even when the two visitors gave her farewell gifts, she didn't even consider the possibility of crying. Mr. Johnson gave her a small dictionary — so small that it could fit in the pocket of her dress — just in case she found her big dictionary too huge and heavy to carry around all the time. Miss Henderson gave her a new set of yellow ribbons from Mrs. Archibald, and from herself, a copy of "The Lady of the Lake." It was small enough to fit in her other pocket, and had a bright red cover, with the title in gold letters. She could read it on the trip, in case Mrs. Hammond didn't want to talk. When her friends left, Anne was able to say goodbye with a real smile on her face. Miss Henderson and Mr. Johnson getting married! Anne felt sad and happy at the same time. And strangely peaceful.

Saying goodbye to Noah was harder. He was watching everything from a little chair in the corner of the kitchen. He was four years old now. When you're four, you know what's going on; and you know how to be unhappy. He was aware that his world was falling apart around him, and he was all closed up inside himself — unable to speak, unable to cry.

Mrs. Hammond had already stood up, indicating that it was time to leave. Anne knew that she couldn't put off the parting any longer. She walked over to Noah's little chair and drew up a footstool beside him.

"I'm not leaving because I want to leave," she said, remembering with an ever-fresh pang that Eliza had *chosen* to leave. "I love you very, very much."

Noah's face was still desolate, his eyes dry. He said nothing. Anne was suddenly stricken by the thought that she had nothing to give him, nothing he could keep and treasure and remember her by. She thought about how comforting it had been to receive the dictionary, the book of poetry, the yellow ribbons.

"I'll be right back," she said, and went over to where her metal suitcase was lying on the floor. Opening it, she looked inside, her mind still not made up. She placed the two books inside, and the ribbons. Then she knelt beside the case for several moments, thinking about its contents, knowing that it held the only treasures she owned. She touched the little bear in the corner, feeling his scratchy fur, running her fingers across his face, over his legs. He'd been almost as good as a doll for her — something to hug when she went to bed, something to remind her that Mr. Thomas liked her. Mr. Thomas — who was gone. She felt torn in two — longing to *give*, longing to *keep*. Abruptly she pulled the bear out of his corner and shut the lid of the case. Holding him close to her chest, she approached Noah and sat down on the stool again. Then she placed the bear on her knee, and spoke to Noah.

"My bear, Boris, is one of my most precious possessions. I love him a whole lot. You can't imagine how much. But I want you to have him, and he wants to stay with you. Hug him when you go to bed at night, and at the same time think about me and how much I love you and miss you."

Noah's dreary eyes slowly lit up, and he held out his arms for the bear. Then he got up from his little chair and crawled up onto Anne's lap, and threw his arms — bear and all — around her neck. In that position, he cried for several minutes, while Anne patted his back and smoothed his hair. When the storm had passed, Noah went back to his little chair, hugging the bear tight, and smiling a small sad smile.

Then came a brief goodbye to Mrs. Thomas. "Thank you, Mrs. Thomas," said Anne, "for saving me from going to the orphanage when I was three months old. Thank you for bringing me up by hand. And thank you for Eliza."

Mrs. Thomas was looking at Anne as she made this speech, wondering how she would ever survive without her help. She was also surprised to discover that she loved her — this strange child of the beloved Bertha Shirley. She would have liked to say, *Thank you, Anne, for all your years of work. I love you. I'm sorry I called you wicked so often. I wish you could come with us.* And Anne would have liked to hear that speech. But the words stuck in Mrs. Thomas's throat as tears gathered in her eyes. She couldn't even say goodbye. She gave Anne a brief hug, and kissed her on the cheek.

There was no one else at home. The empty wagon wasn't expected back until the following day. After Anne and Mrs. Hammond departed, Mrs. Thomas went over and sat on the footstool beside Noah, and cried out loud for a long, long time. Then she took Noah's hand and led him over to the rocker. She sat down, picked him up, placed him and the bear on her lap, and hugged both of them quietly as she rocked up and down, up and down, waiting for the rest of her life to begin.

FIFTY-FIVE

The Journey

Anne climbed up on the seat beside Mrs. Hammond and sat very straight. Her head was still full of everything she was leaving: the house, her little room, the Five Sisters, the Pool of Mirrors, Miss Henderson and Sadie and school, Mr. Johnson and his words and his angels and the pictures on his wall, Mr. Thomas and the three older boys, Eliza and cruel Roger, Mrs. Thomas and her strange ways, Lochinvar, and of course Noah. She wanted to put them all in a large box and keep them in some sort of memory place, where she could take them out and look at them as often as she wanted. But right at this moment, she wanted to put a lid on that box and keep it securely locked for a little while. She needed to look ahead rather than behind.

Even with the loss of her beloved bear and cat and the parting from Noah so fresh in her mind, Anne was almost immediately able to concentrate on the journey. The sun was shining in an almost cloudless sky, and it was an unusually warm day for March. Maybe this was a sign, an omen. *Omen* was one of the last words that Mr. Johnson had given to her. It was something that foretold something that would happen. It could be good, or it could be bad. Anne didn't find this hard to believe. Sometimes she had a strange feeling that something was going to happen. And then it would often come true. So the idea of an omen wasn't an unfamiliar idea for her. Was the fine day, the brilliance of the sun, the warmth, a collection of good omens? Maybe. Maybe not. But in any case, Anne was planning to enjoy this ride. She'd only had about five real rides in her whole nine years, and she was determined to enjoy this one.

As the buggy travelled along, they passed woods, fields, tiny gurgling streams, long views of a river, hills, large lakes, stretches of flatlands. Even without the green of later spring growth, Anne was thrilled by almost everything she looked at — a few newly arrived robins with their rusty breasts; the swift movement of the river, carrying great chunks of ice down to the sea; the flight of a lone heron over the flatlands; the stark forms of bare trees against the vivid blue sky. Something almost like pain filled her chest as she absorbed all the beauty surrounding her.

"I love all this," said Anne to the silent form beside her. "I've lived in the woods for so long, with only one pond and a hill to open up the sky. I love trees, but if they're too close together, I sometimes wish they'd lie down and give me some space. I saw the sea once — just once. It was so open — so wide and high. I don't suppose ... I wonder ... is there a chance that you might live beside a piece of the sea?"

Mrs. Hammond turned her head and looked at the lively little face beside her — a nose so perfect, a chin soft but determined, an expression so eager and hopeful.

She sighed. She, too, would have liked to live beside the sea. It had been a childhood dream of hers. After all, she had known that Nova Scotia was almost entirely surrounded by ocean — with beaches, cliffs, lovely little harbours, green islands. Well, dreams get squashed. She'd have to start squashing one of Anne's, right now.

"We live in the middle of the forest," she said, "in a big house, with stumps all around it. There's a small river nearby, but we can't see it."

So — another house in the woods. But Anne had also heard Mrs. Hammond mention "a big house." She knew she shouldn't ask this question so soon, but she suddenly felt she had to know right away.

"Are there a lot of rooms?" she asked.

"Yes."

"Will I ... have one of my own?" Babies cried a lot. She didn't want a pair of twins in her room.

"Yes," said Mrs. Hammond. "The rooms are pretty bare, but you can take one on the front. All we have for you is a mattress, but Kendrick will make you a bed next week. He can make anything out of wood. He built the house."

"He's a carpenter?"

"No. Not exactly. But he knows how to do those things. He's a *lumberman*." She said this word with a barely detectable tone of bitterness in her voice. "That means he cuts down trees. That's why there are stumps all around."

"What does he do with them?"

"Sometimes he takes the limbs off and then he puts them in the water and floats them down the river to a big mill farther down. Or he takes them to his tiny mill beside the river and makes boards. He sells the trees and he sells the boards."

Anne frowned. "I better not get fond of any particularly special tree. He might cut it down."

"Yes. He might."

"Which would be very sad. I get to love certain beautiful trees. They're almost like people to me. And I make up stories about them." Anne suddenly grabbed the sleeve of Mrs. Hammond's coat.

"Oh, look! *Look!* Over there, right beside that big rock! That huge spruce tree — so perfect from top to bottom, like a giant queen in a long green gown. I can just imagine that all those little bushes are her subjects who've come to pay deeply respectful homage. If that tree was beside your house, I'd never sleep a single wink at night for fear I'd wake up in the morning and see it lying on the ground, the dreadful murderous axe leaning up against its tragic stump. I'm glad that tree is here, in the wilderness, where it'll be safe. If I lived near it, I'd have to give it a name, like Queen Verdant. I looked up that word in my dictionary. It means 'abounding in green foliage.' *Abounding* means there's a lot of it. Like 'my face is abounding in freckles.' Do you have a mirror in your house? I'd love to have one in my room. I find I'm already fond of my room, even though I haven't seen it yet. I suppose I can't expect a mirror in my room, but I'd be *entirely* satisfied with just a very *tiny* one. I need to check my freckles often, in the fervent hope that they're either fading or gone. If I discovered that there weren't so many, I'd feel that there was some hope for me — not hope that I'd ever be beautiful, because I know that's absolutely impossible. But I'm only nine. It was last week that I turned nine, but of course there was no birthday cake, even though Mr. Thomas was still alive. Once I heard him say that he wished he'd got me a doll for Christmas instead of my bear. So I tried not to *expect* a doll for my birthday; still, I have a way of *hoping* for a lot of things. I guess he forgot. And then the train destroyed him. But about the mirror and being only nine — I feel that if my freckles start to fade or go away before I'm ten, there's a bit of a chance that I might have milk-white skin by the time I'm of marrying age. That's why I need a mirror — just to keep a record of my progress. And that's what I mean about hoping for a lot of things."

Mrs. Hammond listened to the stream of conversation issuing forth from the seat beside her. Did she talk like this all the time? Would that constant avalanche of talk be added to the nerve-wracking sound of crying babies? She sighed. She was so tired of being tired, so weary of weariness. But maybe Anne's help would make a difference to all that.

"What kind of work did you do for Mrs. Thomas?"

"Oh. Well, *everything*. I carried buckets of water, scrubbed the dirty diapers, cut up the vegetables for dinner, washed dishes, minded the three terrible boys and the one nice one. I don't expect your twins are terrible yet. They're too young. Even Horace was quite nice when he was a baby. But you may have noticed that babies, even when they're nice, are a lot of work."

"I've noticed," said Mrs. Hammond.

"So I expect that four children are quite a handful, even if they're babies."

"I have six children," said Mrs. Hammond.

There was a long pause before Anne spoke again.

Finally she said, "Six? Did I hear right? You have *six*?"

"Yes. I had two daughters before the first set of twins."

Anne thought about that. Some of the hope was seeping out of her. She completely missed a grove of birches that were almost identical to her Five Sisters.

"How old are they?"

"I almost forget. There are so many of them. But then I count back and I know. I was married in May, when I was nineteen. I had my first baby — Ella — in May of the following year. And Gertie the next year. As regular as clockwork I have a baby every May. Or two. And morning sickness every September and October. Sometimes November, too. By Christmas I'm all right. But tired. So tired. Bit by bit, I'm filling up Kendrick's house."

Anne was silent now, as they drove along. Six children! No wonder the woman was tired. Anne felt exhausted just thinking about it. The oldest — Ella — must be three, going on four. She'd be four in May. The other one, the Gertie one, must be two. And nothing nearby except a forest of endless trees.

"No neighbours?" asked Anne.

"No," said Mrs. Hammond. "Just an old lady who lives in a little cottage all by herself — down by the river, close to Kendrick's mill. But she'd better live forever."

"Why?"

"Because she's a midwife."

"What's that?"

"Someone who knows how to deliver babies."

"But you don't need her anymore. She can die if she wants to. You *have* your family. You *have* all your babies."

Mrs. Hammond looked at Anne carefully. Then she said, "Not quite."

Anne was puzzled. "Not quite? Not quite *what*?"

"Not quite *all*. I'm only twenty-four, Anne. Some women go on having babies till they're over forty."

"But this year? This May? Surely ..." Anne's voice trailed off.

"Another one."

Anne's heart was thumping in her chest. *Seven.* She was thinking about last night's prayer. "Please make it nicer ... *easier.*"

Anne knew she shouldn't ask this, but she did. "Does your husband drink a lot?"

"No," said Mrs. Hammond. "He's too busy."

"Do you have a cat?"

"Yes. Two. For mice. But we have to be careful. They're both very affectionate. They want to snuggle up to you all the time. They could smother a small baby."

Anne took in a long breath. Then she let it out slowly. No drinking. Two affectionate cats. It might all be possible. Not good. Not better than the Thomases. But possible.

Just then, they rounded a corner, and in the centre of a barren clearing — surrounded by tall trees — was a very large house. In front of it were probably twenty-five large stumps. There was nothing in that scene to send even the smallest shiver of joy up and down Anne's spine. As Mrs. Hammond brought the horse to a full stop, and as Anne stared at the wall of trees, she was doing some thinking:

Mr. Hammond must know about a path through those trees, because he has to go to the river and his mill. It might lead to other places. There might be a field out there, maybe, with cows in it. There might be a hill to roll down, or even just to look at. Not that there'll be much time for rolling and looking. But maybe in the afternoons, all six — and then seven — will have a nap. Then I can escape. I'm sure I can find a special place. There has to be one. I'll just keep looking till I find one.

Yes. Anne had a way of hoping for a lot of things.

FIFTY-SIX

Discoveries

Later on — for the rest of her life, in fact — Anne would re-member her first week at the Hammonds' home. They were met at the door by Mr. Hammond, who looked as though he had just returned from a particularly exhausting and bloody war. His face was a mask of anxiety, and the hand that held a bottle of milk was trembling. The bottom of his shirt was es-caping from his trousers, and there were sticky-finger marks all over the front of it. His sparse hair looked as though he'd been sleeping on it while standing on his head. In the back-ground was the sound of crying — obviously coming from multiple throats.

"I'm glad you're back," he said. He didn't even seem to no-tice that Anne was there. He didn't appear to be noticing much of anything. "I'm not used to doing this. I'm not good at it."

"I'm not sure it's a job anyone can be really good at," said Mrs. Hammond. Then she threw her coat over a nearby chair, and went over to a crib to pick up one of the crying babies. "You pick up the other one," she said to Anne. "Pat him on the back. He may have a bubble that needs to come up."

A great deal more than a bubble came up. But Anne had no way of wiping up the stream of supper that was rolling down the front of her coat. But at least both babies — both identi-cal babies — had stopped crying; although wailing could be heard from some far-off room on the main floor. Even though she was smelly and wet, Anne could see that this was a very nice baby. "About ten months old," she muttered. He was chubby, with lots of short curly hair. And Mrs. Hammond was holding one exactly like him.

"What?" said Mr. Hammond, who had just noticed that a total stranger was comforting one of his children.

"He must be about ten months old," said Anne. "Born in May. What's his name?"

Mr. Hammond looked tired enough to die. "I don't know," he said. "Look behind his ear. The right one."

"There's a mole," said Anne.

"Then it must be George," said Mr. Hammond. "Mother," he said to Mrs. Hammond, "I know it's late. But I had no time to get supper ready. I couldn't fit it in. Just a bit of food for the four babies. I hope you ate something at noon."

"I ate nothing at noon," said Mrs. Hammond. "Nothing was offered. I thought there'd be funeral fare."

"The funeral is next week in Bolingbroke. They took him there in a box." Anne was feeling ashamed on Mrs. Thomas's behalf. And on her own. A cup of tea wasn't much to have given Mrs. Hammond after her three hours of driving. They did have bread in the cupboard. And jam. But she'd been too busy thinking about leaving Noah and trying to reach a decision about the bear. *I was too stricken about too many sad things to think about food. And Mrs. Thomas was just sitting there on a rocking chair, totally useless.*

"Can you cut up carrots and potatoes, Anne? Do you know how? And how to put a pot of water on the stove to get it boiling?"

"Yes," said Anne. "Of *course* I know how to do all those things. But not while I'm holding a baby."

"Then put him down in the crib. If he cries, don't worry about it. Let him cry. The only way to look after everything and everybody in this house would be to do twenty-five things at the same time." In the meantime, she was getting the corned beef out of the cold box in the pantry.

George did cry. And then the other twins arrived in the kitchen whining. But their language had been slow in developing, so no one knew what they were whining about. Mr. Hammond was standing around looking helpless. Upstairs, Ella and Gertie were shrieking. One hoped it was with joy.

"Shall I go back to the mill?" asked Mr. Hammond hopefully.

"No time," said his wife. "Supper'll be ready in twenty minutes. Maybe you could go up and make sure that Gertie and Ella aren't murdering each other." All the way home, Mrs. Hammond had been looking forward to a nice hot meal that someone else had prepared. Well, it was not to be. But the Anne girl was proving useful. The vegetables were already cut up and the water boiling. And tomorrow she could help her carry pails of water from the well for the daily wash. With the baby inside her growing bigger — and kicking a lot — she was finding lugging those buckets hard on her back. Yes, it had been a good idea to get Anne. She was thin — almost skinny — but she was strong. Look at the way she'd picked up George — as easily as if he'd been a kitten. And fast. Mrs. Hammond knew she could never have cut up those vegetables that quickly. Not right now, when she was feeling so heavy and slow. But she wished it was quieter. When Anne hadn't been talking in the buggy, it had been so lovely and *silent*. With one baby crying, two whining, and Gertie and Ella shrieking, there was no peace anywhere. And just wait till May, when the new baby came. Never a full night's sleep for six months. Mrs. Hammond closed her eyes. Just thinking about it made her physically dizzy.

"You all right?" asked Anne, as she cleaned off the front of her coat.

"Yes," said Mrs. Hammond. "I was just thinking about May."

Which is exactly what Anne had been thinking about.

During that week, Anne learned just about everything there was to know about her new home. She discovered that she usually had almost one free hour each day, and she spent the first four or five of them exploring. By the end of the week she knew all about the eight bedrooms in the house — what was in them, who slept in them. Her own looked out on the front yard and the stumps. This made her homesick for her old room, with its view of the Five Sisters and the Pool of Mirrors. The room itself was very bare, with just a mattress on the floor, and her own hooked rug, which she'd tucked under her arm and brought with her. That was all. Mr. Hammond said that he'd almost finished making her bed, and that when he had a chance he'd make her a little table for her lamp. Then she could read at night — if she could stay awake that long. Getting four babies and two children up in the morning was hard. Getting them cleaned up and ready for bed was harder. In between, there was the daily wash, which she soon discovered required thirteen buckets of water. There was also helping with the preparation of three meals, the hanging up of the laundry and the removing of it. There were a lot of dishes to wash, bottles to be heated, floors to be swept and sometimes scrubbed, babies to comfort and feed. No, there might not be much energy left for reading after she went to bed.

But Anne missed Katie Maurice. She longed for someone to talk to. On the ride to the Hammonds' house, Anne had thought that she might be able to have nice little talks with

Mrs. Hammond. But it became more and more clear that she was almost always too tired to talk, and even too tired to listen. Possibly *especially* too tired to listen.

Before the week was over, however, Anne made several discoveries that she felt might make life at the Hammonds' bearable. On the second day she was there, she broke into one of Mrs. Hammond's glum silences, and asked, "Will I be able to go to school?"

Mrs. Hammond stopped what she was doing — which was changing George's diaper — and looked fixedly at the opposite wall. It was evening, and she'd already had one full day of Anne's help. She could see already that the extra pair of hands was making a big difference to her life. How could she bear to go back to the way things were before she came? All those buckets of water. Comforting the four twins. Keeping Gertie and Ella from screaming when the babies were asleep. Washing dishes. She sighed.

"I really need you, Anne," she said. "Right now I feel like I weigh about four hundred pounds. And after the baby comes, I'll need you even more. I get really limp and sad after I give birth. And then there's the whole awful torture of not enough sleep."

"If there's a school," said Anne, ignoring this catalogue of woes, "I'm supposed to go. It's the law."

"I know," said Mrs. Hammond, sighing again, and continuing to diaper George, who was almost kicking himself off the table. "I just hoped you didn't know. I'm an American, where the laws are different. I wouldn't be expected to know, because my children are so young. So you could probably get away with not going. I could pretend I didn't know."

"I don't want to get away with not going. I love school. It's what makes me happiest in all the world. It feels like quite a while since I've been happy. Can I go? *Please?*"

Mrs. Hammond suddenly started to cry. When she could speak again, she said, "It's two miles away. In the winter you can't go, once the snows come. That I do know. But you'd be leaving early and coming home late. All those buckets of water ... I don't see how I can do it anymore. And all the dishes to wash, when it makes me tired just to *stand*. Oh, Anne! It was so wonderful to have your help today."

This was the first time that Anne's resolve weakened somewhat. She heard the last sentence. It was nice to hear it. It was almost *exquisite* to hear it. After all, there hadn't been exactly a torrent of thanks coming her way all day. In fact, not a word of gratitude.

"I tell you what, Mrs. Hammond," Anne said. "Get Mr. Hammond to set out the big tubs before he goes to bed. The one for washing and the one for rinsing. I'll get up extra early and fill them. Or do it before I go to bed. All thirteen buckets. And I won't mind the two miles one bit." *Mind it? I'll love it, even if every single inch of it is nothing but trees. But it'll be quiet. And I'll be* alone. *I can dream my dreams and pretend a hundred things. I can* imagine *again. It's hard to pretend* anything *when four babies are all crying at the same time.*

Then, Anne continued. "When I get home, I'll cut up all the vegetables and boil the water — just the way I did the first night I was here. And after supper I'll wash the dishes before I do my homework."

Mrs. Hammond looked at Anne's eager face, and felt guilt wash over her like a muddy river. *What's wrong with me?* she thought. *People sometimes have twenty-one babies and still live to a ripe old age. I'm only twenty-four. Why do I find it so hard? I have only six*

*children, but I don't seem ever to have the time to enjoy them — or even ...
yes ... love them. And this skinny little redhead is offering quite a lot.*

Anne was standing in front of her, her eyes huge with longing, her hands clasped in front of her. "All right," said Mrs.
Hammond. "You can go. In the spring and in the fall. If
there's no snow on Monday, you can start. Just give me the
three days between now and then to rest up a bit."

"Oh, Mrs. Hammond!" cried Anne. "I'm so excited and
thankful that I just have to *move*. I'll take George for a little
walk to use up some of the wild energy I'm feeling in my legs.
He's not heavier than a pail of water, and nicer to carry
around. The other twins are asleep. Maybe you could lie down
for an hour."

Anne got herself and George dressed in their outside
clothes, and lifted him into her arms. There was no snow.
There'd been rain the previous week, and the ground was now
bare and hard. As she passed the barn where the horse and
cow were kept, she peeked in the door to see if the two cats
were inside. They were — sound asleep, snuggled up to each
other in a box behind the cow's stall. This was the first time
she'd seen them. Both were short-haired, one grey, the other
striped. Anne sat George down on the floor while she bent to
stroke them. "Oh, George!" she said. "Isn't a purr the most
exquisite sound in the world? Almost as good as music. Mrs.
Hammond says they have no names. I'm going to call them
Gilbert and Sullivan. Miss Henderson said they were both
very musical."

It was easy to find the path that Mr. Hammond used each
day on his short journey to the mill. It was fairly wide for a
footpath, and easy to navigate while carrying a baby. Anne
walked the length of it, until she came to Mr. Hammond's

little mill. She could hear the sound of the saw whizzing, and the sounds of wood banging against wood, so she didn't disturb him. The river was running swiftly beside the mill, so she was careful where she walked. But soon she found another path nearby, leading once more into the woods. Before she and George had gone a hundred feet, there was a sharp curve in the path and she turned to walk along it. And there, in front of her eyes, was a very small house — not much bigger than Mr. Johnson's — and beyond it a field, with hills rising on each side. Had Anne been dying of thirst in the Sahara desert and discovered an oasis in the near distance, she couldn't have been more thrilled than she was now. First — the house. It must be where the old lady lived — the one that helped bring the babies out of women's stomachs. Second — the field and hills. So she wasn't entirely smothered by Hammonds and forest after all. The old woman could wait. Anne had to place her feet on that field *right now*. She and George set off down the path in that direction.

FIFTY-SEVEN

*V*ioletta and Miss Haggerty

As soon as Anne stepped onto the little field, she knew it was *her* field. If a farmer came in and wanted to use it for cutting hay, or for his cow, or to break up for a new growing area, that would be fine. It would still be *hers*. Why had the trees not crowded into it? What could be in the soil that made that dense jungle of firs and spruces and pines *stay away*? It didn't matter. It was there, and it was her own field. It opened up the sky for her, as well as the view of the two hills. She put George down on the ground, lifted her arms wide, and laughed aloud.

What was *that*? It was a sound that almost frightened her, although it seemed to be a happy sound. It was coming from that hill to the west, and she knew that she hadn't dreamed it up. She shouted a loud HELLO! in that direction. And from the hill came not one but two hellos. Anne knew what an echo was, but she chose to ignore this piece of knowledge.

"It's a friend," she almost yelled to George. And the words "friend, friend" could be heard far up on the hill and into the small valley. "What can I call her?" she whispered to George, who was sucking his thumb with one hand and slapping the dead grass with his other. "When I make up my mind, I'll call her and see if she answers. How about Freda? No. Too short. Annabella? No. Too much like me. Lavinia? Nice, but not a good name to be calling into the hills. Violetta? Oh, George! It's almost too perfect! Four syllables and very romantic. I can see her already, dressed in a filmy green dress that waves around her legs when the wind blows. She'll have dried flowers in her long floating golden hair — hair like Venus in Mr. Johnson's picture — and she'll have rows and rows of bracelets on, made of red rosehips. Around her swanlike neck there'll be a necklace — of what, George? — of stardust. She's part fairy, so she can get that easily by just lifting her slender arms up into the sky. The necklace will sparkle and dance as she moves about, and she moves a *lot* — dancing around the wild rose bushes and leaping gracefully over little brooks and streams."

Anne called up into the hills, "Violetta! Violetta!" and the name came back, four times over. Then she called up, "Anne! Anne! Anne!" The little valley was alive with her name, repeated clearly and then faintly, falling over itself. Anne hugged herself with a new delight. "Violetta," she said more quietly, "I know you're there even when you don't talk back to me. But I know you're going to be my true, good friend, because you called me at least six times. I'll come here often — sometimes with George, sometimes not. And you and I will talk. It'll take a while for me to love you as much as I loved Katie Maurice, and I hope that doesn't make you sad. But I feel sure it will happen. You'll see. It's just that I could *see* Katie Maurice, and that makes a big difference. But she wasn't nearly as beautiful as you, with your pink cheeks and your gentle smile and your regal bearing. Katie Maurice actually looked almost exactly like me — except with auburn hair and almost no freckles — so of course there was no way you could expect her to be *totally* beautiful, although I pretended she was. But I was able to tell her all the secrets of my heart, and I know you'll be wanting to hear them, too. So ..." Anne lifted her head and called, "Violetta! Violetta! I'll come back to see you tomorrow!" The words came floating down over the field, tumbling over one another, "Violetta ... tomorrow ... Violetta ... tomorrow ... come back ... Violetta ... tomorrow!"

Anne had one more errand before going back to the Hammond house. She just *had* to knock at the door of that little house. She had to find out something — anything — about that old lady who knew how to get babies out of their mothers. If she was big and fat and bent over and wrinkled, how could she do that? Wouldn't you need to be young and strong in order to be able to do such an extraordinary thing?

When Anne got to the doorway of the small house, she realized that it wasn't as tiny as she'd thought. There certainly would be space for a bedroom, and maybe a big pantry at the back. Thinking about knocking at Mr. Johnson's door for the first time — which had been a little bit frightening — made her almost brave about tapping on this door. But she did pause for a moment before her knuckles hit the wood. Then she noticed that there were two sleigh bells on a leather rope nailed to the door. She jiggled them.

The woman who opened the door was far from fat and bent over. She was tall and very thin and very erect. Her hair was piled up on her head every which way, and was as white as any hair that Anne had ever seen. And every inch of her that Anne could see was deeply, intricately wrinkled — her face, her neck, her hands, her forearms. So they were certainly right when they said she was old.

"Come in," the woman said, and smiled, thereby rearranging her wrinkles into another pattern entirely. "You must be the new orphan child over at the Hammond place. And this, I see, is George."

"How did you know? Most people can't tell which is which."

"Well, I can. I delivered him. So I know. I saw that mole when he was five seconds old. I see it still. I went out to Kendrick and I said, 'You've got a boy. What's his name?'

'George,' he said. Then I went back to the bedroom just in time for Hugo to arrive."

"I find there are a lot of names in that family to remember. I like memorizing poetry better."

"Well, it has better rhythm. Would you like to sit down for a while? I imagine that George is pretty heavy."

"Yes, please, I'd like to sit down for a *minute*, but I can't stay long. When all the babies start crying at the same time, Mrs. Hammond needs me. To feed them and all. And I'll have to cut up the vegetables for tonight's soup, too."

"You're an orphan," said the lady, "with red hair and freckles. That's why I let you in so quickly. I was all those things, also."

"Even the red hair?"

"Even the red hair." She smiled, and her wrinkles regrouped themselves. "And a lot of it. Also thin. And still am, as you can see."

"Surely not as red as mine."

"Almost."

"Did it change? If I understood about God, I'd ask him for mine to get to be an unspeakably beautiful auburn. But I asked him to make living at the Hammonds' easier than at the Thomases'. And I don't think He heard me."

"Well, sometimes He does seem to turn a deaf ear to some requests. But you never can be sure exactly where his replies may lead. He could surprise you."

"Not if Mrs. Hammond keeps having babies every May. If she keeps on having a baby every May, she could have twenty-three babies by the time she's forty. I'm not good at arithmetic, but I worked that out."

The lady smiled. "That's just simple addition. Mrs. Hammond seems to know about multiplication."

But Anne did *not* know how to multiply. So she changed the subject. "What's your name? Mrs. Thomas said it was rude to ask, but she wasn't always right about every single thing. And it would be easier to talk to you if I knew your name. Mrs. What?"

"Mrs. Nothing. I'm Miss Haggerty."

"Oh! You didn't have a husband? Or babies?"

"No. Neither. My mother had fifteen children, and I was the oldest. They came every one and a half years. By the time I was twenty, I'd changed so many diapers and brought up so many of my mother's babies that I decided that being an old maid would be the nicest thing in the world. It would be quiet, for one thing. And there'd be times when I could be alone."

Anne thought about how she loved walking to school alone. She also thought about children and noise. "I absolutely understand how you feel, Miss Haggerty," she said. "But I'm not that far gone yet. I do want to get married to a breathtakingly handsome man who is gentle and kind, and maybe have two lovely children. Mr. Thomas was breathtakingly handsome, but a lot of the time he got drunk and yelled and hit his wife. Mr. Hammond seems to be gentle, but he saws so much wood and cuts down so many trees that I don't think he has time to be either kind or unkind. He's just sort of *there*." Anne paused for a moment before she continued. Then she said, "You didn't tell me if your hair turned a beautiful auburn colour."

"No. It didn't. When I was twenty-five, it turned snow white — all within three months. At the time, I was working in Eastbury as a midwife. That white hair made the women feel better about me delivering their babies. They believed I was old."

"I just have time for one more question," said Anne. "I should hurry. I don't want to make Mrs. Hammond angry on the second day I'm here. After all, she did save me from the orphan asylum. But I want to know how you could be an orphan when your mother had fifteen children."

"It's arithmetic again. My mother died when I was born. My father then got himself a new wife within six months. Some men can't live for five minutes without a woman. They're so helpless. They can't even make themselves a cup of tea. And other things. They need someone to complain to when they get sick. Anyway, he got married again. Right after their first child was born, my father died of typhoid fever. Then she got married again very quickly. She needed someone to support me and the new baby. She was very beautiful, and she had no trouble finding a new man. She told me they came in droves, begging her to marry them. She was not a woman without vanity. Pretty soon there was a big family, and I was only related to one of them — the son who was my stepbrother. I did call her Mother, even though she wasn't my real mother. But she was all I knew."

Miss Haggerty stood up. "Now you go home to the Hammonds and help that poor woman get supper. Come see me again. But never bring more than one child. And just if he or she is a baby. I don't want them running around and making a noise. At home, I got so I couldn't stand that. Fifteen children! Here I am seventy-five years old, and I still can't stand it."

"But you delivered babies. And still do. I don't understand." Anne was lingering in the doorway. This woman was interesting to talk to. She had stories to tell. And she *listened*.

"Yes. It was the perfect job for me. I delivered the baby, and usually made a woman and often a man happy and grateful. It's a nice feeling to do that. But then, after I'd washed the baby and the mother, and made them both comfortable, *I went home. I left the baby.* Now it was someone else's job to look after it. Or him or her." She paused. "And now," she said, "off you go."

"My name is Anne," said Anne, as she stepped out the door.

"I know," said Miss Haggerty. "I made it my business to find out."

"Spelled with an *e*," said Anne.

"Ah!" said Miss Haggerty, smiling again. "That seems a wise way to do it." Then she closed the door very firmly behind her.

FIFTY-EIGHT

*M*ore Discoveries

The first few weeks at the Hammonds' passed quickly. Even though her days were long and tiring, so many things were happening that the time sped by with abnormal speed. First — except on weekends — were the two hours of walking to school. Anne loved this part of the day. It was very early, so she still felt strong and energetic; and she could also be alone with her own thoughts and dreams. Several small fields opened up the sky for her as she walked along, and she memorized every inch of them — their shapes, the skinny little trees along their edges, an eagle that was often perched on top of one of the tall pine trees, and in one field tangles of stiff sticks where rows of corn had been plowed under. There was even a little brook, which hurried along beside the road as soon as the snow melted. She called it the Giggling Brook, because that's what it was doing. *Giggling*. She loved throwing small sticks into it, and then watching them race away into the distance. She longed for the day when she'd start to see little wisps of pale green on the bare hardwood branches, and a deeper green among the dried grasses of the hayfields. And warmth. Warmth would be nice. It was close to mid-April, but there were often days when wind-blown snow flurries swept across the darkness of the evergreen trees, and she was forced to pull her woollen hat down over her ears.

The school — in the small town of Clareburg — was similar to the one in Marysville, but slightly larger. All the grades were in one room, so Anne would have the same opportunity to eavesdrop on what was going on in the more advanced classes. There was only one other pupil in her class — a little boy who was so shy that he found it hard to answer the simplest of questions, even if they only required a yes or a no. His name was Frederick. Not Fred. His mother had made that clear when she'd brought him to school for the first time, in primer. Frederick was a wizard at arithmetic. He was doing sixth-class mathematics. He didn't have to talk. He could just *do* it. Anne left the arithmetic to him. Her interests lay elsewhere. So they were no threat to each other.

Anne had liked the schoolteacher — Mr. McDougall — as soon as she'd met him. He had a wide smile, a bush of brown hair, and a pair of thick spectacles. He was tall, with long legs, arms, and fingers, and his coordination was terrible. He kept tripping over things — objects left on the floor, like books, boots, mittens — and was forever bumping into furniture and people. But he laughed at himself when those things happened, and no one made fun of him. In spite of his awkwardness and the problems it created, he seemed to be a person who was almost devoid of nervousness or anger. Upon meeting him, Anne immediately felt safe. She almost knew that there would be no Randolphs at his school, no Mildreds. And she was right. There was no time to make close friendships because of the long walk to and from school. But the little building was a peaceful place for her, where she was doing what she loved best — learning new things, reading, memorizing poems, listening to what was happening in the higher classes, working hard to catch up with the work she had missed.

One day, Anne neglected her arithmetic in order to listen to Mr. McDougall teach the fifth class a geography lesson.

"This week," he was saying, "I'm going to start teaching you many interesting facts about Canada. Over the past year, we've spent a great deal of time learning about England; and in the junior class, we'll also study a lot about the United States. It's important that we learn about our neighbours as well as ourselves. And the United States of America is our closest neighbour. But for the rest of this year — and next year, too — we're going to learn about our own country.

"So today," he continued, smiling now in an oddly special way, "I'm going to start telling you about the smallest province in Canada. It's even smaller than Nova Scotia. And it's an island. The sea is all around it."

The sea! Anne sat very still, remembering that wonderful day when Mr. Thomas had taken the whole family to a beach. It was on that day that she had fallen so deeply in love with the ocean. She thought about her hope that the Hammonds might live right beside the sea. But no, it didn't happen. If Mr. Hammond had built his huge house on the edge of a beach, between the wide ocean and the black forest, she would have found it so much easier to carry around all those buckets of water and wash all those endless dishes. She felt that living beside the sea would do so much to lift her *spirit* that it would probably make her *body* stronger, too.

An *island*! And he'd just said that the province was *small*. That would mean that even if a person lived in the middle, it would never be very far from the seashore. Anne stopped thinking and remembering, and started listening. Mr. McDougall was on his way to the blackboard. It wasn't a long journey, but before he got there he bumped into the front of Frederick's desk, dropped the chalk twice, and hit his elbow against his own chair. On the blackboard he wrote:

Prince Edward Island.

"It's very, very beautiful," Mr. McDougall was saying. "It has tidy fields that are almost too green to be believed. There are little white farmhouses, and soil that is so rich and thick that it grows the best potatoes in the world. And it's red!"

"*What's* red?" asked Harold Axworthy.

"The soil!" said Mr. McDougall. "It's red like a brick is red." He looked briefly at Anne's hair but resisted an urge to say, Like Anne's hair.

"Paths are red; roads are red. The red roads and green fields are like a beautiful patchwork quilt." He sighed, folded his arms across his chest, and looked at the ceiling.

"And the sea," said Harold. "Are there beaches? Or just rocks?"

"Oh!" exclaimed Mr. McDougall, sighing again. "The beaches! The beaches! Oh yes! And the high sand dunes with their long waving grasses. Flowing in the wind like a mermaid's hair! Oh such a place!"

There was no chance that Anne's arithmetic sums were going to get done *that* day.

Then Harold, who seemed to be raising most of the questions, asked, "Have you ever been there?"

Mr. McDougall smiled his lovely broad smile and said (almost, Anne felt, as though he was describing his love for a beautiful woman), "I was *born* there. I lived there until I came over to Bolingbroke when my family sold the potato farm and moved to Nova Scotia. Every summer I go back to the Island and stay with my uncle for a while — walking along the beaches, watching the moon make its path across the sea, marvelling at the high waves in the storms, listening to the sound of the breakers at night." Then he stopped abruptly, as though he'd been dreaming and had just wakened up.

"Here!" he said. "I brought some pictures. Have a look. See how lovely the place is." The three fifth-class students passed the pictures back and forth among them.

Anne had to clamp her teeth together tight to keep from shouting, *Show them to me, too!* But she didn't leave the building when school was over. She'd be late getting home, but she'd walk quickly, and then she'd work extra hard when she got there.

"The pictures," she said, after everyone had left. "Please. I want to see them."

He took them all out of his desk drawer, where he'd placed them after he'd shown them to the fifth class. But before he passed them to her, he quickly drew a map of Prince Edward Island, of PEI, on the blackboard. He had clearly memorized every twist and turn of the coastline. "This," he said, "is what it would look like if you were viewing it from heaven."

Anne looked carefully at the map, even though it had been the pictures that she'd been so longing to see. But the map immediately captivated her. "It's so long and skinny," she said, "and such a funny shape. And look at that little squashed place in the middle. It's so narrow that it looks like you could just jump across. From sea to sea."

Then he showed her the pictures. Never mind looking at the Island from heaven. As far as Anne was concerned, the pictures convinced her that PEI *was* heaven. *I am longing to possess one of those pictures*, thought Anne. Aloud she said, "Someday I will go there. It may take a long time to happen. Maybe not till I'm an old lady — as old as Miss Haggerty. *But I will go.*"

Thus was born Anne's love affair with Prince Edward Island.

On that very evening, Anne made another discovery. She told Violetta all about it on the following afternoon.

First, of course, she called her: "Violetta! Violetta! It's me. Anne! Anne!" and Violetta called back in her many voices. Anne pictured her leaping from hill to hill, her long hair streaming out behind her, the skirt of her filmy gown flying in the wind.

"Violetta," said Anne, in her normal voice. "Yesterday I made a huge discovery. It's so great that it will make up for thirteen buckets of water and at least half of the weekend diapers.

"Violetta, my dear, yesterday Mrs. Hammond sent me down to the basement to fetch some apples for a pie she was making. She said they were in a big wooden crate in the cold part of the cellar. I'd never been down there before, and I felt full of fear as I descended into the darkness. The place was dim and chilly and full of shadows. I thought about mice and rats, and I was so frightened that I didn't even want my beloved Gilbert or Sullivan to suddenly run across my feet. I didn't bother working out which part of the cellar was the cold part. All of it felt cold to me. So I opened the first wooden crate I saw. And what do you suppose I found!? Three guesses ... You give up? Well, what I found were dozens — *dozens* — of books. I forgot all about the apples, and kept taking book after book over to the light so that I could see their names — their *titles*, as Mr. Johnson told me to call them. A lot of the books are poetry, and some so small that it will be easy for me to hide one in the pocket of my pinafore each time I do an errand in the cellar. And I'll never again be afraid to go down there. I know now that it's a friendly place.

"So, Violetta, I took a little book of poetry by Mr. Wordsworth and brought it upstairs. I did remember to bring up eight apples for the pie. Mrs. Hammond had a little line in her forehead between her eyes, and I could tell that she'd been waiting and waiting for those apples to arrive. But she didn't scold me or say that I was a wicked little orphan, the way Mrs. Thomas sometimes did. She just heaved a great big sad sigh — which is almost worse — and kept placing the flat of her hand on the small of her back. Her back hurts her a lot these days, what with the front of her being so huge that it sort of drags her down. I felt sorry for her — and of course *guilty* — but I know that you will understand when I say that it was *absolutely impossible* to leave that crate of books one *second* before I did.

"I haven't much time today because I want to fit in a small visit with Miss Haggerty before I return to my vale of toil. She asked me to come. Tomorrow I'll read you Mr. Wordsworth's poem about the daffodils.

"I'm not telling anyone about those crates of books, Violetta. Ella and Gertie might tear out the pages just for the fun of it, or get the beautiful covers messed up with their sticky fingers. Although I deeply want to possess them, I will just borrow them, and then return them with great care to their home in the basement. They must have belonged to Mrs. Hammond's mother, who, according to Mrs. Hammond, was *terribly intelligent*. Mrs. Hammond may be terribly intelligent, too, but she doesn't have time to read a single word from one day to the next. Not *ever*.

"But I have to go now, Violetta. So goodbye! Bye! Bye! Bye!" Anne shouted the words into the air, and the hills sent them back to her as she turned to leave the glen.

Miss Haggerty's welcome was warm and sincere — but constrained. On the occasions when Anne visited her, talked for a while, and then got up to leave, she never said, *Oh do stay a bit longer, Anne!* It was clear that there had been far too many children in her life. However, this time she made her a quick cup of tea and gave her a small ginger cookie. When Anne was settled into a chair and busy sipping her hot tea, Miss Haggerty spoke.

"Anne," she said, "I want you to listen carefully to what I have to say." Anne looked up at her and nodded. "Mrs. Hammond's baby is due in May sometime. It's now the middle of April. This baby could come early. Some of them do. You may be the person who has to come and get me if Mr. Hammond is at the mill when I'm needed. So you'll have to know what to do."

"Tell me," said Anne.

"If she says her waters have broken, come and get me. If she says she has started to have pains, come and get me. Don't ring the sleigh bells on my door. Bring a hammer, and bang on the door — *hard*. We need to make sure that I wake up quickly, in case I've dropped off to sleep. This is especially important if you have to come in the middle of the night."

The middle of the night! Anne tried not to think about groping her way along that dark and twisted path in the middle of a moonless night. Sometimes bears were seen in the surrounding forest. She didn't worry about them in the daytime. But at *night?* What would she do if she looked ahead and saw two bright eyes staring at her through the darkness. She didn't want to hear anything else. She took her empty cup over to the table and started her preparations to leave.

"One more thing," said Miss Haggerty, rising from her chair. "Make sure there's a big saucepan of water on the back of the stove at all times. We'll need boiling water. It'll be easier to get that if we don't start at dead cold." Miss Haggerty paused for a short moment. Anne had already opened the door. "Anne," she said.

"Yes?"

"This could happen at any moment."

Anne turned around and looked at Miss Haggerty before she went out the door. "I'm only nine," she said. "I'm scared."

"Don't be so terrified, Anne. You'll be fine. Women have been having babies ever since the world began. Now go. You're letting the cold in."

"Thank you for the cookie," said Anne. And was gone.

$\mathcal{D}$affodils and Other Things

Anne had trouble sleeping that night. There were too many pictures in her head of the dark path leading to Miss Haggerty's house — with bright, beady eyes staring out at her from the right, the left, straight ahead; roots to trip over; bushes rustling ominously in the still night; the sound of an owl's hoot in a tall tree. Or worse still, being left to look after Mrs. Hammond while Mr. Hammond rushed off to fetch Miss Haggerty. What if the baby started to come while he was away? She didn't even know where it would come from. Through the belly button, perhaps? How would she get it out? What was the boiling water for? Should she put a few more sticks in the stove? What if Mrs. Hammond started to yell — the way Mrs. Thomas had when Noah was born — and all six children woke up? Should she race off to comfort them, or should she stay with Mrs. Hammond — who might be frightened, too, although she'd done this six times before. Oh! This was far, far too much to worry about. There was no point in even *trying* to go to sleep.

Anne had left the oil lamp burning very dimly when she'd gone to bed on Saturday night — for light, for comfort, to limit her overactive imagination. She turned up the wick and reached under the mattress for her book of Wordsworth poems. Then she settled down to make sure that she'd perfectly memorized the first and last verses of "Daffodils."

On the following day, in the late afternoon, Anne raced down to the little glen where she always talked to Violetta.

After she'd called her, she spoke in her usual voice. "Violetta, my dear friend, I promised you I'd come today and read you part of Mr. Wordsworth's poem about the daffodils. It's so cold, with those snow flurries this morning and a big wind this afternoon. A person needs to hear about daffodils on a day like this. Otherwise, you can absolutely lose hope that spring will ever arrive. And it must be particularly hard for you, dressed as you are in that filmy gown of yours, and with just those dried flowers in your hair, instead of a warm woolly hat. So here's your poem." Anne raised her voice a bit, so that many of the words chased each other back and forth from hill to hill.

She didn't need the book. She had learned the first and last verses by heart. As she recited, she was free to throw her head back, place a hand eloquently on her breast, raise one or both arms to the hills and sky. Finally, she recited the last two lines of the poem:

And then my heart with pleasure fills,
And dances with the daffodils.

Anne sighed. "That's so beautiful," she said, "that it gives me a huge and exquisite ache, right in the centre of my chest, which must be exactly where my heart is."

Anne left Violetta and the glen soon afterwards. There was supper to prepare, diapers to change, bottles to fill, babies to comfort, the table to set, hot water to heat for either the dishes or the new baby — whichever came first.

The baby didn't come that day or the next or the next. At one point during those days, Anne took Ella by the hand and led her to the opening in the trees where the path to Miss

Haggerty's house began. She tied string to fir and spruce boughs at the entrance, and then on tree after tree, all the way to Miss Haggerty's front door. She gave Ella a big wooden spoon, and told her to bang hard on the door. When Miss Haggerty opened it, Anne said, "Oh, good! You heard her. I'm teaching Ella what to do in case the baby starts coming while I'm at school." To Ella, she said, "This is the lady who's going to help you if your mama needs her. Her name's Miss Haggerty."

"School!" exclaimed Miss Haggerty. "I'd forgotten about that. I guess you could stay home till the baby comes."

"For maybe a *month*?!" Anne gasped, and hardened her heart. She also completely shut down her imagination. She refused to think about what might happen if Mrs. Hammond's pains started while she was at school. "*No*," she said. "I couldn't. It's the law. I'm supposed to go. The School Man at Marysville said that Nova Scotia needs educated citizens."

Miss Haggerty raised her eyebrows. "I see," she said. "How old is Ella?"

"Four in May. I was washing dishes and cutting up carrots when I was four. Four's older than you think. I've tied strings to all the trees — not too high. She can follow them. I've told her to keep away from the river. And Mr. Hammond is the father. He could stay home from the mill till the baby comes. I want to go to school."

Miss Haggerty gave Anne a long, hard look.

"Very well," she said. "We'll hope for the best." Then she shut the door without as much as a goodbye.

On Thursday, Anne dressed at her usual early hour and packed her school bag. Then she tiptoed down the stairs to get her breakfast and prepare her lunch. Mrs. Hammond was in the large kitchen, rocking back and forth on a straight chair.

"What's the matter?" asked Anne, touching her lightly on the arm. Mrs. Hammond jumped — as much as you can jump when you're sitting down — and said, "Sorry. You startled me."

"Why are you *doing* that?" asked Anne. "Rocking back and forth — like George and Hugo do in their cribs? Are you getting your ... pains? Is your water breaking — or whatever it does? What's *wrong*?"

"I don't know," said Mrs. Hammond. "I just feel ... *odd*. I don't know why. I couldn't sleep. So I came down here. I wanted to be warm." Her wildly curly hair was trailing down her back, with some of it pinned up, some not. "You'd better hurry. You'll be late for school."

Anne ate her breakfast quickly, making her sandwich for lunch while she was eating, adding a cookie and an apple. When Mr. Hammond came into the kitchen from milking the cow, his wife said, "Kendrick. Can you get your own breakfast? I feel ... strange."

Mr. Hammond stopped in his tracks. "You're not going to ...? It's not the ...? Is this ...?"

"No," she said. "I'd recognize the signs. I've done this before, you know." She laughed weakly, with a turned-down mouth.

Mr. Hammond sighed with relief. He spooned out a bowlful of porridge from the stove, slathered it with brown sugar, ate it quickly, cut himself a slice of bread, and spread it with strawberry jam. Carrying it out to the back door, he called back, "I got men coming to pick up an order at one-thirty. I'll need to get some logs ready before they come."

Mrs. Hammond was still rocking back and forth and staring at the opposite wall when Anne opened the door to leave. Then she closed it, and went upstairs to Ella and Gertie's room. She shook Ella's shoulder.

"Wake up and take your clothes downstairs. You can dress in the kitchen, where it's warm. Stay close to your mama today. Just in case."

Ella was only half awake when she staggered down the stairs with her clothes in her arms. "Just in case what?" she said.

"In case she needs you. If you have to go to Miss Haggerty's house, follow the strings. Don't forget the biggest wooden spoon. Bang hard on the door."

"But not yet."

"No. Not yet. Your mama will tell you when. Maybe not today at all. Probably not. But stay close."

Then Anne picked up her bag and left the house. *I can see why Miss Haggerty chose to be an old maid. It might be the only way to be sure of some peace and quiet. But I escaped! I did! And before the other five were even up!"*

It was then — just as she reached the first bend in the road — that Anne heard the screams. Even as she was running back to the house — as fast as she'd ever run before — she knew that the screams were coming from two throats. Mrs. Hammond and Ella were both screaming. While she ran, she was panting out the words, "What did I almost do? I almost left that woman alone with six children — the oldest is just turning four — when she's expecting to have a baby any *minute*. No wonder Miss Haggerty almost slammed the door in my face!"

The screaming had stopped. But Mr. Hammond wouldn't be there. He wouldn't have heard the screams above the squeals of his saw. When Anne entered the kitchen, she saw that Mrs. Hammond was lying on the floor, and that Ella was kneeling down beside her, sobbing quietly and shaking her mother's shoulder. She was pleading over and over again,

"Get up, Mama! Get up!"

Mrs. Hammond was whispering, "I can't. I can't. It's coming! It's coming!"

Anne was out the door again, running, running, through the area of stumps, into the woods, down the path, turning left, racing toward the little house, finally banging on the door with a rock — because she'd forgotten to bring the hammer. But at last, at last, Miss Haggerty opened the door — bleary-eyed from sleep, still in her nightdress.

"It's coming! It's coming!" shouted Anne, as though Miss Haggerty were half a mile away. And then more quietly, "She fell off a chair. She was screaming. Ella is there, but she's useless."

Miss Haggerty was wide awake now. "See if you can get Mr. Hammond. I may need him to help me lift her. Then get back to the house as fast as you can. I'll be right there. Tell her to stay where she is."

The baby might have been coming, but it took quite a while to arrive. Four hours later, Mr. Hammond was still in the kitchen, pacing the floor, wringing his hands. It wasn't clear whether this anxiety was for his wife or on behalf of the wagon he was expecting to arrive that afternoon to pick up the order of logs — which he'd not yet prepared for loading. Anne was busy boiling water, handing out bottles to George and Hugo, and preparing food for the other four children. Periodically, Mrs. Hammond's screams pierced the door of the downstairs bedroom, and then died away again. From time to time, Miss Haggerty's head would appear, and she'd say, "Anne! A clean sheet!" or "Anne! A glass of water!" or "Anne! Another blanket!" Between other jobs, Anne was in and out of that room, rubbing Mrs. Hammond's back, squeezing her hand, passing Miss Haggerty towels, warm water, scissors.

Finally, outside in the kitchen, Mr. Hammond heard the thin, sharp wail of a newborn baby. He shut his eyes, took in a long deep breath, and let it out slowly. Then he stood up and walked over to the door. He didn't knock. He just waited. After a while, Anne opened the door, her face a mask of wonder and exhaustion. She said to him, "It's a boy. But —"

"But what? Is he ... *all right*? Is Mother all right?"

"Yes, but —"

"What? *What*? But *what*?"

"But there's another one coming."

Then Mr. Hammond went over and sat down again. He wished there was someone there who could make him a cup of hot tea. He knew he could go now and cut up those logs. But he wasn't sure he'd be able to do it. He'd been having weak spells lately, and right now he felt dizzy. He rested his elbows on his knees and put his head in his hands.

A few minutes later, Anne came out the door again, her large eyes alive with amazement. "It's a girl," she said. "She's tiny but perfect, and she already has a headful of Mrs. Hammond's curly hair. They're both beautiful babies. I think the boy looks a lot like you. He doesn't have much hair, but he has a sort of neat and tidy face."

Mr. Hammond got up slowly and walked into the front parlour. There wasn't much furniture in it, but against the wall there was an old chesterfield with a broken spring on one side. He put a cushion over the spring, lay down, and pulled an old afghan up over his body. What would he do about the wagon that was coming at one-thirty? What would he do with all those children, six of whom were under two years old? How could he feed and clothe them? He shut his eyes. He didn't know the answer to any of those questions.

SIXTY

*A*fterwards

Anne had seen it all. She'd seen both babies come out of Mrs. Hammond; she had seen Miss Haggerty hold them upside down and slap their backs to make them cry; she'd seen her cut the cords. She'd heard the miraculous first howls of both babies, after a few scary moments of complete silence — when nothing could be heard, not even breathing. She witnessed the exhaustion on Mrs. Hammond's face, and the quiet smile — contented and ... what else? *Proud.* That's how she looked. Anne brought Miss Haggerty warm water for bathing Mrs. Hammond and the tiny babies, and then watched as she wrapped each twin tightly in a small blanket. *Two baby bundles*, thought Anne, and, as she looked at the perfect little faces, knew that she already loved them.

Later, after Miss Haggerty had left, and Mrs. Hammond was bedded down in clean sheets and a warm quilt, sound asleep, Anne went about her work in a kind of trance. She was stunned speechless by the wonder of it all. She felt no weariness of any kind as she fed the children, changed diapers, did laundry, prepared supper, washed dishes. She didn't once think about school. She was too overwhelmed by the thought that because she was a woman — or *would* be one pretty soon — *she could do that, too*. She could make babies. And unlike Miss Haggerty, she intended to do it. If a husband was necessary to the whole process, she'd get herself one. It would be nice if he was handsome and intelligent and unfailingly kind, but if that sort of perfection proved impossible to obtain, she'd settle for less. She wished it was her job to name the new twins. She'd like to do it right this minute. She had two names all ready. They had sprung into her mind the minute she saw those two baby bundles placed in the one crib. But the Hammonds would never let her name them. They weren't *hers*. She'd have to wait until she had two babies of her own. And that time suddenly seemed to her to be so agonizingly far away.

Several days passed before Anne was free enough to go down to the glen to talk to Violetta. Just as she was starting to think that she'd totally *erupt* if she couldn't speak with someone about everything that had happened, Miss Haggerty appeared at the door.

"Hello, Anne," she said, in her usual stiff and formal manner. "I see you're not in school."

"No," said Anne. "Mrs. Hammond's still in bed. She seems tired. Also, kind of *silent*. She doesn't even talk to the new babies anymore. She's lost that happily bewitched look that she had right after the babies were born. And Mr. Hammond is at the mill all the time. When he comes home, he lies down on the parlour sofa as soon as he's had his supper. He says his heart is jumping in his chest. Why would it be doing that?"

Miss Haggerty offered a grim smile. "Probably because he's so worried — wondering if he can cut down enough trees to be able to feed and clothe his eight children, his wife, and his free servant. He should have thought about that a few Mays ago."

Anne had no idea what she was talking about. But she was glad to see her. "Would you like a cup of tea?" she asked.

"No," said Miss Haggerty. "No, thank you. I brought you a couple of loaves of fresh bread. And I thought you might like to leave the house for an hour. You seem to like going out to the little glen in the afternoon. I can sometimes hear you talking to yourself down there."

"Oh, Miss Haggerty! I'd love that *exceedingly*! And I'm not talking to myself when I'm in the glen. I'm having conversations with Violetta. And right now I have so many things I need to tell her. About the new twins and all. And the names I've picked out for them. And a new poem I found in one of the books. She'll be eager to hear it."

"Violetta?"

"Yes. And oh, *please* don't try to tell me she's not real. She *is* — to *me*. I can see her every bit as clearly as I can see *you* right *now*. And I'm sorry I mentioned the books. I was absolutely *determined* not to tell anyone. But it just slipped out."

"What books? Mrs. Hammond goes on and on about how intelligent and educated her mother is, and I must say that she speaks better than most of the people around here. But books? I've never seen a single volume in this house. Not one."

"Well, if you promise to keep it a secret," whispered Anne, "I'll tell you that there's a whole big crate of them downstairs in the dark cellar. Right beside the apples and another big box of potatoes. In the cold section. It's a secret about the books, because I'm afraid the children might tear out the pages or get jam or molasses on the pictures. There are coloured pictures in one of them! And some of them have sort of bendable covers, like the soft leather in Mrs. Hammond's old boots. And gold letters. On the books, I mean. Not on the boots. But you won't tell, will you?"

"Never," promised Miss Haggerty. "And now *go*. Violetta's waiting."

And it was true that Violetta was waiting. When Anne shouted "*Violetta! Anne! Violetta! Anne!*" her greeting came bouncing from hill to hill, with unusual force. It was clear that Violetta was impatient to hear anything that Anne might choose to tell her. And Anne told her everything — from the first scream she'd heard on that morning when she was on her way to school, to the miracle of the double birth, to the way both Mr. and Mrs. Hammond seemed too tired to move or talk or act *alive* anymore.

"Mrs. Hammond seemed proud of herself," said Anne, "and sort of peaceful, after the twins were born. Well, after all, who do you know who ever produced three sets of twins? No wonder she was proud. And why wouldn't she feel peaceful? All she had to do was lie there in her warm flannel nightdress, snuggled down under three quilts. And nothing more tiring to do than accept cups of tea. Then she finally had to get up, and after a few days, everything seemed to make her either sad or cross or exhausted. Or all three. It was as though all the energy juices had been sucked right out of her. If too many babies start crying at the same time, sometimes she just sits down on a chair and cries, too — without even covering her face. She wails out loud, with her face all screwed up, and with tears rolling and rolling down her cheeks. She almost never bothers to put her hair on top of her head, and when she does, it keeps coming loose from the pins and falling down around her face. She never was what I'd call colourful-looking — nothing like lively or sparkly or joyful — except during those few days after my little twins were born. And she never smiles. Not ever. She just sort of staggers around *doing* things — like washing dishes, pushing a mop around — all with a pair of eyes that never really look at you. Sometimes I get the feeling that she doesn't even know I'm *there*. But she'd certainly know it pretty fast if I *wasn't*. Because I feel like I'm the glue that's holding the household of Hammonds together.

"The new twins are so tiny and perfect that I'd like to sit down and just *hold* them *all day*. But that's just a dream that can't come true. Mrs. Hammond is feeding them with her own milk, but that means that no one else can feed them when they wake up in the middle of the night and want a meal. And it's not like George and Hugo never need anything. So I'm the one who looks after their bottles and diapers. Mr. Hammond could do some of that if he wasn't so exhausted all the time — feeling his forehead and pressing his hand to his chest so that he can count his jumpy heartbeats. He works hard all day in his mill, or else cutting down more and more trees. But if that's all I had to do all day, I'd find it easy to pay some attention to my children at the end of it. But he just eats his supper and then lies down on the sofa with the broken spring. *Collapses* on the sofa.

I sometimes feel sorry for Ella and Gertie and the first set of twins. When it gets to be May, those twins will be two years old. And Gertie and Ella just three and four. No one has much time to even hug them, because four babies and *mountains* of laundry and meals to get and dishes to wash don't leave us time for anything else. I told Mrs. Hammond yesterday that she just simply must not have any more babies, especially twins. I didn't know if she'd heard me, because she looks so *blank* all the time, but she started to cry and didn't stop for at least five minutes. So I know she heard. I also know I can't say *that* to her ever again.

"But it feels good to be able to talk to you, Violetta. I miss you and school so much. But I feel that if I left Mrs. Hammond right now, it would be like I was *murdering* her. I want her to hurry up and get better and stop looking so limp and sad, and I want Mr. Hammond's heart to stop jumping around in his chest. And I want it to be spring instead of miserable old April. I want the grass to get green and the early flowers to start cheering us all up.

"Some days I go up to my room and look at my little pink purse with the two five-cent pieces in it; and I pull out my old boot and carefully take out the egg with its entirely exquisite pattern on it; and I flip through my new little dictionary and look for one special new word to learn; and I prop up *The Blue Boy* on my pillow and look and look at him; and I memorize two lines from 'The Lady of the Lake.' Then I feel full of riches for a while. Mr. Hammond made my bed and a little table for my lamp before his heart started making him feel so scared, what with all the jiggling around it does. So my room is now my *sacred* place.

"And this is a sacred place, too, Violetta. I have to go now. Thank you for being here for me."

That evening at suppertime, Anne said to Mr. and Mrs. Hammond, "The new twins don't have names yet. Have you decided what to call them?"

Both of the parents looked nervous and troubled. There was a long silence. Mr. Hammond spoke. "I guess we've been too busy even to think about that. Do you have any suggestions, Mother?" Mrs. Hammond shook her head.

"Me neither," said Mr. Hammond.

Then he said, "What about you, Anne? Have you got any ideas for names?"

Anne felt as though a huge door had opened up for her, leading to green meadows and sunshine. For a moment, she found it hard to speak. Then she said very quietly, "Yes, I do." She was thinking about how she had chosen the little boy baby's name from "The Lady of the Lake" — from the stunning line "And Saxon, I am Roderick Dhu." And Julie Anna just because it was a perfect name.

"Well, let's hear them," he said.

"I do think," she said, "that Julie Anna and Roderick are lovely names. And they're such lovely babies."

Both parents looked distinctly relieved. And both of them smiled. For the first time in four days, Mrs. Hammond spoke. "Perfect," she said.

"Then it's done!" said Mr. Hammond, without holding either his forehead or his chest, "Julie Anna and Roderick are their names. Julie Anna and Roderick Hammond."

SIXTY-ONE

*Time Passes

By the middle of May, Anne was able to return to school. Five weeks had passed since Julie Anna and Roderick had been born. Mrs. Hammond was still sad and quiet, and she often cried when the confusion and noise got to be more than she could stand. But she was stronger. She could trudge through her demanding day and somehow get everyone fed and clothed, the laundry done, most of the dishes washed. Mr. Hammond milked the cow, cut wood, sold it, and drove into Clareburg for food and supplies. He earned what small amount of money they had, and then spent it on necessary things. The two parents were doing as well as they could, but it was a home in which there wasn't time for anything but work.

But Anne found time for other things. Even after the two-mile walks to and from school and the hours spent helping Mrs. Hammond with meals and water carrying and dish-washing, she managed to bring book after book up from the secret crate in the cellar, to read the poems and revel in the pictures before she fell asleep at night. And on weekends, she almost hoped that the new twins would cry, so that she could hold them, comfort them, sing to them, love them. She had helped them be born; she had named them. She felt as though they were almost hers. As Noah had been. But she tried very hard not to think about him. When the thought came up, she squashed it down.

On Anne's first walk to school, she marvelled at the degree to which the weather and landscape had changed. It was almost *warm*; there was a definite feathery green on many of the trees; and the fields were no longer a dispiriting pale brown. With each passing day, it seemed to her that the world became greener and greener. Wildflowers started to appear in the green grass and on the forest floor — her beloved dandelions, clintonea, mayflowers, wild strawberry blossoms; birds arrived back from the south and populated the woods and open areas, perching on the roofs of barns and houses, filling the air with song. As she walked along the road each school day, Anne felt as though she had sprouted wings, too. She was alone, and for the length of the walk no one needed her. She could talk to herself — out loud. She was where she wanted to be — on her way to her favourite place, where she would be doing what she wanted most to do. She felt no one could ask for much more than *that*.

Mr. McDougall was glad to see Anne return to school. Any teacher welcomes a student who is eager to learn; but he had never before had a child in his school with such a voracious appetite for almost anything he chose to teach. He knew she neglected her arithmetic in order to listen to what was being taught to the higher classes. But he didn't try to stop her from doing this. He knew quite a bit about her home life. She had told him enough to make him realize that school was her bright sun in a very dark place. In spite of how seldom she'd attended school, he also knew that her lively mind and intense motivation would enable her to catch up to his other students and surpass many of them. Let her ignore her arithmetic. If she had to learn it later, she could and would.

The geography lessons about PEI were now over — finished while Anne had her long absence from school. But Mr. McDougall had pinned his wonderful pictures of the Island up on the walls of the school, so she was free to look at them whenever she wanted. And she did this often. There were now other pictures — of Nova Scotia, New Brunswick, and Quebec — but she skipped over them and feasted her eyes on the Island's tidy green fields and neat fences, the white farmhouses with the red roads leading up to the barns, the vast beaches and sand dunes, the colourful flowers growing in front of the homes, the lush fields of potato plants. How she longed to be there! How she yearned to own one of those pictures — even the smallest. Then she'd be able to lie in bed and just look at it during nights when she was too tired to sleep.

One day Mr. McDougall spoke to Anne when she stayed behind after school to look at the pictures. "What will you do when you get home, Anne? It's a long walk, so you must be tired. Do you read for a while or have a little sleep?"

Anne laughed. "You're a funny man, Mr. McDougall," she said. "And no. I'm not tired when I get home. I love that walk. I get to see fields and barns and cows and houses, and the sky opens itself up for me. Where I live, we're shut off from the sky by lofty walls of tall trees. It sometimes makes me almost hate the trees, but that would be impossible to do. Anyway, that walk gives the sky back to me."

"So what do you do when you get home?"

"I do whatever Mrs. Hammond needs me to do. Cut up the carrots and potatoes for the night's soup. Or cabbage. Or wash some diapers if there's any water left. Or get the clothes off the line. Or wash the breakfast dishes. Or carry around whatever babies are crying. We have a very large number of babies. One of them nearly always seems to be crying. If I'm lucky, it'll be Julie Anna or Roderick. I love them. I named them. They're very tiny. But if I have to carry around George or Hugo, they're really heavy. The older twins ..."

"Older twins? How many twins *are* there?"

"Three sets."

"So she has six children."

"No. Eight."

"*Eight*?"

"Yes. There are two that were born before she started having twins and couldn't stop."

"How old are they?"

"Gertie and Ella. They're three and four."

Mr. McDougall sat down, as though to rest himself while he tried to absorb this information. He bumped his shin against the desk as he did so, but he didn't even seem to notice. "Are you saying," he said, "that Mrs. Hammond has eight children under four years of age?"

"Yes. They're Mr. Hammond's, too, because they're married. But he must wish she wouldn't keep having so many."

"When were the youngest born?"

"In April. I saw them born. It was wonderful. It was one of my life's most exquisite days. If I absolutely had to, I could deliver a baby. But I don't want to be a midwife. I want to be a schoolteacher and also a mother — even though Mrs. Hammond is sad, and always tired. Julie Anna and Roderick wake her up at *least* three times every night. They're very little, and it seems like they're always hungry. Mrs. Hammond never smiles, and sometimes she cries if it gets too noisy."

This information seemed to be exhausting Mr. McDougall. He leaned over and put his head in his hands. "I'm not surprised," he said. And then, "Do you ever get time for *playing*?"

"Playing?"

"Yes."

"Well, sometimes Miss Haggerty, the midwife, comes over and stays with Mrs. Hammond while I go down to the glen and talk to Violetta. For about an hour. Usually on Saturdays. But not always."

Mr. McDougall sighed. "All right, Anne. Maybe you should start off home. Don't worry if you can't get your homework done. Promise me you won't *ever* worry about that."

Anne looked at the clock on his desk. "Oh, my goodness!" she said. "I'm very late. But I love school and I love your pictures and it's hard to leave. But I'd better hurry. I need to fill the washtubs before supper so they'll be ready in the morning."

"Fill them? How?"

"With buckets. Of water."

"How many?"

"Thirteen. I count while I'm doing it. So that when I get to twelve, I know I'm almost finished."

After Anne had left, Mr. McDougall sat down again behind his desk and stared at the opposite wall for a long time.

May melted into June, and soon school closed for the summer. Anne loved the summer with its warmth, its sunshine, its flowers; but she missed school and the long walk that took her there each day. She no longer had a legitimate excuse for escaping from that huge houseful of noise and people and babies and children and *work*. Miss Haggerty came regularly now for one hour every Saturday. One day when the hour was over and Anne met her on the path leading to her little house, she said, "Anne, that hour in the Hammond house always does me a world of good. It makes me realize that my decision was a wise one."

"Your decision?"

"My decision to be an old maid. You may notice that I never stay in that house one minute longer than one hour. You were two minutes late returning today, and I left. When

I'm in there, I feel that I'm right back in my mother's — my stepmother's — house, helping her look after all *her* babies. No, thank you very much. It's not the life for me. I bring them into the world, and on the very same day, I leave them. It suits me just fine."

"Don't you even love Julie Anna and Roderick? Seeing them get born makes me feel like they're my very own babies."

"Well, they're *not*. And I'm certainly glad I don't feel like that about every baby I deliver. If I did, by now I'd have either a houseful of babies or a broken heart. And — praise be! — I don't have either."

Miss Haggerty looked down at Anne and gently tugged on one of her braids. "Off you go now, and help Mrs. Hammond. She's looking even more frazzled than usual, and it's a hot day. George is kicking up a fuss. He doesn't want to wear a diaper, but if he doesn't, there'll be a new disaster before nightfall. I brought over three fresh loaves of bread, but that's the extent of my good works. I can't cope with George when he starts throwing himself around. When a child is thirteen months old, you need two pairs of eyes and at least four arms, or a battle develops. And there's a big one going on right now."

That evening, as soon as the supper dishes were washed, Anne went into the parlour and sat on a chair beside the sofa. Mr. Hammond was lying down, but he wasn't asleep.

"Mr. Hammond," said Anne, "being as you are so smart with wood, and being as you have so much of it around, could you maybe build a big square fence out in the front among the stumps? A fence that no smart child could climb out of? Would you have time to do that sometime? It's hard to get any work done when there are eight children chasing around in that kitchen. If you built a big square place where they'd be safe, they could play outside on warm days. They could climb up on the stumps and pretend they were mountains. Sometimes I could go in there and read to them. If you could save some old leftover blocks of wood, the little ones could pile them on top of one another and make towers and castles. Six of them could play out there, and Julie Anna and Roderick could stay inside. So far, they're easy." Anne paused for a moment, for what she hoped was dramatic emphasis. Then she said, "*Mrs. Hammond might start smiling again.*"

Mr. Hammond sat up and looked hard at Anne. He rubbed his hand across his forehead. "Most days," he said, "I find it hard just to get through the day. All that chopping-down of the trees and then limbing them. And shoving them through that spinning saw. Orders to fill. Wagons arriving. And everyone in a hurry. And all the while, my heart doing that lurching and stuttering. Sometimes it scares me half to death. I just don't know if I'd have the time or strength to build that thing."

Anne didn't say anything. She just sat there and waited. They could both hear the sounds of too much activity, too much noise, issuing from the kitchen. And one of the new twins was crying. Usually Anne would rush in to rescue Mrs. Hammond. Not this time. She was too busy waiting for a miracle.

"I do like building things," he murmured, as though to himself. "Like the house, to begin with. And the beds. And the little table for your lamp. I always planned to make you a small chair, too. Or a stool. Those are the things I like doing best. But somehow ..."

"We could put a few of them out in that pen *right now*," said Anne. "And bring them in, one by one, to put to bed."

"Hmm," said Mr. Hammond.

"It might be good for your jumpy heart," she said. "It must be hard to rest when everything's all so wild and frantic and *noisy*."

Mr. Hammond rested his elbows on his knees and put his head in his hands. He sighed. Then he raised his head and looked at Anne.

Anne thought about how tired he looked, how worried. She saw how heavy-lidded his eyes were, how creased his forehead. But she showed no mercy. "It would make it a lot easier for Mrs. Hammond," she said, "when I go back to school in the fall. *Because I'm going to go*."

Then she waited.

He rubbed the flats of his fingers across his forehead again. Then he said, "I'll try."

SIXTY-TWO

Another Year, Another Time

Mr. Hammond did try. And he succeeded. What's more, he enjoyed it. He worked on the pen on warm evenings when the mosquitoes were not too bad, and often in the daytime while he was waiting for a wagon to pick up an order of lumber. He nearly always worked on it on Sundays. Just as he had with every other piece of woodwork he did, he built it well. No child could climb out of it. There was a little gate that could be opened only on the outside, or by a long adult arm that could reach over the top. He provided the blocks that Anne asked for. He even fashioned a few toys out of stray pieces of wood — little wagons with wheels, wooden animals. He sanded everything. There were no rough edges. Sometimes he whistled while he worked, or hummed little tuneless songs. He was happy.

The pen was ready by the second week of September; and Nova Scotia has a long and beautiful autumn, with clear blue skies, and a lot of residual warmth. The toys took longer. Some were ready by the time October put on its brilliant show of coloured leaves. The rest would be done beside the fireplace in the parlour, during the long winter months from December to April. But even in the coming winter, when the snow was not too deep, it would be possible to put some of the children out in the pen to play without any danger of their entering the forest. By the next summer, it would become the children's favourite place to play.

The pen didn't solve all the Hammonds' problems. The

housework remained to be done, and babies continued to wake in the night, crying to be fed or comforted. Mrs. Hammond still had to cope with a huge workload and not enough sleep. But the pen eased the general air of chaos in the home, and no one was pleased when the winter weather was either too cold or too snowy to go outside. During the winter after Julie Anna and Roderick had been born, there were six weeks when the children had to stay inside — including Anne, who couldn't walk those two miles to school during the winter months. The pen was sometimes totally buried in snow.

But time — even difficult time — passes, and with spring came school again, and then summer, followed by a long fall, with Anne able to attend school for almost three months before the winter closed down.

One day during that abnormally late fall, Mr. McDougall looked out the window of the school that faced north. It was the tenth of December, and still there had been no snow. But he didn't like the look of the sky. He felt that it signalled an oncoming storm, and a big one. It was only eleven o'clock in the morning, but he stood up behind his desk — knocking a book off the surface as he did so — and addressed the whole school.

"Stop your work, boys and girls, and listen carefully. I think I can tell that there's a big storm coming. The trees are already starting to wave around in an ominous way. Not much yet, but there's a lot of movement. The students who live in town can stay until afternoon. But those of you who live more than half a mile away should pack up your bags and leave."

Then he spoke directly to Anne. "You live the farthest away, Anne Shirley. I want you to pack up *everything* and leave. If this storm is as big as I think it's going to be, this will probably be your last day at school until spring."

The last day. This wasn't enough warning for Anne. She sat behind her desk as though she were paralyzed. The last day! And spring was so very far away. She stared at the pictures of Prince Edward Island on the wall, her eyes filling with tears. It would be months and months before she saw them again. Maybe Mr. McDougall would take them off the wall and never put them up again. The green fields and blue sea and red roads and long beaches — *lost to her forever*. It was so *unfair*. She didn't have a mother or a father or Eliza or a doll or Noah or her old bear or Katie Maurice. And now she mightn't ever be able to see those pictures again. She felt as though she couldn't stand it. She thought that if anyone spoke sharply to her, she might stand up and scream and scream and scream.

But she didn't. She rose very slowly and began to put her books and her slate pencil and her slate in her bag. She knew that Mr. McDougall kept other pictures of PEI in his desk. The drawer was open. He was occupied helping a first primer pupil collect her books. Everyone seemed to be busy. She walked slowly up to the desk and let her eyes slide over the contents of that drawer. There was one picture on the top — very beautiful, very small, with green fields and a little white house with red shutters on the windows. He'd never miss it. He had so many. She watched as her hand moved into the drawer and removed the picture. Then she watched the same hand place the picture between the pages of her Royal Reader. *I'll bring it back in the spring. I'm just borrowing it.* With a mixture of relief, ecstasy, and appalling waves of guilt, Anne put on her coat, said goodbye to Mr. McDougall, and walked the two miles home through the gathering storm.

Anne had already experienced one winter at the Hammonds', with the snow often too deep for it to be safe for any of the children to be outside, with the winds howling down the stovepipe and the fireplace, with that wall of impenetrable forest shutting her off from everything she loved. Occasionally, she took the youngest twins — Julie Anna and Roderick — upstairs, sat them down side by side in one of their cribs, and talked to them. They were almost twenty months old, but very tiny for their age. They were content to just *sit*. They loved Anne better than anyone else in that house, so when she talked to them — saying all those strung-together words that they didn't understand — it was like listening to music. They smiled and chortled and waved their arms around. Julie Anna's curls would jiggle as she laughed — such a lovely soft gurgly laugh. Roderick just grinned broadly — and serenely.

"I know you think I'm your mama," she said to them one day, "but I'm not. Your real mama is the one with all the beautiful curly hair — just like yours, Julie Anna. I'm sure she loves you very, very much. But she has no time to pick you up or play with you. There's just too much else for her to do. I know she never smiles. I really and honestly and truly think that she's forgotten how to do it. Try not to mind."

It was clear that they did *not* mind. They continued to clap and smile, occasionally adding a little hiccupy giggle. Anne loved these one-way conversations with the youngest twins. Sometimes she'd tell them about school, about the way Mr. McDougall tripped over things, about his pictures of Prince Edward Island — although she was too ashamed to show them the picture she had taken from his desk. She told them about Violetta, about her sacred day at the beach with the Thomas family, about the happy times with Eliza, about how sad it was to be an orphan, about the little bear she used to have, about Noah. She wished she could do this every day, but her mornings and afternoons were nearly always too full of chores to permit such a luxury.

January was unusually cold and windy that winter, with snow piled up over Mr. Hammond's wonderful pen and often halfway up the windows. The narrow paths that led to the barn, to the mill, and to Miss Haggerty's house were almost like tunnels. Except for Mr. Hammond, everyone was trapped inside the house.

Then, suddenly, during the first week in February, the sun shone down with unusual force, and before even two days had passed, the remarkable warmth had removed much of the snow, and the drip! drip! drip of melting ice could be heard all day. Anne looked out the window at the pen and the stumps emerging through the snowdrifts and was almost able to convince herself that spring had arrived. The narrow tunnels through the snow and forest widened into deep aisles — shadowy and mysterious but pierced by sunlight. She held Julie Anna and then Roderick up to the window, and said, "It's not *really* spring, but a miracle day like this tells us that it's *coming*. Just look at those exquisite icicles pouring water into the snow and making little holes in it. Look at those trees just weeping for joy."

Mr. Hammond, who was returning to the mill for his afternoon work, whistled as he put on his coat and his cap. A big wagon was due that afternoon to remove the logs he'd been working on, and he was looking forward to a few days when he could take it a bit easier. Maybe he could spend some of that time finishing the little dollhouse he was making for Ella and Gertie, and then try to figure out how to make tiny chairs and tables to fit into it. He gave his wife a pat on the back as he went out the door. "Bye, everybody!" he called. Anne tried to make herself believe that Mrs. Hammond smiled. *Well,* she *almost* did.

Later that afternoon — around three o'clock — they could hear the thunk-thunk of logs being loaded onto the wagon but were unable to see any of that activity, because the entrance to the mill area was from a back road. But suddenly Anne could see a man burst out of the wall of trees, racing up the path toward the house. He was yelling something. Anne opened the door a crack and heard him shouting, "Come! Somebody come quick! Hurry!"

Anne grabbed her coat and boots and ran out the door. The snow had melted enough for her to reach the man quickly, and she followed him as he raced back to the mill. What she saw when she reached the building was Mr. Hammond lying on the floor beside the saw. He was lying on his face, and was very still. "Get somebody!" the man shouted at her, although she was right beside him. "He was carrying one of those large logs, when all of a sudden he just *dropped*. No reason! He just fell down, like *that*! Where's his wife? Get her!"

Anne knew she couldn't do that. As fast as she could, she ran back to the turn in the path, and headed for Miss Haggerty's house.

Miss Haggerty came quickly, in spite of her age and the slippery quality of the path. She examined Mr. Hammond, and then hoisted herself back to a standing position.

"Anne," she said carefully, slowly, with a hand on her shoulder, "it would seem that Mr. Hammond's wobbly heart has finally stopped."

"You mean that he's ...?" Anne stumbled over the words.

"Yes," said Miss Haggerty. "I'm afraid that's exactly what I do mean."

She turned to the men. "Wait here. I have information about the families of Mr. and Mrs. Hammond in my house.

I'll ask you to take it to Clareburg and give it to the pastor. He'll know what to do. Perhaps you'd lift him onto the table; I'll bring you a sheet to put over him. We'd be much obliged if you'd do that for us. I'll go tell Mrs. Hammond. Then we'll wait for help."

Anne went with Miss Haggerty to her house. The old lady made a quick cup of tea with a full teaspoon of sugar and handed it to her. Anne sat at the table, shivering, her mind a jumble of thoughts and fears and half-formed memories. When Miss Haggerty left to take the information and the sheet to the men, Anne stayed behind, sipping the tea, continuing to shiver, feeling as though she would never be warm again.

$\mathcal{E}$ndings

Later on in her life, details of the next four days were a blur in Anne's memory. The first two of those days were particularly foggy in her mind. On the third, however, when the Hammond relatives started to arrive, Miss Haggerty shooed Anne out of the house and told her to go down to the glen and talk to Violetta. "There are enough people here now," she said, "to do our work for us. So take this opportunity to escape to your favourite place and get some rest."

Anne went. The winter thaw had done its work, and it was not difficult to walk past the pen and onto the paths leading to the mill and to Miss Haggerty's house. Once she had reached the glen, Anne stood in the snow and called Violetta, asking her to answer back from the white hillsides. "Violetta!" she shouted. "It's me, Anne! Answer me, Violetta! I'm Anne! Anne! Anne!"

The reply came back — slightly muffled from the two hills: "Anne! Anne! Violetta! Answer! Answer!"

So she was still there. The cold and snow hadn't driven her away. Anne started speaking to her in her normal voice.

"Oh, Violetta! Perhaps you saw it all from up there on the hill. Or heard it all. But in case you didn't, I need to tell you that Mr. Hammond is dead. I thought he was better, I really did. He seemed to be so happy making the wonderful pen and all those blocks and toys — even wagons with wheels. I'd never seen him that happy before. He whistled and sang mysterious songs while he was working. But the men said he was lifting heavy logs all morning. I knew he had a wobbly heart, but I was deeply confident that it would go right on beating forever. After all, he lifted logs and *trees* almost every single day. But it didn't. I mean the heart. It didn't go on beating. It stopped. It makes you realize how important hearts are. If they stop beating, everything else stops. I didn't know that before. Miss Haggerty told me.

"It was Miss Haggerty who sent me out here to spend time with you. I always liked her a little bit — but not *enormously*. She always seemed kind of *chilly* to me. But ever since Mr. Hammond died, she's been almost *soft*, and certainly warm.

"When we came back to the house after Miss Haggerty spoke to the men and told them what to do, Mrs. Hammond was changing Roderick's diaper on the kitchen table. When she heard the terrible news, her hands dropped down by her sides, and for a terrible moment she just stood there, staring straight ahead, not speaking, not crying. Then she walked away from the table, out of the kitchen and into the parlour, leaving Roderick lying with half his clothes off. He could have fallen right onto the floor. Miss Haggerty pointed to Roderick, and said amazingly gently, 'Anne.' So I went over and put his diaper on. Then I lifted him down to the floor.

"Ella and Gertie had heard Miss Haggerty tell Mrs. Hammond that their father was dead, and they were crying. They'd seen the dollhouse he was making for them. They'd discovered they had a real live father, instead of a man who lived in the mill house. But they knew what 'dead' meant. Their puppy had died last August. George and Hugo were crying, too, because one of them was sitting on a toy that the other wanted. And the other twins were quietly building towers with Mr. Hammond's blocks. Julie Anna and Roderick were crying because they were hungry. I looked around at all of them and decided to do the only thing I knew how to do, right then. I started to get supper ready. I pretended I wasn't hearing all that noise. This was hard to do, Violetta, as you can well imagine, because six children make a lot of noise if they're all crying at the very same time. But I started saying the verses from 'The Lady of the Lake' that I'd learned by heart, and doing that filled my head and heart, and also drowned out some of the racket.

"After a while, Miss Haggerty led Mrs. Hammond back into the kitchen — oh, so gently — and said, 'Lottie, it's best you stay in here because it's warmer, even though it's a little bit noisy.' Mrs. Hammond looked both very, very sad, and very, very blank. I went over to her and touched her hand and said, 'I'm sorry. I liked him.'

"But she didn't even look at me. I'd never heard her called Lottie before. Mr. Hammond called her Mother. And the children called her Mama. I hardly even knew she *had* a name. But there it was. *Lottie.*"

Then there was a long silence, while Anne just stood in the middle of the field and cried. Her mind was brimming over with sad thoughts and terrible fears. She cried noisily and wetly. She wished there was something to sit on. *It's so much easier to cry when you don't have to stand. Standing takes energy, and crying this hard pulls the starch right out of you.*

"Oh, Violetta!" she gasped, when she was finally able to speak again. "I just can't understand why it's necessary for people to die. When they go, they leave such a chasm of emptiness behind them. I thought I'd fallen into the pit of despair before, but nothing was ever quite like this. That house up there — that huge house that poor dead Mr. Hammond built — never had a real guest in it before. Then, all of a sudden — after that part I told you about — it started filling up with guests. Now — this very minute — it's full of people I've never seen in my life. There's her mother, who is supposed to be so clever and well educated. That may be true, but she hasn't figured out a way to make Mrs. Hammond smile yet — or even to make her look halfway *alive*. There are three sisters, who are running around picking up babies and trying to comfort them, and *continually* making tea. Of course there aren't enough cups to go around, and there are a lot of complaints about *that*. There are also two brothers who just sit there, taking out their pocket watches every few minutes and looking at them, with deep lines between their eyebrows. Mr. Hammond's father hasn't arrived yet from Kingsport. His mother is dead, and Mr. Hammond was an only child. That's why he built that huge house — so that he could fill it up with children. But there are about five women from Clareburg, whom I'd never before laid eyes on, who are in the kitchen, trying to figure out where to put the food they brought — a whole ham (which we're certainly going to need) and a couple of cooked chickens, and a lot of pies and cookies. And listen to this, Violetta. These are the kinds of things that Mrs. Hammond's family are saying to one another:

"'Which ones do you want to take?' or 'Is there one you prefer?'

"They're not talking about furniture, Violetta, or knives or forks or dishes. They're talking about Mrs. Hammond's *children*. And all the while they're talking and arguing, she's just sitting there with that face that's so *vacant*, not saying one single word. Here's what else they're saying:

"'Well, I want the identical ones. George and Hugo, I believe they're called.' That's the older sister talking.

"'I'll take the older girl,' says the next sister. 'The one they seem to be calling Ella. She has nice wavy brown hair and appears to be quiet. But I'm certainly not going to take two. I have my own life to lead.'

"'Well, if I have no choice,' says the third sister, 'I'll take the other girl — the one that Miss Haggerty says is four. I just don't want to be loaded down with any of those twins.' That's Gertie she's talking about, Violetta. You'd think they were talking about *groceries*.

"No one is asking Mrs. Hammond what *she* thinks. Maybe she's not thinking anything at all. Or perhaps she's just enjoying *sitting down*. She hasn't had a chance to do that since last February.

"The brothers are watching everything, looking nervous. Finally one of them clears his throat and says, 'Marcia and I have no children. Didn't want any — neither of us. And still don't. But sometimes she says she's lonesome. How be Lottie comes and lives with us? Bangor's a nice place. She'll like it once she perks up a bit.' See, Violetta? They're even talking about Mrs. Hammond like she's a loaf of bread or a cabbage.

"Just then, Mr. Hammond's father arrives. He's thin and small, but he has a pretty woman with him. Not young, but pretty. She's handing out instructions to him about where to sit and what to do and what to say, so I figure she must be a new wife. 'Don't offer to take any of the children,' she says, in a voice loud enough for everyone to hear. 'They seem like a noisy lot. Besides, we're close to fifty. That's way too old to start being a parent for the first time. Pay your respects to Kendrick's widow, and then let's get back to Clareburg to make arrangements about the body. It wouldn't hurt to give Lottie a few dollars. But not too much. A burying can be expensive.'

"At this point, Violetta, Miss Haggerty sent me out to talk to you. There were still two sets of twins to be parcelled out, and you'll also notice that no one was mentioning *me*. Miss Haggerty may seem pretty stiff sometimes, but she's smart. She'd know that I wouldn't want to hear any arguments about Julie Anna and Roderick, or anything about what would be done about *me*. If you're wondering why I was standing around in the snow crying, just think about all *that*."

Anne planned to stop talking and return to the house, but she had one more thing she wanted — no, *needed* — to say. "Violetta," she said, "have you ever in your whole life felt *guilty*. I suppose there's nothing for you to feel guilty *about*, as you leap around in these hills with your green gown flowing out behind you and your hair blowing in the breeze. But it's very different for me. I'm *tortured by guilt*. I wish I had known that feeling guilty is far, far worse than longing for something you can't have. I thought that I wanted one of those pictures of PEI so much, so *hard*, that I might possibly die if I didn't have one. That's how much I wanted them. And so I *took* one. I thought I was borrowing it. That's what I *told* myself I was doing. But I'm not even sure I meant it. But I'll never know now if I did or I didn't. Because I won't be going back to that school — not ever. I won't be able to learn wonderful things from Mr. McDougall again, and I won't be able to return the picture to him. He was my friend for two whole years, and I loved him. And what did I do for him to show him all that? I STOLE ONE OF HIS BEAUTIFUL PICTURES. Every night I take it out and try to love it, but I can't even get any joy from looking at it. All I can do when I see it is feel terrible, terrible, *terrible*!"

Then Anne began another storm of weeping.

Back at the house, the older set of twins had been taken by one of the ladies from the town. She was Mrs. Gordon — the one who'd brought the huge ham. She was large and generous and energetic. "They're nice-looking children," she said, "and well past the diaper stage. They'll seem like toys to my Amy, who's just turned twelve. And it'll be nice to have some little ones around the house again. Yes. If you wish, if there're no other takers, I'll add them to my tiny family. All I have is Amy. It seemed like God didn't want me to have any more. But I guess He just changed his mind." Then she laughed at her little ecclesiastical joke.

While all this was going on, Mrs. Hammond continued to sit, as though frozen, on one of the kitchen chairs. She said nothing and her face registered nothing as one by one her children were disposed of.

Finally, just as Anne was returning to the kitchen, her eyes red and swollen from crying, a small shy woman stood up. Her name was Mrs. Granville, and it was she who had brought three apple pies to this gathering. She'd never made a public speech before — or even a private one — but she knew that if you were making a speech you should stand. "I been waiting," she said, "for Mrs. Hammond's mother to make a choice. But it seems like she's going to leave this house empty-handed. So if it's all right with the whole company present, I'd like to ask for the two little babies — the ones they been calling Julie Anna and Roderick. I been wanting them ever since I entered this house today. That little curly-headed child and her brother are some sweet. And I always hungered after having a set of twins. My mother had a set, and so did my grandmother. But all I got is a dog and two cats. This was right disappointing to my husband, but he never said much, nor acted one bit aggravated. He'll be real pleased when I arrive home with two beautiful babies. I thank you, Mrs. Hammond, for the wonderful gift."

This was the first person who had mentioned that Mrs. Hammond had any connection with any of the children. At Mrs. Granville's final words, Mrs. Hammond rose stiffly from her chair, steadied herself, and then walked toward the basement door. After she'd opened it and gone through it, the door closed, and she could be heard going slowly down the stairs. Then the people in the kitchen — suddenly silent as they watched Mrs. Hammond's departure — listened to the loud agonized sounds of weeping and the groans of anguish from the cellar.

Anne went straight up the stairs and lay on her bed, face down. She had no tears left in her that day, but never had her life seemed more hopeless, more rooted in despair.

$\mathscr{A}$nother Departure

On the following day, most of the same people gathered in the kitchen. Where they had all spent the night Anne didn't know; nor did she care. Mrs. Gordon and Mrs. Granville had removed themselves and their chosen twins on the previous evening, along with the children's clothes and other necessities. Their husbands would arrive later that day with their wagons, to transport cribs and beds. But all family members were still present, and a sprinkling of women from Clareburg, bearing more food, along with a considerable amount of curiosity.

From her room, Anne could hear a lot of spirited conversation. But as soon as her footsteps were heard on the stairs, there was a sudden silence in the kitchen. When she came in the room, she saw that Pastor Evans was there. She'd seen him several times in Clareburg. He was going around the room collecting signatures from Mrs. Hammond and from members of her family. She was back on the same chair she had left the day before, looking as though the violent storm in the basement had never happened. She signed her name each time he brought the paper to her, but her hand was the only part of her that moved. Conversation had started up again, but it was subdued. A couple of times, Pastor Evans was heard to say, "For the church records," as he waited for a signature.

One of Mrs. Hammond's sisters leaned across to her and asked, "What are you thinking about, Lottie?"

To everyone's surprise, she spoke. What she said was "Bangor."

Mr. Evans looked up and saw that Anne had entered the room. "So!" he said, his voice oppressively cheerful. "Here's little Anne Shirley. Is there anyone here who might offer to take her in? As you all know, she's an orphan, and the Hammonds have been looking after her for two years. Who else would like to carry on this worthy work? Mr. McDougall says that she's a very bright and pleasant child."

The five women from Clareburg looked at her swollen eyes, her uncombed red hair, her large crop of freckles. Two days of crying had almost closed up her large and beautiful eyes. They thought not. They *knew* not. This was not the kind of worthy work they wished to do. Cuddly babies and little girls of four and five were one thing. Anne was another. She was almost eleven years old. No one knew that she could prepare an entire meal for a family of eleven, and then wash the dishes afterwards; that she'd saved the lives of at least two of the Hammond children when they'd been near death with croup; that she did all the laundry on weekends and holidays; that she carried thirteen buckets of water from the well every evening before bedtime. No one knew, because they'd never been told those things. And it didn't cross Mrs. Hammond's mind to tell them now. For six years, her life had been one long, exhausting blur, with morning sickness, an aching back and painful labours, and with either one or two babies delivered to her every year as payment for those difficulties. No wonder she was thinking of Bangor instead of Anne. So no one knew that Anne could become a perfect unpaid servant — a slave, in fact — in any one of their homes.

There were no replies to Pastor Evans's challenge. The women looked at the floor or at their hands and concentrated on thinking about how much food they had brought along to this house of mourning. After all, they didn't even know Mrs.

Hammond. Surely it was generous enough of them to do what they'd already done. One woman — Mrs. Larsen — was particularly worried. She was a childless widow. She was afraid that all of them — Pastor Evans in particular — might look on her as the obvious choice to be Anne's new adoptive parent. She had no apparent duties or commitments. But she didn't want to take in this freckle-faced urchin. Her husband had been parsimonious, and also fussy about his diet. She was enjoying her quiet life of solitude, with no one making any demands on her energy or time except for her three co-operative cats. Therefore, when Parson Evans said, "Well, then I guess we'll have to consider the Hopetown orphanage as our next step," she immediately volunteered her services.

"I'll be only too happy to take her there myself," she said. "It's a bit of a journey, but I'm not one to shirk my duty. If she can be ready tomorrow morning, we can set off early, catch the morning train, and be in Hopetown by nightfall." She sat back in her chair, hands folded in her lap, her lips set in a small virtuous smile.

Anne slowly climbed up the stairs to her room. After she had feared this outcome — this orphan asylum — for the whole of her conscious life, it was about to happen. She would be installed in an orphanage by tomorrow evening — probably crammed into one giant room with twenty, thirty, maybe *forty* other pathetic orphans. Like her, they would be children whom nobody wanted. There'd be no one to *talk* to. No time — *ever* — to be alone with her dreams, her colourful imaginings. Under those circumstances, there was a good chance that her heart or her brain might erupt. Possibly both. She didn't care if she was needed downstairs. She'd already been needed by too many people in that house. She could hear both George and Hugo crying, and Ella and Gertie whining with that irritating sound they made so often. Well, there were a lot of people downstairs. Let them look after those children — especially the sisters who had volunteered to be their new mothers. It was too late for them to change their minds about keeping them. They'd signed Pastor Evans's paper, and so had Mrs. Hammond. And there was plenty of food. No need for her to be down in the kitchen chopping up carrots and potatoes and putting the corned beef on the stove to boil off the salt. Maybe later she'd go down and make Mrs. Hammond a cup of tea. No one seemed to be paying any attention to her, except for her older brother. He was watching her with ill-concealed anxiety. This wasn't the Lottie he remembered. How would Marcia react when he arrived home with this silent stick of a woman? Just look what they'd all done for her! They'd made sure that every single one of that crowd — that *multitude* — of children would be looked after. And there was absolutely no sign of gratitude on her part.

Later on, Anne escaped out the side door and ran down the path to the glen, to bid farewell to Violetta. But when she arrived at their usual meeting place, she couldn't speak. *I'm too strangled by grief. I can just barely breathe. When everyone you ever loved has been taken from you, what can you say? My parents, Eliza, Mr. Thomas, Noah, Miss Henderson, Mr. Johnson. And Mr. McDougall* — but she could hardly bear to *think* about *him. The stolen picture. Oh! Oh! Oh!* She closed off that part of her mind, and thought instead about Mr. Hammond. She remembered how he loved to build and make things, but was usually too busy cutting down and sawing up trees to have time to do it. And *dead* now. Gone. Before he'd even had time to make the tiny furniture for the dollhouse. She'd miss Miss Haggerty, too, even though they'd seen so little of each other, and in spite of her strange brisk nature.

But worst of all was the fact that on the previous afternoon Mrs. Granville had whisked Anne's babies — Julie Anna and Roderick — out of the house, while Anne was lying face down on her bed. She didn't even have a chance to say goodbye — to kiss their dear sweet faces and hug them till her arms ached. And right now, all her arms felt was *empty*. So *very* empty. What's more, all that lay ahead was the orphanage. No, there was no chance for a conversation today. But maybe she could open up her throat just enough to bid farewell to her friend. Clasping her hands together tightly, she called out, "Violetta! It's Anne! I've come to say goodbye! Goodbye! Thank you for being my beloved friend!" Her words echoed back from the hills, faintly, sadly. "Violetta ... goodbye ... Thank you ... Anne ... friend."

Then Anne turned her back on the hills, and walked along the path to Miss Haggerty's house. The old lady hadn't spent much time at the big house since the family members had started to arrive. Like Anne, she felt overwhelmed by the conflicting family signals and depressed by the way they spoke about the children as though they were *things*.

"Hello, Anne," she said, when she opened the door. "I saw you out there with Violetta — saying goodbye, I suppose. So I warmed up the teapot and put the kettle on to boil."

"Violetta and me ..." began Anne. "We didn't talk. I was too sad, and my throat closed up. But I gathered my courage together and managed to call out a last farewell. It came back to me so faintly, so full of melancholy, that I almost had the feeling that Violetta was going away, too."

"I'm sorry, Anne." Miss Haggerty sat down beside her, and there were tears in her eyes, very nearly spilling over. There wasn't anything one bit chilly about her that day. "Who took your twins? Who took you? Who could be lucky enough to get *you*?"

Anne looked up sharply. She had never heard words like this coming out of Miss Haggerty.

"Mrs. Granville took Julie Anna and Roderick. She's a nice lady. She wanted a set of twins badly. And she *especially* wanted *them*. She'll be nice to them. So I feel a little bit good about that. But only a *little*. Because they're not mine anymore. And worse. I was upstairs lying on my bed, with my face pressed into the pillow when they left. I didn't even get to say goodbye. Not a hug or a kiss. *Nothing*. It's like an evil wizard came and waved his cruel wand. Poof! And my twins just disappeared."

"And you?" Miss Haggerty looked very troubled. "Who's getting *you*?" She reached out a hand and placed it on top of Anne's, which were clasped so tightly on her lap.

"No one's getting me. No one wanted me. I hoped that Mrs. Hammond might say *something*."

"Like what?"

"Something like 'Anne knows how to work hard and could help you.' Then maybe someone would have *considered* taking me. So I'm to go to the Hopetown Orphan Asylum. An *orphanage*! The place I've feared and dreaded for my whole life. I may very well die of heartbreak during the first week."

"Anne," said Miss Haggerty, rising to get Anne's cup of tea. "I want to tell you something. Getting to know you has made me wonder if I made a mistake when I decided to be an old maid. *I might have had a child like you*. I had suitors. Quite a number. I was a pretty woman before my body started to look like a dried-up riverbed. If I'd been twenty years younger, I would have taken you and adopted you as my own daughter. But I'm seventy-five years old. In a few years, you might find yourself having to look after *me*. And you've done far too much looking after in your life. But I *wanted* you."

Anne stood up and went over to where Miss Haggerty was

standing beside the stove, and they hugged each other for a long time. They were both crying — slow, quiet, despairing tears. Miss Haggerty was longing to say, *I love you, Anne.* But she had never said that to anybody, and she didn't quite know how to put the words together. She managed to say, "I'm very fond of you." This, she knew, wasn't quite good enough.

But it was more than enough for Anne. She did know how to say the words. "I love you, Miss Haggerty," she whispered. Then she went and put on her coat, and, with one small wave of her hand, was gone.

When Anne returned to the Hammond house, the three sisters had departed with George and Hugo and the two little girls. Mrs. Hammond's two brothers were still there, and her mother. Anne went over to the stove and prepared a cup of sweet tea for Mrs. Hammond. Mrs. Hammond was sitting silent and limp, but she didn't look entirely unhappy. Maybe she was relishing the silence of the room, absorbing the miracle that nobody needed her. She saw Anne approaching her with a cup of tea. But she didn't care about the tea, and she didn't care about Anne. Her ability to cope had run completely dry.

At that very moment, there was a knock at the door, and Mr. McDougall entered. He walked over to Mrs. Hammond, took her slack hand in his, and said, "I'm sorry for your loss." He nodded briefly to the brothers and mother, but turned his attention to Anne. She was torn between joy and horror when she saw him. Ever since she'd stolen the picture, it had given her pain every time she even *thought* about him. And *there he was*, in front of her.

"I'm sad you're leaving, Anne. I've loved being your teacher. I hope you'll be a teacher sometime yourself. You'll know exactly how to do it. All it takes is a lot of energy, a love of people, and a passion for knowledge. You have all those things."

"It's hot in here," said Anne. "Let me take your heavy coat." She took it over to the back porch and hung it on a hook. She'd already noticed that the coat had large pockets. Then, running quietly upstairs, she took the picture of Prince Edward Island out from under her pillow. After that, she returned to the back porch and inserted it into Mr. McDougall's pocket as skillfully as she'd removed it from his desk. As she returned to the kitchen to get Mr. McDougall a cup of tea, she knew — in spite of all the sorrows that were engulfing her — that she felt an underlying relief and peace that she hadn't felt since she'd left school in December.

"I brought you a goodbye present," he said, and handed her a small flat box. She opened it, her fingers unsteady, relishing the absence of her guilt. It was a framed picture of a beach on Prince Edward Island, showing the sand dunes, the breaking waves, the glistening sea. With a sudden flood of tears, Anne held the picture close to her chest and moved into the comfort of Mr. McDougall's waiting arms.

On his way home, Mr. McDougall thought about what had happened. He had known that Anne had stolen his picture. He'd looked up from his work that day and seen her do it. He knew of her passion for his home province and for his pictures of it; and he was aware that she led a deprived and exhausting life. He was happy for her to have it. But when he prepared his small framed gift for her, it troubled him somewhat that he might be condoning theft. Was it almost like *rewarding* her for stealing the other picture? It worried him. Not much, but it was like a small irritating itch at the back of his mind.

Mr. McDougall was about four miles away from the Hammond house when he reached into his coat pocket for his handkerchief. His fingers closed on a little stiff piece of paper. What was it? He took it out and examined it. When he saw what it was, and when he remembered how long Anne had taken returning to the kitchen after putting his coat away, he knew that she had put the picture in his pocket *before* he'd given her his gift. He brought his horse to a halt in a little siding beside a barn. Then this thirty-five-year-old man, this schoolteacher who had a sensitive nervous system as well as a strong sense of morality that was sometimes at war with his preferences, stayed there for ten minutes and wept. Then he continued on his way, smiling quietly to himself.

Sixty-five

*A*nother Journey

Everything that Anne owned fitted into the metal suitcase that Mrs. Thomas had given her two years ago. Randolph's huge dictionary made it a bit heavy, and Trudy's dress — with its full skirt and petticoats — made it hard to close. But all her treasures were in there — the picture of *The Blue Boy*, the little boot with the egg in it, the small pink purse with its two five-cent pieces, her two Royal Readers, her own slate, her framed picture of the PEI beach, her copy of "The Lady of the Lake," her tiny dictionary. Anne lugged the heavy suitcase downstairs, and set it on the floor by the back door.

In the kitchen, Mrs. Hammond's mother was making breakfast for everybody. It was the first time Anne had seen her doing anything useful. This was the woman who Mrs. Hammond had kept saying was so clever and so well educated. Maybe she felt too intelligent to start being a grandmother — or even a mother. After all, it had been her *son* who had offered to take her *daughter* into his home — even though he'd been regretting that decision for the last twenty-four hours. Still — he'd offered. She hadn't. The second brother hadn't volunteered to adopt any of the children, but he had an eye on the cow and the horses. He was a successful farmer, and he knew the value of such animals. Besides, he had a large barn that could accommodate a number of useful items that he'd discovered in Mr. Hammond's outbuildings. In the meantime, it would be useful to have someone in the house who knew how to milk a cow.

When Mrs. Larsen arrived with her double-seated buggy, Anne didn't wait to discover what was going to happen to the house, the mill, the piles of cut-up wood, the stacks of lumber. She would never know when the remaining people would leave, or how the brother planned to transport the cow, the horses, the large wagon and the many objects in the barn that he hoped to claim as his own. She simply went over to Mrs. Hammond — still stationed silently in her chair, with her wild curly hair unpinned, uncombed — and said, "I hope you have a nice life in Bangor." Anne thought she nodded, but she wasn't sure. Then Anne kissed her on the cheek, and said, "Goodbye. Thank you for having Julie Anna and Roderick." Mrs. Hammond lifted a limp hand, and laid it — ever so briefly — on Anne's arm. That seemed to be all she could manage.

Then Anne picked up her suitcase and walked out the door to join Mrs. Larsen.

It was a sunny day, and there was very little snow on the ground. The horse made good time between the Hammond house and the railway station — which was in the community of Carleton Centre, three miles beyond Clareburg. During that five miles, Anne said very little. For much of that part of their journey, she was travelling through territory that was familiar to her, so there was little to marvel at or to talk about. Besides, her mind was still overflowing with memories, sorrows, fears, partings, regrets. Just after passing through Clareburg, she suddenly realized that she hadn't said goodbye to Gilbert and Sullivan. She let out a gasp that was so loud that Mrs. Larsen looked at her in alarm. But then Anne had to admit to herself that those cats had been little comfort to her during her two years at the Hammonds'. They were kept in

the barn lest they smother one of the smallest of the babies —
and new babies came so often to that house that there was
never time to change the rules. So it was only during the rare
times when she was outside that she searched for them — for
holding, for stroking, for listening to the music of their purrs.

"Are you all right, Anne?" asked Mrs. Larsen fearfully. It
had never occurred to her that Anne might become sick on
the trip, or even unhappy. It's true that she wondered what
on earth she could *say* to an eleven-year-old child on a journey of this length. But she hadn't taken into account the possibility of any emotional or physical hazards. "Are you all
right?" she repeated.

Anne sighed. "Yes, Mrs. Larsen," she said, "I'm more or less
fine, if you don't count the fact that I'm in the rock-bottom
level of the pit of despair. I was just letting out a gasp because
of Gilbert and Sullivan. I clear forgot to say goodbye to them.
But set down beside the other more troubling tragedies of my
life, it probably doesn't much matter. It's not like with
Lochinvar, who always slept with me. Saying goodbye to him
was a truly heart-breaking experience. But my heart has broken so often that it's a marvel there are any pieces left to beat.
And as you can see from what happened to Mr. Hammond,
it's really important that a heart continue to do that. To beat,
I mean.

People in the Hammond house kept talking about Mrs.
Hammond being in shock, so of course I know what that
word means. But the fact is that Mrs. Hammond has been
acting shocked for over a year. It wasn't just from Mr. Hammond dying. I think she was shocked by having far too many
babies and from being almost dead from too much work. Not
to mention losing all that sleep. I've sometimes felt almost
dead myself in that house from too much work, even though

I'm young and very strong. I wasn't doing it with one or two babies in my stomach all the time, and then giving birth to them, and then feeding them milk out of my own chest. She looked really *peaceful* and *content* and *serene* right after Julie Anna and Roderick were born, just lying there on the bed and *resting*. But then she got up and was faced with all those hundreds and millions of diapers and dishes and meals and crying babies, so all that lovely serenity just seeped right out of her. Did you know that I helped Miss Haggerty when she was delivering those twins? It was the most wonderful ..."

Mrs. Larsen knew that she didn't want to hear about *that*. Mercifully, they were just entering Carleton Centre, where she was planning to leave the buggy. Her brother lived there, and would look after the horse. Then she could pick up both horse and buggy on her way back. Already she was looking forward to this. It would be an exhausting trip if Anne continued to talk this much all the way to Hopetown.

After all the arrangements had been made with the brother about the horse, the buggy, and the drive to the station, Anne and Mrs. Larsen found themselves sitting on a cold bench on the station platform, waiting for the train. Anne had lapsed into silence. She was worried about the arrival of that gigantic locomotive. Would she be able to watch that huge monster as it came chuffing and wheezing along the tracks without thinking terrible thoughts about Mr. Thomas? She'd seen trains before, of course, but not since his death. She used to love watching the enormous engine appear around the bend, and then listening to the terrifying but delicious racket it made as it raced by. But that was *before*. This was *now*. How was she going to feel?

"Sometimes," she said, as she stomped her feet to keep them warm, "an imagination can make things hard for you.

You dream up pictures you don't want to look at, and sounds that you don't want to hear. I hope like anything that I won't be doomed to be afraid of trains for my whole life long."

Mrs. Larsen just looked at her. She had no idea what to say. She did not, in fact, have any idea what Anne was talking about.

In any case, there'd be no time to discuss any of that. The train was already in sight, visible at the end of a long straight stretch of tracks. It was puffing its way along, with its clouds of steam rising above the engine; but it was already slowing down as it approached the station. Anne gritted her teeth against the arrival in her head of any terrifying scenes. But none appeared. The train, as it came closer — very slowly — did, indeed, look immense. But it looked friendly. It looked ready to accommodate anyone who would care to ride in it. And this was what they were about to do! She, Anne Shirley, was about to ride on a train! She had known this, but only in a small part of her troubled mind. Now, suddenly, she realized the enormity of it. She was going to climb aboard this train and travel inside it, all the way to Hopetown. If she could just forget where she was going, there was a very good chance that she might actually almost *enjoy* this voyage.

Even with the thought of their destination nagging away at the edge of her mind, Anne found that almost everything about the train interested her. The hissing sound of escaping steam in the station. The little steps that led up to the inside of the train. The jerk and shudder of the engine as the train started to move. The two seats facing each other, upholstered in some kind of exotic fabric. The windows, providing views of the countryside that were more open and vast than anything she'd ever seen before. The other passengers to watch. The friendly conductor. Anne wanted this trip to last forever — never to stop, never to reach the station at Hopetown.

For the first few miles, Anne was too engrossed to speak. Even the forest amazed her. She had spent much of her life in the midst of one forest or another, but to see the dense trees whizzing by the window, so close and yet so untouchable, made the woods into something entirely new. Finally, however, she found her voice again.

"It's very kind of you, Mrs. Larsen," she said, "to take me to this place where I don't want to go — although I can't imagine that it would be a terrible burden for you to be driving on a train. I hate where I'm going. But I love the way we're getting there. Do you want to know one of the things I love about riding on this train?"

"All right. What?"

"*No work.* No carrying thirteen buckets of water every evening."

"*Thirteen?*"

"Yes. But it's hardly surprising. Over thirty diapers a day. Sheets. Gertie was a bedwetter. I bet no one told Mrs. Hammond's sister about *that*. Towels. Smelly socks. So, yes. Thirteen buckets — at least.

"But that was just the *washing*. Never mind the hanging-up and taking-down. And food. A lot of vegetables to cut up. And dishes, dishes, dishes. Babies to carry and comfort. A lot of noise. It's lovely and quiet on this beautiful train. Even with the clickety-clack of the wheels. I love it. And nothing to do except sit and look at things. If there really is a heaven, it must be a lot like this."

Mrs. Larsen dozed a bit as the day wore on. They had eaten the sandwiches she'd brought along, and the food made her sleepy. She was also wearied by Anne's stream of conversation. She wasn't used to the kind of mental energy required to follow Anne's convoluted tales, or to absorb what they told her about a kind of existence that she'd never experienced or imagined. She heard everything — from the death of Anne's parents, to Eliza's love and betrayal, to Miss Henderson and the Egg Man's revelations, to Mr. Thomas's drinking bouts and his struggles to understand life and himself, to her existence of hard labour and noise at the Hammonds', to the wonders of Mr. McDougall's teaching. It was all presented to Mrs. Larsen for her astonished and exhausted ears, and for her mind to try to comprehend. Small wonder that she fell asleep from time to time.

But as the train drew closer to Hopetown, Anne's conversation staggered and stopped. As if in harmony with her mood, the sun set, and fog blew in from the sea — which was invisible but apparently close by. Mrs. Larsen was awake by then, rehearsing in her mind the steps she would have to take to obtain a buggy to take them to the orphanage. Her other brother lived very close to the station, but he might not want to go to the trouble of hitching up a buggy if his horse was bedded down for the day.

The train arrived at the station, heaving slowly to a halt. Mrs. Larsen and Anne walked directly to her brother's house, who announced that he'd just returned from his place of employment and that he'd be happy for her to borrow his buggy. Mrs. Larsen smiled to herself. Everything was falling into place nicely. They could reach the orphanage before dark, and Anne could be installed in the institution that evening, with no overnight wait at her brother's home. Tomorrow she could step back on that train and head to Clareburg, her duty done, her own quiet and solitary home awaiting her, the cats eager for her return.

Anne was *not* smiling to herself. The wonderful train trip was over, and there was no way she could any longer ignore the reality of what lay ahead.

The orphanage was not as close as Mrs. Larsen had thought, and she was confused by the tangle of streets as she searched for its location in the gathering darkness. But at last they turned down a road that was removed from the centre of the town, and she knew that they were going in the right direction. It had to be nearby. She heaved a contented sigh of relief.

But even Mrs. Larsen had a sense of foreboding as the orphanage appeared on a desolate stretch of land as they made their last turn. It was close to day's end, and the plain form of the building was silhouetted against a sky that was only lit by the lights of the town. A single gaslight flickered at the front door, piercing the swirling fog, and on the second floor there were dim lights behind most of the panes of glass. On the floor below, a single light shone in a window close to the door. Someone was waiting for them.

As Mrs. Larsen drove the buggy up the driveway, and as Anne stared with withering hope at the stark building, the lights on the top floor went out, one by one, and whatever was behind those windows was plunged into darkness. All that remained lit were the lamp at the entrance and the light behind the single first-floor window.

When they came to a halt, Mrs. Larsen dismounted from the buggy, and tied the horse securely to a hitching post. Anne followed, staggering down onto the ground, unbalanced by the heavy metal suitcase. Silently the two of them approached the steps that led up to the front door. Above them was a bronze door knocker, in the shape of a lion's head. It was the only adornment that they could discern. The building itself — as much of it as they could see in the overcast night — was as featureless as a wooden box.

Mrs. Larsen lifted the lion's head and knocked on the door. Then they both waited.

SIXTY-SIX

*A*nother Arrival

The orphanage was run by the Baptist Church, and the nominal director was the Reverend Josiah Fairweather. But the matron was Miss Carlyle, and it was she who was effectively in charge. The Reverend Fairweather arrived once a week to perform a religious service. On that day, he taught the children their catechism, told them to mend their evil ways, and offered long sermons and prayers that were too dragged out and complicated for them to understand.

Therefore, it was up to Miss Carlyle to oversee the day-to-day life of the orphans — their behaviour, their clothing, their cleanliness, their schooling, their overall development. It was too huge a job for her, but she didn't realize this. She was not someone who would find it easy to delegate authority. No. If she had to do this work, she would do it herself in order that it be done *right*. It is true that there were teachers who taught, and cooks who provided meals. But Miss Carlyle's careful and critical eye took in every aspect of even these more specialized activities. The children did most of the other work of the institution: the cleaning of the building; the laundry; the preparation of vegetables for the meals; the polishing of the spotless windows; everything, in fact, that didn't require specific skills and training.

Not only was Miss Carlyle a supervisor who had far too much to supervise, but other factors impeded her as well. She had been brought up in a home where she was instructed in rigid morality and in the importance of absolute cleanliness.

She had also learned something that she came to regard as a fact — that anything worth doing was not just worth doing well; it was worth doing perfectly. But she was taught nothing whatsoever about loving or being loved. Ironically, she grew up yearning above all other things to be loved. But unfortunately she didn't know how to make that happen, because she had never been on the receiving end herself. Sometimes she had dreams in which a whole roomful of people crowded around her for hugs. But looking after forty-four orphans — keeping them strictly in line, forcing them to behave themselves — had not helped her in this well-hidden and secret desire for love; nor had her deeply grounded obsession with cleanliness and perfection. For her, *quiet* meant *silent*; *good* meant *perfect*; *clean* meant *shining* and *spotless*. She was willing to squeeze far too many children into that orphan asylum in order to have at her disposal a small army of scrubbers and polishers. Miss Carlyle was so thin that her clothes hung on her like drapes on a window. Even the petticoated fulsomeness of current fashions couldn't hide this fact. She wore thick spectacles and had a straight, cross mouth — even when attempting to smile.

This was the woman who sat in her dimly lit office awaiting the arrival of the new orphan. The train from the Bolingbroke area had arrived in Hopetown hours earlier. She knew the train schedule by heart. *What on earth was keeping them?* She was tired. She also felt irritated, because strict punctuality was another of her rigid goals. When she heard the neighing of the horse, followed by the heavy knock at the entrance, she rose, smoothed her simple dress over her hips and thighs, and went to open the door. With back straight and chin up, she greeted Mrs. Larsen and Anne with what she thought was a smile, and said, "Welcome to our happy orphanage."

Anne was not taken in by this greeting. The scene in front of her confirmed everything she had ever thought about orphanages. It was dark, devoid of decoration or beauty, and obviously ruled over by a stern tyrant. She looked up and down the hall as they walked to Miss Carlyle's office. Even in the semi-darkness, she could see that the floors in the long, wide corridor were very shiny. She had lived long enough to know that floors didn't become like that all on their own. She was missing Katie Maurice and Violetta, and the prospect of forty-four orphans didn't console her. Obviously she'd never again be alone long enough to dream her dreams or talk to herself. *There are worse things than three sets of twins*, she said to herself, as she looked up and down the grim and spotless corridor. Unlike Miss Carlyle, she wasn't even trying to smile.

"Do sit down," said Miss Carlyle, when they entered her office. Mrs. Larsen felt exhausted. She sank back in the one chair that had arms, and told herself that this ordeal was almost over. Anne perched on the edge of a straight chair, her metal suitcase between her legs.

"We are completely filled up as we are," began Miss Carlyle. "I don't know how on earth we can fit in one more child. I wasn't able to contact you about this, but the situation is quite critical."

Anne felt a small stirring in her chest. Was this woman saying that there was no space for her, that she couldn't *stay*? Dared she hope for such a miracle? Mrs. Larsen didn't strike Anne as a thrilling human being, but she had no children, and she did have three cats. This was not a time to set her goals too high. She looked over at Mrs. Larsen and smiled.

Mrs. Larsen saw that smile and felt that she knew what it meant. She could also feel waves of fear passing up her spine and over into her chest.

"You don't have enough *beds?*" she asked, actually stuttering a little.

"Oh, yes," said Miss Carlyle. "We always keep one bed free in case of emergencies. Accidents. Fires. Children who are suddenly abandoned. Those children need a bed instantly, and a lot of care." She looked at Anne's thin arms and legs. "And we need children who can carry their own weight — who are able to work and help support themselves. This is a big building to keep clean. And it takes many hands to prepare food for forty-four children. I'm just not sure that ..." Her voice trailed off. She shook her head.

After all those hours on the train, Mrs. Larsen knew everything about Anne that she needed to know.

"This child," she said, gesturing toward Anne, "is a perfect marvel. In her last home, she helped look after *eight children*. Three sets of twins, mind you, and two more. All under five, if you can imagine such a thing. She looks a mite spindly, but she is actually capable of preparing a meal for eleven. That's how many people lived in that house, and the mother was poorly. Laundry. So much of it. A bedwetter in the family. Anne filled the tubs with thirteen buckets of water every night before she went to bed. A marvel, I tell you."

Anne had been waiting her whole life to hear this kind of praise. And now it was happening for all the wrong reasons. With a sigh, she slumped in her chair and prepared to be accepted into the orphan asylum.

"Well ..." said Miss Carlyle, in a hesitating kind of way, "perhaps we could somehow manage to fit her in. We can put her in the emergency bed. If there's a disaster, we can — if we must — lay mattresses on the floor." Miss Carlyle had known all along that she would take Anne. She just liked people to feel grateful. Possibly this backhanded way of doing things was one of her fruitless efforts to make people love her. Or at least to be grateful — which was, after all, a step in the right direction.

And Mrs. Larsen did feel grateful — more grateful than Miss Carlyle could begin to imagine. Anne's conversation on the train had plumb tuckered her out. "Thank you *so* much, Miss Carlyle," she said, and rose to go. "And Anne," she said, "I hope you'll be happy in this lovely building, with all your new playmates."

Anne didn't think it was a lovely building, nor did she intend to embrace any of those forty-four pathetic orphans as her playmates.

After seeing Mrs. Larsen safely off, amid further effusive expressions of gratitude from the deeply relieved widow, Miss Carlyle returned to her office and sat down. "I see," she said, "that your name is Anne Shirley, and that you are eleven. How long have you been an orphan?"

"Forever," said Anne. "My parents died when I was three months old."

"And two families, with enormous generosity, have welcomed you into their homes and taken good care of you. You must be very grateful, indeed."

Anne said nothing. She stared at her suitcase.

"That's a large suitcase, Anne. What's inside? I'm afraid there's no space for an unreasonable number of personal possessions. No toys or dolls, I hope. Things like that always make other children feel sad or jealous. Angry, even. Open it, please."

Trudy's beautiful dress had been packed in so tightly that it almost sprang out of the suitcase when Anne opened it.

"Well, *that*, of course, will have to go — as well as any of your other personal clothes. We were given hundreds of yards of particularly serviceable wincey, in a practical neutral colour;

and all the orphans wear clothes made of that excellent fabric. I think we have a couple of dresses that will fit you — almost exactly."

"Where's the girl who wore them?" asked Anne.

"She's ... well ... she died. She couldn't seem to ... *fit in.* Wouldn't even *eat.*"

Quickly she changed the subject. "And what is that boot doing in there?" she said, pointing to the open suitcase.

Anne felt something akin to panic. *Oh! Her beloved egg! Gift of Mr. Johnson.* If Miss Carlyle tried to take that from her, she would surely race down that disgustingly clean corridor, out the front door, and run forever into the dark night. Let them catch her if they could, and lock her into a jail cell. At least she'd be alone there, and someone would probably feed her. All these thoughts flew through her mind in one single flashing second. Then she replied, "It's keeping something from being broken. I'll *die* if you take it from me. You can keep the boot. I need the thing that's inside. It wouldn't be good if I died in here. You might lose your job."

No one in this orphanage had ever before spoken to Miss Carlyle like this. She almost stood up and gave Anne the dressing-down she obviously deserved. But there was a fierce intensity in Anne's gaze that suddenly made her feel somewhat uneasy.

Miss Carlyle cleared her throat. "Each child is given a small box," she said, "which is attached to the wall beside the bed. Anything that will fit in that box can go in there. There's a key. You can keep it on your person. In your shoe. Or on a string around your neck, if you prefer. Bring your suitcase upstairs. Then you can make your choices about what you'll keep. Things that don't fit in the box will have to go. We can throw them out or give them away."

Miss Carlyle lit an oil lamp and carried it upstairs; Anne followed her with her suitcase. They opened a door and entered an enormous room where cots were lined up on each side, a sleeping girl in every one. Anne could see, even in the dim light, the boxes nailed to the wall beside the beds. They were very small. At a glance, she knew that she had lost Randolph's huge dictionary. Miss Carlyle sat on the bed, her back as erect as if she was standing, while Anne made her decisions. The items came out one by one and were laid on the bed. The pink purse with the five-cent pieces, the egg, the pictures of *The Blue Boy* and the PEI beach, the "Lady of the Lake," the small dictionary. The readers and the slate might have to go. Everything else was very small. If she packed them in very carefully, she was sure they'd all fit. She thought of the bear she'd given Noah. Miss Carlyle would never have permitted that bear. Anne closed her eyes for a moment and thanked her stars that she'd given him to Noah.

Then Miss Carlyle handed her an old carpet bag. "This is for your brush and comb and toothbrush, your underwear and socks. Keep it under your bed. And make sure you wash things out before they start to smell. There's a rack for drying things under the box."

Then she handed Anne the key to her box and a facecloth and towel. "Here's your nightgown and one dress, too," she said. "I'll give you the other one tomorrow. Make sure you blow out the lamp before you go to bed. Get under the covers, and if anyone speaks to you, pretend you're asleep. A bell will wake you up in the morning. Good night." She picked up the suitcase and left the room. Anne knew she'd never see it or her big dictionary again.

She looked up and down the rows of beds with their human occupants. She realized that her new home, although much bigger in inches and feet than any she had ever lived in before, was going to be the smallest she had ever known. She carefully fitted her treasures into the little box, locked it, and tied the key around her neck. Then she took off her clothes, put her underwear in the carpet bag, put on the skimpy little orphanage nightgown, blew out the lamp, and climbed into bed. After that, she pressed her face into the thin pillow, and cried herself to sleep.

SIXTY-SEVEN

New Beginnings

In the morning, Anne managed to choke down some of the porridge and limp toast in the orphanage dining room. She had lived long enough to know that a difficult day could be made more hazardous if your stomach was empty. And she had no idea what lay ahead. She avoided looking at the other orphans. She concentrated on pretending that she was alone. Otherwise, it would be impossible to swallow a single bite.

What lay ahead was school, after a group of six children — both girls and boys — washed and dried the breakfast dishes. While they were doing that, the others went upstairs and brushed their teeth, washed out anything that needed cleaning, made sure that their beds were perfectly made, and mopped the floor underneath. Anne watched the activities of the other children and tried to do exactly what they did. She asked for no help. Nor, oddly, did anyone offer it. Most children in an orphanage have known what it is to feel sad, lonely, and inferior to other people. The arrival of a new child might have given the others a rare opportunity to feel superior to somebody. Or possibly conversation was not permitted at that particular time. In any case, no one offered to help Anne.

Then a bell rang. Each child immediately went to stand at the foot of her bed. Then, in a seamless and orderly fashion, they moved together in a single line, left the room, and walked down the stairs. They did this as silently and perfectly as if they had been a group of soldiers who had been trained in the operation for several months. In the scrupulously clean lower corridor, a similar line of boys waited, newly arrived from another staircase on the other side of the building. Then, at the sound of a single clap from Miss Carlyle, they all moved down the hall to the two classrooms at the east end of the building. The first six classes were in one room, the juniors and seniors in another. But for the moment, wide sliding doors had been pushed apart, and the classes were open to one another. The first item on the agenda of each school day was about to begin: prayers. In the far room — the one containing the higher classes — someone imperfectly played the opening bars of the national anthem on a tinny piano. Then all forty-four — now forty-five — orphans burst into a wobbly rendition of "God Save the Queen."

Anne was liking the song, and even the faulty piano. She had never heard live music before. She would continue to love the national anthem for her whole life, giving to it more passion than most people ever feel. She knew about the Queen, of course. She'd been to school, had read about her, had seen her picture. She'd been sorry that she looked so fat and old, that her hair was drawn back so severely from her forehead, that her face looked without expression of any kind. But when she heard the anthem, she completely redrew the Queen in her head. She was tall and stately, with a delicately fashioned tiara — sparkling with emeralds and diamonds — above her chestnut-coloured hair, glittering necklaces encircling her high lace collar, her skirt and train thickly embroidered and moving gracefully behind her as she walked — head high and proud. The song was over too soon. Anne wanted at least one more verse. But it was not to be. Miss Carlyle was saying a long prayer in a loud voice, standing at the front of the room, her eyes closed. A picture of the real Queen Victoria stared down at Anne from the wall.

Anne's eyes were not closed. She was sizing everyone up: that big boy who looked like he could be a second Randolph; those two little girls with the dead-straight hair who were certainly twins; two blond boys who were whispering behind their hands; a pretty girl of about twelve, with a mass of curly golden hair, pink and white skin, and eyes that were definitely sapphire blue; another girl with spectacles and two black braids — as long and as thick as her red ones. Would one of those children turn out to be a friend?

Suddenly, Anne realized that in both of those rooms only Miss Carlyle's head was bowed. Everyone else was looking at Anne — sizing *her* up. A lot of whispering was going on, and some barely suppressed snickers. A boy was tapping his own head, pointing at Anne, and then covering his mouth to keep from laughing. Oh! Her hair again. No one in Mr. Mc-Dougall's class had behaved like that. He must have done something miraculous to keep that from happening. But she remembered the taunting about her hair and freckles at the Marysville school. And there was no Sadie at the orphanage to hold her hand. For one terrible trembling moment, Anne thought she was going to cry. Then, almost as quickly, her sorrow and fear were replaced by rage.

By now, Miss Carlyle was well into a long story about David and Goliath. She was looking straight ahead, so the giggling and pointing stopped. But Anne had seen it. Who did they think they were, to mock her so? A bunch of orphans — that's all. She didn't want any of *them* as friends. She was listening to the story with only half her attention, but enough for her to say to herself, *I am David. That crowd of ragged orphans in their horrible wincey dresses and shirts are Goliaths. I feel no mercy for them. I will win this contest! I don't need any of them.* As Miss Carlyle left the room and the teachers entered, the big doors closed between the classes. Anne stood straight and tall, her little pointed chin high and firm, her small perfect nose lifted and arrogant. Anne's huge green eyes were flashing with a fierce confidence. Under her breath, she whispered, "*I'll show them!*"

Miss Kale, the teacher, was fifty-five years old, and weary. She was tired of teaching in this dismal orphan asylum. She'd envisioned something more exciting than this when — as a child — she had planned her future. She had thought of herself as a heroic missionary, ministering to lepers in foreign parts; or as the stunningly beautiful wife of a handsome and wealthy man, receiving breakfast in bed from a uniformed servant; or as a dancer, clothed in flowing, filmy costumes, spinning on one *toe* to the orchestra's rendition of *Gisèle*, the applause of the audience thundering in her ears. But here she was, fifty-five years old, unmarried, overweight, and earthbound, doomed to yet another week of watching James Hinton kicking Harry Woodsworth under their desks. And here was a new orphan — skinny and freckled, with hair that was blindingly red — obviously no great prize. Miss Kale was still capable of dreams, but she hadn't pursued any for a very long time.

It was recitation time for Anne's class. One by one, the five children in the class rose to recite their short poems, haltingly and with no feeling or drama. When all five had finished, Miss Kale said, "Anne Shirley. Have you any little poem that you might like to recite? I'll understand if you don't, because I believe you've had very little schooling. If you find this class too hard, I'll agree to your doing last year's work."

Anne stood up — very straight. "I have a poem," she said. "How many lines would you like?"

Miss Kale felt an unfamiliar optimism stirring in her chest. "It doesn't matter," she said. "Stop when you're ready."

Anne started:

The stag at eve had drunk his fill
Where danced the moon on Monan's hill,
And deep his midnight lair had made
In lone Glenartney's hazel shade
But when the sun his beacon red ...

After Anne had recited twenty-five lines of "The Lady of the Lake," Miss Kale — who could happily have listened to Anne's dramatic recitation all morning — felt that perhaps they should proceed on with the next lesson. "Anne, my dear," she said, "that was wonderful. But I think we'll have to turn now to our arithmetic lesson. But thank you."

Even though she'd vowed not to have any friends in this terrible place, Anne allowed herself to like Miss Kale. She wasn't beautiful like Miss Henderson, but she'd called her *my dear*, and had said *thank-you*. Mr. McDougall had been the last person to say those words to her — way back in December.

The other pupils in the class listened to her recitation with open astonishment. One by one, and in private, they tried to consider what their reaction should be. Were they — or should they be — *envious*? Or even *jealous*? After all, not one of them had ever been called *my dear* by Miss Kale. Or should they decide that reciting a poem of that length was ridiculous — particularly when done by anyone with hair that red. But a few of them were shaken by the beauty of the words, even though they had no idea what they meant.

Joseph Murphy voted for ridiculous. During dinner that day, he made fun of the way Anne had gesticulated while reciting that poem. The other boys listened, laughed, and looked her way. Other children watched her — puzzled. They'd never before seen anyone act exactly like that. There was something fascinating about her — even her strange exotic appearance. But she looked so proud and aloof that they were uneasy about approaching her. However, there were a few brave students who thought they would like to have her for a friend, and began to think of ways they could make that happen. There seemed to be a good chance that Anne might become a teacher's pet, but this didn't seem to bother most of the children. They didn't like Miss Kale enough for that possibility to be of much interest to them. Edna Godfrey — she of the pink-and-white skin, curly blond hair and sapphire blue eyes — watched and waited.

In the meantime, as day followed day, Anne moved through her new life with a hardened heart and a very thick skin of determined self-confidence. She had seen those boys laughing at her, and children talking behind their slates and looking her way. No one was going to puncture that heart of hers — to either soften or break it. And no one was going to strip away her tough armour of courage. She would allow herself to like Miss Kale enormously. She would unabashedly adore the poems she read and the pictures she saw. That was as far as Anne was willing to take love. Anything else would lay her open to the kind of grief that she had experienced too often. She almost never smiled; nor, during this period of her life, would she allow herself to cry.

SIXTY-EIGHT

A Friend!

Anne struggled through her first ten weeks at the orphanage with no large tragedies and few joys. She was holding herself in so tight that it was almost impossible for either of those things to happen. Occasionally she would watch some of the other children and make up stories about their former lives. She had dramatic imaginings about how their parents had died — by fire, under the thundering hooves of horses, by slow disfiguring diseases, from stab wounds by heartless thieves. Then she would wonder about the difficulties the children might have experienced after the deaths of their parents. Neglect, abuse, loneliness, hunger. In the course of imagining all these details, she sometimes came dangerously close to feeling a grudging fondness for the children she was thinking about. But she was careful to wipe such feelings off her emotional slate. She had loved people before. It had obviously been a hazardous thing to do. Just consider how she had felt when those people had left her or betrayed her. Or just simply dropped out of her life. Eliza, Miss Henderson, Mr. Johnson, Noah, even Lochinvar. And then, of course, Katie Maurice, Violetta, Mr. McDougall, Miss Haggerty, her beloved Julie Anna and Roderick. And to a degree Gilbert and Sullivan. She didn't allow herself a single thought about how those people and animals had enriched her life or helped to make her who she was. The soft side of herself was hidden away somewhere, and she refused to invite it to reveal itself. She sometimes wondered if she had become like Mrs.

Hammond, sitting silently in her chair, removed from everybody. But there was a large difference. Mrs. Hammond had been sucked dry of almost every emotion. The fiery explosion of grief in her basement was the last sign she had given that her spirit was even alive. Anne's spirit was very much alive. But it was consciously held in a frigid state by her anger, by her sense of injustice.

Anne couldn't, however, stifle the enjoyment she felt during school hours. All her energies were poured into her lessons in literature, in geography, in history. She had even started to feel a very small pinched pleasure in the balance and perfection of mathematics. She knew she was smart, and this fact pleased her. She felt and looked *proud*, holding herself so straight, her chin up, her eyes looking straight ahead — communicating with no one. She didn't realize that she stood almost exactly like Miss Carlyle, who was so starved for love, and received none. Children often feel drawn to others who are clever and talented — provided they're humble about their gifts. But during this period of her life, Anne felt both pride and anger, and her demeanour seemed to demonstrate the kind of arrogance that other children sometimes find hard to forgive.

Edna Godfrey, however, was intrigued by Anne's clever mind, her haughty manner. People — young and old — had always been charmed by her own beauty, by her ready laughter. But Anne was paying no attention to her. So she longed to make Anne her emotional slave, as so many others had been. Edna found herself envying Anne's unique looks, her perfect nose, her flaming hair. She was intrigued by her apparent inaccessibility.

So Edna started to court Anne.

She gave her little compliments on her work: "Good for

you, Anne! You've cleaned that pot so that it shines like a mirror!" or (after Anne had memorized the catechism in the course of one evening) "I wish I could memorize things as fast as you can." And "Your parents must have been very smart. Else how could they have had such a clever daughter?" And — the very best: "I love your beautiful red hair."

Edna seemed to be exactly what Anne had always longed for in a friend. She was pretty, cheerful, and apparently ready to be loving. How could Anne possibly resist such a stream of open appreciation — even of her *hair*? The answer is that she could not.

It began one day when Edna and Anne were washing the dishes together.

"How lucky I am," whispered Edna, "to have been chosen to wash dishes with you. I never knew before that washing dishes could make me so happy."

Anne was beginning to feel the softening of her hard shell. But she was still careful.

"And why on earth," said Anne somewhat loftily, "are you finding dishwashing so pleasurable today? It's the same old water, the same old dishes."

"Oh Anne!" sighed Edna. "Can't you see that it's because I'm doing it with such a dear friend?"

Such a dear friend. Even with her hands in the hot water, Anne felt a shiver up and down her back. But she had to be cautious. It could be a trap. She'd been betrayed before.

"Exactly *how* dear?" said Anne, head still high, not noticing that her dishcloth was dripping water all over the floor.

"How dear?" repeated Edna. "The very dearest friend I have. I can prove it."

"Do it," said Anne.

"I can prove it by promising eternal devotion," said Edna. "Look! I will put my crossed fingers on my brow, and tell you that I will always be kind and loyal and faithful. I will never lie to you, never be mean, always protect you. Now I'll put my crossed fingers on *your* brow — to seal the promise." She reached over and placed her wet fingers on Anne's forehead.

That did it. With her eyes blurred by soap and by tears, Anne repeated the same words, the same ritual. They were best friends. They had sealed and proved that fact.

That evening — after the pledge of eternal devotion — Anne went to bed in a glow of happiness. She had been introduced to God by Rev. Josiah Fairweather, so she said, "Thank you, God, for Edna." She assumed He was different from the God she'd prayed to on the night before she went to live with the Hammonds. Certainly no one had answered *that* prayer. Then she closed her eyes and once more cried herself to sleep. But this time they were tears of joy. She had a *friend*! And exactly the kind of friend she had always longed for: beautiful, clever, joyful. She could hardly wait for tomorrow.

During the days that followed, Miss Kale marvelled at the new readiness of Anne's smile, and the brilliance of her large eyes. Anne looked out the window and felt tenderness for the pathetic little sticks of trees that had been planted beside the driveway. As April rolled into May, she ceased to grieve that there were no views of fields or flowers or stately trees. None of the work seemed too hard. Scrubbing the main corridor was a pleasure if Edna was working beside her. She lost her rigid stance. She laughed when someone said something funny. The frothy bubbles in the dishwater seemed to be dancing with delight. She no longer fretted the rare occasions when the orphans were allowed to go out, when the only thing they were allowed to do was walk around and around and around the circular driveway; she now had someone to talk to while she did it.

And talk she did.

At last Anne could break her silence. She told Edna everything. "The death of my brilliant father and incomparably beautiful mother was an enormous tragedy. Eliza was a joy to me for a while; but then she chose to depart with the villainous Roger and deserted me, leaving me to the mercies of a houseful of noise and rage. But my walks to school were always a stunning delight, no matter where I lived, and my teachers and the Egg Man — the Word Man — rescued me from the darkest pits of despair. I hope to become a writer when I'm old so that I can share my amazing life with my readers. I will devote a whole chapter to you, because you're my deeply loved friend — as faithful as Katie Maurice and Violetta, but also ... well, *real*."

Edna enjoyed the details of Anne's thoughts and life, and her oddly convoluted way of expressing herself. And she couldn't help being pleased by the stream of adoration that Anne was delivering to her. How could she not be pleased? It was exactly what she'd had in mind when she reached out for Anne's affection. As day followed day, it seemed to be an almost perfect friendship.

But being a bright and observant child, Edna started to notice a disturbing turn of events. The other children were starting to *like* Anne. She was becoming *popular*. And — an even more troubling consequence — Anne was starting to like the other children. This was not at all what Edna had had in mind. To use one of Anne's favourite words, Edna had wanted to *possess* Anne. And now it appeared that Edna was going to have to share her with everybody else.

Edna wasn't the sort of person to just sit by and let things happen. If the other children stopped liking Anne, Anne would stop liking *them*. Then she would belong to Edna alone. It was that simple. By now, Edna was familiar with Anne's excessive responses to both joy and pain. When pain struck, Edna would be there to rescue her. Yes. All these difficulties could be fixed. And easily.

In the meantime, Anne was starting to notice little things about Edna — things that she tried to ignore. The way her laughter was sometimes scornful instead of merry, particularly when it was directed at someone else's shortcomings or peculiarities. The habit she had of making small snide comments about other children: "What a stupid nose she has. She looks like a puffin." "Someone told me that Gerry wet his pants last Sunday when Reverend Fairweather asked him to recite the catechism." "I hate Betty. She stutters. Why doesn't she just *stop*?" Or about the new orphan, Tessa, who'd arrived the previous Tuesday: "I told her to quit bawling. None of us liked this place when we first got here. What makes her think she's so special? Just because her parents were killed on Monday? Huh! Yesterday. Last month. Last year. What does it matter? We're all orphans."

Anne tried and tried not to listen, not to *hear*, not to care. She loved Edna. She shouldn't expect her to be perfect. Look at Mr. Thomas. He hit people and yelled. And she still liked *him*.

Then, one evening when she was washing dishes, she overheard her own name. "That Anne Shirley ..." It was Edna who was speaking. She was helping two other girls set up bowls and cutlery for tomorrow's breakfast. Anne stopped washing and listened. It was noisy, with the clatter of pots and pans and the sound of many voices. But she was able to hear little snippets of Edna's conversation: " ...thinks she's smarter than anyone else ... ridiculous red hair ... she's so *boring* ... and those googly eyes!" Then, during a lull in the kitchen noises, " ...talks so much. And with all those ridiculous big words. She sounds as though she swallowed a dictionary." Edna had even used — *twice* — a word she'd learned from Anne: *ridiculous*.

Anne stared at the wall above the sink and felt her rage develop. She had been in that orphanage for over three months, and she had finally found a person to love. And that person — that *friend* — had turned out to be a villain, a fiend, a devilish demon, a ghoul who was hiding her evil spirit behind her golden curls and sapphire blue eyes. Anne was alone in her part of the kitchen. She picked up one of the plates she was washing, held it high in the air, and threw it on the floor — *hard*. It made a very satisfying noise. "Oops!" she cried,

"Clumsy me!" when someone came into the room to investigate the noise of broken crockery.

Anne dried her hands and swept up the broken china. Then she let her hands dangle in the dishpan, closed her eyes, and clothed Edna in a black costume studded with nails, horns growing out of her head, and two long fangs emerging from her mouth.

"Dreaming again!" snapped Miss Carlyle, who had just come into the kitchen to see how work was progressing. "Open those eyes and get back to work. We're not keeping forty-six orphans in this place for the fun of it. Start earning your keep!"

That night, Anne lay in bed and thought about how her friendship was doomed and dead. She'd continue to work with Edna and occasionally talk to her, because it would be necessary. But she knew that she would never smile at her again. She brought up into her imagination a large box, which she labelled THE ENEMY BOX. She stuffed Edna into it — black costume and all, her horrid blond curls flying in all directions — and then put the lid on the box, slamming it shut with both hands. After that, for good measure, she jumped on top of the box and stomped on the lid.

In the real world again, Anne crawled farther down under the scratchy blankets of her bed, smiling grimly. Never again would she try to find a friend in this terrible place.

SIXTY-NINE

A Revelation

When Edna had made her insulting remarks, she didn't know that Anne was washing dishes only a few feet away. But when she heard Miss Carlyle scolding Anne, she realized she was nearby. If *she* could hear *Miss Carlyle*, the chances were good that *Anne* had heard *her*. This possibility made Edna uneasy; but she assumed that Anne's slavish devotion to her would be able to survive that small onslaught. But when Anne walked right past her on the following morning and went to sit with someone else, Edna knew that life was neither as simple nor as predictable as she had thought. Later on, when she and Anne would be working on the same project — preparing food in the kitchen, washing dishes with a cleaning brigade, or just in school — Anne spoke to her when the situation required it. But her comments were as brief as she could make them. "Yes." "No." "I don't think so." "I can't." Anne's hot avalanches of words had shrunk to a slow, cold drizzle. And she never, never smiled.

Edna was as disturbed by this as she would have been if Anne had physically attacked her. She missed Anne's public proclamations of adoration, her private confidences. Life was not nearly as interesting as it had been. She had cringed at the idea of sharing Anne's friendship with others. To lose it altogether was a blow of another dimension.

However, there were no fireworks, no open explosions. Each of them dealt with the situation in ways that were predictable. Edna continued to make devious comments about

Anne's deficiencies. When not doing this, she treated others
to unfailing sweetness, letting her radiant smile light up the
dark halls, filling the air with her musical laughter. Many of
the children saw through her strategy, but no one stood up to
her. They were familiar with her sharp tongue. They knew
she was a dangerous person.

Anne's way of coping with Edna's betrayal was to retreat
into herself again, dreaming her elaborate dreams, taking
refuge in her imagination, vowing to keep aloof from any further overtures of friendship. She wasn't happy and she wasn't
unhappy. She still had school and Miss Kale. No one could
take that away from her. Most of the time, she was existing in
a sort of emotional limbo.

One Saturday morning, Anne and Edna and Tessa were on
their hands and knees, scrubbing the vast corridor of the first
level of the building with large scrub brushes. Buckets surrounded them, along with three large bars of bright yellow
soap. This was the floor that Anne had found so alarmingly
shiny on her first evening at the orphanage. Tessa had been
doing little except cry during the days that had followed her
arrival. On a dark night, her parents had been killed instantly
when the carriage in which they were driving plunged over a
cliff on the Eastern Shore. They had been wealthy, but left
behind no relatives and no will. And no one offered to take in
the fat little girl with her unattractive haircut, her small blunt
face, her lack of confidence. Someone packed a large suitcase
with her dolls and her beautiful dresses and delivered her to
the orphan asylum. Miss Carlyle immediately confiscated the
dolls, but allowed her to continue to wear her own dresses.
They had no wincey uniform that would fit her tubby little
body, so until two of them could be made for her, there was
no alternative to her own clothes.

After watching Tessa sit on a chair and cry almost constantly, Miss Carlyle was starting to feel as irritated as Edna had felt. "Tessa," she said. "I've had enough of that crying. Everyone in this orphanage is an orphan of one kind or another, so it's time you stopped thinking that you're different from all the others. You're a very lucky girl to be here. We had no space for Anne Shirley when she came three and a half months ago. So you can imagine how difficult it was for us to squeeze you in. Therefore, today you'll have to start pulling your weight. You'll join Edna and Anne scrubbing the floor of the main hall. We have to be clean here, and cleanliness doesn't just happen by magic." Tessa didn't know what "pulling your weight" meant, but whatever it was, she could see that she was going to have to do it.

So there she was, down on the floor beside Anne and Edna, pulling her weight. She was no longer crying, but she didn't feel one bit better.

Anne stopped scrubbing for a moment and looked around. The long hall was lit by bare kerosene lamps that hung from the ceiling, giving off a glaring, merciless light. The walls were a dark beige, and empty of pictures or any other decoration. Anne sighed.

"Would it really be so hopelessly hard," she said, "to put pretty little lampshades around those stark, naked lamp chimneys? If you look at one by mistake, it's like staring right at the sun on a July day. And any dumb person knows that if you do that, you could go blind in less than five minutes."

Tessa stopped scrubbing and looked at Anne, her eyes full of fear. "Anne," she said, in a whispering voice, "will I go blind if I look at those lamps?"

Anne looked at the scared little face and felt ashamed of herself. It was true that she'd been feeling sorry for Tessa. *You'd have to have a heart composed of solid granite*, she mused, *not to feel sad for that wailing little girl, wiping her eyes and her nose on the skirt of her dress, hour after hour. And only eight years old.*

But Anne had also discovered that she envied Tessa — yes, *envied* her. Tessa had had both a mother and a father for eight years. That was about seven years and nine months longer than Anne had had even one parent. And she couldn't even remember them. Wasn't that a good reason for envying Tessa?

It tortured Anne that Tessa was allowed to wear her own clothes. Just look at them! The dress she had on yesterday even had puffed sleeves, and she couldn't be wiping her eyes and her nose on her skirt if it hadn't been soft and full. Anne had felt so envious at that time that she couldn't even hear Tessa crying. Her ears were stopped right up by the thought of Tessa's wardrobe.

Yesterday Anne had even felt a tiny crumb of dislike for the sad little figure on the chair — her hair so straight and short, her face so pale and wet.

But when that same little face looked up at her today, with fear written all over it, Anne wished she could drown her own shame in the scrub bucket. She was suddenly remembering how much she'd missed Katie Maurice when she left Mrs. Thomas, and Violetta when she had to leave Mrs. Hammond. She guessed that missing your own parents must be one thousand million times worse than missing a reflection or an echo, no matter how deeply she'd loved them and how real they'd seemed to her.

Anne reached over and patted Tessa on the shoulder. "No," she said, "you won't go blind if you look at the lamps. But they're pretty bright, so it can't be *good* for your eyes to stare at them. Poor little bare glass chimneys with nothing to wear! I'll just have to dive down into my imagination and dream up some beautiful shades. I can see them so clearly, made of pink silk with long fringes and silver tassels. Can you imagine anything more beautiful than that?" Tessa actually smiled.

By then, Anne had set her scrub brush aside and was sitting on the floor, leaning against the beige wall, with her thin legs stretched out in front of her. Her eyes were closed, and her mind was full of elegant lampshades.

Suddenly Edna stopped scrubbing and stood right up straight. "Anne Shirley!" she cried, her voice cold and sharp. "You get right back on your knees and help with the work. I'm twelve years old, and Miss Carlyle said I was to be in charge. Tessa's so little that she's useless, and I can't scrub this whole hall all by myself!"

Anne was so busy thinking about lampshades that she didn't give much thought to what Edna was saying. And even if she had, she might have thought it would be perfectly fine with her if Edna scrubbed that floor all by herself.

"Oh, *Anne*!" snapped Edna. "You make me *so, so angry*! What's more" — and here Edna paused for effect — "you'd better make sure you do everything right today and tomorrow, because Miss Carlyle will be watching you extra carefully."

Anne opened her eyes. "Why?" she asked.

"Because Monday morning something very special is going to happen."

Something very special! A special day! Anne thought about all the special days she'd heard about but never experienced — not even once. Even at the orphanage, the other children talked about wonderful things that had happened to them before they'd come to live there. They went on and on about concerts and Sunday school picnics and weddings and birthday parties and fireworks.

"Oh Tessa," she gasped, ignoring Edna, "I'd give anything to have a special day. I'd scrub this floor three times over, all by myself, if I could have a special day. I've read about them and heard about them, but I've never had a single one of my *own*. Birthday parties with candles on a frosted cake — little tiny candles, all lit up, the same number as your age —and people singing lovely songs, just for you. Weddings, with brides in filmy, flowing, flouncy dresses, and long, languid veils. And an organ playing delicious music. Oh, how I would love to attend such a magnificent spectacle! And concerts with people standing up on a stage and reciting my favourite poems, or singing songs with maybe someone playing a mandolin. I've never seen or heard a mandolin, but it's such a magical and musical *word* that I just know it would sound almost too beautiful to bear."

Then Anne was silent for a moment. She'd forgotten exactly why she'd launched into this praise of special days. Then she remembered. Anne's curiosity was forcing her to speak to Edna.

"Edna!" she cried. "Tell me what the special day will be."

Edna looked smug. "It's not a *whole* special day. It's just something special that's going to happen. And it won't happen to everyone. Just to two people. But it could be you. Or me. Or Tessa. But it certainly won't happen to anyone who's being an old lazybones and sitting around with her eyes closed. It *might* happen to someone who's working so hard scrubbing the floor that Miss Carlyle would know how *useful* she is."

Anne had already returned to her position on her knees and was digging her brush into the yellow bar of soap.

"How do you know all this?" she said over her shoulder. "And what's the special thing?"

"I heard Miss Carlyle speaking to Minnie, and telling her

to bring two cups of tea into her office on Monday morning at ten o'clock. And to wear her black uniform with the little frilled apron. And to starch it. The apron, I mean. Because ..."

Edna paused and let the suspense grow.

"Because *why*?" Anne almost yelled it.

"Because a visitor is coming. A fancy lady from Prince Edward Island called Mrs. Spencer."

Prince Edward Island! Anne's brush fell from her hand. Her dream place. Neat green fields and little white farmhouses. Beaches with dunes and long grasses and sand. When the minister came to the asylum Sunday school and told the children to pray for good things, Anne always prayed that sometime, somehow, she'd get to see that place, would get to walk on those beaches in her bare feet, and lie down in those green fields and sleep among the buttercups.

Why would that lady be coming here? It seemed to Anne that it would be like inviting the Queen to visit a chicken coop. What would that fine lady from the Island — probably with an elegant hat and high silk collar and pearl buttons all up and down her front, above a crackling taffeta skirt — oh, and of course with puffed sleeves — what would that fine lady think of all the pathetic little children in their skimpy wincey dresses and shirts, these dismal halls, the bare lamps?

Anne said most of these things inside her head, but all she actually said out loud was, "Why?"

Edna smiled with her perfect pearly teeth. She knew that what she was about to say would be a piece of high drama, and she'd seen Anne react to exciting things before.

"Because," she said, and then repeated, "*because* she's going to take two of us girls back to Prince Edward Island with her. One for herself. A *pretty* one. And one for a farmer's family. A *useful* one. They'll be *adopted*." Edna smiled complacently. She knew *exactly* who the pretty one would be. And she'd heard Miss Carlyle scolding Anne several times for dreaming. No one would choose *her* for the useful one.

Anne received this news in absolute silence. This was an occasion for which words were completely inadequate. It was as though a powerful and magic pair of hands had set the gates of heaven in front of her — all shining and golden in a warm unearthly light — and said to her, "Someone's going to go through those gates — straight into heaven — and *it could be you*."

Pretty. Well, that wouldn't be *her*. In all of her eleven years, no one had ever once told her that she was pretty. She was smart. She knew this to be true; and she hoped it wasn't too sinful to admit that fact, as long as it was only to herself. However, the farmer and his wife wouldn't care if she was smart. But *useful*? Useful was a very different matter.

Anne started to scrub that floor so hard, so quickly, so violently that it's a marvel the shellac surface didn't wear right off. Edna was disappointed that Anne hadn't reacted to her news about Mrs. Spencer more hysterically. In fact, Anne didn't really seem to react at all. But Edna did take some satisfaction from the fact that she and Tessa didn't have to do much work on that floor whatsoever. Anne did most of it. Miss Carlyle, who looked out the dining room door at ten-thirty, was impressed by how hard that little Anne Shirley was working. And apparently with no motivation at all. Maybe she'd misjudged her. Possibly she was more useful than the little dreamer, the procrastinator, that she often seemed to be.

On the following evening, Anne fell into bed as though someone had pushed her. She was that exhausted. Never in her entire life — including the time when she was helping to care for the three sets of twins — had she ever worked as hard as she had worked during the last two days. After the floor on the corridor was scrubbed, she'd offered to help wax it — and then polish it. She scarcely touched her food at noon because she was far too excited to eat. It was Saturday, and there was no school in the afternoon, so Anne suggested that she help wash the dishes. She did this job more quickly and more thoroughly than any orphan had ever done it before — according to Minnie and her sister, who marvelled at such cheerful efficiency. Then Anne worked for several hours in the laundry, ironing their hateful little dresses and the boys' shirts and handkerchiefs. Later she offered to peel potatoes for the next day's soup and to beat the million eggs for that night's tomato scallop. And after supper, she attacked the dishes again with the same speed, the same care. On Sunday, she worked with the same intensity.

Once she was in bed, however, sleep would not come. All around her, from the cots lined up along the wall, came little snorts and snores, and indications that everyone was asleep. Anne could tell that it was safe to whisper. She felt that if she couldn't speak at all, she would burst or break or explode. In fact, *erupt*. She thought about maybe asking God for what she wanted, but she didn't feel that her past prayers had been very productive. Certainly, three sets of twins hadn't been a good answer to the prayer she'd said the night before she went to live with the Hammonds.

Anne crawled out of bed and stood on a chair to look out the high window. It was a warm June evening, and the sky was alive with stars. Words came into her mind: *Star light, star bright...* Yes. She'd pray to the stars. If there *was* a God, and if He *was* listening, He'd maybe figure out why she'd lost confidence in praying, and would understand why she was talking to the stars instead of to him.

"Beautiful stars," she said, "oh, dearly beloved stars, please understand why I want so much for Mrs. Spencer to choose me. I know I should be willing to let her choose someone else, but the fact is that I'm not even a little bit willing for that to happen. I've washed so many diapers in my life, and carted around so many crying babies, and looked after so many cranky children that I think it would be only fair of you to give me a little bit of childhood myself before I get too old to enjoy it. After all, in six years I'll be seventeen and might even be married — not that any handsome man would ever choose someone with bright red hair and six thousand freckles and skinny legs.

"But look at yourselves up there in the sky — twinkling away, and obviously having a wonderful time every night of your lives. Couldn't you persuade your shining selves to pick me up and place me down on that gorgeous little island in the middle of the sea? Is that so much to ask? I'd work hard on that farm. I'd learn how to milk a cow and make butter with that churn thing. I'd wash the lady's dishes and do her laundry and make it extra white. But I could look out the window of my very own room and see the trees and the flowers and all the neat green fields that I saw in those pictures of Prince Edward Island. And it would surely make you twinkle all that much harder to look down and watch me walking on the beaches and picking apple blossoms and hanging out the wash. I'm just positive that seeing that would make you even more joyful than you already are.

"I'd like to be fair. So although there have been too many runny-nosed children and wailing babies in my life — as well as Mr. Thomas's drunken rages — I know that you've also given me some truly wonderful things. Here. I'll make a list. First, thank you to you, or God, or whoever did it, for getting me born in the first place. And for the following very excellent gifts for which I am exceedingly grateful: for Eliza before she left; for Mr. Johnson for telling me how to use my imagination so that I needn't be sad or mad or bored all the time, and for words and eggs; for the day the Thomases took me to the beach; for giving me Katie Maurice and Violetta when I didn't have anyone else to pour all my love into; for Miss Henderson for being so beautiful and for teaching me how to read; for Noah and Julie Anna and Roderick; for the box in the Hammonds' basement that had those books in it; for the Five Sisters and the Pool of Mirrors; and for all cows, crows, and cats, especially Lochinvar.

"So thank you for all those good things. But please, my dear generous stars, lift me up now out of this dreary, pathetic, miserable asylum, where nothing is pretty and nobody really loves me, and put me down on Prince Edward Island so that I can live happily ever after. Thank you very much for attending to this matter."

Anne then climbed down off the chair and slipped quietly into bed. She was asleep within five minutes.

SEVENTY

*M*rs. Spencer

Mrs. Spencer's carriage — borrowed from her brother in Hopetown — arrived at the orphanage at 9:55 sharp on the following day. After driving halfway around the circular driveway, the horse and carriage came to a halt directly in front of the entrance. The driver rushed around the back of the vehicle to help Mrs. Spencer as she stepped down to the ground. Then he returned to the driver's seat while she mounted the steps to the front door.

Mrs. Spencer always dressed carefully when she was away from home. She never chose clothes with an excess of decoration — fringes, hanging ornaments, a plethora of bows — although she would embrace bustles and side panniers for very special occasions, when those styles reached Prince Edward Island's rural areas. In spite of visiting Charlottetown frequently — and occasionally Hopetown, where fashion was even more extreme — she tended to avoid clothes that used layers of lace over unseemly bright colours. On any kind of journey, what she wanted in her dressing — even on an errand to pick up two orphans at an orphan asylum — was a sense of simple dignity. And she achieved this. For this particular event, Mrs. Spencer was determined to look like a woman of some social significance — like an important person. She wanted to be sure that she would get exactly what she had come for — one pretty child and one useful one. She didn't want to have to make this trip twice, in case the matron's choices didn't work out well. For this trip — which would involve short and long journeys in carriages, trains, and a ferry, she had chosen her second-best dress — a gown of fine beige wool, fitted tightly at the waist, and featuring a dark brown stand-up collar of velvet and buttons that were covered with the same material. Her long sleeves ended in wide cuffs of the same dark brown velvet. Only the narrowest of brown velvet trimmed the bottom of the wide skirt, complementing the beige wool of the dress. The garment was warm, simple, and undeniably elegant.

After using the lion's head door knocker, she waited — composed, confident, erect.

Minnie answered the door, her full figure resplendent in its carefully ironed black uniform, starched white apron, and white lace collar. Even Mrs. Spencer — not given to being overly impressed with the good qualities of others — immediately felt that this must be a well-organized and efficient institution. Minnie led her to Miss Carlyle's office door and knocked. When the door opened and the matron appeared, Minnie disappeared as though by magic.

"Mrs. Spencer?" inquired Miss Carlyle, although she knew, of course, precisely who she was. And when Mrs. Spencer inclined her head in a dignified nod, Miss Carlyle added, "How do you do. Please come in." She gestured to the one comfortable chair in the room; and Mrs. Spencer — gathering the folds of her gown around her — sat down, her feet pressed firmly together, hands and small bag in her lap.

"Now," said Miss Carlyle, "what can I do for you?" in spite of knowing exactly what she could do. Well in advance of this visit she had been warned about what was expected of her. She hardly listened as Mrs. Spencer spelled out her requests for "a pretty little girl of about five for me; and a useful and hard-working girl of about eleven for my friends the Cuthberts." She didn't specify anything about the appearance of the second child. Miss Carlyle did notice that, and was relieved.

Miss Carlyle had spent several hours yesterday and another hour or two last night trying to make up her mind which children to choose. It hadn't been easy. What did Mrs. Spencer mean by "pretty"? With some children, the issue was clear. Edna, for instance, was *undeniably* pretty. *No one* could be disappointed by her appearance. But Edna was twelve. This little girl had to be "about five." None of the four girls of that age were stunning beauties. But none were hopelessly plain, either — like Tessa, the new arrival. She finally chose Lily Jones, because of her cheerful nature. And she did have naturally curly, nut brown hair — an obvious plus. She hoped she had chosen wisely. It was important that she do so. Mrs. Spencer was obviously a person of some influence in her community. You could be confident that this was so just by *looking* at her. And she seemed to have an air of unruffled authority that went hand in hand, as it were, with her elegant appearance. If she was pleased by the orphans she took for herself and the Cuthberts, other adoptions might follow. She would spread the good word in her own rural community and in Charlottetown. It was part of Miss Carlyle's job to attract adoptive parents. Neither the church nor the province wanted to support the orphans forever. Miss Carlyle wanted — no, *needed* — to keep this position. But there hadn't been an adoption for eleven months. She longed for Mrs. Spencer to be pleased with the two children she was going to take away with her.

It was particularly difficult for Miss Carlyle to choose the "useful" orphan. Grudgingly, she admitted that most of the children were more or less useful. It had been required of them. She had *made* them be useful. But some were undeniably more useful than others. On Saturday, for instance, she had witnessed at first hand the extraordinary performance of that skinny little Anne Shirley. Miss Carlyle had been *very impressed*. Maybe Mrs. Larsen's assertion that she could cook a meal for a family of eleven was true. But she also seemed to be a dreamer, a procrastinator, someone who seemed cheerful one week and then withdrawn and almost *haughty* the next. This was a worry. It was odd. Maybe that one day of astonishing work had been a fluke. Therefore, Miss Carlyle had determined to keep an eye on Anne on Sunday, too. And she did. Not once did Anne lean against the wall and close her eyes. When washing dishes (which she did — voluntarily — *three times*), she didn't dangle her hands in the dishwater and stare at the ceiling. At no point during the obligatory walk around the circular driveway were her lips moving — as though having long conversations with herself. Maybe all those shortcomings were a phase that had passed. Possibly Miss Carlyle's excellent training had knocked those undesirable qualities right out of her.

Miss Carlyle sought out Miss Kale and asked her opinion. Everything the teacher said was positive. Anne was apparently clever and hard-working, and also produced excellent work. That she could recite seventy-five lines of "The Lady of the Lake" was of no interest to Miss Carlyle. But it wasn't a *negative* quality. The Cuthberts — and Mrs. Spencer, for that matter — might feel some alarm at her appearance (that hair, those freckles, those skinny little legs), but Miss Carlyle decided — in a rare, reckless move — to take a huge leap and recommend Anne.

Minnie arrived with the tea. Someone had willed an ornate silver tea service to the orphanage twenty years ago. It was seldom used, but that day it was lavishly presented.

Before Minnie left, Miss Carlyle said to her, "Please fetch Lily Jones." While the women drank their tea, Lily was quizzed by Mrs. Spencer, and Miss Carlyle surreptitiously bit her nails. Her whole future as the matron of this orphanage might depend on the success of these two adoptions.

"What do you like doing, Lily?" This from Mrs. Spencer.

"Playing."

"Ah. Do you have dolls?"

"No. We're not allowed. I had one, before. But she took it." She nodded toward Miss Carlyle.

"Would you like to come to Prince Edward Island and be my new daughter?"

"Yes."

"Splendid! I'm sure we'll get along beautifully. Maybe we can find a doll around the house somewhere. My older daughter had several."

Miss Carlyle emerged from her uneasy silence and said, "Run along, now, Lily, and pack your things. Don't take the towels. They belong to the orphanage. And leave your key in the box after you've emptied it."

"And the useful one?" inquired Mrs. Spencer, after Lily had gone.

"Ah, yes," began Miss Carlyle. "The useful one. I have a child here who's been with us for only four months. The woman who brought her said that she was a wonder. Before coming here, she washed dishes, did laundry, helped look after three sets of twins and two other children, could assemble a meal for a family of eleven, and is smart at her schoolwork."

"I'll take her," said Mrs. Spencer, looking at her watch. "Say no more. I don't need to see her. Appearance doesn't matter."

"Still," said Miss Carlyle. "I think you should meet her." If Anne was returned to the asylum, it would be *she* who would be blamed for an unwise choice. Mrs. Spencer should have some idea what she was being offered before she made her decision. Miss Carlyle rang for Minnie, who was then told to find Anne and bring her to the office.

Before she arrived, Miss Carlyle tried to sweeten the deal. "Her parents were clever and respected schoolteachers." She had no idea how clever or respected they were, but she had taken the plunge, and was determined to continue swimming. And then, "Although quite thin, she is enormously strong."

Mrs. Spencer didn't notice Anne's thinness when she entered the room. Nor did she discern the large number of freckles. All she saw, as Anne entered the room, was a face that was alive with a blinding joy, an agonized hope. Anne assumed that she had not yet been *chosen*. She suspected that there would be questions, some sort of *test*. She had already memorized what some of her answers would be. But the call to the office must mean *something*. It had to mean — *at least* — that she was being *considered*. She approached Mrs. Spencer as one would a queen or a goddess, her large and beautiful eyes fixed on Mrs. Spencer's studied elegance and careful smile. She actually curtsied. Mrs. Spencer, somewhat taken aback by this entrance, was finally able to observe that Anne's hair was a brighter shade of red than any hair she had ever seen. But she astonished both Anne and Miss Carlyle by saying immediately, and with a high degree of courtesy, "Anne. We have chosen you to be the Cuthberts' adopted daughter."

Anne was rendered speechless by this announcement. She just stood there staring at Mrs. Spencer, breathing in short gasps. Miss Carlyle was standing behind her. Mrs. Spencer had said "we" — not "I." Therefore, Miss Carlyle must have recommended her. In one quick, unrehearsed movement, Anne spun around and hugged Miss Carlyle in a gesture of fierce gratitude. For one brief transient moment, Miss Carlyle knew what it felt like to be loved.

Then Anne turned slowly around and faced Mrs. Spencer again.

"How many children do they have?" She didn't really care. Let them have sixteen. She would be on that beloved island, close to the sea, in her *own home*.

"There are no children," said Mrs. Spencer. "The Cuthberts are brother and sister, not husband and wife."

Anne came very close to fainting. She did, in fact, drop into a chair that she was standing beside, and put the palm of her hand on her forehead.

"Are you all right, Anne?" asked Miss Carlyle, with genuine concern. Anne was, after all, the only orphan who had ever hugged her.

"Yes," breathed Anne. "Oh, very, *very* all right. It was just that for a little moment there, I was rendered dizzy with joy."

"How soon can you be ready, Anne?" asked Miss Carlyle, already sorry that she would be leaving. "There's a train to be caught."

"In five minutes," said Anne, who had already packed her belongings in the canvas bag the night before, in a gesture of unreasonable optimism.

SEVENTY-ONE

On the Way

Anne was silent as she followed Mrs. Spencer down the orphanage steps toward the waiting carriage. Prince Edward Island was her goal, her destination, her brand-new life. She was on her way to a home that contained no children. In her mind was a swirl of what one could call positive negatives: no diapers, no crying babies, no sleepless nights, no crises over colic or croup or bedwetting. Anne's breathing was shallow, and she was almost paralyzed by excitement. Certainly her vocal cords seemed to have seized shut. Mrs. Spencer was pleased that this odd-looking child was said to be clever and a tireless worker. But she rather dreaded a voyage of this length unless Anne showed some signs of *speaking*. Lily was proving to be a very quiet child. But this was good. A fractious five-year-old could present enormous problems on a long trip. But the apparently stunned silence of this Anne child was making her feel a bit nervous. Should *she* start a conversation? No, she should not. This shouldn't be expected of her. Doing this complicated errand for the Cuthberts was enough of a good deed, without having to turn it into a social situation.

After Anne had climbed up into the carriage, her mind started moving about a bit more. She suddenly realized that she had not given a single thought to how she would get to this land of her dreams. And here she was, in the company of a woman of such apparent dignity, in a *carriage*. Not in an express wagon or even in a farm wagon or a buggy. Never would her imagination have dreamed up the possibility of travelling in a vehicle that was so grand. She had seen them in Bolingbroke, but that was long ago. Surely the Queen must drive about in something like this. It had a *driver*. There was no need for Mrs. Spencer to manage the horses.

But their ride in this wonderful conveyance ended before Anne could fully appreciate its wonders. There hadn't been enough time for her to pretend that she was one of Queen Victoria's daughters, waving languidly to the cheering throngs who lined the streets. No. She had to follow Mrs. Spencer and Lily as they stepped down from the carriage onto the ground below them, and then into a building and thence onto a wooden platform. And there, in front of them, was a *train*. Anne closed her eyes, and sighed with a profound joy. *Another train!* But this one was different. It would be taking her to somewhere wonderful instead of to a deeply dreaded destination. She whispered those words, liking the alliteration. All those *d*'s. Her interest in words was piercing her stunned ecstasy. They mounted the steps into the train, and found two double seats, facing each other. A uniformed man took Mrs. Spencer's suitcase from her and put it away. But although Lily surrendered her bag, Anne held her canvas carpet bag close to her. Its handle was undependable, and she didn't want *The Blue Boy* or the little pink purse or the carefully wrapped egg or the little dictionary to spill every which way over the train floor. Then the train gave a big lurch, and the wheels started to move. They could hear the hissing steam escaping from below them, the rhythmic puffing of the engine. People on the platform were waving and throwing kisses. Anne knew that they weren't saying goodbye to *her*, but she waved and blew kisses all the same. She ignored her wincey dress and shabby little coat that she was so ashamed of, and reclothed herself in a gown befitting her status as a princess, waving eagerly to her loyal and adoring subjects. It was as though the bump and lurch of the starting train, the escaping steam and clicking wheels had restored Anne's ability to think and move.

Anne cleared her throat. "Mrs. Spencer," she began, " I just wanted you to know that I am in a state of absolute bliss."

Well, well. So the child could talk. She had, of course, spoken a few words in Miss Carlyle's office, but the exit from the orphanage had seemed to silence her. However, it appeared that this state of affairs had passed.

"You cannot imagine," continued Anne, "the degree to which my life has so often been mired in the depths of total despair. So therefore it may be difficult for you to realize that this trip is, to me, a voyage into the very heart of heaven."

Mrs. Spencer, not often at a loss for words, paused before she spoke. After this speech, she wasn't sure what to *think*, let alone *reply*. Where had this eleven-year-old urchin, in her appalling orphanage uniform, dredged up such an unusual way of expressing herself? She didn't know that Anne had rehearsed that little speech during the ten minutes before she delivered it.

"I'm glad you're enjoying the trip," said Mrs. Spencer. She cleared her throat. This little girl in her skimpy wincey dress, sitting so straight and composed with her hands in her lap and with her large bright eyes radiating a kind of subdued ecstasy, was making her feel just a touch uneasy.

"Oh, Mrs. Spencer!" exclaimed Anne. "*Enjoying* is a word that doesn't even *begin* to describe what I'm feeling. It has been my lifelong dream — well, for the last two years — to just *see* Prince Edward Island. The pictures I have seen of it have made me so *hungry* to look upon it with my very own eyes. And *now*, I am actually on my way — not just to *see* it, but to *live there*. So you can see that *enjoying* is really an inadequate word in this case. Oh! Do look at those little lambs in that huge field, all snuggled up to their mothers. I've so missed not having a mother. Are you one?"

Mrs. Spencer, taken aback by this stream of unexpected talk, was not prepared for the question. "Am I what?" she said.

"A mother," said Anne.

"Yes," said Mrs. Spencer. "I have an older daughter."

"Oh," said Anne. "Older daughters can be lovely. Like Eliza, until she betrayed me. But when your daughter was small she must have loved to snuggle up to you. And that must have been a lovely feeling for both of you."

Actually, Anne couldn't imagine anyone, no matter how small, snuggling up to Mrs. Spencer. Curtsying to her was one thing; snuggling was another.

Mrs. Spencer, for her part, was thinking that Flora Jane, now in her late teens, had never been much given to snuggling; but then neither had she.

"It's a nice thing to be a mother," said Mrs. Spencer, groping for something to say.

" ... A nice thing." Anne pondered this disturbing understatement. Mrs. Thomas and Mrs. Hammond hadn't presented perfect models of motherhood, but after all, they had problems that had probably hindered — even damaged — that ability. But even the apparently chilly Miss Haggerty had admitted to wishing she was young enough to adopt Anne. And her own mother had thought her "perfectly beautiful." What was wrong with this elegant Spencer woman? Why was she so *held in*? She was likely just pretending to be elegant and perfect.

Well, she'd try another topic.

"Mrs. Spencer. I loved the carriage. It was so grand. Like

the Queen's, I'm sure. And now I'm loving this train. I've been in a train once before, and I loved it, too. But I knew it was taking me on a tragic trip. I'm sure you can imagine that this made it somewhat less than perfect. But this — this is a magical train that is transporting me to everything that is wonderful. To Prince Edward Island, to a real home, to a place where it's very likely I won't have to carry thirteen buckets of water every day or listen to noise all the time or see people hit one another. So even if I get to have a thousand train trips in my life, none will ever seem as excellent as this one. Look! Look out there at the blossoms on those trees. They're smothered in flowers. What are they?"

"Maybe apple blossoms. Possibly cherry. I haven't thought too much about flowering trees. If the fruit is on them, I know what they are." Mrs. Spencer hoped that Anne wouldn't ask too many questions that she couldn't answer. She was a lady who was used to being *in charge* of things. Some of Anne's conversation was making her feel — of all things — mildly inadequate; and she didn't like the feeling.

Anne had a more important question. "How do we get to the Island? Is there a big boat? Does the train go onto it, and then continue on when we get there? Will we see the open sea, reaching out, out, out until it reaches the sky?"

Mrs. Spencer was relieved. Answering those questions was easy. "Yes," she said, "we go to the Island in a big boat. No, the train doesn't go across on the ferry. We get off, and then go onto the boat on foot. And yes, you'll be able to see the horizon — the place where you can't see any land."

Anne was hugging herself. It was the only way to keep from trembling with anticipation. Mind you, there were ways in which she didn't ever want to leave this train. It had solid oak panelling and strange-shaped windows. On her first trip to the washroom, she'd found solid brass taps and fixtures, and the seat of the toilet was of a glorious warm-coloured wood that she would later learn was mahogany. She, who had been used to outhouses and chamber pots for most of her life — not to mention water that you had to drag out of a well in a heavy bucket — was deeply thrilled by the little bathroom with its church-like windows. She kept thinking of reasons why she should go in there — frequently offering to take Lily. Being only five, Lily might need to go often. At least Anne hoped so. But the thought of the boat was even more exciting.

Suddenly, to the left of the train, there was a large river; and ahead she could see it widening. She knew, without being told, that the river was flowing into the sea, and that the entry to the ocean was not far off. So — at last — she was about to see part of the 3728.4 miles of Nova Scotia's coastline, even if it turned out to be only a very short section. She sat up straight and looked out the window hungrily. This was, after all, her native province, even though she was about to leave it. It had been the home of Bertha and Walter Shirley. She needed to see at least a small slice of that seacoast before she left. Anne had always known — ever since the single Thomas expedition to the beach — that the parts of Nova Scotia she'd love best would be the areas that were beside the ocean. She longed to witness a rising tide, to smell the seaweed, to watch the water breathing in and out. As the river became wider and wider, she knew that she was almost there.

As the train rounded a bend, the trees thinned, and before Anne's betwitched eyes was the most compelling of sights — a *horizon*, far, far away in the place where the sea forever meets the sky. As the train slowed, she could hardly wait to step out onto the wooden platform — to inhale the pungent sea smells; to follow the flight of the squawking gulls; to watch the fishermen unloading their catch; to feel a longing for and a belonging to a part of her province that she'd never seen before. Here was her last chance to do this before she left — possibly for the rest of her life.

But alas, when the trip was over, Mrs. Spencer pushed the girls along the aisle, and then down the steps of the train. When they reached the wharf, she hurriedly guided them onto the ferry. She wanted to do this quickly, in order to get a seat in the warm interior — three seats in a row, in fact. Besides, the train was late; so there was no time for Anne to investigate the pier or the small and large buildings that surrounded it. At first Anne was wild with frustration. She'd come all this way from the dense woods of Nova Scotia to get her first — no, second — view of the sea, and Mrs. Spencer wouldn't allow them enough time to stand on the big wharf to see it, smell it, think about it. When they found their seats on the inside, Anne left her place immediately, in order to press her nose against the window to see the seagulls, the busy harbour boats, the men loading their own vessel with parcels and bags. This was almost as good as watching from the pier. *Besides*, she told herself, *I'm going to live on an island forever. I can spend the rest of my life close to the sea.* Then, just as the vessel left the pier with a heavy shudder, she heard a man say to his wife, "I'm going out on deck." Then he disappeared out a heavy door.

Anne rushed back to Mrs. Spencer. "What's 'on deck' mean?" she asked.

"There's a deck outside, with a railing. Some people who don't mind the cold winds like to stand out there. Or sit. I can't imagine why."

"But it's June," said Anne, her eyes pleading. "Please let me go out."

"It may be June," said Mrs. Spencer briskly, "but it feels like April today. And once we're on the open sea, it will feel more like March. No. Stay in here. I don't want to deliver you to the Cuthberts with double pneumonia."

The open sea. And she had to stay imprisoned in there, in order to be *warm*?

Anne had lost her stunned awe of Mrs. Spencer. The time for curtsying had passed. She wasn't a queen-like person after all. Anne sat down and put her hand on her arm. "I beg of you," she said. "I *beseech* you. Let me go out there. I've only seen the sea once before in my whole long life. Just imagine *that*. But I knew when I saw it that it was my very favourite thing. Even better than the maple trees in October, or the Pool of Mirrors, or cats, or even poetry. I knew I'd forever love the sea best. Please, Mrs. Spencer. I'm warm. I never feel cold. I lived in freezing cold houses for most of my life. The Thomases' house was so cold that sometimes we wore our woolly hats indoors. I'm never sick. So, *please*. I'll be careful. I won't fall over the railing. But I know I'll reach the absolute height of rapture. Surely, Mrs. Spencer, you wouldn't want to deny me the chance to experience *that*."

What Mrs. Spencer was thinking was that she didn't want to experience any more of Anne's conversation for a while. Best to let her go. She could check on her safety from the window. There were plenty of people out there who would make sure that she didn't fall into the water. She wasn't a child who wouldn't be noticed. All that red hair. The ridiculous straw hat. That awful dress. Those freckles. Yes. She'd be safe.

"Go along, Anne," she said. "But try to take some reasonable care."

The day was sunny but chilly, with a driving wind. But Anne felt none of that. She watched the retreating coastline

of Nova Scotia, bewitched by the limitless expanse of sea, the galloping whitecaps, the wheeling gulls, the smell of salt and seaweed. *This is what I've been waiting for my whole life.* Anne walked and ran up and down the vessel, inspecting its fittings, enjoying the chug of its engine, loving everything she was seeing. Even a crying baby delighted her because she knew she didn't have to carry it, comfort it, or feed it. She made up stories about the people around her. She saw a parade of porpoises, and almost cried out with the delight of it. She didn't notice Mrs. Spencer watching from the window, or making brief journeys out the door of the cabin to check on her safety — looking more irritated than elegant. Anne was totally closed up inside her own joy. When the Island itself became nearer and more visible, she found herself grabbing the railing with white knuckles, and weeping with something approaching ecstasy. By the time she returned to the cabin — when it was clear that the boat was about to dock — she felt as though she'd absorbed enough happiness to keep her warm and safe and satisfied for the rest of her life.

Then, almost immediately, there was another train to catch. And once again they had to hurry in order to be on time, in order to get a good seat — close to the washroom and with a clear, clean window. But as Anne stepped off the ferry and then off the wharf onto dry land — onto *red soil* — she stole a swift moment to think, *I'm here. I'm on my island. I'm on THE Island. I will be here forever. It's my home.*" Then she boarded the train, and sat very still, smiling quietly.

As the train puffed along on its winding and circuitous route, Anne felt an unfamiliar peacefulness descend upon her. She looked out both sides of the train, and knew that all Mr. McDougall's pictures were *true*. There, out the windows, were the neat green fields, the white houses with their bright picket fences, their rust-coloured roads, their blossoming trees. Here and there, from time to time, were glimpses of the sea, sometimes sparkling with almost a whiteness, at other times the deepest of cobalt blue. It was all there, and it was all going to be *hers.* For a long time, she didn't speak. But then she did start to talk. She had a sudden feeling that she wanted to get her old life *out* of her so that she could put it far back in her memory and start again with a new one. She began to tell Mrs. Spencer about her early days, her middle days, her recent days. Like it or not, the weary woman heard all about her parents' early death, her turbulent life with the Thomases, Eliza, the betrayal of Roger, the noise, Horace's violence, the two-sided character of Mr. Thomas and his tragic death. Then came the exhausting years with the Hammonds, the multitude of children, the exhausting work, the strange withdrawal of Mrs. Hammond, Mr. Hammond's heart attack and death. She also spoke of some of the joys of that life — her teachers, the Egg Man, Miss Haggerty, Lochinvar, the precious gifts she had in her bag, her love for Noah, and the miracle of the birth of Julie Anna and Roderick. She merely listed these joys. Somehow it made her feel uneasy to speak in detail about those people and things that had helped to keep her spirit alive during difficult times. About Katie Maurice and Violetta she said nothing. Some memories were too sacred to be shared with someone she scarcely knew. But all of it was there, and she wanted to leave it behind, on the other side of the Northumberland Strait — the good and the bad. She wanted to forget the bad and stop missing the good. Her account of the orphanage was short.

"It was the worst," she said, and told of Edna's friendship and treason, of the way she could never be alone, of her escape into herself. And then of Mrs. Spencer's visit and her release from that terrible place. "You saved me from a kind of dying," she said to Mrs. Spencer.

Then, in what seemed to Anne to be an astonishingly short time, she could feel that the train was slowing down. Anne literally jumped out of her seat, and cried, "Are we *there*?"

"Oh, no," said Mrs. Spencer. "We're just stopping to let off some passengers. But the rest of the trip will be very short." *And thank heavens for that,* she thought. *I don't know what has wearied me more — Anne's early life, or her telling of it.* Exhausted, she had pretty well turned her mind right off during Anne's summary of her past. But at least checking on Anne's safety on the ferry had kept her too busy to feel ill. However, she patted Lily's hand, and thought about how lovely it was that she'd chosen for herself a quiet child.

As soon as the train started to move again, Anne lapsed into silence. The time, she knew, was at hand. Suddenly it was as though her old life had slipped away — just as she had hoped it would. And now she was faced with the fact that she was just minutes away from her new one. When the conductor would come in and announce that Bright River was the next station, she would know that her future home would be just a buggy ride away. She'd see the house, her room, the view from her window, the strangers who would be her new family.

But Anne was abruptly aware that she might have to leave the train quickly. The wheels did seem to be doing their clickety-clack very rapidly. So she broke her silence and turned to Mrs. Spencer.

"Thank you very much," she said, "for taking me out of my old life and putting me into my new one. And, Lily, I hope you'll love Prince Edward Island as much as I do. Try to be happy."

Then Anne sat very still while the train travelled on in the direction of the next station. She was no longer seeing the green fields and tidy houses and flowering fruit trees. She was in her head, trying to imagine what lay ahead. Her quietness was not the result of any sort of nervous dread. It was rooted in a quiet certainty that her previous long voyage of difficulty and uncertainty was almost at an end, and that what she was about to experience would be altogether wonderful.

When the train slowed, and the conductor called out "Bright River!", Anne rose without a word or a backward glance, and, clutching her bag with both hands, walked along the aisle and down the steps of the train into her new life.

Acknowledgments

There are many people whom I need to thank for the help they gave me during my preparation of this book. Monika Sormova took six hundred pages of my handwritten text and put it on her computer — cheerfully and with amazing accuracy. For various legal reasons, it was necessary for someone to read the first third of the book before it was finished. Diane Wile Brumm did this for me, along with lending me a number of Royal Readers and other textbooks from the time when Anne went to school in Nova Scotia. Another person who filled in a lot of educational background through books and spoken advice was Archie Killawee, a former teacher at the Truro Normal School. Karen Vonmaltzahn lent me her collection of the Montgomery Journals and made no complaints when I kept them for five months. A number of people who had a detailed familiarity with the Anne books were able to enlighten me when I was searching for references to what took place in Anne's life before she met Matthew Cuthbert at the railway station in Prince Edward Island. Among those knowledgeable fans were Mary Jane Copps, Carol McDougall, Glynis Wilson Boultbee, Lorraine Hurtig, Kathleen Martin, and Lisa Doucet. They would give me titles of the relevant Anne books, chapter numbers, and specific pages within ten minutes of my query. Andrea Wilson drove me around various areas in Nova Scotia while I attempted to find suitable locations for Bolingbroke, Marysville, the Hammonds' home "up the river," and the orphanage. Marian Hebb and Sally Keefe Cohen generously offered their expertise, and maintained unwavering interest in the project. Karen McMullin of Penguin was a constant and reliable support throughout the process of creating the book.

I must give special thanks here to Jane Buss, Executive Director of the Writers' Federation of Nova Scotia, who spent many hours studying contractual matters in connection with the project, and giving me explanations and advice.

Dr. Elizabeth Epperly, noted authority on the life and work of L. M. Montgomery, and Professor Emerita of the University of Prince Edward Island, was of enormous assistance to me in my effort to be consistent and accurate in my treatment of times and places and people that were referred to in Montgomery's books about Anne Shirley, and was always generous with her time and her vast knowledge of Montgomery's world.

The idea of publishing a prequel to *Anne of Green Gables* originated with Helen Reeves, Senior Editor at Penguin. I am very grateful to her for her sound advice and listening ear throughout the time when I was working on the book. She gave me free rein in the writing of it, not even complaining when I wouldn't let her — or anyone else — see a word of it until I had finished the first draft. She does her editing with insight and with grace.

I would also like to thank Alison Reid, who did her usual careful job of copy-editing, catching the smallest flaws with her eagle eye, but always with respect for my own voice and preferences.

My husband, Alan Wilson, deserves the most thanks. He unflinchingly received my long lists of questions, and consulted libraries and the Internet for answers. He then typed up many pages of information about the history of Anne's time — with details about fashion, transportation, inventions, medical beliefs, religious practices, gadgets (egg beaters, safety pins!), employment opportunities, social customs, and anything else I wanted to know. He also cooked all the evening meals, listened to my anxieties about the project, and put up with the piles of Anne materials that were cluttering up our home.

I wish it was possible to thank Lucy Maud Montgomery for writing the Anne books in the first place, and for making Anne such a feisty and fascinating and articulate child that I was tempted to try to solve the puzzle of how — coming out of a grim and deprived early life — she managed to become who she was when she first stepped off the train in Prince Edward Island. I would like to thank L. M. Montgomery's heirs for giving me the opportunity to do this.